HUNTING BY STARS

a MARROW THIEVES novel

Cataloging-in-Publication Data has been applied for and may be obtained from the Library of Congress.

ISBN 978-1-4197-5347-3

Text © 2021 Cherie Dimaline
Book design by Hana Anouk Nakamura

Printed and bound in U.S.A.
10 9 8 7 6 5 4 3 2 1

Amulet Books are available at special discounts when purchased in quantity for premiums and promotions as well as fundraising or educational use. Special editions can also be created to specification. For details, contact specialsales@abramsbooks.com or the address below.

Amulet Books® is a registered trademark of Harry N. Abrams, Inc.

ABRAMS The Art of Books
195 Broadway, New York, NY 10007
abramsbooks.com

For Lydea, Miles, Tarquin, and every kid in, or running toward, community. And for the grown-ups working to make sure it's there for them to find.

The last thing I remember is standing on the edge of the clearing looking up. The tops of the pines looked like black lace over the full yellow moon, the constellations stitched into velvet. The whole sky was dressed for a feast. Around me, the calls of crows reported on the darkness, a mocking song of reunion with pauses full of loss. I should have listened harder to the crows. Anything that when gathered is called a murder is bound to speak prophecy.

CHAPTER 1:
PROOF OF LIFE

French

I DREAMED ABOUT MY BROTHER.

In the dream, we were still kids—the same age we were the last time I saw him, gangly and uncoordinated. We were sitting on the wooden floor of a tree house, the walls buckled and thin, the same tree house he was stolen from all those years ago. I tried to speak, to warn him that the Recruiters would be coming and he was going to be taken and I would be left in a tree like a forgotten ornament. But I couldn't make a sound, just empty speech bubbles like an unfinished comic that popped around my head. Mitch was laughing as if I was telling the best jokes.

"Frenchie, you're hilarious," he said, his words swooshing through the air, shaped like paper planes folded out of weekly flyers.

Set between us on the floor was a small green figure of a plastic army man, one knee bent, a crooked rifle held at shoulder height. The swoop of the word *hilarious* tumbled to the ground and knocked the man over. That small violence of plastic on plank sounded like lightening bursting an oak to wood chips.

Outside, the world was sped up, the sun and the moon exchanging seats like a game of musical chairs set to fiddles. I saw us in the tree house, and then the tree house in a field, and then the field in the middle of a forest, and then the towns and highways beyond, haphazard like a snapped string of beads over green fabric. Water slid down mountains clotted with pines, and soil rushing after like black vomit. Hail the size of dinner plates bounced over cracked pavement and smashed into buildings. People blipped onto the land like faults in film and then disappeared just as fast, leaving shadows and holes. Lakes, poisoned useless, glinted like coins in the sunlight, then moonlight, then sunlight again. Icebergs melted, and everything warped as if the ice had been the solid frame of it all. Trash in the oceans was beached in tall waves, leaving deserts of water bottles and decorating the trees with the confetti of faded wrappers and pull tabs. Disgorged grocery bags spun down wrecked roads like the crinkly ghosts of tumbleweeds. This was the world now. And that wasn't even the worst part.

Then we weren't in the tree house anymore. We were outside, in a brick-and-vinyl suburb with dandelions to our knees poking out from cracks in asphalt like bristle on hide. I was holding Mitch's hand, and we were standing on a street in front of a row of emptied houses, their windows dark as punched-out teeth. People walked by us coughing blood onto their shirts, clutching their bellies and heads and sides, medical masks hanging from their ears like hand-me-down jewelry. They had the plague. The trash cans at the end of each driveway were heaped with syringes, so many vaccinations and cures thrown out because none would work. The people stumbled into one another, knocking over cans and crunching through the needles. They had that look, the one that let you know they were dreamless, that they were halfway to crazy, that they were the most dangerous animals in the field.

Fear pinched my guts, and I squeezed Mitch's hand. Now the dreamless were starting to walk different, stooped, their fingers held strange, always in mid-grab. They had nowhere to go now. They'd stopped showing up for their shifts on rebuilding projects. They'd stopped loving their spouses. They hung themselves from the confetti trees like heavy ornaments. At the edge of my sight, I could see them now, bloated faces pointed down, sightless eyes like coins in the sunlight, then moonlight, then sunlight again. I heard their shoes hitting against each other, hollow chimes in the breeze.

The people on the street were starting to notice us, turning on awkward feet to amble over, fingers flexing open and shut. I closed my eyes and buried my face in Mitch's shoulder. I could hear his breathing loud in my ears, but I had no words to calm him or myself. They saw us now for what we were: dreamers, providers, fuel. I knew what they wanted. I'd watched a pack of dogs once, breaking bones apart in a parking lot and snarling over the marrow, chewing and growling through exposed teeth at the same time, a cacophony of glut. A woman in a beige sweat suit approached, her long hair pulled back tight in a high ponytail, head held at an odd angle, her face twitching. She took small steps toward us on white sneakers until I could feel her breath on my cheek. I closed my eyes. I could hear her teeth snapping open and shut and then the low rumble of a growl, like a spool of ribbon uncoiling up her throat. That's when my voice returned and I screamed and . . .

My eyes opened.

There was no light. I lifted my hands in front of my face but couldn't make them out. I touched my arms, stomach, the front of my pants, wet down to the knees. A sting of humiliation when I realized I'd pissed myself, even now in the heavy dark, even through the massive weight of the headache, there was room for this small embarrassment.

Then pain swept in, cutting through my scalp and stabbing into my brain. I pulled my chin to my chest and slouched my shoulders, trying to back away from it. Eventually, it spread to a thud and pull, matching my pulse, and I knew that my heart was still beating somewhere under the dull throb of bruised ribs. Living, as it turns out, is the ability to ache.

What had happened? Where was I?

I sat up and assessed the back of my head. There was stuff stuck in my hair, like I'd been rolling around in the bush. I hissed through closed teeth, trying to untangle the mess. I grabbed what felt like a leaf and started to pull.

"Jesus Christ!"

There was a kind of tearing that I heard from the inside of my skull. It wasn't a leaf; it was dried blood and the beginning crust of a large scab. I dropped my hand to my eyes to look for evidence of the bleeding I knew was there, but there was only darkness.

Standing on wobbly legs, cold pushed through the holes in my socks. Where were my shoes? And why was the ground so even? There were always branches to step over, roots bubbling under the soil, making walking a careful dance. I'd been out in the woods and on the run for so many years that my feet didn't recognize a floor. I shuffled forward, arms outstretched, the ground smooth under each step. Seven slow paces forward and my fingers crunched into a wall. I flattened my palms and followed it until it met another at a ninety-degree angle.

That's when the panic settled into the bottom curve of each throb; I was inside. I'd spent the last eight of my seventeen years outside, running, trying to stay on the other side of walls. Walls only slowed you down. Walls left you without options. Walls kept you still. And these days, stillness was death.

I called for the others. "Miig? Rose? Rose, are you there?"

I followed the wall all the way around, my shaking fingers, sticky with drying blood, making out the seams of a door, a sink, a toilet, my clumsy feet ramming into the metal frame of a small bed. I collapsed there on the thin mattress and whimpered, winding up like a kettle into shrill. The only thing that made capture more certain than walls was noise that would give your location away, anything from a heavy footstep to a loud cry. But I had no sense, not then, not trapped in this room in the complete blackness.

Hearing yourself fall apart makes it happen faster. Back when I was with my family—maybe hours or even days ago, who knows—we worked hard to hold each other up. Tree and Zheegwon, they had a special way of doing this for each other; maybe it was a twin thing, but something as simple as a glance or a hand on a shoulder and they were brought back to calm. It was dangerous to be anything but calm. Calm is strength performed. Weakness is like a loose sweater string caught on a nail and you're running in the opposite direction. Eventually, you unravel the whole thing and you're left naked.

Somewhere in the middle of the undoing, I fell asleep, curled fetal, my broken head resting on the podium of a knee bent like a plastic army man. And I dreamed; the other thing besides pain that assured me I was alive, truly alive, all-the-way-dialed-up alive.

♦♦♦ ♦♦♦ ♦♦♦

I opened my eyes back into the black, scrambling to my feet before I remembered I was inside. The back of my messed-up head shrieked from the movement, and I sank back to the bed. I smelled wet rot and metal rust—the mineral waste of my own blood. Every muscle hurt, and I was cold. I didn't know if I was shivering or if the room was vibrating, as if a large vehicle were revving nearby. I folded myself so small my hands were sandwiched between the crescent bones of my ankles. All over, my skin was slippery. Had I pissed myself again? No, I was sweating. I could taste it on my lips, salt and sick.

"Not dead. Not dead," I reminded myself.

And then I knew where I was. There was only one place I could be. If I was with my family, Miig and Wab and the others, I wouldn't be inside, and I certainly wouldn't be hurt, and I would never, under any circumstance, be alone. I knew then that I was in the place we ran from, the place where Indigenous people were brought and never seen again—I was in one of the new residential schools, just like the old ones the government stole us away to, where they conducted experiments, where they tried to kill the Indian in the child. The realization hit me like a punch to the stomach, and I struggled to breathe, each gasp sending shards of pain into my head and down my neck.

Then I did something I hadn't done in years, something I really had no memory of ever doing: I called out for the one who had left so long ago, the one whom I hadn't seen since she climbed down from the roof beside the Friendship Centre looking for supplies. Leaving Mitch and me alone and hunted in the middle of a splintered city to run until we found the tree house, where only one of us would be left to continue that run.

"Mom! Oh, Mom. Pleeease . . ." It didn't make sense to try, and it did nothing but amp up the panic pouring into my lungs.

There was the sound of metal turning on metal and a click, loud and sure like fingers snapping. The solid air in the room shuddered; I felt it in my ears.

A slice of light appeared, so clear it made me squint, so electric and pitched I could hear it. It grew so massive I lifted an arm across my face and sucked in my breath. There were footsteps. I pulled my arm away and only opened my eyes enough to see that the door was swinging wide open.

My first response was shock, then an almost hysterical relief. I could see!

And then a dark figure appeared in the light, a hieroglyph of a man blocking the way out. His shoulders were broad, the hair on his head short and bristled, and the outline of a holster at his hip came into focus. And I understood that not being dead could be a very temporary state after all.

I wanted to sit up, but I had no way to operate the joints and muscles needed to move. Then a voice, unmistakable, one I'd heard since the very beginning, whispered from somewhere close to my head, as if I had tucked her under my pillow like a worry doll.

"Without the magic in the marrow, we're just machines," my mother said. "And you can't reason with mechanics."

I tried to call out but only managed to exhale all the breath out of my body. I closed my eyes, eager to get back to the certainty of the complete darkness. It came right away. And this time, there was no dream.

CHAPTER 2:
LOSING THE FINDER

The Family

THE FIRE WAS SURROUNDED BY THE TIRED AND HYS-
terical, all of them breathing heavy from exhaustion or frustration,
each of them finding it hard to keep their eyes focused without
jumping to the trees all around them. Not one of them had slept.

"What in the hell happened?" Miig sat as close to Isaac as possible, their arms threaded, fingers braided at every bend. Even now,
the spots where their skin connected was electric distraction. But he
was a leader, an Elder in his group, and he needed to stay focused,
now more than ever, even with his newly returned husband, someone he had thought long dead in the schools, beside him.

"Not sure. He was there, and then he just wasn't." Bullet, a
long-time member of the resistance camp Miig's group had found
weeks ago, rubbed her palm across the top of her shaved head. "I

saw him in the grass, and then everyone came out of the camp, and then . . ." She motioned with the same hand, lifting it to the sky with her last words. "And then he was just gone." She was crouched in the grass, bouncing slightly against her heels. She hung her head, pressing her fingers into the back of her neck.

"I should have been paying attention. I should have noticed French was missing before we left the clearing." Miig was beating himself up, the dark bruises on his face from the absence of sleep like black eyes. Frenchie had been in his family since they'd found him in the woods at ten, half starved and all alone after his brother was taken. How could he have lost him? The weight of his guilt was almost unbearable. If he hadn't been so distracted by finding Isaac—by Frenchie finding Isaac for him—he would have been paying more attention.

"We all should have been more careful." Wab was pacing, a hand on her lower back, her swollen stomach pushed forward.

Chi Boy, always the doting partner, shuffled down the log and patted the space beside him for her to sit. She shook her head and paced. He kept his mouth shut but his eyes open, taking in each line on her face, every falter in her step. Not that he spoke much to begin with. This last month had been difficult now that the baby was asserting its presence. He wasn't sure she'd make it to full term, not with all this stress: the regular day-to-day stress of being hunted in a broken world, and then this new anxiety over a missing relative.

"But what are we going to do?"

Rose was frantic, had been since the scout had jogged back with news of a Recruiter van sighting and they'd realized French hadn't made it back to the camp. They had all been laughing, dancing almost, at Miig's miracle, the return of his Isaac, and what that meant for all of them, the beautiful possibility of it all. Now she was rushing around the outside of the circle, all twitch and adrenaline, checking and rechecking the sharpness of the blade on her belt knife with her thumb. "We need to do something . . . and now!"

"No, that is exactly what we shouldn't do," Wab answered. "That's how we make mistakes."

"Oh, like misplacing a whole boy, you mean? That kind of mistake?"

Her black eyes flashed, her curly hair bouncing at her shoulders with each movement of her head. Rose was always quick to any emotion. It was one of the things French loved about her, this intense and deep ability to feel, even when every hour was filled up with just getting by. She was just sixteen, but she'd already lived a life made long with grief. She switched directions, exasperated at her own inability to do anything of use. Her heart was breaking at the potentials of what might have happened. They had been ready to be a real couple—finally, after all the careful dancing around each other, all the running that stopped conversation short. And now he was gone.

"'S no one's fault, Rose." Chi Boy spoke just louder than a whisper.

"It's everyone's fault!" Rose shouted back. "Every one of us."

She'd unsheathed her knife in one quick motion and used it to point at the group around the fire—Miigwans, Isaac, Chi Boy, Wab, Bullet, Derrick—pausing at each one so they understood they had been implicated. She placed the tip of the blade over her own heart to include herself in the accusation before pushing it back into its case.

"French would never have left one of us behind. He never did. Ever!" Tears broke loose and made tracks down her cheeks, cutting through the dust and dirt of a frantic search.

She swiped the back of her hand across her face. There was no time for tears. There was never time for tears. Not out here.

"Things don't happen right away," Isaac spoke up. His voice was melodic, made deeper by fatigue. "In the schools, I mean. If they have him, he should be okay . . . for a while." He shivered, and Miig rubbed his arm. The school would probably never leave him, even though he had escaped with the help of a network of nurses for whom harvesting humans was just not an option.

"Has anyone told his dad yet?" It was Rose's turn to almost whisper. When his makeshift family had found the camp, French had been reunited with his father, a reunion neither had dreamed was possible after so much time. And now, in one moment of dropped defense, there were miles and maybe the boundary of death between them again.

"I did," Derrick answered. Like Bullet, Derrick wasn't a part of the original family who'd wandered into their camp, but he, like Bullet, felt close to them. He felt especially close to Rose—or at least, he was hoping to get closer. "He's lying down. Spent the whole night in the bush, looking."

During their time apart, French's dad had lost a leg after taking a bullet from vigilantes. That, coupled with age, diabetes, and life on the run, meant he had to rest often. Put grief on top of all that, and the group wasn't sure he'd ever leave his cot again. And for a moment, that seemed to Rose like a perfectly reasonable response. Maybe she should just lie down . . . just for a moment, or maybe until this was all over, regardless of how it ended.

"Fuck this." She slapped her hands against her thighs and spun on one boot, stomping off into the trees.

"Where're you going?" Derrick looked up from braiding his hair. Chi Boy held Wab by the forearm lest she get any ideas about following the girl. Rose had joined them years into their never-ending journey to evade capture, but she was, without a doubt, one of them.

"The road," Rose tossed over her shoulder, moving fast.

Derrick sighed, let his hair fall down his back, the thick strands loosening from the design, and picked up his rifle. He spoke to Miig. "I'll keep an eye on her." Then he jogged into the shadows, leaving the depleted group to their worry. Derrick's concern was amplified by his feelings for Rose, even though it had become clear she and French had a thing.

"Rose . . . Rose . . . wait up!" he called out to her, but she didn't slow down. Finally, he reached out and caught her shoulder.

Her round face was dark, all angles with anger. "Don't try to stop me, Derrick. I don't expect you to understand."

"I don't understand? Just because I wasn't with your little crew until you stumbled into our camp doesn't mean I don't understand family." He refused to let her go, making her stop for a moment. "Rose, you've gotta calm down a bit."

"Don't tell me to calm down! I need all this—all of this." She patted her chest and her arms to show the twitch and tightness of her muscles. "This is how I get shit done."

"Yeah, and it's also how you get caught." He looked at his feet. "Or worse."

She paused. Derrick had been there when they'd tried to rescue their Elder Minerva, the one who carried the language, the one who had burned down an entire school with her words. That had ended in the old woman bleeding out in the road from a Recruiter gunshot. Things hadn't been the same since. Rose just couldn't find the right ways to mourn. She cried, she cut her hair, she spent hours focusing on everything Minerva had ever told her, every word she'd pushed into her vocabulary, but it wasn't enough. A loss like Minerva was monumental. A loss like Minerva these days was unimaginable.

Still, maybe Derrick was right. Maybe rushing headlong into another confrontation with the Recruiters would only mean another one of them—maybe her this time—lying in the road, failing lungs grasping at breath like a fist already clenched.

He took the pause as an opportunity to continue. "Just sit for a minute. After that, if you really want to head off on your own with no direction and no backup, well, then, I'll let you go." Still holding on to her, he directed her to a tree trunk snapped near the ground and lying horizontal by moss and splinters. She allowed herself to be lowered, and their weight pushed the wood to creak.

Sudden rest filled her limbs with fatigue, and she couldn't hold out anymore. She leaned over and put her forehead on Derrick's shoulder, the tradecloth of his jacket rough against her skin. And then she began to cry. He put his arm around her and pulled her closer, eyes trained on the expanse of forest around them, just in case.

With this beautiful, broken girl finally soft against him, Derrick couldn't help but wonder if maybe French leaving wasn't such a bad thing, an opportunity instead of just a loss. He'd been out here on the run with other Natives since the government had started hunting them, since people had gotten raddled enough by the Plague sickness and the inability to dream and started believing that Indigenous people were the answer. And he'd been alone, even in the increasingly crowded camp. There had never been someone who had moved him the way Rose did, who had reminded him that life in this apocalypse was more than just survival, or at least it could be.

He shook his head, swearing to himself under his breath. No, that's not how he should be thinking right now, not ever. It was them against the world, and every man counted. Every man deserved to be found. But still, Rose's body against his made thinking . . . complicated.

◆◆◆ ◆◆◆ ◆◆◆

The last flames were flickering orange in the mid-morning grey. Chi Boy put an arm at Wab's waist and guided her back to their tent to rest. She shouldn't have been up all night, walking around, but Wab was not the kind of person you directed. She was always in charge, especially of herself. When he'd suggested she lie down, she'd fidgeted with the beaded patch covering her permanently closed eye, then run her finger down the heavy brocade of a keloid scar that split the side of her face. She should organize another wave of searchers. She should find those who could climb as well as French could to take to the trees to get a better look at the landscape. It was foggy, but there might be something. Maybe she should gather the Council again to see if they could call in their informant. It'd been a long night, and many were just now grabbing some sleep, but she could rouse them. Finally, though, the baby made the decision for her, sucking the last bit of energy from her muscles, and she allowed herself to be led away, back to camp. She'd rest, but only for an hour, and then they'd set out again.

Bullet took over pacing when Rose left. She was uneasy in her skin. As one of the founders of the resistance camp, she felt responsible. Years ago, at the height of the hysteria, she'd traveled across the border from her Menominee community before the schools had started opening. Back then, she knew only that she had to get to family, and that meant finding her partner in southern Ontario. She had arrived too late to save Olivia, but she had stayed once border crossing became impossible, and by then she had found others who were building a place of safety. It was empowering to have a plan and likeminded people to carry it out. Now she felt diminished. Not quite weak, but less than she should be. Once Miigwans and his small group had been welcomed into the camp, they'd become her responsibility. It was one of the most important teachings, that they all looked out for one another without hierarchy, without question. And now one of them was gone. It had been hard enough to lose an Elder after the failed rescue mission, let alone one who carried an Indigenous language in a time when so much was lost or in danger. But now a youth? It was almost too much.

She sighed. "Gonna do another perimeter check, then grab some supplies and recheck where we last saw him." She turned into the trees, leaving just Miigwans and Isaac at the fire.

The men sat quietly for several minutes, watching the embers, holding on to one another in this small, damp clearing. It was the first time they had been alone since the night before, since Frenchie had brought them back together. The group Isaac was travelling with had set off an alarm, and French set out with the scouts sent to find them. He was the one who had recognized Isaac's tattoo from Miigwans's stories. He was the one who had run back to tell Miig that his love wasn't dead after all, that he was right here. And any reunion

18

in this time was a miracle for all of them. If Isaac was alive, anyone could still be alive, could still be out there breathing, searching.

"How long since you got free? How long have you been out here now?" Miig needed to know more, needed to get caught up on the time since he'd last seen his husband being dragged out of a Recruiter van and into a school while he sat, zip-tied and frantic, under guard in the cargo section until it was his turn to be "enrolled."

"A few weeks, maybe. Hard to say."

"Time is different now, eh?"

"I'm not sure it exists anymore." Isaac sighed, dipping his head to fit on his partner's shoulder. "But we exist. At least there's that."

Miigwans turned his face to the side, and Isaac lifted his head to meet his gaze. "Do we?"

"Yeah, baby. We do. And we're together. And I'm going to take whatever minutes we have to be grateful for them."

They leaned together and kissed, breaking apart only to gasp at the power of that small act of resistance: love despite it all, love because of it all.

Eventually, they walked back to camp, to Miig's small tent set at the far side of the circle, to lie, grateful, in each other's arms, but only for a few hours. Only long enough to give their bodies the sleep they needed to search again.

CHAPTER 3:
PRISON

French

I WAS BACK WITH MY FAMILY.

Miigwans lit a sprig of white sage and placed it to burn on a rock in front of the small fire. White sage was precious because it wasn't from this territory. It was one of the ways we knew how important we were, even now, especially now. We were worth that cumulous smoke. We were as necessary as this medicine. We leaned in closer, our shoulders touching, reminding us we were a circle, no matter how much smaller that circle had become.

"It's time for Story."

I sat beside Rose, the only girl who'd ever made my chest expand so much I could breathe bigger, which meant I could be bigger. Maybe even better. I pushed my knee up against the outside of her leg.

She kissed her teeth. "Move, na?" Her father was from Barbados, and in some moments she borrowed his cadence. She was missing him, and his words brought him a little closer. It was a luxury for her.

Beside her, Slopper slouched, his chin resting on his chest. He drew foliage in the dirt with the tip of a branch. He was still a child, but he was working to carry language, and the words he had memorized made him taller. He was becoming a giant and deserved the respect one affords a giant.

Wab rested her head on Chi Boy, who rubbed her pregnant stomach while staring into the flames. She absentmindedly stroked the lines on the ruined side of her still-beautiful face, feeling the memories raised and scored into her skin.

Tree and Zheegwon, identical in every way save the hand-me-down clothes they wore, kept all four eyes on the near distance, on the trees where they turned to shadows and sway. They were posted lookouts for the next five hours, and that job didn't end, even during Story. Their fifteen-year-old bodies were lean to the point of sharp beauty. You had to look close to see that one of them was missing the outer shell of an ear, or a pinky finger, or to make out the dents in their legs, the painful movement of a badly healed elbow, all injuries suffered at the hands of people looking for a cure, trying to dig one out of these remarkable boys and their fragile skin.

Miigwans was elegant even in mourning, even in dirty pants, even without adornment. He was our Elder, the only one we had left in this found family, though there had once been two. He was elegant in his rupture and repair. He spoke now:

"Story is a home, it's where we live, it's where we hold everything we'll need to truly survive—our languages, our people, our land. And you could say, but we're out on the land, now more than ever. So why worry about it? Because we are not all one people, and this land that we walk, we are so often guests in these territories. We are different people. Even though now we are one group—Dreamers—we are still also separate nations. Lumping us together makes us easier for the outsiders to catalog, easier to dismiss, to devalue, until we are only single-colored containers for the thing they want the most. We are one box to check and stack.

"Like any home, Story has to be renovated—extended or repaired or even torn down from time to time. For us, the repair and renovation is not always pretty. Sometimes it's unsound, but we do it the best way we can when the time comes. We do it with sticks if we have to. We hold them together with blood when we have to. Now, here are those sticks, and to it we add our own blood."

I stretched my arm behind Rose, not holding her exactly, but just letting her know I was there, that I had her. In truth, I may have needed her more than she needed me right then. All I saw was Minerva's blood on the road. My mother lying facedown in a ditch. My favorite uncle bleeding from the ears and nose, alone on a cot.

"Earthquakes in fracked landscapes. Tornadoes through pipeline-riddled fields. Tsunamis across poisoned waters. The coasts broke and sank. The weather turned manic. And the sicknesses were released. A virus, a pandemic of plague, a cure, and then another would step up to replace it. Depression as the markets crashed. Despair as the young and old died. Desperation when they could no longer rest at night with no dreams to hold them together. Madness, madness everywhere, and not a dream in sight. Until they saw us—maybe for the first time in a long time, *really* saw us. And suddenly, we were needed. Or rather, the marrow where they thought we kept the dreams. That was what they thought they needed. The very marrow from our bones. The very dreams from our heads."

He turned to me, quiet but louder than I'd ever heard him speak out here in the green expanse of our world. "Don't let them take them, French. We're counting on you."

♦♦♦ ♦♦♦ ♦♦♦

Something tickled my face, like I was walking through a spider-web. I couldn't lift my arms to brush it away. I heard an electric buzz and felt a weight being dropped and pulled against my head. Each time it was lifted, more webs fell on my face. It took a minute before I realized it was my hair. Someone was cutting my hair. I fell back asleep.

I woke up with tears in my eyes. Had I fallen asleep crying? I tried to speak, but there were no words. My throat was too dry to drag one up. There were voices. Then I was gone again.

I opened my eyes. A man in a white lab coat stood at the foot of the bed. He glanced up once to regard me, then went back to scribbling on a clipboard.

The next time I came round, there were two men. One of them was hanging an IV bag of clear liquid from the pole at the side of the bed. I moved my head, trying to shake the sleep off, and he spoke.

"Don't fuss. You'll loosen the bandages," he said, his voice small and tight, the words too close together. I had to concentrate to force them into sequence so I could make sense of the message.

Everything was soft around the edges, like the room was backlit by moonlight. I smiled, then closed my eyes again, remembering a yellow moon cut through with pine lace.

I finally woke up, back in the dark.

"No." It was a croak. I felt the shape of my body tucked under a rough woolen blanket. "No!"

I was back in my godforsaken room, back on the small bed, back in the dark. Had I ever even left? I reached up and felt the stubbly contours of my shaved head. My skull, just above the neck to the top curve, was covered by a large padded bandage. My hand was sore; I felt the edges of a smaller Band-Aid above my knuckles. I remembered the IV needle, now gone. So I had been out of this room—that much was true. How long had I been here? And then I wondered if I was the only one here. Oh, holy shit, had the others been brought in? That pushed adrenaline into my veins, and I jerked into full consciousness.

I yanked the blanket off, the cool air rushing to replace it. I was wearing a T-shirt and loose cotton pants with a drawstring waist. There were different low socks on my feet, ones without holes. I felt like a baby learning how to control my movements as I swung my legs off the side of the bed and stood. I turned to the right and, with arms stretched out, felt my way to the door. I knew it was delusional, but I tried the handle.

Locked. I pushed and pulled, and there wasn't the slightest give. Then I knocked.

"Hello?" I coughed a few times and tried again, louder. "Hello, is anyone out there? I need to speak to someone."

Hearing my voice, small and beseeching, just made me angry. What if my family was here—Chi Boy and Slopper and Rose . . . oh god, Rose. I had a quick vision of her in a dark room with a faceless man in the doorway. I banged again with my fist, then two fists.

"Answer me, goddamn it!"

Anger decanted into my limbs, thick and powerful. It made me slam into the metal, to kick and yell. "You cowards, you fucking cowards! Why don't you show yourselves?"

And that's when my mother came back.

"Oh, my boy. What is all this yelling around?"

The sound of her voice shoved me to the ground as sure as if it had grown hands to push me. "Mom?"

"You know what marrow looks like under the microscope? Like the entire universe, just full of planets."

"Mom? Where are you?"

I stretched my arms out and rushed around the space like a frightened bird in a cage, crunching numb fingers against the walls, slamming toes against the toilet. I was frantic.

"I am right beside you, my boy."

After scratching the paint off the bricks, crawling around on my hands and knees and searching the ground, I knew she was being figurative. She meant "beside you" the way other people said "I'm behind you." They were rarely ever at your back, even when they said they had your back.

"Mom, I can't find you!" I was sweating, and I couldn't get on my feet, so I sat hard and leaned against a wall, trying to even out my breath. Lethargy was pouring cement over frustration. I must have been concussed or drugged . . . maybe both.

"Here. I'm right here."

"Where?" I couldn't stay awake, my sore head tipping toward my shoulder.

"I'll reach for you. Reach back."

I slid down until my cheek was on the floor. I turned to face the wall and stretched out my hand. And there she was. She grabbed my hand and laced our fingers together. There must have been a vent between rooms, hers and mine. Maybe that was how she'd found me. I brought her hand to my face and rubbed my lips against the cold metal circle of her wedding band.

"Why are you here? Where's Dad? I found him, you know. He's alive. We're alive. We're alive, right?" I couldn't project past a whisper, getting softer with each word.

◆◆◆ ◆◆◆ ◆◆◆

In what I can only assume was morning—there was no way to tell time and no sunlight to suggest an hour—I woke up knowing she wasn't really there, that there was just me and the memory of her, the massive want of her. Cold and stiff on the ground, I woke up holding my own hand, one inside the other, under my cheek. I dragged myself back to the bed, pulled the blanket up to my chin, and understood that until now, I had never truly been helpless. Out in the bush, I could hunt if I was hungry, I could run if I was being chased, I could stand my ground and take a life if that's what was necessary. I had done all of those. But in here, what could I do? For now, I just closed my eyes and counted the stars that bloomed and arced across my lids, praying on each one that I was really alone, that no one else from my family was locked in here.

My mother returned every now and then in the innumerable dark hours. Eventually, her voice stopped breaking my heart.

"Hey, Frenchie, did you know there are eight hundred billion more cells in your body than there are galaxies in the known universe? Can you imagine that? You're bigger than everything we know."

"You're dead," I told her for probably the tenth time since we'd started this broken conversation through the wall.

"I was just lost."

"Where am I?" I'd asked this so many times now, first with a frantic screech to the words. Now it was more of a challenge to her voice. It always went unanswered in any real way. It was like trying to map a forest without true north.

"With me, Francis. You're with me."

"Yeah, yeah. A lot of good that does either of us. And why is it you right now? Why couldn't it be Dad? At least I know he's still aboveground." Oh god, I hoped he was still aboveground. Who knew what had happened out there.

A darkness like this was a place full of lost and found. Every fear you'd ever had found you, and you lost your entire mind in return. I counted my fingers and toes over and over as a way to know I was actually real, because I was worried that maybe I was not. I tried to piece it all together, to remember every detail that had brought me here, to this non-place where my mother was now singing an old song about a girl sleeping in the pines.

The last thing I remembered was going on a mission to intercept strangers who'd come near the camp. I'd slung the rifle, pulled my courage out like a prayer ribbon, and run toward the danger. But instead of Recruiters or those Natives who pretended to be refugees but who turned out to be school informers, we'd found real community. And among them, there was Isaac, long lost to the schools. Those last starlit moments outside of this dark cell had been in the clearing where Isaac and Miigwans were finally reunited.

That night, I had sat in the grass and cried. At that moment, there was only Miigwans and Isaac in the entirety of the broken world. I saw joy and the hope for more. I had laughed when they embraced, each searching the other's face with hands and mouths, because I'd needed to feel the biggest I could, and that was with laughter, especially out here, right now. Laughter made space. And after a while, when they'd gathered enough sense to return to camp, I'd stepped out of the clearing for just a moment to relieve myself in the woods. Just one moment—alone and caught up in that elusive joy . . . and then a sound, like a cedar trunk being hit with a bullet, and then nothing. Everything went away. I remembered only the feeling of my limbs folding up like cracking knuckles, and I'd woken up here, in this place, in this impossibly dark room, more alone than I'd ever been in the bush.

I thought maybe it had been a bullet after all. Again, I considered that maybe I was dead. That would explain Mom being here.

"The magic of the entire machine is in the marrow; that's where cells snap into existence and can become anything to anybody." The voice sounded dry, so the words were like a coughing hacked up a parched throat.

"Shut up, please." I turned on my side and toward what I knew was the wall only because my fingers had traced it so many times. My breath was sour in that space. I used a ragged nail to scratch plaque off my fuzzy teeth.

"A tooth is not a bone. Did you know that?"

I paused, hand near my mouth. Could she see me in here? I pulled my knees up toward my chest. No. No one could see anything in here. And she wasn't real, I reminded myself. "You're not real." I said it out loud so the facts would stay straight.

I opened my eyes, slow and without hope, and besides the physical push of air against eyeball, there was no change in sight.

"A tooth can't be a bone. It's just a sharp thing that tears and rips. Because it has no marrow."

"Neither do you." It came out weepy, wavering under another surge of panic. I tried to breathe through it. "Your marrow is gone, s'been sucked out. So all you can do now is rip me to bits."

Tinny laughter from the corner of the room. I stood up and paced. It kept my mind off the hunger. I had water from the sink and a toilet, but so far, there'd been no food. It was getting desperate. The last time I'd bitten a broken fingernail off, instead of spitting, I'd swallowed it.

"Hey, Ma, you got any grub up there in my head?" I laughed at my own joke. There was no answer, which was even funnier to me. I laughed until tears squeezed down my cheeks, until there were no sounds coming out, until I had to hold my sides to keep from busting wide open.

I was losing my damn mind. And then it hit me: the only people I knew who couldn't control themselves, who did things like scream at nothing and have conversations with the dead as if they were sitting beside them, were the ones who couldn't dream. I tried to remember the last time I'd had a dream, but everything was one continuous sigh in the dark. Then I remembered waking up in the bed, getting my head shaved, the man in white writing on the clipboard, the man hanging that bag, tubes going into my arm. Maybe the liquid wasn't going in . . . maybe it was being sucked out . . .

"They took it." I was sure of it. They'd taken my marrow. And without my marrow, how could I dream? That's where they said it was hidden, in our bones, like sleepy bees in a hive. "I'm empty."

I had to go, one way or the other. I had to get out. I searched the room again, looking for anything loose or sharp—a broken brick, a bed spring, a cup I could smash into a cutting edge. All the while, the tears I'd laughed loose kept falling. I would get out of here, even if it meant leaving in a body bag.

After a while, I lay down, hugging myself and pretending my arms were someone else's. "It's okay, Frenchie," I whispered into my pillow. "It's okay. You'll be okay."

◆◆◆ ◆◆◆ ◆◆◆

There was a fire, the kind of fire that we never would have made—high and hot. We built Dakota-style fires in holes with tunnels underneath so the smoke was pushed away from the camp and no bark on the wood so it burned cleaner. I watched the flames jump and fume. The abandon was beautiful. I walked toward it, waiting for the waves of heat against my skin, but there were none.

Stepping over the ground, my feet made no noise. Noting its absence, I listened for the cracks and hum of the fire eating wood. Again, there was nothing. I tried my voice. "Hello?" It echoed around the clearing.

"Hello." This time I was louder, almost yelling in the comparative silence of everything else.

I was at the edge of the fire, bright orange and burning tall. Still, no heat. I tipped forward, pushing my face closer. Nothing. I reached out, tentative and ready to pull back as soon as the heat jumped against my skin. Eventually, my fingers were directly in the flames. It was as if it wasn't there, like the whole thing was a projection. I put my other hand in, then sank them up to my elbows. Finally, I pushed my head in.

Not a sound or a change in temperature. What kind of fire was this? I looked up; miles away, the sky blazed blue. I looked down. Beyond the top flames in shades of yellow and orange, the bottom burned blue, as if reflecting the sky itself. And below the blue was the fuel—wood chewed to solid grey ash, and there, in between the branches and burn, was something else. What was it?

I crouched down, getting on my hands and knees, still submerged in the pit from the shoulders up, nothing but my own breath in my ears even though the flames were jumping and the wood was breaking apart. What was it?

Something round and charred black, almost carved with dark filigree. I grabbed it—it was light—and turned it around in my hands. On one side it was like an egg where the fire had eaten it smooth. Then it got bumpy, and then there were odd formations. It was a skull, a human skull, the teeth and orbital holes intact. In my shaking hands—I couldn't drop it—the clotted mess stuck on the front started to grow back and reshape: a nose, then a chin, then lips to form a smile around the edges of the teeth.

"No." It was becoming familiar. "No, please, no."

Eyes molded themselves back into the holes like blown glass, so dark they shone maroon.

"No!" I stood, the skull fused into my palms.

The ears spiraled out like seashells. Hair—loose dark curls—pooled out of the restretched scalp like vines.

"Please stop!"

Finally, I was left with the head of Rose, my beautiful Rose, staring up at me. Her eyes found mine, focused in and glinting with life, and for a second, I was happy. And then her eyes changed, her brow pulled up, her mouth opened wide, and she began screaming. And that's when the heat returned to the fire, and I was consumed.

◆◆◆　◆◆◆　◆◆◆

I sat straight up in bed as if I'd heard a gunshot, covered in sweat.

"Oh god, oh good frigging god." I put a hand on my chest and tried to slow my breathing, throwing myself back against the damp pillow. "Good god, no."

There are images and words and memories you can't recall without getting gut-punched. They're the things that haunt you for years, the feelings that get trapped despite your best efforts to set them loose so you can run away from them. They are the most horrid things, because they come from inside you. This—Rose being burned alive, nothing more than a piece of herself, in pain—this was as bad as it could get, and I couldn't find a way to shake it off.

And then I realized what it really was. I clasped my own forearms where the veins were the bluest. They hadn't taken it, not yet. After all, a nightmare is still a dream, isn't it?

Click.

I spun to face the door, and sure enough, a line of yellow light appeared. I should have jumped to the side, ready to spring out at whoever came through. I should have been exercising, keeping limber, pumped up for action. I could hear Wab—"Stay ready, Frenchie. As a wise sage once said, if you stay ready, you ain't gotta get ready." But the sad truth was, I was grateful—grateful that someone was coming, that someone was even out there, and hopeful that they had a granola bar in their pocket. So I cupped my hands over my brow to shield my eyes from the harsh light and waited.

Once the door was fully open, I had a hard time looking up, so I took in as much of the room as I could before hands grabbed me.

I was dragged down a hallway. Not that I didn't want to go just about anywhere if it meant being out that room, but the lighting out there was too bright, and I couldn't see past a squint and blur and needed to be held up and pulled ahead. Toward what, I couldn't have imagined. And that was saying a lot, since I had been imagining my long-gone mother in this place.

What did I know at that point? I knew from the small glimpses I'd seen before leaving that my room was white—white walls, white bed, white sheets, white toilet, white sink. Only the blanket had color, a soft blue that didn't match the rough scratch of its texture. And fingerprints of dirt and old blood smeared on the walls.

I knew that the hallway was painted a light grey, that ahead, every ten feet or so, there was a bright fluorescent light buzzing on the ceiling, and that the floors were cement buffed to a high polish. I knew that my escort was not a Recruiter. He was some kind of new danger we hadn't named yet. Instead of shorts and a windbreaker, he wore a black coat and dress pants in the same material. His shoes were black and low heeled. I couldn't keep my eyes focused long enough to consider his face.

"Aaniin." I tested out my rudimentary Anishinaabemowin on him. Nothing. It was a long shot, but even now, hope forced me to try.

"Where are we going?"

Again, he didn't answer. He just tightened his grip on my arm as he picked up the pace.

I tried once more, this time low and quick, because I didn't want to know the answer. "This is a residential school, isn't it?"

He straightened his arm so suddenly that I banged into the wall, my head, already tender from the earlier injury, connecting with the frame around a door. Then he yanked me back to his side, never pausing or slowing down.

I hung my head and tried to keep pace. Looking down, I saw that I was wearing a white shirt and socks and that my pants were light green with a yellow logo on the right thigh. I couldn't make it out with my legs moving and my eyesight wonky. So I concentrated on paying attention to the directions we turned, the length of each hallway, the closed doors we passed. I wondered if there were more Native kids behind them. I wondered if I knew any of them, loved any of them.

There was a smell in here like wet metal and chalk. It brought back the outside world to me, not the woods, but the before time, when I was in abandoned towns and cleared-out cities. It was the smell of industry, of more structure than flesh; it was the smell of a new kind of decay as we inched back through the Industrial Age. It made my stomach hitch up like I had to use the bathroom. Because I knew it as the scent of dark change and brutal theft.

Two right turns, each new hallway the same as the last—empty and lined with closed doors. Then a left into a large space, skylights up top, concrete pillars spaced throughout. I stared up. It was grey out, the kind of grey that falls at midday this time of year. There were no trees in that small section of sky, no birds flying over, no obvious way to escape. There were a couple of brown couches pushed against the walls and a low coffee table in front of each. It felt lived in, but in that way waiting rooms feel lived in: temporary and impatient. In the corner, on the floor, was a ragged teddy bear, one eye missing. It watched us pass with his mouth stitched shut.

We walked through double doors at the other side of the room and into a smaller area. There was a booth with two security guards sitting behind glass. We turned right again, and my escort swiped a card in front of a small sensor on the wall, and a door without a knob slid aside.

We were in a stairwell with white metal railings going up and down. We took the upward set; I almost fell on the first few steps until the man in black decided I'd move better without broken legs and slowed down.

"Thanks," I told him. I was genuinely grateful, but then immediately angry with myself for feeling gratitude. I should be fighting him, pushing him, tripping him down the stairs; Wab would have, and Chi Boy probably would have snapped his neck already. But here I was, meekly being led without so much as shrugging off his grip, with a "thank you," even. The shame of it made me timid.

Two flights, and then through another door, opened with the same card, into another area watched over by two security guards behind glass. I was sluggish, weaving a bit with every step. We took a left and walked down a hallway wide enough to have little sitting areas outside the rooms, one chair and a round table each. We stopped in front of a closed door with a small plaque on the front: MEETING ROOM 3.

My escort rapped on the door, and we waited. I started seeing spots and shifted my weight from foot to foot. I needed food or I was going to pass out.

"Come in," a voice called out.

Even if I hadn't been guided through the open door, even if I wasn't under guard and too weak to make any sudden movements, I would have gone in. Something in that voice hooked itself under my ribs and pulled me toward it.

CHAPTER 4:
THE PLAN

Rose

"WHY DID I EVEN COME BACK?" ROSE WAS EXHAUSTED, but her anxiety held her straight like scaffolding. She shouldn't have let Derrick bring her back. She should have left on her own when she wanted to, gone way out, all the way to a school, if that's what it took, instead of sticking around here for two days with the others only searching close to camp.

"Because heading out on your own is suicide," Bullet sighed, like she was talking to a child instead of a grown-ass woman. She turned back to the table. "Father Carole, we'd like to thank you for coming out to help us once again. You continue to be a tremendous ally."

Father Carole was the Council's man on the inside. Officially, he sat on a board of directors for the school system. Unofficially, he carried information to the resistance. He was the reason they knew anything about the schools and the people taken inside. That's how they'd found out when Minerva was being moved and why they'd been able to attempt a rescue, even if it had failed in the end.

He sat next to Frenchie's dad now, across from Bullet, her counterpart Clarence, and Miigwans. Rose, Derrick, Wab, and Chi Boy had been invited to observe from a bench behind the main table. Bullet had made clear at the beginning, "Observing is not shouting out whatever the hell pops into your head whenever the hell you want."

"I don't know how much help I can be. It's only been a few days. The weekly report hasn't even come in." Carole spoke slow and soft. He knew the missing boy was Jean's and tried to maintain the calm in the camp that he knew was temporary, perhaps even pulled together for his visit.

"What *can* you tell us?"

"I can tell you that in the last four days, six young people and two adults have been . . . collected from this general area. There are no specifics yet, only statistics. Are you certain the individual is no longer in the vicinity?"

Jean spoke up. "We've spent the past two days and nights searching every inch of the woods. We took turns, so there was someone looking every hour. The only things we found were small amounts of blood on the edge of the clearing and a few snapped branches on the path."

"Low branches?"

"Yes," Bullet picked up. "Suggesting something or someone had been dragged."

Father Carole placed a hand on Jean's forearm. "I wouldn't worry too much about the blood. If it's his, he's not likely to be too injured. It doesn't fit the needs or rules of the organization."

Rose scoffed. Bullet cracked her neck by tilting her head toward one shoulder, then the other. "Of course, we are grateful for the reassurance." She spun around in her seat, making eye contact with the girl. "And the help. We know you come here at great expense to your own safety."

"It is the only choice I have. I couldn't live with myself otherwise." He folded his hands on the table, his white cuffs peeking out from underneath a dark coat. "I will get word to you as soon as the details are released. I can tell you that two regional schools have added four people to their population charts—no names or descriptions yet. Four more were added to the DOA list." He lowered his gaze.

"DOA?" Jean repeated.

"Four didn't make it out of the woods," Bullet told him in a low voice.

"Which schools?" Jean leaned in, refusing to consider the possibility that maybe his boy was on the second list.

"St. Brebeuf and Sir John A. MacDonald."

"Hmm, both are about eighty miles from here," Bullet said. "Hard to say which one they'd take him to."

"Yes, since the decision to make the facilities coed, it's really anyone's guess."

Rose couldn't hold back. Words popped out like a crow had been released, loud and aggressive. "Well, let's make a fucking guess, then! I'm tired of wandering around the woods and sitting up in trees with shitty binoculars. Or, better yet, let's split up and go to both!"

Bullet stood up so fast her log stool fell over. "That's it. This Council meeting is closed to outsiders. Now." She pointed toward the main cave, nostrils flaring.

"Outsiders?" Rose was also on her feet in a flash. "Is that what we are now? Outsiders?"

"Well, you're not Council members, so yes. Outsiders." Bullet wasn't backing down. She kept her arm out straight, the other one at her waist. They were in a standoff, neither one budging. Chi Boy broke it, getting up and helping Wab to her feet.

"Let's go," he said. "We can get the details later." The rest of the group stood and followed him. Rose was the last one to go, sneering the entire time, not breaking eye contact with Bullet until she was halfway to the cave. She veered left at the opening, walking fast toward her tent.

"You're leaving again, aren't you?" It was Derrick.

She spun around. "Why are you always following me?"

"Well, you're not good at taking others, so this is the only way anyone can get close to you." He caught her arm. "Seriously, you are, aren't you? Leaving?"

"Eighty miles is a three-day hike in this terrain. I saw the map. I know which direction to go."

"But toward which school?" he asked. "What, you gonna flip a coin?"

"Maybe." She was stomping now, wanting to get away, to get to her tent and pack up. No one was going to stop her this time. "Better than sitting on our asses doing nothing."

"Planning isn't doing nothing, Rose," Derrick tried to reason with her. "Planning is doing something the right way."

"Jesus, listen to yourself," she scoffed. "You might as well start wearing your pants high and napping, mosom."

"Hey, you know Cree? Nice." The infatuation was back in full force.

"Not much. Just enough to insult you."

"That's all anyone needs. It's like you really understand the Cree soul," he joked.

"And yes, I'm leaving. And no Cree is going to stop me this time." She placed her gun against a woodpile and started hauling blankets and supplies out of her tent so she could pull it down.

Derrick sighed. "When do we leave?"

She paused, checking his face for signs of trickery or doubt. Finding only resignation, she answered, "First light. Not a second later." She pulled the main pole, and the vinyl dome fell.

CHAPTER 5

CHI BOY'S COMING-TO STORY

Chi Boy

CHI BOY DIDN'T HAVE TO DO MUCH CONVINCING TO get Wab to lie down. She was tired all the time now. The women kept saying that soon enough the nesting instinct would kick in and she'd be up all hours moving, so they'd better enjoy this time of rest, both of them, while it lasted.

He sat near the doorway, which he zipped up to try to give her some quiet. It was never loud here; the people knew they needed to remain as soundless as they could. They reserved their noise for important things like hunting and drumming, and the rest of the time they communicated mostly with gestures and carefully placed wood and supplies, as if everything were fragile. He put her swollen feet in his lap and rubbed them. He felt useless these days, so when there was something he actually could do to help, like massaging her feet, he did it. Right now, this new life was Wab's burden to carry. All he could do most of the time was watch over her, but not too closely, or she'd get antsy.

A gauzy sun filtering through the blue tent walls cast her in a somber light so that she resembled a statue. He took her all in, in these moments of stillness, the curved beauty of her. When her breathing was steady and even, he lay down next to her so that his head was at her distended belly. Carefully, he ran the palm of his hand over her stomach. Her belly button had recently started to protrude, and he smoothed the fabric of her shirt over it. Without putting any more pressure on her skin, he leaned forward and placed a kiss just above that button, where he imagined his child's head to be.

What world would welcome this baby? How would they survive? What could he possibly give to ensure that survival? He would give anything. In time, he could teach them to shoot and run and deliver messages without words. He could share trapping skills and how to get clean water and the best ways to hide. But for now, in these early days and the ones to come, what could he possibly do?

The first thing anyone needed to make the right moves toward survival was the truth—the lay of the land, the history of the place, the people they could trust and the ones they had to run from. This generation would be the first one born during this new epoch. So it was his responsibility as a father to give his child the map to find a way forward. There was no forward movement without truth. So then, that was what he had to give, as hard as it was, as much as he wanted to keep the darkness at bay.

Taking one last look at Wab's sleeping face, he lowered his lips again and started to tell his story for the very first time.

✦✦✦ ✦✦✦ ✦✦✦

I tried to get help. I tried to get them to help me. And then they reminded me of who I was. What I was.

People called me quiet, or sullen, or stupid. But when you're alone, it's easier not to talk. Why start a conversation when it's going to be one-sided? Why get to know someone if next week they'll be replaced by someone else? My life didn't have a soundtrack, you know? Because it wasn't a movie. It was more like a bunch of scenes stitched together.

Scene one: Eating corn syrup on white bread from a paper bag. Sitting at a Formica table. My feet don't touch the floor, which is good, because this home has a dog that wants to sink its broken teeth into my bare legs. I keep as immobile as I can and still be chewing.

Scene two: Carrot sticks rolling around on a Styrofoam plate. From the back porch, I watch two boys who belong there play badminton with loose-stringed rackets in the yard. One of them looks over, sees me, flips me the finger, and goes back to playing.

Scene three: I am so grateful to be back in the group home, because this one has bedroom doors that lock. I lie flat on my back and watch the car lights draw stripes up the white walls. An average of ten cars an hour pass down the street. I keep as quiet as I can and still be breathing.

Scene four: Things have gone weird, and kids are disappearing, but no one is looking for them. I wander off after school and never go back. Soon, one of the straps on my backpack breaks. I tie it together with a shoelace and keep walking.

Scene five: Outside a small town, there are farms. Their fields lie against one another like patches on a quilt, smoothed out and equally divided. I like crossing their boundaries from the road. I disrupt their polite geometry. A truck rumbles behind me, slowly passes, and then pulls into the ditch in front of me. Both doors open, and men in old hats and new sunglasses get out. One of them has a knife in his belt. But it's the second one who scares me; he's smiling real big. I jump over a low fence and into the field. They're shouting, calling me a dream smuggler, calling me a coward, calling me an Indian, and closing in behind me. I run so hard I have to close my eyes. I run so hard I can't hear anything but my heart in my head and the wheat at my knees. I run until the only thing left in my body is burn. I run as fast as I can and still be thinking.

Scene six: I'm at a house after so many fields. I know the men aren't behind me anymore, but I don't know where they've gone. Maybe they went back for the truck. Maybe they are hiding. Maybe the knife is in a hand and not a belt now.

On the front stoop is a small mat that says WELCOME TO OUR HOME and a large red planter full of bright daisies. I lean on the wood cutout of an old woman in a blue polka-dot dress who's holding an apple pie. A sign hanging around her neck on a brass chain reads, THE LORD PROVIDES. FOR EVERYTHING ELSE, THERE'S GRANDPARENTS. I catch enough breath to knock on the door and tell the woman who answers that I am scared and I am being chased and I need help. She tells me to sit on a small bench beside the cutout and goes back in to get her husband, says he can help me.

I sit on the narrow bench and put both hands flat on my chest, convincing my lungs to slow down. A minute passes. I rub my legs to ease the ticks. Another minute. Then the door opens again, and this time it's the husband, only I don't see him, I just see his handgun. He tells me he knows what I'm up to and I better get the hell out of there before he puts a hole in me.

I stand and fall back down on my butt. I try to say I'm not up to anything. I stand up again and start backing away. I tell him I'm scared.

He tells me he knows all about "you people," that I'm only there to rob him. That I'd better get my buddies and hit the road.

I'm alone. And I'm scared, I say, and hear myself getting quieter. *Scared* is barely a whisper.

He takes a shot. The bullet lands beside my foot. The wife yells from inside, "Don't go getting dirty blood all over the front walk, Harold."

"Sorry, dear," he says to her over his shoulder, his voice full of the kindness I was searching for. He turns cold eyes back to me. Tells me to move . . . now! To grab the others and take our party somewhere else. He knows how we are, what we do to poor farmers like them.

I tried to get help. I tried to get them to help me. And they reminded me of who I was . . . what I was. And I ran.

I'm not sure if it was an accident, or if he was too full of adrenaline, or if he just hated me that much, but I was at the end of the front walk when the bullet tore into my calf. Maybe he was going to shoot me all along and was just trying to respect his wife's pressure-washed cobblestones.

Scene seven: Trees. Blood. Ache. At least the bullet went straight through. More trees. So much time passes that eventually I forget to run. Then I find an old trailer, all rusted out and quiet, a fifth wheel without a truck to pull it. It's leaning a bit to one side, but all the windows and the door are intact. I think it's a fine place to rest up, to give my leg a chance to really heal. I'm too loud in the bush with a limp. I sit in the low brush and watch the trailer all night, waiting to see if anyone comes out or goes in. Once I think someone must be inside because it starts to shake, but it's just a massive raccoon lumbering over the roof. His nails scratch into the vinyl top when he rears up on his hind legs, sniffing me out. But he's not afraid that I'm there. I'm bleeding. And just a boy.

At first light, I cross the ferns and rocks to the trailer and open the door. Once inside, it's the first time I notice the forest is full of noise—leaves, bugs, wind, birds—because it's suddenly gone. It's all muffle and hush in here. When the door closes behind me I let all the air out of my body and feel light.

Scene eight is really a bunch of scenes. I took it all in—the dirty shelves; a stack of plastic cups stuck one inside the other; the floor, crunchy with old leaves; a mattress covered in messy sheets and a blanket with a yellow cartoon bird on it—all so filthy they practically crack in half when I move them.

I sleep on a lawn chair pushed into the corner.

I eat a box of stale raisins from my bag.

I piss out the window.

I sleep again.

It doesn't occur to me that I am alone. Until I realize I'm not alone.

I push the mattress up and against the wall, planning on cleaning up a bit, settling in for a few nights. But underneath the mattress is a hatch cut into the floor. An old storage space. I lift it. And there's a body.

I don't scream. I don't think I ever have, even when I should have. I back away, stumble, even, but I make no sounds. Then, eventually, I creep back over. It's a woman, an old woman. Her hair, where it peeks out from around the folds of a flowered kerchief, is grey and matted, her face lined with dirt. I can only see her from the chest up. She's wearing like three different sweaters with a brown turtleneck underneath. I should be scared, or maybe grossed out, but I'm just sad. So sad, I reach out and touch her cheek. It's warm.

Her eyes open, all big and at once. And I fall back on my ass. And then, if you can believe this, she laughs. Laughs so hard she starts coughing. Laughs so much I have time to get back up on my feet.

"What the hell are you doing?" I ask.

She takes a minute to shimmy and groan and sit up so that she's halfway up into the trailer. "Hiding."

Then she holds out a hand so I can help her up.

That's how I met Minerva. She was already pretty old when we found each other, but not as old as when the Recruiters did her in. She could still follow a conversation. She could still remember where she was most of the time. She didn't slip between Anishi-naabemowin and English without warning so much. We stayed in the trailer for a week, then left together. She said we needed to keep moving because sitting ducks never make it out of hunting season.

We traveled together after that, collecting more of us along the way. Miig was the first one we found together, then the rest kind of fell into place while we were on the move. I guess this story can end on scene nine. This is my favorite one, anyway, scene nine.

I have never seen a beaver lodge before. It doesn't look like it was made by animals as much as very smart children. We're hunting, so we've split up, and I am alone, standing on the bank of a creek with a sharp stick. That's all I have, no gun, no bow, but it's enough to make me brave. Because I am eleven years old now, and I am brave, I tell myself. I tell myself this a lot.

I leave my shoes on the bank. Wet feet are too dangerous out here. Catching cold could be the end. I wade in, holding the stick above my head, the water reaching to my ribs. If there's a beaver in there and I can kill it, we'll eat well. We don't trap out here, so it's hard, but if anyone can do it, it's me. Minerva will tell me she's proud of me and call me her boy. I'll do just about anything to be her boy.

This lodge is small. Probably a young beaver's first digs. I'll have to dive to get inside since the doorway is underwater. That makes me nervous. It means my head will pop up in the dark before anything else. It means I'll be in a vulnerable position. Miig tells us we are already vulnerable out here, so don't take chances. I circle the structure, listening. The creek is low, and the lodge is sticking up pretty high. On the far side, there's a crack in the dome. I push the sharp end of the stick into the soft ground around the lodge, pull myself up, hook fingers and toes into the branches, and climb. I get to the crack and stop. I look up; the sky is bright blue, the sun is full and blurry behind a haze. I take a deep breath, like I'm going underwater after all, and look down and inside.

There's a girl. She's curled up, her face turned toward the ground, limbs over bones, bones stacked over curved muscles, a dark bud in a streak of sunlight. And then, as I'm watching, she starts to pull apart, stretching until her fingertips hit the muddy wall. She's on her back, and I can see her entire face, and it's the most beautiful thing I've ever seen. She's soft like that, looking up at me, for a few seconds, and then she pulls it all back and in and gets hard, like she can do so quick. She cups one hand over the side of her face and puts the other one on a cleaver by her side. Then she kind of smiles, no fear at all, and says:

"What the fuck is this, now?"

I feel something in my chest start to unravel. It's a new space, and it opens quick. My heart gets real wide, so big. As big as it can go and still be beating.

◆◆◆ ◆◆◆ ◆◆◆

Chi Boy pushed his lips right up against Wab's belly so that his words are a tickle over tight skin. "That's the day I met your mom. The day I started dreaming you into existence. Nothing matters before that. This is where the story really starts."

Eyes still closed, pretending to sleep, Wab turned her head slightly into the pillow so the tears would have somewhere to fall.

CHAPTER 6:
CATALOG AND CRUCIFY

French

I WALKED IN, AND THE ESCORT STAYED BEHIND IN THE hallway. In the whole room there was only an empty desk and two chairs—one behind the desk and one in front. In the one behind the desk sat a young man in a brown suit. The room was too bright, and I winced. The young man stood up and pulled the blinds so that we were in a blue kind of half dark.

"There, that should be better." He sat back down, his face in the new shadows, one hand on his tie so that it sat flat against his chest. He looked like he was wearing his grandfather's suit; it fit him all wrong. His arms weren't big enough and too long at the same time so that his bare wrists settled on the wood desk. He looked like he's just hatched into this baby executive.

"You look like a bird, man," I told him, and started giggling. He sat quiet until I settled down.

He opened a drawer and pulled out a small laptop, opening it in front of him, smoothing down his tie over and over as if it were a snake he was trying to charm. He typed for a moment, waited for another, then glanced up at me, fingers poised over the keys.

"Name?"

"What?"

"Your name, please."

"Why in the hell would I give you my name?"

"Why would you not?" His voice was even, practiced.

I was cold. I rubbed my shaved head. "It's breezy up top now. Hard to think."

He looked down at the screen. "According to your file, you sustained a severe concussion and dehydration and required a dozen stitches, so hair removal was necessary."

"Oh, so you were helping me? I mean, it's not like your goons cracked my skull open to begin with, right?"

"Name?"

I sat back in the chair and felt every one of my bones rest on the frame. My vision was kind of zooming in and out, making me lightheaded, but I didn't want to look like I felt. In the bush, you never show your underbelly.

"Not gonna happen, dude." I smirked, trying to look sinister. I had the feeling I maybe just looked like I was in pain, which I was. But I did manage to lock eyes with him before he looked back down to his computer.

"Are you Nish?" I asked. Things were a bit blurry, and the

sunlight had been blocked out, but there was something about his structure, about the way he held himself in his borrowed suit.

"Are *you*?" he countered without looking up.

"Why else would I be here? This is a school, right?"

"We prefer institute. And I don't see how that detail matters right now," he said, fingers steepled under his chin.

"You're right." I slid down in my chair. "We don't need details like names of schools—sorry, *institutes*—or people."

He sighed. "Okay, then. I'm just trying to get this file done so we can properly catalog inventory, but I think maybe you need some more time to think about how you want this to go."

I sighed and stretched out my legs till my feet hit his desk. "Sure thing, I'll just get comfortable. Inventory likes to relax every now and then."

"Oh, no, not in here." He stood, pushing his chair out. "This room is for people who work and those who cooperate with people working. No, I think you should go back to your quarters." He reached behind him, in between two windows, and pressed a small white button. There was a high-pitched buzzing outside the door.

The panic that kicked up my throat matched that sound. It was sharp and sudden. "Back to my quarters? Now, hold on—"

"No, it's become quite clear that you need a little more time. Not to worry, we'll book another round in a few days."

I tried to stand, but my legs were jelly. "But I'm starving in there. You can't be serious."

"Oh, I'm afraid I am serious." He had two hands on his tie now, like the snake was trying to strangle him. "It happens—don't feel special. Sometimes it takes three or four tries." He paused, his hands moving to his belt.

Breathing was getting hard, and black spots were swarming over my vision. "No wait, wait—"

"I don't think I would believe any sudden change of heart you might have now. It's clear you're resistant. And that's okay, buddy. It happens."

"Buddy?" The door behind me clicked open, and the light from the hallway streamed into the semi-dark. My escort had returned, and this time he had another man with him, one even bigger and wider than the first, both in black. "Wait!"

They each grabbed me by an arm, easily prying my fingers off the arms of the chair. And then I was up and on my toes, almost levitating in their grasp.

"I'll expect you back here in a better mood soon." The interviewer stepped around the desk, buttoning his suit jacket. "And then we can talk." He had a pronounced limp that did nothing to diminish his malice.

"NO! NO! Wait!" I struggled against being pulled backward from the room. I was through the door when the interviewer walked into the hallway light after us and I saw his face for the first time.

Short dark hair, closely cropped around the sides, narrow brown eyes—not unkind, even now—and a small chip in his front tooth. I heard his voice again, but this time as a child. *Too late, buddy; they know someone's up here, just not how many someones.*

"Mitch?"

His eyes narrowed, nose scrunched the way it always did when he was really thinking. His mouth opened, and he pulled a hand out of his pocket to cover it before reaching out with the other to grab the door frame. His eyes got all big, like they did when he figured something out.

"French?"

"This one's gonna be a problem," the new escort said. Then he bent down and grabbed my legs in one arm, effortlessly throwing me over his shoulder like a folded tarp. "Easier this way. Get the doors," he told the first man.

His shoulder jostling under my guts cut the air out of my body. My head was already spinning, but now it was also heavy, too heavy to lift. I had no more voice to call out to my brother, the brother I hadn't seen since he'd sacrificed himself so I could get away so many years ago. The brother I last saw being dragged off into a Recruiter van destined for one of these schools while I hid in the trees. How? Why?

By the time we hit the first set of stairs, I was quiet and still. I might have even blacked out for a moment. Small mercies, I guess.

Everything was a blur of turning and climbing and muffled conversation between the two men and then with the security guards. Could this all be a dream? Another nightmare, maybe? First I heard my mother through the walls, and then I saw Mitch?

"Easy there, little guy. You gotta walk." My feet touched the floor, and four hands were standing me upright, leaning me against a cold wall.

"Whew, those stairs are a bitch." He stood upright and stretched out his back. "Wish they'd let us use the elevators all the time."

"Oh, c'mon, Franklin, you gonna let a little cardio with a bone bag get you all winded?" The second man slapped the first on the shoulder and chuckled.

I pulled myself together while they bantered. We were just past the final staircase, inside the hallway on the third floor, my floor. I was minutes away from being back in that room. In the dark. Alone.

But what if I wasn't alone? If Mitch was actually here, then maybe—just maybe—so was my mother.

They say adrenaline floods into your body. But a flood is gradual and rising. Adrenaline is more like electricity, sharp and sudden and random with its placement. It stabs into your muscles and needles you behind the eyes. It sets your lower guts quivering and makes your breath fast and shallow so that you have to pant.

I knew the way. I knew the door. And I had to know if she was here. So I did what I did best: I ran.

I pushed off the wall and easily darted past the men, who were tired and distracted and absolutely not expecting the skinny kid with the banged-up head to go all-out down the hall.

"Hey!"

I ran straight and fast, all my senses narrowing in on the task. I streaked through the big room, barely seeing the bodies that filled the corners, slumped on the couches, staring out the windows, all in similar muted clothes. I did hear one yell as I passed, "Yeah, niijii! Give'r!"

A right turn. Then a left. I could hear the men behind me, shouts and heavy footfalls, but it was all shades of an echo mixed in with the ringing in my ears. The edges of my vision blurred, my throat closed up. I couldn't go much farther. I hadn't eaten in days, and adrenaline will only take you so far. But I was in the hall with my room, the hall where my mother had spoken to me. And now I knew which room it had been coming from, to the left of my door, right before the hallway split off in either direction. That's where the voice was coming from, that's where she was.

I turned the corner, crashing into the wall, falling to my knees, her door directly in front of me now.

"Mom!" I meant it to be a shout—heroic, even—to let her know I was there and I was getting her out, but it was a nothing but a lip movement and a wheeze.

The escorts were coming. I could hear them now and imagined their popped veins and red cheeks just around the corner. I scrambled to my feet and lunged for the door.

"Mom." This time it was a whisper. I put a shaking hand on the silver knob, and it slipped off. I couldn't even grip it. One of the escorts rounded the corner.

"Stop right there!" He skidded on the slick floor.

I reached out again, two hands this time. And, holy hell, it turned, clicked, and opened. I used what felt like the last breath in my body to push it wide.

A light flickered and hummed to life. My eyes jumped around the space: brooms, buckets, boxes stacked to the ceiling, a metal shelf full of bottles and containers, folded rags and packages of sponges.

"Mom?" No, she had to be here. I'd heard her. She was talking to me. And it was real. If Mitch was real, she was real.

"Mom!" This time it had volume. But there was no answer, no movement. Not even a shadow. Not even a sigh. This was a broom closet, and she was not here.

And then the escorts were on me, tackling me to the ground. And it all went away.

Darkness.

CHAPTER 7:
MILES TO GO

Rose

THEY DID LEAVE AT FIRST LIGHT, MAYBE EVEN A moment before. Derrick slept light, so when Rose started moving around, he was up. She'd spent the night in her sleeping bag dragged close to the fire, her tent already tied and ready to go. By the time she'd rolled up her gear and put on her shoes, he was up and on his feet.

"You coulda slept in here," he mumbled, stretching out in front of his pup tent.

"And you coulda just slept in the cave like normal," she retorted. "I don't need a babysitter. Never have."

"And let you slip off by yourself? No siree." He laced up his boots and dragged his prepacked bag out of the tent, which he then folded down in two quick movements. Then he scooped up his hair and spun it into a messy bun at the nape of his neck.

"You think anyone's going to try to stop us?" She looked around nervously.

"Quit doing that. You're gonna break a molar," Derrick said.

When she gave him a quizzical look, he continued, "When you get nervous, you clench your teeth, and your jaw muscle gets all twitchy." He looked away, suddenly shy. "Anyway, no one is really paying much attention these days. Too busy planning and searching. Besides, your spot is pretty secluded."

It was true. Rose had purposely set up camp far from any neighbors. It was enough having to be around everyone during the day; she could do without hearing people fart in their sleep all night. She put her pack on, gauging the weight distribution. They had a long way to go, and she needed to make sure everything was in place. The tent shifted around, so she took it off and retied it. Now it was too high up on her neck and made it hard to turn her head.

"Shoot." She took it off again.

"What's wrong?"

"I have too much stuff. When we were on the move, everything was distributed among the group, so we were all even, but this is too much." She sighed, pulling off the tent and opening the bag's flap to rearrange the items inside.

"Can you leave anything?" Derrick was wrapping his own tent in a ground tarp.

"Nah—knife, change of clothes, hatchet, food . . . we'll need all of this." She was getting frustrated.

"Listen, why don't you just leave your tent here? It's too big. You don't need all that space, anyway. We can use mine. Look." He shouldered his bag and turned around to show her. "It's already packed up nice, no worries."

"Share a tent?" She looked at him suspiciously. "Why are you trying so hard for that?"

"Why not? We both have sleeping bags, so we'll have our own space." He tried to sound nonchalant.

Leaving the camp a few minutes later with her abandoned tent stashed behind a tree, Derrick tried even harder not to smile.

◆◆◆ ◆◆◆ ◆◆◆

They left quietly and kept up a steady silence and a quick pace for the first few hours. The key was to get out of range of any potential searchers sent from the camp. Once they got to the main road, they'd have to decide which school they were going to. In a dense circle of pines where they could see the road, Rose finally stopped, pulled off her bag, and retrieved a water bottle from the side pocket. She sat on a moss-covered boulder, stretching out her legs with a sigh.

Derrick sat back on his heels and took the water when it was his turn. "Well," he said after a long drink, "where to now, oh navigationally gifted one? Since this is the mission of the century, I assume you have some sort of game plan, right?"

Rose squinted toward the asphalt, then took in their surroundings, rubbing her palms across her thighs.

"I would do anything to hear music right now," she said.

"I can sing for you," Derrick offered, dropping the sarcasm for the opportunity to impress her.

"No, no, not like that." She waved him off. "Not to be rude. Sorry." She threw the apology at him like an afterthought.

She placed a hand on his shoulder for a second. He moved to touch her, but her fingers were already in her hair, pulling its thick weight into an elastic band.

"I mean, a song, a full song with lots of pieces. Like a symphony, you know?" She stood up. "It's been forever since I heard one of those. But sometimes I can still feel it—that way you feel when the music breaks apart into all its separate instruments and melodies, the way they move through your ears and settle in your muscles."

"Breaks apart?"

"Yeah, you know—the piano plays in your ribs, the flute in your stomach . . . but that's not the best part. The best part is after each piece digs into a different part of you, and then it's like they're carrying magnets in their pockets. Because then all the pieces, they do their damnedest to find each other, to get back together." She wrapped her arms around her waist and watched the tops of the trees sway. "That's what great music does."

"And what's that, exactly?"

"Forces you to feel every part of yourself—parts you didn't know existed—because it's moving every last piece from the inside, just trying pull itself back together through muscle and time and the darkest spaces."

Now they were both watching the trees.

Rose closed her eyes for a moment. "They do whatever it takes to be back together, no matter how impossible that might be for tiny notes stranded in an unknown body."

Derrick watched her face, relaxed into the satisfaction of a remembered love. "Sounds like family," he finally said.

Rose lowered her gaze and smiled at him. "Now you know why I couldn't wait around for another day. Not for another minute. Why I have to find him no matter what. I need to hear his notes. Just even one more time."

A pained look flickered across his face, but he didn't respond.

After some stretching and reshouldering their loads, they made their way to the side of the road. Rose looked back and forth. Both ways looked lonely and hard. She closed her eyes and took a deep breath. "Sir John A. MacDonald. That's where we go."

"You sure?" Derrick asked. Truly, it didn't matter; it really was a bit of a coin toss. "I sure as hell don't want to have to backtrack to another school if we choose the wrong one."

"No," she answered honestly. "But that's where we're going."

They crossed the road and scurried back into the bush, then turned right and followed the long highway from the cover of branches.

"About this family thing . . ." Derrick loud-whispered over the crunch of their boots on fallen leaves and old wood. "So, would that make French like your brother, then?"

Rose didn't answer.

"I'll take that as a yes."

That first day was all about covering ground. They ate dried meat from their stores and kept things at a brisk pace. It was easier not to talk, but they did anyway, sharing stories of the worst things they ever ate (Rose: grilled acorns; Derrick: a moss sandwich), the craziest nights they ever spent (Rose: sleeping in a tree; Derrick: running through a marsh), and the things they missed the most (Derrick: Spam; Rose: well, that one was obvious and started a long bout of silence while Derrick sulked).

"One time, I got the shits so bad I had to travel with a plastic bag on my butt," Derrick told her.

Rose scrunched up her nose. "What, like a diaper?"

Derrick mimicked holding a grocery bag by the handles. "No, like a friggin' *bag*. Like something that could hold a load, but, like, a real load."

Rose squinted, imaging for a moment how this would work. "Waaaaiiittttt . . ." And then she laughed so hard they had to stop for her to catch her breath.

Derrick waddled around her, legs bowed as if he were clutching something between his butt cheeks.

"Stop!" Her cheeks were shiny with tears. "Oh my god, stop."

Derrick righted himself and put an arm around her shoulder, pulling her forward. "Come on, Morriseau. We gotta keep moving. If I could do it then, you can do it now." He pretended to be interested in the twisted trees they passed under, but it was all he could do to hold himself together while her laughter pulled him to pieces.

CHAPTER 8:
A GIRL AND A GUN

The Family

NO ONE BACK AT CAMP PANICKED. THEY KNEW exactly where Rose had gone and why, and they knew that Derrick had followed after her. They knew because they knew these kids so well, but also because Derrick had left behind a note, scribbled in pencil on the back of a tear of birch bark paper.

Gone to the schools to find the kid. We're all good. Took a rifle. I'll bring them back—Rose and the gun.

"Fools," Bullet hissed. Despite all the clamor and gnashing of teeth, she liked the girl. It was a fondness born out of respect, which was even rarer than straight-up kindness or having things in common. The truth was, they did have things in common—they all did. That was why it was so hard to be removed and skeptical these days. Survival made a hell of a social glue.

It would be six more sleeps until Carole returned with an update. Then they should know exactly which school the boy had been taken to and could set out to recover him. And even then, it wasn't like they could just walk up to the building, knock on the front door, and politely ask for him back. It wasn't like they had the manpower or the weapons to storm in. But once they knew where he was and got details on the property and routines, then they could scheme. Maybe the Recruiters would move him. They could try to highjack the convoy, like they had for the old woman. That one hadn't turned out so well, but there were lessons to be learned from it, and they had, they had learned. At a terrible cost. But now they had to worry about where these two idiots had gone? She spoke her worry out loud.

"How are they even going to choose to the right school? And that's even if they make it there," she sighed. "But I cannot think of a good way of getting them back. I mean, how do we know which way they went?"

"I'm going to kill her." Wab went from concern to anger in the blink of an eye.

"I should have given her more of my time," Miig sighed. "I was so caught up in French and in Isaac . . . well, I wasn't a very good relative. I didn't seek her out. I didn't calm her down. I just . . . didn't."

Isaac grabbed his hand and gave it a squeeze. "She seems like a capable girl. I'm sure she'll be smart about it."

"And Derrick, he's a good hunter, him," Jean interjected. "And I appreciate that kind of determination focused in on my boy."

The group fell quiet. Jean had just been reunited with French, the only remaining blood family he had, and now he was in limbo again, wondering if his blood was alive or dead. And here they were, arguing over the logistics of an attempted rescue?

"If anyone can do it, it's Rose," Miig agreed. "She's braver than most, that one."

Bullet put a hand on Jean's shoulder. "We all agree. Francis is too important to sleep on. And that girl, she sure as hell didn't waste any time sleeping. We wish her the best, and in the meantime"—she looked around at those assembled—"we will start preparing to leave. Because we will. Just as soon as Father Carole brings us word and a destination."

CHAPTER 9:
BEDRIDDEN

French

"MAYBE DREAMS WERE ALWAYS IN THE MARROW. Maybe not. Maybe they used to be everywhere—muscles, skin, voice—and then we learned how to hide them better." She was sitting on an upturned bucket in the back corner of the storage room.

"Mom?" I was in the supply closet doorway. My head jerked to the side to check the hall behind me—clear and quiet. Now there were no escorts chasing me down, no inmates screaming from the main room. And the light seemed to soak in through the walls from somewhere outside.

"Yes, yes. Why is it so hard for you to see me, son?" She looked exactly like she had the last time I'd seen her—dark eyes and hair a little wild, face too flushed, dressed in jeans and a thick green sweater, scuffed work boots on her small feet. She was smoking, flicking the ashes toward the cement ground and watching them spin into little twisters like weather in the room.

"Why are you here?"

"Because you need me to be here." She shrugged. "So, here I am."

I tried to move into the room, but my feet wouldn't budge. I struggled against the inertia, but it only shot pins and needles up my calves and made ache and rot out of my knees.

"Bone marrow, the way it's built up, the way it rests, can change over time, you know. It's not supposed to. But things like tuberculosis can do it. Could be that's when we first had the idea to stuff our dreams in there, when they stuffed Natives into the tuberculosis wards to die." She opened and closed her fists where they rested on her thighs.

"Maybe that's when we noticed there were new places opening up in our bodies, each just big enough to hide a dream." She lifted her right boot and stomped out an ash twister that was getting unwieldy. It collapsed into a small pile but still shuddered and jerked like a dying insect.

"And then, when they tossed us into boarding schools to kill the Indian in the child . . . well, then we had to hide them so we wouldn't just shrivel up. So we'd still fight for the things that made us who we are. And now, here we are again . . ."

"Mom, are we going to get out of here?"

She looked me in the eye for the first time, and I saw infinite mourning there. It made my heart race and then slow to a heavy thump in my temples. "No, son, *we* are not. But *you* might."

"I'll take you with me! We can leave together." I was crying.

She smiled, tight and small, holding back more than she put out. "Too late, buddy; they know someone is up here, just not how many someones."

"Buddy?" I grabbed my head; it was throbbing something terrible now. And I was remembering: the room, Mitch, the mad dash to get to my mother, finding what turned out to be nothing more than a storage closet and a hallucination . . .

"Mitch." I said it out loud.

✦✦✦ ✦✦✦ ✦✦✦

"I'm here, French." He put a hand on my shoulder. I wasn't sure if it was his hand or my shoulder that was shaking. Maybe both.

I woke up back in the medical room, in a narrow bed, hooked up to another IV, with more bandages on my head.

"What . . . what . . . happened?" Everything was in pieces, and none of them fit together.

"Well, I'm told you pulled a runner." Mitch was standing by the bed, wearing that ridiculous suit and that stupid tie he couldn't stop fidgeting with. "Which makes no sense. Why would you run in the direction you were going to begin with? You ran pretty much all the way back to your own room. Apparently you're terrible at getting away."

"When . . ."

"What happened? Were you trying to escape and got turned around?" He chuckled. The sound made me angry. Anger brought the pieces together.

"I was not trying to escape. I was trying to find her!" Raising my voice only made my head hurt more.

"Who, French? Who were you trying to find?" He leaned over me, ready to take in any information I was willing to part with. Unbelievable. Here I was, laid up, again, with a busted head, again, and he was still trying to extract intel?

I strained and pulled my neck off the pillow, getting as close to his face as I could before I spat it out. "Mom, you jackass. I was trying to get to our mother."

Our eyes were locked now, and it made me happy to see my words hit him like a slap, like paper airplanes whipped at close distance. He took a deep breath and pulled away, lowering himself into a metal chair beside the bed. He crossed his legs at the knee and folded his hands on top of them, like a proper gentleman. But that was wrong. There were no gentlemen left in the world.

"She is not here, French. As far as I can tell, she has never been here. And there are no records of her in the system." He looked out the frosted glass window behind me and cleared his throat. "Of course, back then, the system was less than efficient. Not that anyone is to blame, really. Those were early days, and we were just learning . . ."

"We?" Oh, if I could get up right now, the things I would do to him. "We? So you're one of them now?"

He sighed and dropped his chin to his chest, speaking into his shitty dress shirt. "We are all one people, French. We always have been. All separations are false. There is but one God, and we are but one people under him."

"God? What kind of god allows some people to be harvested so others can live? How is that godlike?" I sneered. I turned my head; I couldn't even look at him. I wished he would just go, just get the hell away from me. What was the point of finding your brother when your brother had become the thing you hated and feared the most?

"You do know the story of Zeus eating his own children, don't you?" He was so calm it made me tense.

"Oh, just get away from me." I closed my eyes. My whole body hurt, my chest, my back, even my face.

"You're upset—" he started.

"Upset? Upset?" I faced him again. "Oh, I am more than upset. I am a prisoner, and I am hurt, *and* I am probably going to die. And that's not even the worst of it. No, no. The worst of it is that I get to see you again, and you're not my brother. You're not even close to being my brother."

We sat in silence for long minutes. From the beds around us came coughs or groans. Men and women in white coats gliding between bodies like efficient ghosts. Then he tried again. "Well, you need to know that the Watchmen had to subdue you with some amount of force. During the recovery operation, you sustained quite a bad fall. There are six stitches in your right cheek where you came into contact with the floor. I'd advise you to keep your facial movements to a minimum for a while."

"Yeah, thanks," I scoffed. "And be sure to thank your Watchmen for me, too. Apparently, they did a bang-up job of *watching*. Who are they, anyway?"

"The Watchmen?"

"I thought Recruiters ran the show."

"Out there"—he nodded toward the glass—"Recruiters run the show, as you say. They're actually Supply Chain Management Officers, but the nickname stuck. In here, the Watchmen are the security."

"How many layers are there to this bureaucracy?" I could dig for intel, too.

"In the institutions, like this one, the Watchmen are the front line. Then the Agents—that's where I'm headed. They're the managers. Then the Clergy are kind of like the board of directors. They used to be more involved in the day-to-day operations, but we've built in some layers to maximize their time. And the residents play a part, too."

"Yeah," I couldn't resist saying. "We're the supply."

"Well, depending on how you behave, there are options, especially within an evolving system." He sounded like he was reading from a script. "You start off in general population, as a resident. If you show promise, like I did, you get drafted into the Program: those with the potential to join in the meaningful work once they've proven themselves."

I wanted to cut him off. *Meaningful work like bringing in others? Traitors, you mean, like the ones who killed Riri?* I bit my tongue; it was better to let him keep talking.

"Some residents can stay in a school for years, helping—janitors, orderlies. Back when the staff was still thin, there were lots of reformed residents doing odd jobs."

This must have been what had happened to Isaac, I thought. He'd come in in the early days of the schools.

Mitch prattled on. "And then there are the doctors and nurses, of course. Those who do the extraction work, and the medical researchers who are taking us to the next level." He clapped his hands together on his lap. "It's all very intricate, and we all work together like a well-oiled machine."

"And what happens to people who don't get into this program of yours?" I already knew the answer, but I wanted him to say it, dared him to acknowledge the monster in the house.

"Well, if you can't join the higher cause, and not everyone can, then you are part of the solution in other ways. You supply medicine to the population—"

"You get your marrow sucked out?" I blurted. I had to know. "Mitch? Did you . . . did they take your marrow?"

He grew quiet, put a hand over his lips. Oh god, even now, I didn't want it to be true. It was the most horrible thing I could imagine. Small sounds started to come from him. Oh god, they took it. "Listen, man, I'm sure—"

I was cut short by the small sounds turning to giggles. He stifled harder laughter behind his fingers.

"What the . . . are you laughing?"

"I'm sorry." He composed himself. "It's just, I'm not a zombie, am I?" He stretched his arms out in front of him, tilted his head, and moaned. "Jeez, French. If I'd had the procedure, I'd be in the lot out back . . ." It was his turn to break off. "Uh, you're hilarious." He fidgeted with his damn tie and continued with his spiel on how things worked.

"If you're not in the Program, you have the privilege of being part of the ongoing research, so you're put into isolation so that data sets can be monitored. Or on to the more high-level rooms, where the work is undergoing change." Suddenly, his shoes were so interesting he had to examine them—anything to avoid making eye contact.

I took a deep breath to scream at him, but pain cut it short. My cheek was definitely messed up. I felt the pull of the stitches and raised my hand to touch them. It reminded me of Wab, my real sibling, the one who would have burned this whole ward to the ground to get me out. I secretly hoped I'd be left with a scar. It would be an honor to resemble her, even though this wound was a thousand times less grievous than her own. She'd gotten hers in the city, from the men who had wanted her to shut down her courier business after the world went dark. That cut had taken her business and her eye, but it had also brought her out to the bush. That scar was the map she'd used to get to us. Maybe mine would also give me a direction.

"We die from the extraction? That's it? You take it all till we're dead?!" I couldn't let go of the image of a lot, a mass grave, in the back. I was loud, but I didn't scream like I was in my head.

"Shhhhh. Calm down, now." He glanced around the room, gave a fake smile, and waved someone off. "Not right away. It takes a month, maybe two. And it's not the extraction that kills a patient. It's the inability to heal without bone marrow. Basic science, sad but true."

I could not believe he was saying these words the same way one might say "good morning." My mouth was opening and closing like a fish; I had no response. How did you sanely respond to insanity?

"I understand this must be a bit of a shock." He was really working on that merit badge in patience now.

"A bit of a shock? I couldn't be more surprised if you removed your own head and flew around the room."

"But here we are, both of us, we are alive. We really beat the odds on that one. And now we can start rebuilding a life. Together." He leaned in. "You'd like that, wouldn't you, little brother? To stay together?" There was a softness around his eyes, or maybe that was just what I wanted to see.

I didn't answer him; what was there to say? In the pause, I gazed around the room. It was a big space, divided up into cubicles by curtains and glass walls. I saw dozens of other beds, each one occupied, bodies big and tiny covered with stiff green sheets. I didn't know what was more heartbreaking, the tiny bundles or the larger ones, some heavily pregnant bodies or men with still-youthful jawlines. At each bedside was at least one machine or IV pole and, in a few cases, laptops on carts with webs of wires slipping up under the sheets. There were moans and beeps and the shuffle of nurses walking between curtains. No one was running; no one seemed in any big hurry, not even when one of the monitors started screaming. An orderly just walked over—swinging his arms, even—and shut it off. High up on the walls, along the edges of the ceiling, were narrow windows, embedded with thin bars and frosted so that only light got in and nothing got out.

I'd heard so many stories about the new residential schools over the years. There were variations to the tales. Some said they were straight-up prisons without food or clean water. Others said they were where the government siphoned our ability to dream for mass production and we died in the process. Others spoke about a community of donors living the good life with books and clean water and the freedom to make noise. These ones talked about living through the donation, about reintegrating into the societies that were carrying on, and a world being rebuilt with enough room for us all. These were the stories planted by traitors to try to get us to come in on our own.

Years ago, when I was boy and Mitch was a boy and we were the kind of boys who still had parents, we had a distant cousin come to stay with us. She was what other people called an activist and what

she called "being sane." She told us stories about animals in slaughterhouses, how eating their meat was one of the reasons we got weak
as a species, more susceptible to illness.

"They're terrified. Wouldn't you be? Yanked from your mother,
watching and listening to your relatives being butchered day and
night? Smelling their blood in the air?"

Mitch and I huddled together on one big chair while she talked
to us, leaning in like it was a ghost story at bedtime, which it kind
of was.

"Some companies try to do things quick, to make life near the
end less miserable so the animals won't know what's coming. But
it's not some kind of charity. No, like everything the bastards do, it's
for profit. Makes the meat better. Reduced fear equals better taste.
Because fear is poison, and it gets transferred from animal to meat
to human."

When Dad told us about the call for healthy Indigenous donors
in the early days, before some escaped with the truth, this was what
I thought of: slaughterhouses. Now I wondered if the dreams from
those who had walked in of their own free will instead of being
dragged in by white vans, were better, full of sunshine and wing-
less flight.

"Just think about it, French. We can go back to the way things
were. Even better. You can finally stop running." I heard him stand.
My eyes were closed, and I was already drifting off. "You can finally
be still."

He put a tentative hand on my shoulder. I felt it as weight and
absence. I felt it for what it was, something meant to hold me down,
to break me. I had to get out of here.

"Mitch, do you still dream?"

"It's . . . quiet now. I'm not really sure." He sounded sad. Or maybe that was just me projecting.

"I'd rather be dead." It was no more than a whisper, and it didn't matter anyway. He was already gone.

For hours, my thoughts alternated between hoping my family was on their way to get me and hoping my family stayed away. It would break me to know they were stuck in here; it would absolutely kill me to know that I was the reason why.

♦♦♦ ♦♦♦ ♦♦♦

Mitch slipped back in that night. The room was dark and marked with small constellations of electric lights from the machines, punctuated by the sobs and coughs of the patients. His outline perched in the chair at my side, backlit by security lights out the window. The yellow glare was softened by the frosted glass and cut the dark like rolls of old muslin unraveled onto bodies and machines alike. I turned my head on the pillow, my busted cheek settled now into a steady pulse. He cleared his throat and began his story.

CHAPTER 10:
MITCH'S GOING-AWAY STORY

Mitch

REALLY, I SHOULDN'T HAVE PUT UP SUCH A FIGHT. IT was nobody's fault but my own that my leg got broken, snapped clean through. I was lucky for that. My calf could have been a bag of shards. If I had only listened to instructions when they found us in that tree house, nobody would have gotten hurt—it is neither the mandate nor intention to cause hurt. It never was. But I recognize that I was different back then, more focused on individual freedom than collective survival. I was a child.

I was blind. But now I see.

Things were rough, and I was convinced I was going to die. But I clung to the idea that you were out there, that you were going to make it. I felt like I'd done my job as a big brother, creating a distraction, letting you slip away into the godforsaken woods. Now I'm embarrassed that I left you out there to fend for yourself. Anything could have happened. How could I have told you to climb into the trees? To hide? You could have fallen. And what if they didn't hear you fall and you were just out there, broken, at the base of a tree? Or what could have happened if you had managed to climb down? Over the years, I think I've imagined everything—you eaten by bears, taken by the insane who didn't find help for their sickness, starving to death in the pines . . . I should have kept you with me. It would have been better to have you with me. Then we'd have been saved together. I was selfish.

The early schools were really nothing more than warehouses. There were fence cages full of metal bunks and no plumbing, and we were just kind of stored in there. It wasn't all bad, though; there were regular meals, and the pastors involved gave us sermons and teachings every night before lights out so we had something to think about other than our pain, our loneliness. It's weird to think that so many of us had been alone, and now there we were, hundreds of us all together, and yet still we felt lonely. That was before our hearts were relieved. Before we found grace. We *were* alone. Somehow, all together we were more alone than ever.

It was a few days before they really did anything about my leg, but what could they do? They had to wait for the doctors to show up. See, back then, the institutes didn't have their own staff. People covered whole regions, so sometimes we'd go a week without a doctor or a dentist or a nutritionist. That was really the horror of it all—the waiting. If someone got sick or hurt in between visits, well, there was nothing that could be done. Sometimes releasing someone from their misery was the only kindness that could be afforded. But I was young and tough. In fact, it was how I dealt with and survived those first days that made them consider me for a higher calling in the first place. Though I was only a boy, a confused and lowly wretch, I was saved. Isn't life wonderful sometimes?

The first year is kind of a blur. There was a lot to get used to, and things were changing as fast as you could acclimate. And then there was the way you haunted me. I couldn't close my eyes without seeing you, either still swaying in the wind, clutching a thin trunk, or lying on the ground, just a splayed-out skeleton, too small to be real. The group formed friendships—that's inevitable in any situation, but especially in ours.

After a while, we learned to let go, to not be sentimental about things or people. Things and people were one and the same—they could be lost, moved, taken away, broken. No use in getting attached. It was much better to form a friendship with the one thing that couldn't be taken, someone who went with you when you moved: God. He was our friend and our father. He listened. He watched. He was constant. In fact, it was He who finally gave me peace about you being left out in the wilderness. If He was watching over me, then perhaps He was also watching over you. Perhaps you had been found, too, and taken in. Or perhaps the end had been swift and painless. I found peace in that.

After that, I was separated from the herd. A few others and I, all around twelve or thirteen years old. That's when they start training us for the intelligence program. All of us were still stuck on our *before* lives, of course. So at first, we wanted to escape, to burn everything to the ground, as it were. But after some time, after being taught the reality of the world and the important role we could play in it, well, we started to see the light.

Mind you, it was an intense program. We spent a lot of time isolated, away from the others who were too old or too stubborn to change their minds and hearts. Sometimes we were even kept away from one another. But I had the Holy Bible to keep me company. I must have read it front to back four times in that first year alone. Now, of course, I understand that's not such a feat. Now I understand it was just desperation. We carry the words in our hearts. There is no need for paper and ink. That's a crutch, an introduction.

I didn't get to go on any of the early missions; my leg kept me grounded. But again, small graces. It gave me more time to be mentored. I stayed in the offices and labs. I heard things. I learned things. I was brought in to help in other ways, ways that gave me insight into the future of the REM recovery mission.

It wasn't all admin work and running errands, either. I had my trials. I joined the doctors when they did procedures. I helped deliver vessels to the crematory. I tried to calm new students, especially the very young ones who were alone for maybe the first time ever. Some days I had questions; most nights I questioned everything. It's hard to devote yourself completely to logic when you have to face yourself alone at night, knowing where you came from, knowing your own family members had met the same fate as those you helped lay to rest.

But what could we do? Let the whole world crumble into madness and violence? How could we let that happen when there was a chance, a solution, right there in front of us? And how could we, the dreamers, begrudge any of God's children the opportunity to rebuild and move on? You see, eventually everything would right itself. The world would settle, and the networks and systems would return, and then there would be no need to sacrifice anything. Then we could all live together again. It was almost too beautiful to be true, that we could play such a huge role in it all.

It took years before I could sleep without nightmares, years before I could truly look at my own reflection in the mirror, but I got there. Eventually. And just in time, too. What a gift it is to be here, to be a part of the solution, when we have only just made the kind of breakthroughs that change the game for everyone. I'm excited again, for all of us.

Things are going to change, and we are going to be here to see that change through. Oh, French, you wouldn't believe me if I told you, but the days of hunting and sacrifice are nearly over. Wait and see. Believe and witness.

We once were lost, but now we're found.

CHAPTER 11:
A SLIM LIGHT IN A DARK WORLD

French

IN THE MORNING, I FOUND HIM SLEEPING IN THE chair, his elbow on the arm, his head held up with a palm.

"Were you really quoting 'Amazing Grace'?"

He roused, stretching and blinking rapidly. The imprint of his hand was red on his cheek. "What?"

Seeing the doctors in the room, he pulled himself upright quick, smoothing out the front of his shirt, tugging the seam on his pant legs straight. Then he ran both hands through his short hair and used his fists to rub his eyes.

"You know it was written by a slave trader, 'Amazing Grace.' Someone who literally delivered thousands of people into torture and death."

He paused, remembering his story from the night before. "Well, a slave trader who later reformed and fought for the well-being of all the people." He opened his hands wide, smiling, more than a little smug. "You know that song predicted our time, where we are now?"

"You don't say." I was tired, down-to-my-soul tired. Tired of all this horseshit. I slumped farther into the bed till my feet hit the footboard. The sheet was scratchy on my chin.

Mitch stood in front of the chair, cleared his throat, placed a hand over his tie and heart, closed his eyes, and began to sing:

"The earth shall soon dissolve like snow,

the sun forbear to shine;

but God, who called me here below,

will be forever mine."

"Nice pipes," I teased.

"Thanks," he answered in earnest. He must have forgotten I was his brother and real compliments would be harder than that to come by. "I'm part of the staff choir."

I rolled my eyes. "Yeah, well, there aren't many opportunities to sing when you're running for your life."

He sat back down, playing with the crease down each leg of his grey trousers. "French, I'm real sorry about how things went for you. Honestly. If I could take it all back and make sure you went with me, I would."

I sat up quick, too quick, and the blood rushed into my head, pushing black spots into my vision. "What the hell, man? That was the bravest thing I've ever seen, the bravest thing I've ever even heard of! You saved me! I was actually saved, not pretend-gospel saved."

He leaned forward, placing a hand on the bed near my arm, which I jerked out of reach. "Easy, easy, now. You'll pop your stitches." He looked around the room, smiling at the frowning white coats watching us suspiciously with their clipboards and magnified eyes. "Don't go getting all charged up, or you'll get strapped to the bed. I've seen it happen for less."

"You've watched a lot of kids being tortured? And you just keep watching, eh?"

I didn't want to look at him, but I couldn't help it. In between each word I was searching the planes and curves of his face for the Mitch of my memory, the one I'd held on to all these years. He should have taken me with him? And behind it all was the deep humiliation of being robbed, robbed of the reunion I had played out in my head so many nights before sleep. Robbed of Mitch. Could I not even have this one moment of relief, of happiness?

"French . . ."

"I think you should call me Francis."

"Francis . . ." He said it as a sigh. He paused. I might not know him anymore, but I knew that taking away my name hurt him. "I understand your frustration. I really do." He sat forward on the chair, his hands clasped between his knees. "You're at the beginning of a long journey, but I'll be right here by your side."

"I'd rather you weren't."

"And it won't take as long as it did for me. We've changed the Program, revised the timelines. You could be out of containment in weeks instead of months. You could even be in the field before the year is over."

Wait . . . out of containment? In the field? Now I was truly interested. "Like, the actual field?"

He laughed. "Yeah, little brother, into an actual field." His face turned serious. "But there's no gaming the system. Your dedication has to be real. They'll know if it's not." His eyes got dark. "I'll know if it's not."

I tried to swallow everything I wanted to say. I longed to both tell him to stop calling me "brother" and beg him to help me escape, even though it was becoming obvious he would never do that. I couldn't help it, though: even now, I had a small, bright piece of hope. If he'd been changed once, maybe he could be changed again.

"What is the Program?" I had trouble maintaining eye contact. Maybe he really could tell when I was being insincere. When we were little, he always called me on my lies. "How do I start?"

He smiled, small and quick, but it betrayed actual happiness. "Leave that to me."

The good thing about Mitch not being Mitch was that he seemed to have lost his ability to see my tells—the way I started shifting in bed, the way I pulled my lips tight. Even Miig knew those. I had to pull myself together, to get past the ache in my head and visions of my dead mother and terror for my family, for Rose, Chi Boy, Slopper, Tree, Zheegwon, Wab, and Miig. I had to get it all the way together if I was to have even a hope in hell of pulling this off. So I laced my fingers and forced myself to meet his gaze. I had to be even: no sudden changes, nothing he could doubt.

"I'm not actually interested, you know. I'd rather die than convert."

He smiled again, this one more perfunctory than the last; no more reveals for now. "I'll do you the favor of not repeating that."

He bent down to pick up a black binder he'd left beside the bed. On the front was a small white label that said, 656987: 17-YEAR-OLD

METIS, MALE. That was me. That's all I was right now. But better that the label was on a binder than a vial of marrow.

"Okay, then, first things first. I'll go talk to the supervisor, and you get some rest so we can get you out of here." He wagged his finger in front of my nose like an old lady. "And no more smart mouth."

That one cut. Oh man, I wanted to pop him in the jaw. Instead I just rolled my eyes. He scurried out of the room, binder under his arm. I closed my eyes, but sleep wouldn't come. Instead, I ran through the building again and again in my mind, memorizing each corner and counting the doors. It was obvious there were no classrooms. This place was as unlike a school as you could get. There was nothing here but medical gear, offices, and Indigenous bodies in locked rooms. It was a prison. I had to get out. And now Mitch had given me a small sliver of light to chase.

But could I pull it off? Could I convince not only my asshole brother but the people who pulled his strings that I had "turned"? I pictured myself in my own nerdy suit with a tie I couldn't stop fidgeting with. I could do that. Then I pictured myself with a binder under my arm, detailing all the specifics of some other poor sap on a bed. I imagined walking past suffering prisoners, whistling "Amazing Grace" like I hadn't a care in the world. I thought of singing in the staff choir while kids cried for their moms. I couldn't do that. But I had to try to make it look like I could. There was too much at stake.

Then I imagined holding Rose's hand, walking over the spongy ground through bright ferns, the sound of water trickling nearby, the way her hair smelled when we'd been running hard. And I knew that I could. I could do anything—I would do anything—to get back home.

✦✦✦ ✦✦✦ ✦✦✦

I woke up to two nurses, one checking my pulse, the other sliding the thin curtain along its curved pole so that my bed was surrounded by fabric and the suggestion of privacy.

"How you feeling?" The one holding my wrist with gentle fingers smiled. It was such a rare and true smile that I suddenly had space to not feel okay.

"Lousy."

She released my hand and wrote some numbers on a clipboard, then placed it at the foot of my bed. Her long braids were held back with an elastic, revealing small gold hoops up each earlobe all the way to the cartilage. "I bet."

The second nurse wore pink blush on her dark skin and had kind eyes. She rubbed the metal circle of her stethoscope on her own stomach to warm it up before placing it under my shirt. These small acts of kindness were tearing me apart.

"I'm May, this is Alice, and we're here to help. Now, do me a favor and take a deep breath." She filled her own lungs to demonstrate. When she was done listening to my chest, she added data to the clipboard, and they both stood, one shorter, both in pink scrubs, side by side at the foot of the bed.

"You get brought in by yourself?" May asked.

I hesitated. Was this another trick? Another way to pump me for information, only this time with niceties? Maybe they were a part of the underground network that helped Natives escape. Or maybe they were using the system to catch us before we made the first move. Them being here now, right after Mitch brought up the Program . . . it just seemed a little too convenient. I had to keep my head on straight, especially now that Mitch had shown me a way out.

"Yeah. So?"

They exchanged looks. Alice spoke next. "No one's out there waiting for you? Nowhere to run back to?"

"No. I'm alone." I folded my arms over my chest. "You can tell Mitch that. I have no intel to give. And I'm all-in for the Program, so he can stop checking." I turned over in my bed and closed my eyes. If this was another test, I intended to pass.

I heard the curtain being pulled back, and then I was alone once more. I smothered the small spin of panic and regret in my stomach with a palm pushed against my belly button.

Just before dark, the same Watchmen as before came to collect me. I was put into a wheelchair and strapped down. They were silent as they loaded me up, signed a form on a clipboard held out by a doctor, and took me out into the hall. This time we took an elevator. When the door slid shut, the larger one, who was pushing the chair, leaned down until his mouth was beside my ear.

"I wish you could run again. I should cut these straps so you can try. You'd get more than a busted cheek this time."

The other man stood in front of us, his back to me. I saw his shoulders bounce as he chuckled. "It's like they think they're all great athletes now or something. Too many years spent on their asses, living off the taxpayers. Now all of a sudden they're all Olympians."

They both laughed.

"Yeah," said the big guy. "They finally get a chance to provide something to society, to pay us back for centuries of free school and special privileges, and they're even trying to get out of that."

"Typical."

I kept my eyes on the lit-up red arrow above the door, trying not to hear them.

"You hear me, niijii?" He said it through gritted teeth, gripping the handles of my chair again and shaking it. "Or are you too stupid to understand?"

"Ah, leave him." The Watchman in front turned his head. "He's pretty much just a ziplock for what we need. We just gotta keep the bag from tearing before it's time to break the seal."

Ding.

The doors slid open, and they went back to their stoic stance. All professional-like. The elevator was on the other side of the guard station, so we had to swipe through into the hallway. I used every second of the journey to take in details about the place. The windows were all high up on the walls, so trying to use one to get out would involve finding a way to reach them.

The hallways were empty, but the doors were all open. I strained to see in each one, looking for any familiar faces, but there were no people at all. Each room, identical to mine, was empty, the bed made and the light on. There was nothing differentiating one from the next, no posters or knickknacks, no books or even a clock. A few had a pile of folded clothes at the foot of the bed, mostly pale green but one or two grey, but they could have belonged to anyone. There was nothing about any room that indicated an individual and nothing to tell me if I knew any of the people who were kept there.

And then I heard a noise I had no real memory of hearing before. A cacophony of voices mixing and weaving, punctuated by laughter and a few small currents of despair, all joined and set loose from throats with abandon. We turned into the main room, and there they were, about sixty people of different ages and sizes, all in white T-shirts and pale green scrub pants like me, all Indigenous like me. They gathered in small groups around the space. Two boys tossed a red ball back and forth. There was a lively card game happening at one coffee table, and a group of teary old men in serious conversation at the other. Teenagers stopped talking to watch us pass. The general volume lowered as I was wheeled through, but there was no moment of silence. I was so happy I could have cried. Here we were, taking up space, filling it with our bodies and with our voices. It was more than I ever could have hoped for in any place, let alone this one.

Two men with scraggly moustaches and longer hair lifted their fists in the air as I passed, eyes solemn and connected to mine. The Watchman in front flicked his wrist, and the small tube he held snapped into a long rod. He wound up and cracked the guy closest to us in the side of the leg so that he went down on one knee. Still the man maintained eye contact with me, arm bent now, his fist still raised.

"Stay strong, brother!" someone yelled from the crowd, and a few others sent up a short *who-oo* in response. As we left the bright and noise of the room, I turned my head back to take in every last face I could see.

"Morons," the man pushing me sneered.

"Fucking idiots," agreed the other, collapsing his rod back into the handle.

We traveled the rest of the way in silence. I noticed it was silent because now I knew what the opposite of silence was. Just like I knew how light my room was when we entered because it had been dark for so long.

"All right kid, no funny business." They unbuckled my restraints. "Get out."

"Can't I go with everyone else?" I climbed out of the chair.

"No way, not after that shit you pulled, running off. The main room is for better-behaved animals." They pulled the chair out into the hall and slammed the door.

"Good night," one called through the door.

"Good night? But the sun's out," I answered.

"Oh, there's no sun for you." And then the light snapped off.

The room had never been more quiet or more dark. So I closed my useless eyes and dreamed of home.

CHAPTER 12:
THE DEATH TREE

Rose

THE FOREST OUT HERE WAS UNENDING, GREEN DRAPED over green woven with brown. There were few things as certain as the forest these days. Death. Movement. Hope. All three of them could be found hidden in the wet give of the woods.

Animals were less shy here than near the camp. Out here, there was less to be afraid of—not so many predators or change for them. Squirrels chased each other in the treetops like light-footed toddlers. Bugs big enough to have to crunch with your molars climbed over rotting logs. Derrick used this time to hunt on the go. Sometimes that meant running ahead of Rose, finding a blind, and waiting for prey.

"You'd better not mistake me for a moose," she called after him as he set off.

"No chance," he shot back. "A big gopher, maybe a skunk, but definitely not a moose."

She laughed. It was easier to forget the potential danger, immersed as they were in the woods, a bit easier to put down the anxiety that had made her rush out here in the first place. The world around them was lush to the point of opulence, and they were once again kids left to roam the garden.

Flowers twisted on slim vines along the forest floor and up the trees. Whole canopies of orchids had braided together over hollows in too-damp trunks. Earthworms slid slow bodies over one another like busy fingers in the soil. And everywhere was the smell of dirt. Real dirt, rich dirt, dirt meant for growth. Rose and Derrick relaxed and filled the space as much as their conditioning would allow them, still pausing at each sound but no longer jumping.

Derrick found small game. They didn't have time or room for anything bigger than a rabbit. He even picked some herbs to go with the wild meat and was able to cook gourmet over a spit. The first two days passed this way—food and walking, sleep and walking, games bored children used to play on road trips switched up to fit their surroundings and more walking.

"I see an ant, *a-n-t*. Your letter is *t*."

"Over there—a tree." He spun around, pointing in all directions.

"No, jackass, that's cheating. You have to be specific."

"Okay, okay," he answered, scouring the ground as they walked. He pointed to a small shrub. "Taxus, *t-a-x-u-s*. Your letter is *s*."

"What the hell is taxus?"

"Did you do any learning during the last few years? Jeez, Morriseau. You'd better spend more time with the bush master here. It's a kind of yew tree."

She thought for a moment, the term familiar. "Isn't yew called the tree of death?"

"Yeah, it is."

"Aaannd aren't they found only in the south?"

Derrick stopped. "Well, I mean, things are changing, right? Climate's all messed up. They must grow up here now." He shrugged, a smile playing at the corners of his lips.

Rose caught up to him and gave him a half-hearted shove. "Yeah, right. Sounds like 'the bush master' could do with a little more schooling."

Derrick overexaggerated a tumble from her push and then recovered into a full pirouette. He seemed to be a fine mood today. Last night, they'd shared his little tent, and when she'd woken up in the early morning, she had her back to him, feet touching his, and was sleeping under his arm. She'd immediately thrown him off with an annoyed grumble but wondered if it had contributed to his sudden sunny outlook.

He pushed aside an overhang of moss ahead of her, and caught sight of something bright in the distance.

"Tent." Derrick stopped altogether, his neck at its full extension, his body held on tiptoe.

"And what's that, another death tree? Besides, it's my turn, unless you concede that taxus was bullshit."

He thrust his arm out behind him and lowered his hand at Rose without looking at her. "Shhhhh!"

She crouched, an automatic reaction to the universal symbol for "get down." After a moment, she whispered, "What is it?"

"I told you," he hissed over his shoulder. "A tent."

He stood like that, not even moving his chest as he breathed, for two minutes before resuming his normal posture and taking a deep gulp of air. He whispered, "Okay, no movement. Let's go slow."

They both got down as low as they could and moved in a kind of commando glide, cutting through the thicker foliage. Crawling under a knot of old oak and maneuvering around an overgrown blueberry bush, Rose finally saw the tent. It was green, and the front flap was open and blowing in the breeze. The movement startled them, and they held their breath, but when no one emerged, they moved forward.

There was no use in avoiding a settlement. It was always better to find than to be found. If you were the finder, you set the rules of engagement. Being found meant being surprised, and all power was lost. Beside the first one was another tent, orange and crushed under the weight of a fallen branch so that it sagged and billowed like a plastic bag. Opposite the pair was a third, yellow and zipped up tight. On the ground was some debris—a cracked plastic pail with the handle pulled loose, a striped sweater sprawled out like a chalk outline, an empty juice bottle. None of it was a good sign. It had the feel of quick abandonment. Out here, you didn't leave your trash behind, let alone your shelter. Only one thing could've made people leave that fast.

Rose felt a rush of excitement in her dread. If Recruiters had been through here, so deep in the bush, maybe that meant they were getting close to the school. Surely they wouldn't have ventured too far on foot, and there was no way a van could have gotten through this tangle, not even close.

Derrick caught her eye and silently motioned for her to take cover behind a massive trunk several feet away. That way they'd have two sight lines. She lowered to her belly and made her way over. Once she was hidden, she turned back to the camp, watching, waiting. And then a feeling was released into her blood. It was cold and heavy and moved quick like a hungry snake. Panic—useful when you have to run, but deadly when you have to think. It wound its way up her spine and made her fingers numb. Something was up.

When Rose was young, she had lived with her grandmother and two great-uncles. They'd taught her everything she needed to know about what was to come by teaching her everything she needed to know about what had already come. It had been a childhood full of lessons, like Bush Life 101. Her grandmother, always the most stubborn person in any room, had sent Rose off with her uncles when she became too frail to travel, insisting she'd be fine. It was almost a year before Rose had been able to accept that the old woman wasn't playing bingo with her friends on the rez, that she wasn't cooking bread in her small woodstove, that she was, in fact, dead in the shed where they'd left her. She'd stayed with the old men until, one at a time, they'd gotten sick and died. She'd buried her last living relative before setting off on her own, wrapping his old bones in his favorite Pendleton before returning them to the earth. And then she was alone, out in the woods and getting by just fine. Maybe not fine, but well enough. She ate when she was hungry. She bathed when she found water. And she listened to everything—the way the wind turned around a body, the way the birds shifted their songs depending on incoming weather. The way a footstep echoed like ground thunder if you really didn't want to hear a footstep. The one sound she had never learned in all that time alone before she found Frenchie and the others was the way your heart beat in your ears in the moment you prepared for your worst fears to come true.

That was the sound she heard now, her heart like heavy hooves running, when the thought occurred to her that French's body could be in one of those tents. Panic insisted that she consider the possibility. Maybe the Recruiters hadn't grabbed him. Maybe it was traitors. Maybe he had put up a struggle. Maybe he'd bled out and they'd left him behind. She looked over at the yellow tent, zipped up tight so that no smell would leak through, so that no animal would be drawn in. What if what she had been searching for was in there?

Once the image was clear, she couldn't wait. She stood. Derrick's eyes got big. He motioned her down again, but this time she ignored him. She stepped between the trees, out in the open, and walked into the camp.

"Rose!" he hissed from his position. "Hey, Morriseau. What the hell are you doing?"

She kept walking. If she could hear him, she gave no sign.

"Jesus, woman, are you trying to get us killed?" He was louder now, having given up on stealth. "Arrggghhhh. Fine." He stood and rushed to catch up. She was already standing in front of the yellow tent.

"Seriously, what gives?" he shouted now. If this was an ambush, they'd already surrendered the element of surprise.

"Shut up." She couldn't explain. Not now. There was only the pulse in her head and the feeling of mud in her limbs. She had to make them work, had to grab the zipper and pull. She had to know. And there was a part of her that was sure what she would find. Something bad was coming. There was danger nearby, or maybe its ghost; maybe it had already passed through. But something bad was close. She knew it. And her instincts had never been wrong before.

"What is it?" Derrick was annoyed more than alarmed. His eyes moved around the space. This whole thing could be a trap, an elaborate stage set to lure in passersby. He kept the rifle cocked and moved it around with his gaze.

Rose grabbed the zipper of the yellow tent and, taking a deep breath, yanked it down. It caught and hitched a bit, but she managed to open it all the way. The wind caught the flaps, and then she could see the entire interior at once. A sleeping bag rumpled in the corner, a lantern tipped on its side, and a stack of tin mugs. Nothing more. No body, no blood, no French. She released her breath, and her shoulders dropped from her ears.

SNAP!

It sounded like an ax hitting a young trunk, one wet and sinewy enough to resist. Then a scream filled the clearing, so solid and sharp it was like river ice cracking. It made her duck and lift one foot off the ground at the same time. She recovered quick and spun.

In between the other tents was Derrick, his head thrown back, mouth open, eyes a color she had never seen—so wide, so dark. Both hands clutched his right thigh, his body rigid as if he'd been electrocuted. And there, ripped into his calf, were the metal teeth of an activated bear trap.

"Holy shit!" She ran over, skidding to a stop on her knees in the dirt. She grabbed the trap and tried to pull it open. It jostled around its bone like a rabid dog but remained clamped shut. He wailed in a different tone.

"I'm sorry, I'm sorry," she babbled, trying from a different angle, only to jiggle it some more.

"Stop, stop, stop!" He swatted at her. "Listen, just listen to me." He took a minute to catch his breath.

"There should . . . be a spring."

"A spring?"

He pointed down at the half circle of metal clamped around his leg. "On either side. Either side!"

"Okay, stay still."

"Where the hell am I going to go?" He was trying to look away, but the wound kept pulling his gaze back. His pants were ripped, and through the holes were oozing circles of blood, the metal tips buried in his skin.

"Gimme one second," Rose said through her panic. "Just one minute to find them . . . ah, there. Got 'em."

"Push them down."

"Both of them?"

"Yes, at the same time." He gritted his teeth in anticipation and turned his upper body away.

Rose pushed, and Derrick tensed, mouth open with no sound coming out, but neither spring budged. She pushed harder, and the teeth tore bigger holes where they had found purchase.

"Jesus, be careful!"

"I am!" She shook out both her hands as if she'd touched something hot. "They're stuck."

He looked down at her, his whole face bright red and sweaty. "They can't be stuck. The trap wouldn't have sprung."

"Okay, well, Mr. Trap Expert Who Somehow Got Caught In A Trap, they are stuck." She put both thumbs on the springs again and pushed out her breath in a small puff. "Alright, here we go."

This time she pushed with all her strength, ignoring the pressure of the metal against flesh.

"It's not working!"

"Keep pushing!" Derrick shouted through his teeth.

After what seemed like forever, the trap snapped, and the springs gave way. The teeth stayed where they had bitten, but the pounds of pressure were gone.

"Done!"

Derrick collapsed to the ground, holding his leg at an odd angle. "Oh Jesus. Oh God."

They were on their backsides in the dirt, now watching not the injury but the shattered quiet of the forest. If anyone was near, they would have heard. If they had heard, Rose and especially Derrick were done for. This potential was more painful than anything else.

"Derrick," Rose whispered.

"Yeah?"

"We gotta get it off."

"I know." He closed his eyes.

"Now."

"I know, I know. Just give me a minute." He worked to make his breath even.

"No, I mean, ASAP. Look at it." She motioned with her chin to the trap.

It was rusted to a jagged edge, rusted to a burnt-orange finish, rusted to death.

"Rose?"

"Yeah?"

"Did you bring any antibiotics?"

She shook her head. They pulled themselves up quick.

"Okay, I'll grab this side," Derrick said, placing his fingers carefully around the left side. "You take the other. Watch your hands."

Rose pulled the sleeves of her black hoodie over her fingers and used the fabric to grab the right side. Then she nodded to him.

"Okay, on three. One . . . two . . . THREE!"

They yanked back, and immediately the blood started flowing, soaking into the dark green of his pants, filling his shoes with thick wet. Once he'd pulled his foot through, Rose tossed the sprung trap into the bush.

"Who the hell leaves a bear trap in a campsite?" She was worried. Out in the woods with no meds and a deep cut from a rusty trap? It was looking more and more like they wouldn't make it to the school, or maybe even back to the settlement.

"We would." Derrick lay flat on his back, arms flopped out at his sides, chest heaving.

"True." She pursed her lips and raised an eyebrow. "It's actually kind of ingenious, now that I think about it. Even with the Indians gone, this still could have messed up a Recruiter real bad. Like bush warfare."

After a few minutes, the birds returned to their songs, and the insects clicked and slid over the cunning green. All around, a soft drizzle fell like a reprieve.

"Derrick? We gotta do something fast. As much as we can with whatever we have."

"I know." He was like a little kid who didn't want to take his medicine. He pouted and slammed his fists into the ground, but eventually, he sat back up. Rose dug through their bags for whatever she could find.

"I don't see any gauze. Oh, even better—a clean sock." She pulled a single black sock from Derrick's bag and placed it on her shoulder so it wouldn't touch the ground while she kept looking.

"I need those," Derrick protested.

"You're only gonna need one sock for one foot if you don't let me take care of this now."

He nodded, but she didn't wait for an answer. She pushed aside items and tried to take stock.

"Water bottle . . . no saline . . . no antiseptics . . ."

"Great. I can already feel my jaw tightening up." He touched his face with one bloody hand, leaving red finger marks behind.

"You can not. Quit being a drama queen." She shook her head. "I have some salt."

"Oh great."

"I know, I know, but we need something to sterilize the wound." She put the small restaurant-size packet of salt in her pocket and tied the bags back up. "Let's get you in one of the tents. This rain is picking up."

They dragged their stuff and themselves to the yellow tent. It was the most intact, and the zipper still worked. Rose went in first, placing their tarp on the bottom, then layering it with the sleeping bag they'd found inside and then her own. She set up the packsacks against the back wall and helped Derrick inside, leaning him against the bags. She placed her gear on top of an open plastic bag smoothed out like a medical tray and then turned, her hands clasped in her lap.

"Derrick, none of this is going to be fun for either of us. But I need you to cooperate. We've gotta get this done." She reached over and placed a hand on his forearm.

He looked down at her hand, then up into her face. As much as this sucked—and it sucked so hard—she didn't mind caring for him. She had nothing but concern: no pity, no annoyance, no urge to cut him loose and leave him.

"I know. I trust you." He meant it.

She patted his arm and went to work. She sliced his pant leg and peeled it back—a painful removal, since some of the blood had already started to clot with the fabric in it. Then she poured the water from her bottle first over her hands and then over the leg, rinsing it as best she could. Then she added the salt packet to the last third of the water in the bottle and shook it up. This she poured close to the skin, making sure the solution drenched each puncture. Derrick threw his head back and screwed up his face, but he stayed quiet. Now that he had some of his wits back, he sure as hell wasn't going to whine.

Rose tore the top elastic from the clean sock and used it to dab at the edges of the teeth marks; ten in all, two of them deep enough to require stitches. They hadn't brought any needles or thread with them. They'd left in too much of a hurry for a thorough pack.

Annoyingly, Rose could hear Wab in her head, reprimanding her for trying to rush off. *That's how we make mistakes.*

"Yeah, yeah," she whispered under her breath. "I know. You're right."

Derrick raised his head. "What's that?"

"Nothing." She pushed him back down.

◆◆◆ ◆◆◆ ◆◆◆

She'd done her best to clean up the area and cover the open wounds, but the leg was already looking bad. The sides of the bigger punctures couldn't meet to start stitching back together, and there was no medicine to stave off infection. But Derrick was asleep now, his sleeping bag opened over him. And they were warm enough in the yellow tent with layers underneath them, keeping the ground cold from seeping in. Rose couldn't sleep. She had a hard time even relaxing, but she stayed in the tent. She had to try to rest her body, and she wanted to keep an eye on Derrick, who had already kicked the blanket off twice. She worried about a fever setting in. A small injury could mean death out here. And she was the one who had brought him along—against her will, but she hadn't exactly insisted he stay behind, either. So she slept on and off, sitting up, the rifle across her lap.

The last thing Rose remembered before falling into a deep sleep, the kind with dreams and amnesia and resetting, was thinking that maybe Derrick was right, maybe there was a death tree in these woods after all.

CHAPTER 13:
PROGRAMMING

French

I GOT WORD THAT THE PROGRAM WAS STARTING THE moment they switched the lights on, so that the news was delivered while I was switching from disorientation to relief. And so it became good news in my body. And I supposed it was. This was my chance, the only one I could see. What I couldn't see yet was the cost of it.

"You commence activities tomorrow," the man at the door called in. His voice was low and quiet. I hadn't seen him before. He wore grey scrubs, and as far as I could make out, he was unarmed. He stepped just inside the room carrying a canvas sack and threw it onto the foot of my bed, where I was still lying. "Be ready. And be presentable."

Then he turned and left, the door slamming and clicking behind him. I waited for the dark to return, but this time, it did not. The first thing I did was look at my hands, fingers outstretched. There were a few old cuts, broken fingernails from scratching the walls, but otherwise, they were mine. I was still me. I put them to my face and winced. Six small stitches held a split over my cheekbone together. My head felt a bit better. It was bruise sore but not trauma sore anymore. I reached for the sack and sat up to check it out.

I pulled out folded scrubs, grey like those of the man at the door, a pair of white boxer briefs, a bar of green soap, a toothbrush (!) and a small tube of toothpaste, and a clean pair of white socks. At the very bottom were grey canvas slip-ons. No laces, no buckles. Oh, I was so happy to see clean clothes, to see a toothbrush, and the soap smelled strong and good. I rechecked the empty sack, hoping for a comb. My hair must have been a mess. Then I remembered it was gone. I ran a hand over the stubble and really felt that loss for the first time.

There was a sudden burst of sound, and then water shot from the ceiling over the toilet. Embedded in the ceiling with no pipe to hang a noose on, there was a shower, the controls somewhere outside this room. The flow was steady over the sink and toilet, splashing onto the cement floor, but not strong enough to make it to the bed. I watched it for a moment, and then, realizing this might be my only chance to get clean, I rushed to throw off my clothes and step under the stream. It wasn't hot, but it also wasn't cold, and it lasted just long enough for me to lather up and rinse off. I contemplated brushing my teeth under it, but just as suddenly as it had started, it stopped. I looked around for a towel, but I guessed that was a luxury item. So instead, I used the scratchy blanket to dry off and mop up the water that hadn't gone down the drain beside the sink, then hung it over the toilet to dry so I could use it later tonight to sleep.

I tried on the scrubs. They were a bit baggy, but the elastic waist kept them up. I had to keep adjusting the top to stop it from slipping down one shoulder or the other. But the shoes were the right size once I put the socks on. I could run in these shoes. I tried it out, running from one wall to the other, back and forth, back and forth, until I realized I was sweating up my new clothes.

"Be presentable, French. Be presentable," I repeated. I stripped down to my socks and underwear and folded the garments, placing them on my pillow, then made my bed without the blanket and went right back to running. I had to get in shape. Outside, you had to be quick, both in your body and in your mind. It was never one or the other. One or the other slowed you down enough to get caught. Like I had been, like I still was.

The rest of the day was for sit-ups and thinking. By the time I fell asleep under my still-damp blanket, I thought I might just be ready.

◆◆◆ ◆◆◆ ◆◆◆

First there were tests: sense-based tests, reaction time tests, math tests, which I was sure I'd failed, and physical stamina tests. I must have run on the treadmill for an hour before it slowed to a halt. Then I was put in a small room no bigger than a closet and exposed to extreme temperatures that almost broke me—so cold I could have snapped my hair in two, if I'd still had any, then so hot I wanted to crawl out of my skin. I was never given any feedback.

"I did okay?" I asked the man in a full hazmat suit who handed me dry scrubs to change into after the closet torture. He didn't even bother to nod.

"Okay, then, I'll take that as an A plus, if it's all the same to you," I shouted after him as he walked away with my sweat-soaked clothes held out from his body.

After that, I was escorted down endless hallways and left to sit in a meeting room like the one where I'd talked with Mitch before I knew he was Mitch . . . which was before I knew he wasn't Mitch at all. The blinds were open, and sunlight poured in over the empty top of the desk. I wasn't restrained, and for a minute, I thought I should try some of the drawers, maybe open the laptop sitting in the corner. But what if there were cameras in here? Maybe this was just another test. So I folded my hands on my lap and sat still. The door opened behind me.

"Stand up," a woman's voice commanded.

I stood, not turning to look.

She walked around my chair and took her seat behind the desk. She opened the laptop and began typing. Still I remained standing. She wore a black suit with a slim tie. Her red hair was pulled back into a severe bun. She wore no jewelry, no accessories other than the dark tie.

After a few minutes, she looked up over the rim of her glasses and regarded me. "Good. Now sit."

I did as I was told, though the smug note in her voice made me wince. "My name is Agent Mellin. I will be your direct command for the duration of your time in the Program. As the in-house Agent with the most experience, and someone who has contributed significantly to the development of the Program, I should be able to move you quickly and successfully through the stages."

I didn't know how to answer, so I stayed quiet. She was impressed enough with herself that my words were meaningless.

She waited a moment, then looked at the screen and continued. "I understand that you are related to Agent Dusome, is that correct?"

"Yes." I held back my laughter over the Agent business, like Mitch was part of some cool secret service and not just a loser kid pretending to be something he wasn't.

"Ma'am. Yes, ma'am." She said each word slow, like I was somehow impaired.

"Yes . . . ma'am," I choked out.

"And you have been separated for"—she looked down again—"seven years now?"

"Yes. Ma'am."

"And just what were you doing for those seven years, then?" She placed her fingers on the keys, awaiting my answer.

Maybe they didn't know about the others—about my family. Was that possible? That would mean they weren't here, and I sure as hell wasn't going to give this Agent any information that could endanger them.

"I was wandering on my own out in the wild. I mean, every now and then I'd come across another person and we'd team up for a bit, but I always left. It's better to be alone when you're trying to survive." I kept my eyes on my folded hands as I spoke. When I did look up, I saw that she wasn't typing. Instead, she was staring at me. I kept talking. "I found a gun at some point, so I could hunt. That kept me alive. And I got good at making shelters."

Her glasses clattered on the desk as she put them down. She closed her eyes and pinched the red marks at the top of her nose. "Mr. Dusome, you know, you did so well this morning."

"Thanks." I meant it. Why did I mean it? "Thanks a lot."

"But now you are wasting both our time." She stood, grabbed her laptop, and made her way toward the door.

"No, wait . . ." I tried to stand, but before I could make a move, two different Watchmen were on me. "Wait!"

But she didn't wait. She moved quick down the hall, the sound of her heels on the floor like gunshots. The Watchmen dragged me behind her. I kept trying to reason with her.

"I . . . I'm just confused. A bit confused, that's all."

She stopped just past a set of steel double doors. "One hour in the Correction Room to start." Then she walked away.

The Watchmen opened the doors and tossed me in. I landed on the floor in a heap and scrambled to my feet. The doors closed, and then there was the familiar sound of an electric lock clicking.

I spun around. The room was empty. One wall was covered in a large mirror, cloudy like polished metal. I was shocked by what I saw. There was a skinny boy—no hair, no color in his skin, eyes wild and mouth open—staring back. I rushed over, stumbling in my panic so that my hands hit the surface.

This was me now: bald, weak, caught. I recognized my eyes, but they too were different. I felt tiny. I felt young. I was the boy who had almost died after losing his brother, in death throes in the dark woods, before Miigwans had found me all those years ago. And then a loud screech filled every molecule of air in the room, so high and so precise I felt it in my throat. I slapped my hands over my ears and dropped to the ground, gasping. After an interminable amount of time, the siren stopped, but I was already hollowed out from it. Gutted. I crawled on hands and knees to the middle of the room. At least the lights were on. Then I realized I didn't care if the lights were on. Everything had been taken from me. I had nothing left to lose, not even light. They couldn't reach me, not really, if everything was already gone.

And then the siren started up again.

◆◆◆ ◆◆◆ ◆◆◆

"Shall we begin again?" Agent Mellin asked back in the office. Once more, she waited with her fingers on the laptop keys.

I wasn't sure if I could talk anymore. There was nothing in my head but the echo of the siren needling my brain. What even was time if it had only been one hour before they'd let me out of that room?

"Mr. Dusome? Do you perhaps need a bit longer in solitude?"

I shook my head. "No."

"No?"

"No, ma'am."

"Good, then let's continue. What were you doing for the seven years after you were separated from your brother?"

I went all the way back. Not because I wanted to tell her everything, but because I needed to keep talking. If I stopped talking, they might bring me to the room again.

"The Recruiters came in their white van. Mitch told me to get out of the tree house, to hide. I went out the window and into the trees. I stayed there for . . . a long time, I don't know how long, really. Then I got down and ran into the woods. I didn't have much food or water or anything. So I just kept going. No plan. No solution. No hope. I just moved."

The sound of her typing was soothing. *Click, click. click*. Such a small, polite noise. I needed it. It was like Morse code tapping into the memory, reminding me, leading me onward.

"I don't remember days, exactly, but I do remember pain and exhaustion. And then one day, I woke up, and there were people. Native people. They took care of me."

"How many, exactly?"

I counted their faces as they pushed through the fog in my mind. The Elders, Miigwans and Minerva; the kids, Slopper and Riri; the twins: Tree and Zheegwon; the older kids, Chi Boy and Wab. "Eight. There were eight then."

"Then?"

"We lost two along the way." Riri's face disappeared over a cliff. Minerva closing her eyes forever on a road that went nowhere. I watched them fade.

"Continue."

"We were together for a long time. Hunted together. Slept in a circle. Walked." I held Rose back, refused to share the night Chi Boy caught her lurking around the camp and dragged her into the light, into our family. No one could shake her out onto the table for the taking. I held her in a small pouch at the back of my mind. I wouldn't even allow myself to imagine her face right now.

"Isn't it true that you were with this one group for the entirety of your time out of captivity?"

Mellin already knew the answer.

"Yes, ma'am."

"Are there many families out there, eking out some kind of existence?"

"No." It was the truth, and it hurt. "Not many."

My eyes were fixed on my feet, turned on their sides, big toes together through the rubber soles of my slip-ons. I remembered the way food tasted when we harvested it ourselves, like a feast each and every time. I remembered the way laughter felt when you stifled it in a sleeve, like extra padding between your skin and the cold.

She snapped her laptop closed. I jumped.

"That will do for today."

"Where am I going?" I was frantic. I could hear the siren being wound up with a crank somewhere, which of course was only in my head.

She stood and answered, "Why, you're going back to your quarters, of course." She smiled. There was so much in that small baring of teeth, everything but joy. "Get some rest."

I didn't hear the Watchmen come in until their hands were on my shoulders. I let them guide me back to my room without a fight. I didn't even really look up as we walked. I was lost in the memory of my people, my family, out there somewhere. I was sure, in the same way I knew my mother was long dead and gone, that they weren't in here. And that meant they must be looking for me.

The thought of them creeping closer to this place brought me nothing but anxiety. Maybe it would be best if they forgot all about me.

That's when the image of Rose burst to the front of my mind so that all I could see while we walked back to my room was her dark eyes, her flashing smile. It's hard to put one foot in front of the other when your sight is blurry with tears.

That night, I fell asleep to the sound of sirens pushing the trees to the ground, exposing every person I loved to watchful eyes above bared teeth.

CHAPTER 14:
NEWS

Miig

FATHER CAROLE ARRIVED, ESCORTED INTO THE CAMP by the scout who had spotted him from the trees, where she'd been perched with a rifle. Miig knew as soon as he appeared that the news would not be good. Like most people, Carole carried bad news in his posture. Today, his shoulders were curved toward his chest, as if shielding his own heart. Even subconsciously, people sought to protect themselves, their most vulnerable places. In almost everyone, that place was the heart. It was why people carried them in bony baskets of ribs.

"He was on the record at Sir John A. MacDonald."

"Was?" Miig pulled the word out slow, like something sharp.

"Was." Carole sighed, looking around. "Is there a place we can sit? Some water, perhaps?"

"We don't have time." Jean was uncharacteristically rude. His boy's fate was carried in this man, and he needed it to spill out.

"Of course we have time," Bullet responded. "This way. Maybe just Jean for now." She looked around at the hopeful and terrified faces that had already gathered and paused on one. "And Miigwans."

The four of them walked into the cave and made their way to Jean's space, kept private by only a thin bedsheet tacked to an overhang. Carole and Jean sat on the cot, Bullet handed over her thermos, and Miig stood by the door to make sure they weren't interrupted.

Carole drank deeply, then handed the container back. "Thank you."

"Is he not on the records anymore? Has he been moved?"

"If he had been moved, he'd still be in the system. There would just be a note in the location column and details about transportation." Carole hadn't yet been able to look the man in his eyes. "But there is just nothing, like he was never there."

"What does that mean? What *could* it mean?" Miig felt his legs go numb.

The older man sighed again. He was full of pause and thought. Then he shifted on the cot and finally faced Jean. "It could only mean one of two things."

Miig's knees folded before the words even hit the air, and he crouched close to the damp ground.

"The first is that he's been converted to work for the schools. They go 'dark,' so to speak—they're taken off the official records, and their information is held internally in the Special Recruitment Office. Or . . ."

"Or what?" Jean asked.

"Or he's deceased."

All the blood in Jean's face drained out, and the cane he'd been clutching clattered to the floor. Bullet hung her head. Miig cradled his face in his palms.

"But there's no saying which one it is for now," Carole offered, rushing the words as if applying balm to a burn.

"Yes, there is." It was Miig who answered. "There's no way French converted. So we know . . . oh dear god, we know."

When Miigwans came out of the cave, he saw the rest of his small family gathered near the entrance, waiting for him, waiting for word of French. Miig held himself together until he saw them. That's when he broke. Isaac stepped forward and gathered him up in his arms, whispering Cree into his ear—the only thing soft in this hard moment, in this rigid world full of monsters and the dead kids in their wake. He led him outside into the light, the family following close behind them.

They made their way, a solemn procession behind a weeping man, to the clutch of their tents. Isaac put Miig in a folding lawn chair, and the group naturally slid around him in a circle with too many open spots. Isaac crouched beside him, arm encircling his contracted width, rubbing his shoulder.

When he could speak, he did. "Someone tell a story. I'm not ready to talk just yet."

They knew it was bad then. It was the twins who stood.

"We'll tell our story," Zheegwon said, his hand on Tree's arm. "Our coming-to story, of how we came to be here. It's time."

When they were done, Miigwans would add a new chapter to the bigger tale, the one about their family and the world, a chapter of loss and grief. The part of the tale when they got to the end of Frenchie.

CHAPTER 15

TREE AND ZHEEGWON'S COMING-TO STORY

Tree and Zheegwon

WE LIVED IN A SMALL CITY. NOT ONE OF THE BIG ONES that fell first, but one of the smaller ones that kept on being crappy, sliding from level to level so slow that people forgot it hadn't always been that way.

We lived with Uncle Tim. Uncle Tim was a pretty small guy with a huge voice. He was known for a two things, hunting and dancing, and he made the gods jealous in both. In both, he moved with silent grace. In both, he was successful in providing for our house. He could catch a rabbit with a shotgun and just nick its neck so the meat was still good. He could spin you in circles to Hank Williams Jr. till you were a blur, and you wouldn't even be dizzy or nothing. There was never a lack of meat or women to cook it. They stayed for a short time or a long while, dusting the shelves we forgot were on the walls or filling the rooms with new smells and sounds. They also kicked his ass when he needed it and reminded us to bathe more. Some sat in the cracked vinyl kitchen chairs and watched him cook. Others left before the morning school bus arrived.

We were happy. We had enough. There was always enough. Sometimes, if he didn't time his "friendly visits" right and they overlapped, the windows shook with raised voices and thrown shoes. And at the end of it all, Uncle Tim would sit with us and laugh so that the windows shook again. He was thunder in a flannel jacket.

"Doreen would've been proud of you boys," he'd remind us, always in moments you wouldn't expect—like when we were shoveling the long driveway to our cabin or at a commercial break during *Jeopardy*. "All tall and polite. Real proud."

We lived on the outskirts of the small city, where the farms were cut down and buttoned up into large lots and the houses were wood and not so fancy. Still nice, with big decks and reshingled roofs, but not all braggy about it. We were almost from somewhere else, as far as the city could imagine. Almost invisible. Almost, but not quite. Not enough.

We had this old hound, Max. He lived outside because he was what Tim called "all business." He hunted birds and wandered off to impregnate the neighbor's poodle and that was it. Except that he was also an alarm. When we used to have wolves, he'd let us know they were close, and then Tim would go out and shoot off a round and Max would sleep in the mudroom.

One night in March, a year after we stopped going to school and Tim stopping bringing women home, Max warned us about a new danger. Tim was snoring away on the couch, and we had just turned off the bedroom light when Max started. It was a bunch of quick barks on a string of growls—the alarm.

"Wolves?"

We went to the window. He stopped sudden, and we knew something was wrong. Turned out these predators had hands that held knives and no sense of what was right, and they cut his throat mid-howl while he was on his lead. No animal would do that. It wasn't fair. Max never had a chance. If he'd been loose, he could have chosen to stand his ground or run into the bush. These predators had a crooked sense of fair.

There was movement out by his pen, just past the vegetable patch. We went down the stairs and shook Tim awake.

"Huh, whatisit?" He rubbed his eyes, sitting up.

"Max," we said together.

"Shit's sake." Tim threw the crocheted blanket off his lap and pushed past us to the door. He grabbed the rifle from the umbrella stand and a jacket off the hook, the screen door slamming behind him. We watched from the side window, his dark body lumbering across the grass toward the back corner where the trees began. We waited. After almost an hour, we found Max, throat slit, blood already thick in the gravel. No Uncle Tim. We walked the tree line, flashlights bouncing back to us off the trunks—nothing. We went back to the cabin and waited some more.

When the sun was up but behind clouds so the air itself was grey, we went back out. We walked for hours, weaving into each other's paths through the bush, into a neighbor's abandoned cornfield, the stalks all crispy so they broke when we pushed against them. Empty.

We stayed on the couch that night, TV volume turned down,

listening for him cussing, dirty and maybe with a few pelts, making his way across the yard. We fell asleep there. Sometime near midnight, we heard them: footsteps. We watched at the window, but there was nothing to see.

"Might be hurt."

We decided to go out, to meet him where he needed us. One went out the front door, the other out the back. We'd meet up and head to the back if we didn't come across him. Neither one of us expected the way your neck crunches when you're hit on the top of your head. The last thing we heard was:

"Got one!"

And then a loud whoop.

And then static.

We woke up hanging from ropes in a barn that still smelled of horseshit even though the horses were long gone. Maybe the voices woke us up, talking just outside the gapped walls.

"Wasn't enough for one family."

"You wasted it."

"We gotta get better at it. Take our time."

"Spoiled the whole midsection when the guts were punctured. Gotta treat it like a deer."

"We'll take our time this round. Learn from our mistakes."

They came again and again over the next few days, taking a finger, taking a chunk out of a thigh. They didn't know yet what they were looking for—blood or flesh or maybe bone. They hadn't yet heard the marrow theory.

They were pale, filthy, eyes all wild. This was the Plague, then. We examined the way they examined us, looking for what was buried inside or missing altogether.

They didn't feed us. Every morning someone would hold a ladle of metallic water up to our lips, and every afternoon they'd hose us down clean. Clean enough. We spent hours in the dark of weakness, of grief, knowing Uncle Tim wasn't going to bust down the doors and two-step over their rifle-riddled bodies. We were losing too much blood. We were losing too much hope.

And then one day, the doors did open, and a man slid in, a hood pulled over his head. He drew his knife, and we winced, knowing what came next. Except we didn't know. He cut the ropes and lifted us down. He wrapped quick strips of fabric over our open parts. He pulled back the hood and whispered for us to follow. And we did. We've followed Miig ever since.

CHAPTER 16:
A HOUSE IN THE WOODS

Rose

THE HOUSE WAS HUGE, OR AT LEAST IT LOOKED THAT way to eyes that had only seen the inside of a tent or the darkness of a cave for so many years. It was spread out like a cluster of mushrooms on a tree, low and full, the roof covered in leaves. In this new weather the walls were coated in green and brown, moss and vines and even ferns in the gutters. That's probably what had kept it safe—the forest working to reclaim it. From a helicopter, it would have looked like another hill, just another blank spot teeming with flora and bugs. But under the heavy eaves, the mold-dotted windows flickered with lights: candles lit on the inside. Lit candles meant someone was home to light them.

"We need to get out of here *now*." Derrick was already turning back into the bush.

"No, we need to check it out. Maybe we can overpower whoever is there. We have a gun." Rose rubbed her hand along the barrel of the rifle, looking at his wound, now oozing through the fabric of his pants. "We can't go on like this. You won't make it."

"Are you crazy? I'm hardly any help right now." His face twisted from his hurt pride as much as his hurt leg. He couldn't stand being vulnerable, let alone being a danger to anyone else, least of all Rose.

"Don't flatter yourself. I don't need help." She was serious, but she still said it with a smile, giving him the gift of her confidence behind humor.

The crickets out here were loud, like they'd made the overgrown front yard into a band shell and the entire orchestra was tuning up. Fireflies as big as butterflies flickered across the expanse like cameras flashing.

Rose sighed and sat back on her heels. "All right, look. I'll go check it out, peek in to see who's in there. You stay here with the rifle." She was already pulling the strap over her head. "You're the better sharpshooter anyway." That was another gift.

"Are you serious?"

"Yes. Stay here and keep six. If you see or hear anything, you get ready to shoot." She handed over the gun. After a moment's hesitation, he took it, using it as a crutch to hobble over to a tree where he leaned. There was no arguing with her when she had an idea. This time wouldn't be any different, and he didn't have the strength to resist, anyway.

"Fine. But you have two minutes, no longer. And try to stay in sight. I can't exactly skulk around." He was looking at his leg; the shirt they'd used to try to stanch the bleeding was crusty and dark.

It was obvious, even though Rose wouldn't admit it, that infection was setting in.

"All right. I'm going in." She shrugged off her backpack and checked her bootlaces. Then she lifted her sweater hood over her dark curls and crouched through the branches like massive drapes, pushing into the tall grass.

The crickets' music shifted in tone but not in volume, like they were singing from the prows of small boats riding the waves made by her movements. The fireflies were always just up ahead of her, scrawling a broken calligraphy into the dull sky. Rose walked bent low, her knees almost hitting her chest with her high steps. She kept to the perimeter of the house, rounding it like it was a wild horse she was trying to sneak up on, knowing that Derrick had lowered himself to the ground, keeping an eye on her.

The candlelight was hard to trust; it moved, casting shadows without allowing any real view inside. Rose had to go right up to the house, push her back against the grey wood, and slide, careful to keep her feet high and light in case there was any debris or, god forbid, any more traps set in the grass. She looked toward the bush and made eye contact with Derrick. He was barely visible, crouched down, gun ready.

Rose ducked under a sill and waited a beat, then lifted her head so that she was eye level with the glass. She was looking in on a large room stuffed with furniture—armchairs and lawn chairs jostled for space with bookshelves stuffed to overflowing. A long orange couch was draped with mismatched blankets and bed pillows, stained and without cases. In front of it was an uneven coffee table laden with candles and random dishes. The walls were wood paneling, the kind Rose's great-uncles had in their hunting cabins, cheap and splintery.

On the floor, in between the chair legs and more pillows, she could make out the threadbare remains of actual carpet. And then shadows morphed and slid against the far wall—people approaching from a back hallway.

"Fuck." She dropped her head and got low, turning to motion to Derrick, a quick chop downward signaling that he should back away. Stubborn asshole that he was, he just moved back an inch so that his face disappeared into the foliage, but the gun muzzle stayed trained.

She heard rustling through the window, chairs being moved, ceramic bowls clattering, and laughter. Someone coughed, deep and mucky. It sounded like metal shovels hitting gravel, real sickness. She buried her face in the crook of her sleeve without even thinking. Too many memories of the early days, when people became vehicles for bacteria just hitching a ride. She had a vision of Minerva crouched over the youngest girl, Riri, before they'd lost her. She'd spent long hours caring for the sick, Minerva. She had always boiled cedar tea and put together ingredients she collected on the trail for plasters and cough syrup. The memory hurt, and Rose pushed it away. She had no time for the past. Not now.

She lifted her head to look back through the window. Shadows crept tall and thin along the hallway walls, so many at once. They moved slowly, a pace she hadn't much seen in years. They clapped each other on the back, and one grabbed the other around the waist. One threw its head back and laughed, teeth pointed in silhouette. She was mesmerized. The candlelight made the shadows into marionettes, all stretched and oddly jointed. But when their sources stepped into the living room, they lost their menace.

Here was a young person, hair closely cropped, dressed in an old velvet blazer over a stretched-out T-shirt and cargo shorts. They looked like a bored child, a few years younger than Rose at least, and better yet, they looked Native. Rose caught her gasp before it was audible. Behind them was a man, about forty, with hair loose and long to his waist. He was the laugher, the last remnants of the joke caught in the wrinkles around his eyes. He wore no shirt, and his belly was small but round. He wore some kind of a wrap knotted at his waist, patterned with green leaves against a yellow background. He tucked a strand of hair behind his ear and revealed an earring of deep red beads cascading to his shoulder. He, like the youth, was visibly Native.

Rose had learned the hard way, like many others, that not all Indians were Indians these days. That the schools had converted some to go out and trap those who let their guard down when they saw a community member. It had happened to them. Two Native men, an inviting meal, and a few words in the language was all it had taken, and they had lost their little girl, Riri. Every time she closed her eyes, Rose could still see her in the tall man's arms as he ran, her arm dangling at a sickening angle, headed for the edge of a cliff. So for now, she stayed where she was. It was hard to combat the natural pull of potential, especially with the state of Derrick's leg, which she had been lying to him about. They needed help, and fast, or he wasn't going anywhere but in the ground. It was starting to stink.

The man in the wrap sat on the couch, spreading out his arms and legs so that he took up half the space. Had you looked hard enough, you could've seen right up his skirt. Rose did not look hard enough. The youth stood beside him, leaning against the armrest to his right. From the hallway, six others entered, all wearing white, some of them draped in what looked to be bedsheets knotted like togas. They placed themselves around the room like wilting flowers, languid and slightly off. When all the chairs were taken, the last one poured onto the floor, supine and slightly curved like a bright comma against the dark carpet. The couch remained empty beside the man. He smiled at each person in turn except the one beside him in the dinner jacket. Then he opened his arms, palms up, and brought his hands together as if beginning a prayer.

"Oh, my lovely swans, my sacred creatures, how lucky are we to be together for another day?"

They whooped in return, a sad echo of the war cry Rose remembered from her great-aunts. This sound was skinny by comparison. It didn't have legs to move around the room.

He clapped. "Ho, ho, yes, my warriors, yes! Oh, that fills my heart with such joy!"

He placed his elbows on his knees and leaned forward. "We begin tonight the same way we begin every night, with appreciation. Tonight, I'll ask our radiant Owl woman to start us off."

He pointed at a figure in a lacy white sundress, her thin shoulders covered with a crocheted shawl of cream wool. Her yellow hair was twisted into messy dreads tied around her head, making her small skull look like a bobble on her thin body. She had a small tattoo on her neck that looked like a swallow, and several more taking flight down her arm. Around each ankle, she had tied what must have been the leftover wool from her shawl so that she wore short leg warmers.

She stood and wiggled her bottom, pointing her fingers down at the floor, as if she were an excited grade-schooler. "Well, as usual, I am eternally and meaningfully grateful to Chief for bringing us together and keeping us all safe and full."

She couldn't have been talking about their bellies being full, Rose noted. Everybody in the room, save for the Chief himself, looked like they must click and clack when they moved.

"I am grateful to my sisters, all these beautiful women, for their support and love." She moved one stiff arm over the room to indicate the others in white, each of whom smiled or bowed her head, hands in prayer position as she did. "I am grateful for all Nam provides us, from help around the house to being such a bright spirit. They are such a gift." She ended with her hand outstretched toward the youth, who did not respond in any way, eyes down cast, limbs perfectly still.

"And I am thankful that our mother has decided to keep spinning like the magnificent dancer she is. Oh, and I offer thanks and praise to Grandmother Moon and ask that she bless me soon so that I may pass into the next phase of womanhood in her name." She ended with a high pitch, one hand on her flat stomach, and then sat down abruptly.

"Excellent, Owl, excellent." The Chief looked to the woman on the floor. "Wren?"

Just then, there was a flutter of movement near the tree beside Rose. She turned her head quick. A large crow, feathers iridescent in the waning light, landed on a branch that bobbed under its weight. It turned its head to the side in that odd way birds do so that he could regard her with the full orbit of its black eye. She glared back, lips pursed. *Shut up*, she thought. *Shut the hell up.*

"Caw!" It screamed in return. Crows were prone to assholery.

Her head still above the edge of the sill, Rose turned to look back inside. The crow's call had drawn the attention of the youth, who was now looking directly at her with quiet intensity. The women were still chatting, the Chief leaning on his knees with a benevolent smile on his face, but all it would take was one word from the youth and Rose would be caught. She dropped to the ground but knew it was too late; she'd been spotted. She needed to make a decision, and fast. Run or stand her ground. At least she had a sniper of sorts lying in wait.

And then she realized that all decision-making time had disappeared. Because there, crashed through the bush, hand still clutching the stock of their rifle, was Derrick's prone body. She sighed, clutching the sides of her head and pulling at clumps of matted curls. "Come on, come on . . . think!"

"You don't want to be here."

Rose fell back on her ass, then scrambled up, hands seeking solid wall behind her, getting away from the window. In front of her was the young person in the blazer, arms crossed over their chest, a long shock of bangs brushing their nose.

Rose took in their dark knees, small hands, and the unreadable features set in a wan face. Then she looked back over to where Derrick lay still, mostly hidden, and wondered if he'd passed out or been taken down. Then she sighed.

"I don't think we have much of a choice."

✦✦✦ ✦✦✦ ✦✦✦

It took them a while to pull Derrick out of the tangle of brush once they'd assessed that he was indeed still breathing. Then they had to carry him between them, his toes digging small trails into the dirt.

"This guy really busted up his leg."

"Bear trap."

"Yikes."

They conserved their words. They needed breath more than words, but they did manage a quick introduction.

"I'm Rose. This is Derrick."

"Nam."

They started up the overgrown stone path to the front door, and it opened before they got there. They were greeted by the Chief, bare-chested and shrewd-eyed, all the women in white huddled behind him like a bouquet. "And what do we have here?" He took a step outside and put a finger under Derrick's chin, raising his face, looking him over like a fruit at the market. Then he turned his attention to Rose, narrowing his gaze. He reached out and, before Rose could protest, grabbed one of her loose curls.

"Where are you from? Originally, I mean."

"A land called None of Your Fucking Business."

He released her hair, and it bounced back against her forehead. Then he threw his head back and laughed. "Oh man, I wasn't sure, but that accent—it's unmistakable." Still chuckling, he stepped to the side and waved them forward.

"Ladies, what we have here is a true gift. Even better, two gifts!" He followed them back inside and closed the door. Then he opened and lifted his hands. "Ladies, please welcome our two new First Nations friends."

Upon hearing the words, the women reacted as if a boy band had just waltzed in. They laughed and gave little cries, hugging and clutching one another's arms. One of them began to jump up and down, and soon they all were. They were like water on a hot skillet, all hiss and pop.

"He's hurt." Nam motioned to Derrick's leg with a tip of their chin. "Bear trap." Derrick was still draped between them, his arms slung over their shoulders.

"Rusty bear trap," Rose added.

"Oh my. Bring him into the back room." The Chief went ahead down the hall, and the women formed a single white line behind the newcomers, quiet now that new instructions had been given. Rose noticed ornate frames around cloudy pictures hanging crooked on the walls. No one in the pictures resembled anyone she saw here. Stacks of pulpy magazines were piled against the walls decorated with peeling wallpaper and water-damaged wainscoting. It was as if the house had been pulled from the depths of the ocean and lifted into the woods with a crane. The smell of decay and disintegration hung over everything like mothballs and rotting lace.

The hall opened into a kitchen. Rose saw a wooden table surrounded by mismatched chairs, piled high with cans and jars. A single yellow rose sat in a slim vase in the center. The Chief turned before the kitchen doorway and led them into a darkened room. It was tiny, barely enough room for a twin bed and wobbly nightstand. The two makeshift paramedics struggled to get him onto the bed. Then one of the women came forward, but Rose stood in front of Derrick protectively until she saw the woman had nothing in her hands. She knelt in front of him and removed his shoes, placing his feet up on the bed as she did. Another woman went to the opposite side of the bed and guided him back onto the pillows. Derrick moaned.

The Chief watched from the doorway.

"Fever. Smells like infection," he assessed. "If we're lucky, there's no tetanus." He turned to Rose. "Has he been complaining of stiff muscles? Any spasms?"

She shook her head.

"Good, good." He absentmindedly stroked a redhead's bare arm while he spoke. She fluttered her eyes up at him. "I have some antibiotics in the pantry we can give him. But first"—he snapped out of doctor mode—"a drink to celebrate!"

"Celebrate? Is that a joke? I really think we should get him medicine before we do anything clse," Rose protested.

No one seemed to hear her. Instead, they skipped and collided like moths around a sudden light, following Nam out into the hall and pouring into the kitchen. Their excited whispers echoed in the damp space like small bubbles rising to the surface. Only the Chief stayed behind, facing Rose in the small room.

"I am the Chief here, young lady. And I say a drink is in order." His voice was still friendly, but edged with authority.

They stared at each other for long seconds, neither one wavering. He smiled slow and wide and said, "Before he partakes of *my* medicine." It was clear that this was not up for discussion.

Rose looked down at Derrick, tucked under a stained quilt with a design of autumn leaves and cross-stitched pumpkins, his forehead shiny in the wan light from the hall. The quicker she downed a drink, the quicker he'd get his meds. So she pushed past the Chief, refusing to make eye contact.

In the kitchen, the women were dancing, though there was no music. Nam, sweaty from helping Derrick, poured purple liquid from a mason jar into small glasses. And on every wall were drawings of dream catchers in crayon, marker, and what looked like jam, or perhaps even blood. Rose leaned against the laminate counter and sighed, watching the chaos and wondering just what in the hell kind of place they had stumbled upon. She started to think perhaps their better bet would have been sweating in the dark of the woods, under the moon, surrounded by flora and the kind of impending danger she could at least understand.

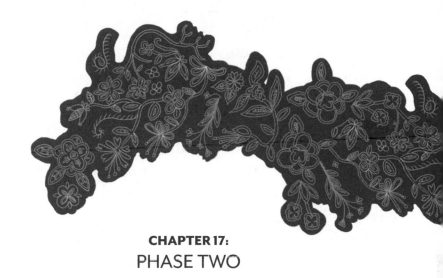

French

SOMETIMES THE SIREN WENT ON FOR HOURS. OTHER times, it never went off at all. The threat of torture, after enough torture, becomes the torture itself. Even the mention of the Correction Room made me drop to my knees and beg. Even turning into that hallway made vomit burn in my throat. After the first ten days, they stopped locking my door. After eleven days, I stopped checking it. I knew when I was expected to be up and ready. I knew what they wanted me to say. There were only two things I wasn't forthcoming about: Rose, and the nature of my capture. I held the truth of them so tight, I started to believe my own stories.

"I wanted out," I told Agent Mellin as she moved her fingers over the keyboard. "I'd tried to leave earlier and was stopped. That's why the bag you brought me in with was so well packed." It was always best to use material from the truth when constructing a lie. I actually had been leaving, but with Rose, to start again on our own. But then the alarm had gone up that there were strangers nearby, and we had both joined the scouting party. Of course, in this version, the version I was sharing for the "official record," there was no Rose. And I was bitter. And I had been leaving on my own, disillusioned by a long, hard life in the bush. I was a resentful old soul at the age of seventeen. I thought letting Agent Mellin know how much I loved my family would make them irresistible, so I held back.

"So I waited it out, and when the rest of the group decided to go one way, I went the other. I'd just stopped to take a piss when your Recruiter conked me out, and then, well, then I was here."

"And did anyone notice you were not with them?"

"Probably not," I answered truthfully. "They were too busy with the newcomers."

"Describe these newcomers for me."

This part was tricky. I wasn't prepared for it, so I hoped I was convincing. I couldn't give up the nurses who had helped Isaac and his fellow runners. Nurses might still be a way out, if not for me, then for others. If the Agents didn't know about this network of allies, I wasn't about to reveal it. I had already tried to keep the group in my rendition small, to leave out the resistance camp we'd joined, but they already knew about them. That omission had gotten me two hours in the siren room. I'd almost pulled my own teeth out that time, trying to distract myself with a different kind of pain, the kind that lives in meat and nerve. I couldn't risk that happening again, so I decided that instead of leaving out the nurses, I would recast them.

"Indians. Six of them. All adults. Scared but in good health." I knew these were the details they wanted.

"And mentally?"

"Sound. Dreamers, obviously."

"Fantastic." She typed faster.

"I needed a way out. Nothing made sense anymore. Why were we always running? And why did we stay in groups? If I had to run, which I thought I did, then why take on the extra responsibility of others? I had my own rifle. And skills. I could hunt, I could get by. I figured I might as well do it on my own."

"It seems that maybe your *family* felt the same way about you," Mellin offered in a conversational tone.

"How do you mean?"

"Well, I mean, come on." She folded her fingers in front of her face, then opened them up as if she were offering me something. "If they really felt the way about community and family that you say they did, wouldn't they have kept a closer eye on every single person, yourself included?"

That thought, casually dropped before she asked me to go on, stayed with me all day. I woke the next day with a pit in the bottom of my stomach. It felt like I could fall right inside it.

It was on day fifteen that I finally saw Mitch again. After so many hours spent stitching careful words around electric panic to keep myself from shorting out, I was genuinely happy to see him. He must have seen it on my face when he came to get me that morning, because he smiled back, big and genuine.

"Hey, little brother," he called in the open door. He hadn't knocked. No one did around here. They didn't want people thinking they had the privilege of privacy, after all. That would've meant they might've have other rights, too.

"Mitch!" I jumped off the bed, already dressed, teeth brushed, shoes on. "Where have you been?"

"First half of the Program needs to be done in solitude."

"I'm halfway done?"

"It wouldn't normally be this fast." He looked over his shoulder before continuing. "But I got word that they're amping things up. Time's of the essence, apparently."

"Why?"

"Not sure," He shrugged. "They don't tell me everything." He continued on to save his pride. "That's standard—they don't tell any one person more than they need to know. It's safer for us that way."

"Sure, sure." I crossed the few paces between us and put an arm around his shoulder. He stiffened at my touch. "Listen, do you think they'll let me do a mission on my own, so I can really prove myself?"

He patted my back awkwardly. "Well, we don't get a say in how missions are set up until we have experience out in the field. That's the goal, to get out there and do the real work of saving civilization."

He made it so hard to stay in character, this character who wanted to pitch in, to be a good soldier, this character who had forgotten who he used to be.

"Hmm. I should really ask Mellin about it," I said.

"Hold on there, Francis. You have to take this one step at a time. You're just starting the next stage."

"And what's that?"

"Integration."

"Integration? Into what?" Lord, how could this get any worse?

"Into life at the institute, of course." He pulled away and sat on the bed, patting the space beside him to indicate I should do the same.

I was confused. "I haven't been integrated yet? I've been here for weeks."

"No, no, not as an occupant." He pulled a slim folder out from under his right arm and opened it across his lap. "As a helper."

The room suddenly seemed smaller than ever before. I had trouble finding air.

"And what does that mean, exactly?" I looked down at the pages in the folder. One on side was a schedule, color coded and laid out in blocks of twenty-four hours. On the other side was a map of the building, not too detailed—no security, and nothing below the second floor, but each room was labeled with a number.

"Just what it sounds like," Mitch answered. "You have to prove that you can take on a leadership role with the residents and a helper role with the doctors and administrators."

He walked me through potential daily duties: cleaning the common areas, serving lunch, assisting in the "health zone," which I assumed meant the infirmary I had visited twice now.

"Do we get to interact with the others?"

"Other Program participants?"

"Well . . ." I considered. "I was thinking more about the other inmates, but yeah, are we like a group, the Program participants?"

"First of all, we never speak to the residents." He tapped his paper with a finger as he said each word, a soft emphasis from his place of non-power. "Secondly, we do carry out some duties as a larger group, but it is not a time to socialize."

God, *not a time to socialize*? He was such an insufferable wiener. Instead of voicing this opinion, I asked more questions. "Are you a part of that group?"

He smiled. "No, no, I have moved up from that. I am kind of a supervisor. I do advise on the Program, since I was part of the inaugural class. I've yet to take the final step into the field, but hopefully soon. And hopefully with you."

He crossed two fingers for good luck. I mimicked the motion.

"But no real interaction with the inmates—"

"Residents."

"Residents? Like, I can't hang out in the common room with everyone else?"

He chuckled. "Definitely not. Besides, why would you want to? Those people have no hope of moving into the system. They are the rejects, the holdouts, the past. We"—he put a hand on my shoulder— "are the now, the future."

He snapped the folder shut and placed it on the bed, stretching to his full height. "We're going to make sure future generations will be safe and well and whole."

"Yeah, but honestly? Whose future generations?" I couldn't help it.

"Oh, brother. You have a lot to learn." He walked to the door, then turned to say goodbye. "I'll be seeing you around."

I saluted his retreating figure before picking up the folder to read the schedule in full. And there in the back folder, I found a pen. Just a simple, cheap plastic ballpoint pen, but I knew it was off limits—I could get punished for having it. I should call Mitch back and return it. I stood up, moving toward the open door, before I

shook off the programming and stashed it under the toilet tank, balanced on a coil of pipe.

✦✦✦   ✦✦✦   ✦✦✦

At eight A.M. sharp, I met the grey-scrubbed man who had brought
me the bag of clothes and supplies weeks ago. He walked alone down
the hallway, paused at my door, then carried on without a word. I
hesitated at first, then shuffled alongside him. It was weird to be
alone with another Native in the hallway. I felt giddy, but a new kind
of giddy cut with fear. I was scared a lot these days. I jumped when
the shower started and picked my nails bloody in conversations with
Mellin. I moved to the side of the hallway when someone passed
and kept my eyes on my feet. It was safer that way. But now this was
someone like me, someone in grey scrubs, with a shaved head, with
my skin. I had to try.

"Aaniin," I ventured before switching to Cree, just in case, then
Mohawk. "Tansi. Shé:kon."

He didn't answer, but his shoulders stiffened. I regretted the
words immediately. They could be taken as a sign of dissent, of
rebellion. The words were powerful. After all, Minerva had used the
language to escape the machinery of the school, the one that had
ended up burnt to the ground. The siren whispered in my ear from
somewhere not too far away, always waiting, always calling to me.
We walked the rest of the way in silence.

The kitchen was on the second floor, accessible only through a
locked door, so we had to be buzzed in. It was eerie in there with
the noise of water and porcelain and steel but no voices to meet the

culinary rhythm. A dozen residents in their pale green uniforms worked cutting vegetables, washing fruit, putting bread dough into the huge wall ovens, sweeping stray crumbs from the floor. They worked with their mouths shut tight, with only their eyes moving around the space, always taking in everything. I searched their faces as much as they searched mine, looking for family, for friends, for possible allies. I knew they were doing the same. I held my breath until I had scanned every last body and I was sure not one person from the resistance camp was there. More than a few of them looked away when they saw I was in grey; two even scowled. It was clear I was not one of them anymore. I was something else entirely. I just wasn't sure what that was, exactly.

"You are to supervise the isolation meal preparation," my guide said, handing me a clipboard. "Make sure these residents put them together correctly, with nothing extra, not even one cracker more than the allotted four." He held up four fingers as if I needed a visual aid to count.

"And then you deliver them to the isolation ward. No talking, no responses, nothing. You can slide the meal trays in and leave. Then, later, collect the empty trays. That's all."

I looked at the paper on the clipboard. It was a list of numbers with check boxes beside each one. "What's this for? To make sure they each get one?"

The guide stabbed at the page with his finger. "First row indicates that they received their meal. Second column indicates they ate it."

"Some people don't eat them?"

He sniffed. "Some people think the best way through this is to just wither away and die. As if that option is open to them. Those are the ones who get taken to the Feeding Rooms. Not a place I'd want to end up."

A teenager walking behind us coughed into his bent elbow. A cough that sounded like the word *traitor*. Two men operating a bread oven giggled into their gloved hands.

The guide spoke louder. "And keep an eye on your crew. Any disobedience at all, and they are headed to the Correction Room." The men went quiet and turned back to the control panel set in the wall. "Got it?"

"Yup."

He looked at me, waiting. "Oh, uh, yes, sir?" I wasn't sure of the hierarchy at this point, and I figured it was better to err on the side of deference.

He gave a slight nod, satisfied, and walked back to the main door. When he got there, he bent to talk to a Watchman posted on a stool, reading a paperback. The Watchman stood, placing his open book on the seat, and walked to the resident who had coughed. He grabbed him by the arm and dragged him out the door. The resident didn't protest; he just dropped his head as he passed the others and, before he got out into the hall, held up a middle finger behind his back. I couldn't help but think it was specifically for me.

CHAPTER 18:
VAMPIRES IN THE WOODS

Rose

BY THE TIME THEY'D FINISHED THEIR GLASSES OF bitter mash and listened to a few of the women trill a thin backup to his version of a welcome song, Rose knew that the Chief ran his house with an iron fist hidden in a sleazy silk glove. The women—his Wives, he called them—were useless in all respects. They lay around most of the time, vacant-eyed and soft-limbed, getting up only to follow him when he left the room. Rose was pretty sure they wiped his ass for him.

The Chief didn't have any more questions for her, which was odd. Out here, the first thing you did was try to make connections—to your old home, your lands, your family. Instead, he held forth on the topic of gifts and rewards. He remarked on his unique ability to shine so bright he could be seen from the spirit world.

He declared this house holy and offered up the idea of opening it as a church for lost souls. None of this seemed new to anyone other than Rose. Everyone else cooed and clapped on cue like trained monkeys.

"I had a dream," the Chief began, like he was a different man, a great man. "I want to tell you about it, because it goes beyond a dream and enters the realm of prophecy . . ."

He went on to talk about a round house in a field, circled by horses and strung with bear skulls hanging from the gutters. When he got up to "peruse the pantry," the assembly moved with him. Only Nam, who resembled the Chief around the eyes, stayed behind. Rose used the opportunity to ask them some questions, frantic for answers, desperate for the aid promised to Derrick that still hadn't appeared.

"Hey, thanks for the help with my friend."

Nam looked at Rose quick and sharp, as if she'd pulled a gun on them. They answered in a low voice. "No worries."

"How long have you and your dad been out here?"

"Chief's not my dad," Nam scoffed. Rose collected the resentment they threw down and put it in her back pocket in case she needed it later.

"So, what, are you one of his spouses?"

"No!" They scrunched up their nose. "God, no. He's my uncle." They paced a short trail by the fireplace. "We've been here for years now. I don't know. I don't keep track."

Rose, sensing that Nam was a bit of an outsider here, decided to get closer. "I'm from Treaty 3. Last name is Morriseau." She paused checking if her words were landing—she needed to get through, then added, "My pronouns are she and her."

Nam stopped moving and studied her face, connecting for the first time. "Williams. Nam Williams. They/them."

They nodded at each other slow, seeing one another more clearly now.

Through a dozen inquiries, Rose was able to ascertain that back on the rez, the Chief had cooperated with the new government until his own safety was compromised, and by then he'd betrayed so many people, sending them out as "volunteers," that there was no one left who would shield him. Only Nam remained unwillingly on his side, and they were too young to offer any protection. For some reason they were never quite clear on, he kept them away from the Recruiters. The Wives were all the women he'd collected since they'd been on the lam, the ones who were too "liberal" to take part in the marrow consumption but too ingrained in the system to find a different way to survive.

"They're all like, 'Oh, I would never take marrow from your people' and 'I'm anti-government and against the death camps, so I refuse the dream serum on principle.'" Nam imitated their voices, exaggerated their movements. "As if they could even afford treatment. That's what it is—lack of choice, not principles. So they took the middle ground, finding a real live Indian to chirp after like baby birds."

"Gross." Rose kept an eye on the hallway, watching for the return of the group, hoping they stayed occupied long enough for her to get the real scoop.

"The women, they have this idea that he can save them. That he's some kind of medicine man." Nam put air quotes around this. "And I think he really thinks he can. Pfft, idiots. All of them."

Nam was quiet in voice but strong with opinions, and Rose liked that, even if getting them to spit them out was like pulling teeth.

"Listen, does this guy even really have meds at all?" She had taken a quick and discreet stroll around the living room, looking for weapons and clocking the exits, just in case. "Is it a lie? Like, should I be dragging my friend out of here before he croaks?"

"Not in here." Nam had noticed Rose scouting the room. "But yeah, he does, in a different room. He cleaned out the reserve health center before we left."

Rose stopped searching. "He took all the medical supplies? There was no one left who would need them, right?"

Nam looked at their feet.

"Right?" Rose repeated.

Just then, the Chief returned with his flouncy circle of admirers. Seeing them so jovial, without a care in the world, while Derrick sweated through the mattress in the other room took the last of Rose's patience.

"I need to check on my friend." She pushed past them, shoulder-checking the Chief on the way out. "Someone has to take care of him."

Derrick didn't get any antibiotics until nearly midnight, if the clock on the living room mantel was to be believed. Even then, it only happened after Rose threatened to drag his broken ass back into the woods. The Chief insisted on administering the drugs himself, removing them from a locked closet and then closing the bedroom door after him. He took one Wife in with him, the blond one with dreads who he called Owl. The other women pouted as they waited outside in the hall. One girl, younger than the rest, with short brown hair and a heart-shaped mole on her cheek, actually cried.

"It's okay, Robin. One day you'll be chosen," the one known as Wren consoled her, but with an odd smirk on her pallid face. She moved as if underwater, trying to be seductive even now, without an interested audience. Her mullet made the theatrics almost comical.

"What the actual hell?" Rose whispered to Nam. "What's up with these women?"

Nam shrugged and carried a load of dirty dishes into the kitchen. Rose followed.

"Need help?"

"Oh, we only do dishes when there's rainwater collected. It's been a few days, so, it'll have to wait." They pointed to the counter, crammed with chipped mugs and sticky plates.

"Oh. Gross."

"Yeah," Nam agreed. "And these puppets are real lax on the house-work. Until he snaps his fingers, they don't do much of anything."

Rose leaned against the table, biting her thumbnail, her leg jiggling with nerves. "Listen, you don't think I should be worried, do you?"

"About what?" Nam scraped food scraps into a metal bucket near the back door.

"About whatever the hell he's doing to Derrick in there." She motioned with her lips toward the door into the hallway.

Nam followed the point, then went back to work. "Nah. He'll be fine. You're Indigenous, you got nothing to worry about." They paused and scrunched their nose a bit. "I think. I mean, yeah, I'm pretty sure it's all good."

It was the last part that got Rose's leg moving even faster.

That night, she was put to bed in a dorm-style room shared with five of the six Wives and Nam, all crowded on single beds or folded into large chairs pushed back against the walls. Rose wasn't sure she'd be able to sleep. For one thing, she was worried about Derrick. For another, she was inside. She hadn't slept indoors since she and her family had found an abandoned resort. Thinking about the Four Winds Resort made her miss Frenchie in the pit of her stomach, maybe a bit lower. Eventually, with her hand on her lower belly and her mind spinning through memories like a flip book, she did fall asleep.

◆◆◆   ◆◆◆   ◆◆◆

At all times, but especially in her dreams, Rose felt the threads. They extended from her skeleton, poking through her flesh as innocuously as birthday candles on a cake—no blood, no pain. They connected her to who she was, where she had been, where she belonged.

Every now and again, one would get tangled, and she would have to stand still, turning slow and paying attention, to figure out where it started in her and where it had become snagged. Every now and again, one would snap. When this happened, the thread dragged behind her, collecting dry leaves and hollow insect casings so that she sounded like a wedding car festooned with ribbons and cans when she walked. So that she lost her stealth, her ability to slip and deke.

Lately she had noticed a new snag, already picking up the tin and crackle of debris and celebration at once. It slowed her down, made her unbalanced so that she leaned into her walk, one side tense and pensive, the other slack and excited. It made her uneasy, changed the tone of her thoughts, made her stutter over words and steps.

The third night in the Chief's house, Rose woke up with an incredible thirst. The last two nights had been rough, and water was scarce, since they were still waiting on rain. She spent the days sitting and talking with Derrick or scavenging the woods and ignoring the Wives as they sighed and huffed and giggled around the house like adolescent ghosts.

She lay quiet for a moment, trying to summon saliva so she didn't have to get up. Her head was as dry as a cotton ball. Finally, she threw the blanket back, only to find the threads pooled around her bed. It was like she'd turned into a cat overnight and had fallen asleep in a knitter's basket.

She sat up and pulled her fingers through the mess, feeling where they tugged, loosening words that had caught in the mess like a poem spilled. *Hunt* fell off the side. *Home* held four threads in the angles and nooks of its consonants.

"God, I need water."

So she stood, gathering the strings like a cape and tossing them en masse over her shoulder. They trailed behind her. She was too thirsty to think about their nature right now. She had to get a drink, and then maybe she would find some scissors to cut herself free.

She tiptoed past the sleeping Wives, curled into their blankets like doped-up cherubs, their fingers intertwined, their hair loose over arms they used as pillows. It was dark. The stars were a weak night-light tonight, barely filtering through the lacy curtains. The floor creaked and moaned on her way to the door, which groaned like a woman stretching. She tripped across the threshold and stumbled into the hallway.

"What the . . .?"

One string had freed itself from the others and looped around her ankle. She tugged and felt a pull in her chest. There, her right breast was where it started. She grabbed it in both hands and gave it a few tugs. No pain. In fact, it felt satisfying, like touching a bruise in your mouth with the tip of your tongue. Of finding the itch in your ear with a long fingernail. She tugged once more, sliding her hands down the string's tension. It continued out in front of her and around the corner. Moving down its length hand over hand, she followed.

The silky length tumbled loose down the stairs, and she picked it up as she went, gathering a handful of thread, then an armful. Around another corner and into the hall. It must have been taking her to the kitchen, a lifeline to water. Her mouth opened in anticipation. So thirsty.

She walked faster, one bare foot stepping over a torn page from a home decor magazine, her elbow knocking a framed portrait to the ground so that the glass shattered on the hardwood. She tried to make out the face behind the broken glass—a tall man, his long hair pulled back in a single braid—but the break began in his face, and she couldn't tell who he was.

She walked ahead, eyes on the small window above the kitchen sink like a buoy in the dark. But two strides from the linoleum, the thread pulled, and she stumbled. She collected its length in the basket of her arms and used a hand to tug. The tension turned right, not straight. But the kitchen . . . the water . . .

Obediently, if reluctantly, she followed the thread under a door, which she opened with the push of a shoulder. This was where she was snagged. This was where she belonged. She was standing in Derrick's room. And the other end of the thread climbed the bed, fell across the sleeping body of the boy, and disappeared into an invisible hole in the center of his chest.

Hand over hand, the thirst gone, Rose picked up the length as she moved to the side of his bed. The final tug pulled it tight, lifting the slack off his blanket, and he opened his eyes. She gasped . . .

. . . and woke up in her cot. She threw back the blanket. There was nothing in her bed but her own sweaty limbs and a puddle of moonlight. She breathed heavy, ran a hand over her forehead and into her hair, her fingers tangled in the curls.

"Oh god," she turned onto her side and whispered to the moon. "I have to get out of here."

She fell back asleep picturing French, tall, a long braid down his back, but the features of his face had started to blur.

❖❖❖ ❖❖❖ ❖❖❖

The next morning, it rained. It was the kind of rain that was common now—sheets of water, unrelenting, moving the earth where it fell. The Wives screamed in the halls. Nam and Rose got out of the way, standing just inside Derrick's room, watching them rush about collecting slivers of soap and bits of cloth and then running outside into the front yard.

"They shouldn't be so damn loud," Rose remarked. "It's not safe."

"Wouldn't it be tragic," Nam replied, "if they got caught and taken in . . ."

The two smiled conspiratorially.

Rose had been introduced to each of them by the Chief while they'd shared a bowl of boiled peas at the dinner table last night.

It was weird to her that he took it upon himself to tell their stories. Miig had told them that every person is responsible for their own story, of who they were and how they'd gotten there: coming-to stories. Not that these ones were much in the way of stories—it was more like reading short bios in a magazine—but still . . .

"Owl is the wise one, the one who came to us with her own lessons about the stars and their positions and how to make vegetables grow." He pointed at the one with dreads, who bowed her head, her cheeks scarlet with pride.

"So, an astrologer? I'm a Cancer; tell me my fortune," Rose said sarcastically. The Chief ignored this.

"Next we have Wren. She's the sensual one of the bunch. Reminds us all to find the beauty in the moment and that it's okay to act on our impulses." The brunette with the mullet, who was wearing a stained silk nightgown, leaned in and stared into Rose's eyes with a manic intensity that made the younger girl look away. Weirdo.

"Robin is our youngest and also our newest. She hopped into our path just before we found our temple here." He gave her the look a father gives a child he's proud of for doing the smallest thing. It was even creepier because it had recently become very clear that the Chief's relationships with these women were not platonic.

"Grouse is the matron." He pointed opposite him to the older woman sitting beside Rose. She stared at the pile of green mush she had made on her saucer, smashing the peas with the back of her spoon without putting a single one in her slack mouth. "She's quiet but strong in her convictions."

"Of course she is," Rose remarked, pulling her chair half an inch away, watching a string of shiny drool start a slow descent from the woman's chin.

"Cardinal is our treasure. Right now, she is carrying the next generation." Chief sat up straighter, puffing out his bloated stomach so it smooshed against the edge of the table.

The redhead, wearing an oversize men's dress shirt unbuttoned to show ample cleavage, teared up. She grabbed the Chief's hand and placed it on her flat stomach. "I am so blessed."

"Wait, you're pregnant? How far along?" Rose hadn't heard that the settlers were fertile again. Word was that the mainstream was slowing down, maybe from the sicknesses, or maybe from all the failed cures. It had been a whisper for years, but lately, any news that came through to the runners was full of concern for the birth rate.

"We're not sure. Uh, it's early."

"Cardinal is almost always pregnant," Wren purred. "They don't last long, but we're hopeful this time." Her words had a jealous tinge to them. One tear snaked down Cardinal's face, landing with a plop on the top of her boob.

"And finally, there is Chickadee. Chickie is a remarkable hunter. She brings in meat at least once a week, and always when we need it the most." He pointed at a woman who was short to the point of dwarfism, a mass of almost-white curls piled up on her head. She fixed Rose with eyes so blue they looked backlit, but said nothing.

Rose memorized the points that mattered: who seemed the closest to the throne—that was Owl and Wren—and who was clearly going mad—that was Grouse and maybe Chickie. She wasn't sure which of the categories Cardinal belonged in. She was either delusional or really dumb. These were things that could be weaponized, should she need to fight. The jury was still out on Robin. The Chief was a different story. Did he really believe himself to be a healer who would usher in the new age one baby at a time, or was he after something else, something darker. She thought Nam might be able to provide that information, but Nam, as much as Rose liked them, was secretive and prone to disappearing for lengths of time.

Together, Nam and Rose washed Derrick as best they could with rags and some water brought in by a rain-soaked Grouse, who had to be reminded to leave the room. Even after that, she stood just outside the door, looking confused about which direction to turn, her long greying hair and long greying sheet toga dripping onto the floor. Nam left to go change Grouse's clothes before she got sick.

Rose tiptoed to the door and gently closed it, then came back and sat on the edge of the bed. Derrick's wound was still oozing, and his fever was high, but at least he wasn't alternating between screaming and comatose anymore. Mostly he slept. When he was awake, Rose fed him soup and made him drink ungodly amounts of water, and then, maybe because of all the water, she had to help him hobble to the bathroom, which was really just a series of buckets in the closet since he couldn't make it to the outhouse yet.

"Where exactly are we?"

"Dunno."

"And who are these freaks?"

"They're freaks for sure. Not sure of much beyond that."

He listened while she rattled off potential plans and went through the pros and cons of leaving at various times. They had to get back on the road as soon as Derrick was well enough to walk. He had started taking little jaunts around the room, but the infection made him tired and weak.

"Good thing I'm the real hunter in this duo," she teased. "When we get back to the bush, I'll show you how it's done."

"Great. Hope you like rock stew," he countered.

At least he was joking.

Rose leaned in close. "Listen, Derrick. Nothing . . . weird happens when they come to give you antibiotics, does it?"

"Define weird. Like, an old Indian with a serious beer gut mumbling nonsense while random white girls do interpretive dance? Is that weird? Because if so, then yes, weird stuff definitely happens."

She wasn't surprised. "No, that's not what I mean, exactly. They don't do anything . . . invasive, do they?" It had occurred to her just that morning that maybe they were amateur marrow extractors like the ones Tree and Zheegwon had run into before they'd found the family.

"No. I mean, I don't think so. I kind of, like, fall asleep while they're in here."

"Every time?"

He sat up a bit more. "Yeah, it's weird. I cannot keep my eyes open. And I try because, like I said, it gets strange in here."

Rose sighed, thinking. "Well, try to stay awake tonight, and let me know what happens. They don't let me in here, so my hackles are up."

He agreed. They shook on it like kids over a bet, and she went to help with the kitchen cleanup now that there was water to be had.

◆◆◆ ◆◆◆ ◆◆◆

Someone was standing at the foot of the bed. Rose woke up and knew it before she even opened her eyes. And sure enough, though blurry from sleep, Rose was able to make out the form of a woman standing in the shadows, naked except her underwear and staring straight ahead.

"Grouse?" she mumbled. "Is that you?"

"There is much to be found. Almost as much as there is to be lost." Her voice was low and monotone.

Rose mulled this over, rubbing the sleep out of her eye. She knew Grouse by now, knew it was better to just go with the gibberish than question it. "But isn't there the exact same amount? To be lost and found, I mean?"

Grouse only stared, not moving a muscle, not breathing deep enough to see.

Rose tried again. The sooner this was sorted in the old kook's head, the sooner she'd move her naked ass from the foot of the bed. "Aren't there just as many things to be found as things that are lost?"

Grouse laughed, short and stuttered, through her nose. "Silly. Then there wouldn't be the turtle's back of tragedy for beauty to ride on."

Rose stared back. The woman blinked once, hard, robotic. The Plague had turned her mechanical.

"Time to go," she quipped, then turned on a heel and marched out of the room.

"Indeed," Rose agreed, knowing she had reached the end of putting up with this place. "It *is* time to go."

But it was too late. They had missed the opportunity for an easy departure.

✦✦✦ ✦✦✦ ✦✦✦

The next day, the Wives and the house were as clean as Rose had ever seen them. They shone. Everyone was in a better mood, even Nam, who relaxed on the couch with an old comic about an awkward redheaded boy with two attractive girls inexplicably fawning all over him.

The Chief sauntered in, and the Wives sat up straight like buds seeking the sun. He pointed to Rose, who had been reading over Nam's shoulder.

"I am going to check the garden, and I would like for you to keep me company."

Rose put her finger to her chest. "Me?"

"Yes, yes. Please, if you will." He swept his arm out beside him like a gentleman. But that was a lie—there was nothing gentle about him, just a soft malice that she could almost smell, like fire in the distance. Nam's comic trembled a bit like a rattle. Rose stood and followed the Chief out the front door, ignoring the glares of the Wives as she passed them.

The garden was a small plot of mismatched plants surrounded by a border of tall weeds. There was no order, no sense to the patch. Pumpkins spiraled around cornstalks, beans withered under drying tomatoes leaves.

"You really need to organize better. The three sisters should be together," she pointed out. "That's squash, co—"

"There is nothing forced about this garden. It is exactly as the Creator wants it to be. Who am I to tell him how to grow his gifts?" the Chief cut her off to pontificate.

"Well, uh, maybe *she* gave us specific teachings so we could do things right instead of just all willy-nilly." Rose hated this kind of man, this kind of overexplaining, condescending man. She'd been so long with men like Miig and Chi Boy that she had almost forgot this type of broken man existed. Every day she was realizing just how lucky she had been, even while running for her life. She also remembered that there were indeed gentlemen still left . . . just not any here.

The Chief laughed. "Oh, you are a firecracker, aren't you?"

How was she supposed to answer that? Oh right, she wasn't. She walked the perimeter of the patch to kill some time. It did bug her that they would be lucky to get even one third of what this yield could be, but as a firecracker, she supposed her only role was to pop off—*bang!*—and not to offer any useful advice.

"So, tell me, Rose. Where are your people from?" He bent to fondle a leaf, like just caressing the plant was actual gardening. As if it were one of his Wives.

"All over." She didn't owe him anything. "What about you? Where did you get these people, some kind of lost and found? Maybe a mental hospital?"

"Basically, yes, I did." He grunted as he stood, ignoring the barbs in her question. "They were lost out here in this unhinged world, and I found them. After the last round of flus, when the armies moved into the reserves, I was on my own, just Nam and me. This Two Spirit kid of my sister's is the closest thing I have to a son to help out around here. Well, for now, anyway, until sons come from the angels we've collected."

"By angels, you mean hippies, right?"

"You are very judgmental, aren't you?" He tipped his head to the side, one eye closed against the sun, with his hands laced together over his hard, round stomach. "It's a lonely place to be, sitting at the judge's bench all the time."

"It's a powerful place to be." She wasn't going to break in either direction. She wasn't about to give him the satisfaction of making her truly angry. And she sure as hell wasn't looking to be his friend.

"I'm not your enemy, you know. I have done nothing but provide a roof and care for your friend, who, by the way, wouldn't have
lasted much longer with that infection," he said. "And I haven't even
gotten so much as a thank-you."

Rose bit the inside of her cheek. "Thank. You."

"You are truly welcome, sister." He turned back to the plants.
Rose resisted the urge to point out that she was not his sister, not by
any stretch of the imagination. Instead, she pulled some dandelions
and pocketed the greens for later.

"Can I ask you something?" he said.

"I guess." Anything to make this be over soon.

"Do you not feel that we have an obligation to help?"

"Help who? Help ourselves to breathe? Our families to survive?
Our children to have a future beyond having everything taken from
them? Then yes, of course I do," she answered.

He chuckled. "Classic victim stance. No, no. Do you not feel
that as the chosen people, the ones who have lost nothing important, nothing we can't find elsewhere, we should help those who are
truly without?"

Rose stood to her full height and placed her hands where they
fit the best, on her hips. "Where exactly do you think our dreams
come from? My dreams are full of lakes and the small islands that
skip across them like a heartbeat. They are all that I am. They are
my land. Yours are different, I'm sure. If you're from the north, they
are all the colors of freeze, as deep and devastating as their stories.
In the south, they are red sand and hills cut from the glass formed
under a red sun. Our lands are who we are. That's not something
easily replaced."

He smirked, and she raised her voice to finish. Despite the subject matter, it felt luxurious to be loud outside for once. "And what have the colonizers lost, exactly? The ability to steal? Their loss is not our responsibility."

She walked back to the house—there was nowhere else to go, since Derrick was still recovering inside. She paused by the stone path, angry the Chief had goaded her into popping off, just like a firecracker, but continuing nonetheless. "And for the record, I am nobody's victim. I am my own savior. And I take *that* responsibility very seriously. It's exactly what I owe my grandmother."

She left him in the broken garden with his withering plants.

"And you planted your seeds too shallow," she yelled. "You gotta get deeper than that if you want them to survive." She slammed the door behind her with a real bang.

◆◆◆　◆◆◆　◆◆◆

Rose visited with Derrick when the Chief pulled out his drum in the living room and asked for volunteers to join in a song, which every Wife jumped at with their reedy voices and exaggerated gestures.

"Shit's wacky out there." She carefully closed the door. The Chief didn't like the two of them "segregating themselves." If he knew they were locked in alone, he'd send one of the Wives to check in.

"Shit's less wacky in here. I walked for twenty minutes last night, just back and forth down the hall, but I got it done."

"That's great! I think we need to set a goal. As soon as you can go for an hour without puking or turning into an old man, we leave. I'm good with taking breaks on the trail." Rose was getting excited.

She felt the weight of departure like a pack full of meat, with hunger and anticipation. Especially after Grouse's visit last night. "Do you think there's something wrong with this group?"

Derrick wrinkled his nose. "You mean, do I think they have the Plague of madness?"

Rose nodded.

"Hells yes, I do." He pulled himself up against the headboard. "I mean, who lives like this, in a waterlogged house in the woods with a fake medicine man? I mean, do they, like, take turns being his wife?"

"At night they do."

"Gross." Derrick crossed his arms over his chest. "I'm more of a one-woman kind of man."

Rose laughed. "Uh, I think at this point you're more of a no-woman kind of man."

Derrick looked out the cloudy windowpane at the abstract green beyond. "So, I stayed up for a bit last night when they were giving me medicine."

"And?!"

"And a few minutes was all I could manage. But I think it has to do with this stuff he uses to wash me. They put on surgical masks, and then he wipes my face with a damp rag, and last night, I noticed that it really stinks, like nothing else I've ever smelled. And then that's it, I fall asleep." He looked concerned and almost sheepish.

"Oh my god." Rose jumped to her feet. "Do you think it's chloroform or something? I mean, why, though?"

Derrick shrugged. "No idea. Maybe they just want to touch my sweet abs while I'm under," he tried to joke, but the reality was too creepy for real mirth. What they could be doing to him while he was out was too dark to consider.

Rose folded back onto the bed, grabbing his left arm. "Derrick, what is this?"

He pulled his arm back and stretched it out. There on the inside, in the bend of his elbow, was a blue bruise and, in the center, a bright new scab. "Isn't that just where they give me the meds?"

"You don't mainline antibiotics. Not like that." Rose was starting to panic. "Are they taking something from you instead of putting something in?"

"Only as much as we need. We're not greedy," the man said.

They jumped. Neither had heard the door open. Neither had seen the Chief leaning against the doorway, and so neither one had bothered to lower their voice.

"You're taking his marrow?" Rose stood, blocking Derrick's prone body with all the stretch and muster of her small frame.

"Oh, silly girl. No, no. I'm not some colonial monster." She could see the Wives pooling behind him like half-erased ghosts. He smiled, big and full, showing so many teeth. "We're not stealing marrow. We're simply borrowing blood."

CHAPTER 19:
MOCCASSIN TELEGRAPH

French

A WEEK INTO KITCHEN DUTY AND STILL NO ONE would talk to me. I got a lot of eye rolls and subtle shoulder checks, but no words were exchanged save for the orders I gave. I kept delivering meals to the isolation ward residents, and that became a reprieve from the rest of my day. I got to know many of the residents by their first names, so at least there was that.

"Kirby. Soup today, not too cold this time. Sorry, no utensils again, but at least you can drink it."

"Marsh, come grab your tray. I don't want it falling again. I can't get you another, and you don't want to get reported."

"Shell, last chance before they take you in. Please eat everything, Shell. You need to eat."

Saying the names felt like medicine, felt healing and precious. I wasn't supposed to know them, but some of those who still had voices had whispered them to me the first few days, missives pushed through the metal delivery slots where I slid in the plastic trays. Some breathed them from the dark like sighs; others spat them through the openings, the whites of their eyes glinting with an inner fire. The names haunted my dreams at night, and I woke up with them rattling around in my mouth, stuck in my teeth.

I made sure I said them at each meal. It was probably the only time they heard them, and I knew that after even a few days in isolation, we needed to be reminded of who we were. We forgot. We were always so close to the underlying condition of death that our minds could tip off the brink if we were not called back by name.

Saying them felt like resistance, small and solid.

There were a few residents who never said anything. I tried to reach them in different ways. Sometimes by whistling an old song, sometimes by remarking on the weather I saw through the thick glass. Each exchange was quick and low. If the Watchmen outside the ward door had any idea I was speaking to these people at all, I would be pulled off duty and sent to the Correction Room. I didn't want to think of what would happen to the residents. Then again, I wasn't sure what could be worse for them than this. But it was more than just the siren for me; I could be putting my one chance at escape in jeopardy.

I thought saying their names was the most I could do before I decided to risk small bits of conversation. Then I thought that was the most I could do. But by day eight of this new role, I was proven wrong. Because it was on day eight that the letters began.

"Keep the napkin," Kirby whispered as I gathered his tray from the hatch. "Don't throw it out."

He sounded frantic, so I made sure he saw me take the folded napkin and slide it into my breast pocket. I smiled into the darkness, humoring him. Maybe he thought I could use extra tissue. Maybe it was the only gift he could give me. "Thanks," I said.

At the next door, Marsh waited with his tray all ready to go. When I pulled it out, he whispered, "Wait," and handed over his napkin, folded between extended fingers.

"Oh." I squinted. "Uh, okay. Thank you."

This continued down the line. Not everyone had a napkin for me, but I started taking each tray slower in case they did. Soon, my pants pockets were full; I didn't keep any in my shirt pocket, since the Watchman might notice. Leaving the corridor, he only remarked, "Took you long enough today."

"Sorry about that." I hurried off with my cart of dirty dishes, rattling with movement.

"Don't start getting lazier than usual."

"Right. Sorry." I turned the corner into the kitchen.

It was easy to be unseen in the kitchen even though the space was high and open and sterile—nothing but steel appliances, white walls, and brown people. All the stock was in the huge pantries, behind lock and key. People went out of their way to avoid acknowledging me. But still, I left the napkins in my pockets. I thought about throwing them out—I really didn't need them—but that might've drawn attention. I didn't want anyone getting in trouble, not the residents for gifting them or me for accepting them. And I didn't want to be escorted on my rounds. Obviously, my visits were doing some good, names and pleasantries pushed through metal slots like balm. I didn't want to lose that.

After final cleanup, after I'd gone around my area with a clipboard and checked that each station was spick-and-span, after I'd walked the empty halls back to my room and closed the door behind me, only then did I take out the gifts.

"So weird," I said to myself as they tumbled onto the bedspread like kindergarten paper snowflakes. "So random." But still I was touched by the gesture, even if it was starting to look like none of the napkins were really clean.

"Gross," I grabbed one with edges were stained in watered-down pasta sauce. Today's dinner had been a mass-produced version of spaghetti in a can. I had eaten my own ration sitting on a stool by the sink. I was about to throw the napkin into the toilet when something caught my eye. A pattern. No, a letter. The letter *e*. I pulled the napkin open, the centerfold offering some resistance as the sauce had dried and held.

James King from Birchbark Island. 7 y.o. 5 years ago. Dad is okay. Love you. Stay with your mom.

Suddenly, the napkin was heavy, too heavy to hold in one hand. I walked it carefully back over to the bed and laid it down. What was this?

I picked up the next one and opened it.

Shelly A., Hilly Narrows. Tell my sisters to hide, keep running!

Oh god.

I opened them all in a flurry, reading as fast as I could, though the script was often wobbly or soaking into the paper or misspelled in the dark.

I have to get out. Help me. I am forgetting the words. I forget my chil-dren's faces.

They're changing the game. Tell the leaders to burrow. Tell them to take up arms. It's the only way.

To Bella Dawn from Rainfall River: DON'T COME FOR ME. Stay safe. XO, Mom.

They weren't gifts. They were bombs, and they threatened to blast me to pieces. I backed away from them, both hands over my mouth, until my shoulders hit the wall. So much hope. So much pain. And now it was documented and spread out on my bed. Maybe they weren't written on paper or signed with a flour-ish. They didn't come in envelopes or have stamps affixed to the corners. But they were letters, and I had been assigned the role of postman.

I didn't want them. I didn't want the responsibility. I didn't want to actually hear their voices any more than a just quick word pushed through a locked door. Because really hearing them meant I had to do something.

I ran to the bed and gathered up the missives in my arms. I had to get rid of them. There could be no evidence. I went back to the toilet, only to pause again.

What would I say tomorrow and the day after and the day after that? That I'd flushed them away? That I couldn't do anything for them? Here I was, thanking them for their gifts like I was some Good Samaritan, but for doing what? For saying their names? Tell-ing them it was fucking sunny outside? They didn't need my shal-low platitudes. And really, I was taking no great risk. What they needed was action. They needed me to do something real. I burned with shame. I had actually felt smug, like I was some kind of savior handing over shitty spaghetti and a few words to people who were dying in the dark.

I sat on the floor and folded each napkin as small as it could go. Then I used the pen I had pocketed from Mitch's last visit to work a hole in the mattress and stuffed each one inside.

It was difficult getting to sleep that night on top of all those dreams, all those wishes, all that torment. It seemed like there was no room in the bed for my body, certainly not for my own thoughts. Whatever I did next was going to be bigger than me. It had to be, for all of us. And so maybe these messages were gifts after all. Because in a way, they started delivering me back to myself.

More napkins appeared over the next few days. I realized that the inmates weren't saving their words just for me, that they had a way of communicating with one another as well. It was a small mercy, to have community even in the darkest of prisons. I collected the messages, saying thank you for each one, and carried them back to my mattress depository. I didn't read them all; I couldn't. Some were for family members, a few were for the Creator, and more than one read like a diary. They were written in mustard, in soup, sometimes in blood. They used shorthand, and some were in different languages. These felt like prayers, even if they just recounted the day. That was real resistance, small and impactful. The words existed even now. I believed they always would, even if we didn't. Because the potential of us was in those nouns and verbs, the belief that we could exist, that we had before and would again. Soon there were so many napkins under me that it was like sleeping in a chapel.

After a while, I grew used to the routine: when I'd be met in the hall, the timing of my showers, the menu that would be prepared. I came to expect the sneers and the avoidance, found ways to recognize the kitchen staff by their posture, or their ability to grow facial hair, or the way they put a hand on the small of their back as the day trudged forward toward dinnertime. I knew that twice a week, I had to check in with Agent Mellin to deliver details about the hardship of my time in the woods and that twice a week, Mitch would swing by to sit in my room and talk about his time in the Program and how amazing it all was. It was like listening to the most boring story ever told, but like a TV show when you only have one channel, I got used to it and even started to look forward to the installments.

Any break in the routine became alarming. And so the day I came back from my afternoon shift in the kitchen to find Watchmen tossing the rooms, I almost swallowed my tongue.

There is an excruciating moment when you are confronted with an emergency—an ambulance on your street, or ominous smoke somewhere up ahead—when your body and your mind fight each other. Do you speed up or slow down? How fast do you really want to know what's wrong? How long can you avoid the inevitable? The impulse to do both brought me to my open door at the same pace I usually walked, which in hindsight was probably for the best.

"Can I help you?" I asked, keeping fear and anger out of my voice. It was best to remain neutral, if not subservient, at all times when addressing the Watchmen, who were always looking for any excuse.

"Routine check," said one of the pair, the one who was yanking off my sheets without looking at me.

"Let's see what you're hiding," the other one remarked, running his hands under the edge of the sink.

I felt the blood leave my head. I felt sweat prickle under my arms. But to them, I just shrugged and walked into the room.

The one by the sink put a hand on the rod nestled in his belt and put the other one out in front of him. "Whoa, whoa, whoa. Just what do you think you're doing?"

I shrugged. "I don't know, just coming in?"

"No way. Out in the hall. Now. And stay to the right of the door until we're done." He walked a few steps forward, as if ready to physically push me from the room.

I did as I was instructed, happy to avoid what was to come but also wanting to be present. Every second out there was torment. How long until they found the napkins? What would they do to me when they did? Would I get kicked out of the Program? Would I join the residents in the isolation wing, using my own blood to send SOS messages to the person bringing me Spam sandwiches? I listened for anything that would let me know they were ripping open my mattress, that they were bagging the evidence for Agent Mellin. I could already hear the siren winding up.

"All right." I jumped at the voice. "We're done."

I exhaled. It was the first time I noticed I'd been holding my breath.

"Okay, well, thank you." I gave them a tight smile and started to push past them into my room.

"Not so fast, Chief," the taller man said. He grabbed my arm. "You're coming with us."

"But—"

"Did you think we wouldn't find your contraband? How stupid do you think we are?" He pulled me back into the hall. I looked into the room. Everything was on the floor—blankets, pillow, my clothes—and the mattress was flipped up against the wall.

I had no words. This was it. It was all over.

They marched me down the hall to the stairs. We were headed to wing that held both Agent Mellin and the Correction Room. I wasn't sure which one I'd prefer. All I could think was how I was responsible for the misery of the entire isolation block. Every one of those people had trusted me with their letters, and I had done nothing but get us all caught.

CHAPTER 20:
MOVING ON

The Family

"WE'RE MOVING INTO THE NORTH." BULLET ADDRESSED the entire camp from the base of the hill. "This spot has been good to us for a long time. But in light of recent events, the Council feels it's best to pick up and find a new base."

The grumbling began right away.

"We cannot leave our home!"

"Why now? We should stay and fight!"

"And what about the markings? We've left syllabics in the woods so other travelers can find us," a young man in a faded plaid shirt asked.

Clarence cleared his throat and took a step forward. As a member of the Council, he tried to help Bullet with what was bound to be a barrage of concerns.

"We'll carve the marks off the spots where we left them. And when we have a new home, we'll leave new ones."

"We've made a home here. When the world went to shit we found each other, and then we found this place. We have the cave, the hill, and the road's close, so we can keep an eye on the Recruiter movement. How are we going to find someplace else this perfect?" The woman stood holding her partner's hand, concern lining both their faces.

"You know what's perfect? Not dying." Bullet was overtired. The Council meeting had been heated, and she wasn't really in a congenial mood right now. Bullet understood—they'd all come from something broken and dangerous and disappeared. This small piece of land was the first place in a long time where so many of them could breathe and sing and sleep without the constant nightmare of capture. But it was in danger now, which meant that soon, the nightmares would find them here.

"When would we leave?" a woman holding a small child on her hip asked.

"A week, maybe two. We need to repatriate the space so the Recruiters have nothing to go on." Bullet looked around, considering the scope of the work. They'd have to get rid of so much that couldn't be carried. And then there were the structures they'd built. It hurt to even think about tearing down what had taken so much effort to put up.

"What if we don't want to move? What if some of us decide to stay?" Plaid Shirt challenged.

"Then you stay. We can't, but we won't force anyone to do anything they don't want to do." Clarence shrugged. "You do as you see fit."

"I call dibs on the back cave space!" Plaid Shirt's declaration was met with raised voices and groans.

"People, now is not the time to fall apart and turn on each other." Bullet was exasperated already. "And it most certainly is not the time to be selfish. We are a community. It's how we get by. Remember that."

From the front, Jean struggled to stand up from his upended log seat. The crowd fell silent. He was a Council member, and he had just lost his son. This afforded him a kind of solemn respect, more so than the others in his group. So many of the people, too many, understood what it was to truly mourn. They knew how deep that pit was dug in your chest.

"My son, he found us because we were here. Because we survived, and we survived long enough to welcome others. If we had made foolish decisions way back, well, we wouldn't have been able to settle here, to send out signs to others like us." His voice wavered between resolute and broken. "We need to do that for other children, for all our relatives who may need us. We need to be strong; we are the stronghold in the north that people are looking for, and we need to move so it stays that way."

He lowered himself with the help of Clarence. His speech was met with a few "aho"s from the assembly and a lot of nods. Even Plaid Shirt lowered his head in consideration.

"I say we sleep on it. Tomorrow, we'll gather again after midday meal to discuss where we're at. I would just advise everyone to consider their own families—both the one we have and the ones that might still be out there." Clarence clapped his hands, calloused from years of bush work even before it became the only way to survive. The meeting was adjourned.

Miig and Isaac held hands as they walked back to their tent.

"What do you think?"

"I think it's the smart decision," Miig answered, "but it's not going to be the popular one. People are tired. Hell, I'm tired. Everyone is just looking to stop moving."

"Agreed. What are we going to do?"

"Well, let's call our people together and make our decision." Miig rubbed his eyes. It had been weeks since the news about French, and he was still having a hard time coming to terms with the reality that he would never see him again—not in this lifetime, anyway.

"Jean doesn't look like he's in any shape to pick up and move," Isaac considered. "I wonder if he'd even make it."

"I don't think he cares at this point." Miig squeezed his husband's hand. "I don't know what I'd do if I lost you again. It's too terrible to even put thought to."

"I know what I would do," Isaac answered.

"Oh yeah? And what's that?"

"I'd swan dive off the nearest cliff." Isaac said it in all seriousness.

"No. You can't do that. You can never do that. What would that say to the others? Everyone is fighting to live. You can't just decide to die." Miig was angry even at the comment.

"At that point, my love, I wouldn't care about anyone else. Not even myself."

They were already at their tent when the scout jogged back with a sighting, when the rifles were shouldered in preparation, and when two visitors walked into the camp.

✦✦✦ ✦✦✦ ✦✦✦

Bullet and Clarence entered the clearing where Miig's family had set up their tents when they'd first joined. The settlement was communal and open, but families usually stayed close together, especially those who had journeyed in together. Miig was finishing up Story, so they waited on the periphery for him to finish before intruding.

"For so long, we as a species were violent. Our violence was neglect; our violence was arrogance. The wasp sting of capitalism was left to grow malignant without proper care. And wasps can keep on stinging once they begin. They don't die like bees, so they don't have to be as committed to the damage. We as humans forgot our *specific* place and spread into *every* place instead. As if we were removed from consequence. As if we were untouchable. We couldn't even imagine the Earth retaliating. And then it did."

Miig acknowledged their guests with a tilt of his chin. "Come in, join us."

"Miig, sorry, brother. We wanted to bring some people who just arrived to meet you, Wab especially. Is that okay?"

"Yes, yes, of course." Wab sat up a little straighter. Chi Boy eyed them with suspicion.

Clarence waved two newcomers forward and introduced them. They were nurses. Theo was from Boston and had been working in the schools for the past year. Rania came from Pakistan before the closures had begun of the North American borders and had been transferred from a Toronto senior care facility to the schools shortly thereafter.

"I didn't know what was happening—none of us knew. We just thought, hey, here's an opportunity to keep working in health care when so many others have lost their jobs, you know?" Theo explained.

"I stayed on once I saw what was going down." Rania looked tired, the kind of tired that takes years to build. "I figured I could help, first just by being kind inside, and now by organizing the network to get people out." She sighed, passing a hand through her short hair. "There's not enough kindness in the world to make what's going on better. We need to do more. We're trying."

Clarence put a hand on her shoulder. "We know. We see what you're doing, and it's working."

"I'm proof of that," Isaac said. "You're the only hope any of us has while we're in there. The network is the reason I'm out, the reason I'm alive."

A single tear escaped down her cheek, and she wiped it with the back of her hand. "Thank you. It means a lot."

"We brought Theo and Rania to you because they have some information that directly affects your family," Bullet explained. "It concerns those who are with child."

Chi Boy instinctively put his arm around Wab's waist. Even though she hated public affection, especially in front of newcomers, when it was important to look tough, it was clear his concern went beyond her and to their shared child. She allowed him that.

"Right." Rania took a deep breath. "Things are changing. The schools are changing. And we need to get you out of reach."

"How far out of reach?" Tree asked, driven to uncharacteristic questions by a new urgency in the air. "We're pretty safe here."

"As far as we can get," she answered. "Over the border."

"Into the States?" Zheegwon reached for the hat Tree was already pulling off his head, a gesture that revealed their unease. The twins shared the hat like a teddy bear when they were nervous. "We're already talking about going farther into the bush. Maybe to the north."

"Yes, into the States. The government is still enforcing the no-harvesting law there, and they're making headway into synthetic dream cures. There's an opportunity to get across before the real danger hits too close, but we'd have to leave pretty much now."

"Besides," Theo added, "the north is going to be crowded soon. There's new construction planned—big construction, covering acres at a time, like farmland."

"You'd better sit down for a moment." Miig gestured to the fire. "And tell us everything you can." He was starting to feel as tired as the nurses looked. What now? What could possibly be going on now, and how much more could they take?

Rania began her tale, and by the time she was done, they were packing their bags.

✦✦✦ ✦✦✦ ✦✦✦

"We'll stay until she shows up. You have my word." Jean embraced his old friend after handing him a bundle of wooden matches and braided sweetgrass. "I'll make sure."

"And make sure she gets the instructions, yeah?" Miig was torn, but he had to do what was best for the group, what was best for Wab and her baby. There was no way they would let her take the journey by herself, but still, leaving before Rose made it back felt like admitting she was dead, especially after French.

"Of course." The two men held each other at arm's length for a moment, each one memorizing the details of the other's face in case it was the last time they saw it.

"We have to come up with a new route anyway, never mind a new destination," Clarence added. "The north is out of the question now that we know about the new builds."

Miig shook his hand. "The hospitality and safety you've shown us . . . well, it won't be forgotten. It's a story that will be shared. It allowed me the return of my partner, and for that alone, I am indebted to you."

"It was a pleasure, one of the few I have left. Truly."

They left that night while most of the camp slept. A single scout walked them to the perimeter under the milky moon, blurred to a soft spotlight. They waited while she climbed a tree and whistled down the all clear. Then they slipped into the denser trees, Rania and Theo in the lead, and headed toward the imaginary line in the sand that might offer them a chance at safety, that might give Wab's baby the chance to take its first breath in freedom.

They had no choice, not anymore. They had to leave now. They had to leave Rose behind.

CHAPTER 21:
A LITTLE BIRD BRINGS DEATH

Rose

"LET ME GO!"

Rose's scream echoed in the empty room and fell back on her, pinning her limbs like heavy blankets, useless weight making it harder to breathe. All the cots belonging to the Wives had been pulled out except for hers, where she lay strapped to the metal frame.

"THIS IS SERIOUSLY MESSED UP!"

She struggled against the leather restraints until her skin was rubbed raw and pinched. After she and Derrick had been caught talking, the women had grabbed Rose. One at a time, she could have taken them, but all at once? It was like fighting a giant, pale spider. At some point, the Chief had put the same rag he'd used to drug Derrick over her face, and the rest was gone. They must have carried her up here, made their renovations, and left her to wake up alone. The sky outside the window was grey. It was hard to tell how long she'd been out. Minutes? Days? She finally settled down, banging the back of her head into the thin pillow until a wave of nausea overtook her. She felt terrible.

What now? Derrick was sure to be tied up downstairs, and she was locked away up here. There was nothing nearby that she could use to free herself, and she was starting to panic.

"*Nam*," she called out. "Nam, please. I . . . I need some water!"

The room was so much bigger than she remembered now that it was empty. The wallpaper hung down in long strips, and the ceiling was spotted with brown rings and sagging so that the entire space felt like being inside a rotting ribcage. She moved her joints at different angles and pulled, trying to slip them through the loops that held them. They tightened and refused her movements.

Long minutes passed before she heard someone on the stairs. Minutes during which she imagined what might be happening to French, to Derrick, to herself, scenarios that ended with them dried out like corn husk dolls, discarded in different desolate rooms on different stained mattresses. When the footsteps echoed down the hallway, she lay perfectly still, trying to quiet her hysteria, trying to look like she still had a mind to lose.

The door opened, and Nam entered with a red plastic cup. "Brought you water." They wouldn't meet her eyes.

She licked her lips. They were starting to chap and peel. "Nam, listen, I . . . I'm scared. I'm really, really scared. And I need your help."

Rose talked so fast the words tumbled into one another. She didn't know how long Nam would stay, and she had to get through to them. Plus, her voice felt smaller by the minute. She was weak, and that made her even more frantic. "This is not fair. It's not fair. And it's not right."

"I can't help you," they said after a moment of pause, standing just inside the door.

"You have to! You're the only one here."

"But I'm not. I'm not the only one, and the others . . ."

"Those women have the Plague," Rose hissed, cutting them off.

Nam was across the room in a flash, clamping their fine-boned hand over Rose's mouth. "Shut up. Just shut up. Don't say that word. It's forbidden."

Rose shook them off. "Drinking our blood is not going to give anyone dreams! That's just madness!"

"Jesus, I'm not stupid. It's not the blood. He knows that, I think." Nam separated themself from the Chief in one sentence. "It's not about that, anyway. It's about hope."

"Hope?"

They placed the cup on the floor and sat on the edge of the mattress. "People can't dream because their way of life is gone and they can't accept it. They lived through pandemics, but they didn't, not really. He wants to give them hope that there is a different way."

"What does that have to do with us?"

"We *are* the different way." Nam's shoulders slouched. They looked so slim and young, like a willow in a white tank top, the outline of a pentagram charm showing through the material like a birthmark. "So he gives them us. One drop at a time. And I guess it's enough."

"Enough to give them dreams?"

"I'm not sure there's enough blood in one skin for that." They rubbed their chin in a thoughtful gesture. "It's enough just so they'll wait around for the dreams to start."

"Why doesn't he give them his own blood, his own dreams?"

"He doesn't have enough to go around," Nam admitted. "Of either."

"What? But he's always going on about his visions—all colorful and sacred and Indian-y."

Nam laughed. "You've obviously never read much. Those are stories. Stories I remember from Maria Campbell and Waub Rice . . . and some are just my dreams."

Rose held her breath. "He's telling your dreams?"

They nodded.

"Why doesn't he have more?"

"Before he was the Chief, he was just plain old corrupt Chief Henry Williams, a stereotype. He had the biggest house on the rez and two brand-new boats. He was in tight with the oil dudes, living a good life with the consultation money meant for the Band."

Rose's head started to spin, and she had to close her eyes. She felt the cup at her lips and tried to drink. A thought occurred to her.

"Nam, did they already take some?" She kept her eyes closed. "My blood? Did they take it?"

There was no answer. There didn't need to be. Rose twisted in her starfish position to see her arm. There was a bandage on the inside of her elbow. If she'd had anything other than a mouthful of water in her stomach, she'd have thrown it up.

◆◆◆　◆◆◆　◆◆◆

"I don't know how much longer we'll last." Rose felt her heart in her throat, too small a place to comfortably hold such a muscular organ, even weakened as it was. It had been four days since Nam had first appeared with water, since she'd been captured and tied up with her arms out like some kind of Christ, and already she was losing hope of ever getting back to the woods, let alone to the school to find French. That mission felt like a dream from another life. Nam had been coming in every day to take blood. At first, the Wives showed up to drain her: Wren, who stabbed at Rose's arm with wild abandon, and Cardinal, who cried from the second she walked in until the second she was chased out by a string of profanities. Neither approach was particularly successful. The Chief came once, but Rose made sure he knew exactly what she thought of him.

"You're a cult leader, that's all. You are no real Chief," she spat at him. If she'd had more saliva, it would have landed on his face. Instead, he wiped his arm on the front of her T-shirt and left, unharmed.

"I hope your ancestors are watching. I hope your grandma has a front row seat to this bullshit," Rose laughed. "If I were you, I wouldn't step outside. You might find wolves sent by your own relations waiting for you."

"I don't have time for all this negative energy you're spewing," he replied from the safety of the doorway. "Good thing we have sacred medicines to clean all the foulness from your blood."

"You think the medicines will be on your side? Our blood isn't like Tylenol, asshole. It's not gonna help you and your sick concubines. You're done for. Sooner or later, you're all done for!" He slammed the door on his way out, but Rose's laughter followed him down the hall.

So he started sending Nam to do his dirty work. Rose preferred it this way. Sure, it hurt to have someone you considered decent slowly killing you, but at least she could talk to Nam. Every day, she tried to get more information about the house and the inhabitants and made desperate attempts to get them on her side. And Nam seemed to like being with her, taking their time to do the extraction, then hanging around after, fiddling with the vials and the sheets—any excuse to stay a bit longer.

"We can leave together. We can be your family, a real family." Rose teared up thinking about her own group, but she told Nam all about them anyway. About Wab and the baby on the way; about Miig and his husband Isaac, how they'd found each other after years apart; about the language Slopper had been collecting like beads on a string.

"You don't need a house, Nam. You need a home. I have a home. I can take you there." She wasn't used to pleading, and it was hard to know if it was even having an effect.

"I tried before, to leave." They got a look in their eye that Rose recognized. It was the look a deer got when it smelled you close by, knowing your intention before you raised the rifle. It was an understanding of menace. "He's always watching. He's got a lot of eyes to watch with, all those Wives jumping at any chance to be his number one." Nam removed the syringe and pressed down on the puncture spot on Rose's arm with a small piece of cotton. They tried to be gentle, but every touch was unbearable pressure at this point.

"I took less than before," they whispered. "I'll add some water to the vial before I hand it over so neither of us hears about it."

Rose rolled her eyes to Nam's face, trying to push gratitude into her look. She was sure she just looked nauseated. But she really was grateful. This was the only spark of hope she'd had in days.

"I'll start weaning them onto the watered-down shit." Nam checked the door before digging in the pocket of their velvet dinner jacket. "And take these. I got some to Derrick, too."

They pushed a couple of pills into Rose's hand. One was a huge oblong horse pill that looked physically impossible to swallow. Then they picked them back up and popped them in Rose's mouth before feeding her the water to swallow them with.

Rose had tears in her eyes, but not the strength to shed them. "This is exactly it—you get it. It's exactly the thing you do for family . . . anything . . ." She couldn't finish the sentence.

Nam picked up the harvesting supplies and the blood. "It's iron and vitamin B-12. You need to get your strength back, start rebuilding your blood and muscle, before it's too late."

For the first time in days, Rose didn't feel so alone in the room after the door closed. She drifted off, wondering what they had meant. Before it was too late for what?

◆◆◆　◆◆◆　◆◆◆

It took a full week before Rose had enough strength to think of a plan, days when Nam came by more and more often, bringing her comics and reading them aloud. Slowly, Rose went from silent prisoner to asking to see pictures or commenting on the storyline. "How the hell does he go from football player to nerd from one book to the next, and why can't he be both at the same time?"

By the tenth day, Nam was releasing one limb at a time so Rose could flex and rotate and stretch, getting her range of motion back. Rose had asked them to start pilfering things, slow and easy, one at a time, things they would need when they made a break for it.

So far, Nam said they had some bottles of pills, gauze, and a few tins stashed.

Nam reported that Derrick was looking good. Since they'd been smuggling him vitamins, his leg had gotten better. The wound was closed now, and the fever was completely gone. The Chief had told the Wives it was a sign from the Creator, that their dedication to traditions and their family ways had pleased him, that he had healed the bringer of blood so they would have a long-term supply. Nam told her all about what was happening downstairs.

"Blood regenerates. We just need to treat the vessel with care, and the holy water will continue to flow," the Chief explained. He tipped a few drops onto each woman's tongue from a slim decanter every night while Nam watched from the corner, reading a comic book.

"What of the girl?" Owl asked, waiting patiently on her knees for her communion.

"I haven't had a vision for her yet. But besides her blood contribution, I do think she might finally provide us with a viable pregnancy." Here, Cardinal, who had miscarried again—if she had even been pregnant to begin with—burst into fat tears. The hydration in the woman was admirable. "And then," the Chief spoke over her sobs, "we will all benefit from the new life, especially one with so much Indigenous blood."

Several women clapped their hands together in prayer. Grouse wiggled a loose molar and grunted around the dirty fingers jammed in her mouth.

"Can we afford another stomach to feed?" Wren asked, her leg draped over one arm of the moldy barrel chair by the front window. She traced the outline of her lips with the tip of a finger as she talked. "Not to be blasphemous, but we barely scrape by now."

The Chief dropped blood into Owl's mouth, and she swooned in supplication, the back of her head lightly touching the floor before she pulled herself back up. He paused for a moment and looked around at the women, delicate and fragile, surviving on expired tins and squirrel meat. His eyes landed on Grouse, who at that moment managed to free the loose tooth. Red drool dribbled down her chin and onto the front of her filthy toga. She regarded the brown stump, then popped it back in her mouth and swallowed.

"Yes, perhaps you're right, Wren. We should consider making some adjustments." Nam watched the cords in his neck flex. "Let me sleep on the question tonight, and tomorrow we'll have action."

"He's going to kill Grouse," Nam whispered, their back turned so Rose could use the chamber pot. "Tomorrow." They rubbed their chin. "But maybe it's better that way. How much of her, of any of them, is really left, anyway?"

"What? Why?" Rose asked, well beyond any embarrassment over nudity or bodily functions by this point. She figured if anyone in the house should have shame, it was the man downstairs with his collection of dolls. But she did feel new fear. She hadn't considered that he might be evil enough to kill one of his own members. Clearly, the Plague was deep in this house.

"She's too far gone," Nam said over their shoulder. "And he's made other plans."

"Other plans?"

They paused. "He's going to try to give you a baby, and there is barely enough food for the bodies we have now. So Grouse has to go."

The two of them were silent for a minute.

Rose shifted on the bed. "I'm done."

Nam cleaned up while Rose chewed her lip in thought.

"Nam?"

"Yeah?" Their voice was flat, eyes far away in thought.

"We leave tomorrow, before the sun comes up. We gotta get away from them as fast as we can, especially if they're talking about murder. We might be next." There was no telling when the Chief might decide they had outlived their usefulness or that they were more trouble than they were worth. Rose thought about all the things she'd said to him. It was now or never.

"You sure you can make it?" Nam sounded calm, but their eyes were wide, darting to the closed door and back.

"Yeah, I feel a lot better, thanks to you." She smiled. "Early or late?"

"What?" Nam's hands were shaking, so they shoved them in their pockets.

"The group, do they go to bed early or sleep late?"

"Those assholes, they sleep in. Pretty much up all night."

"Okay, good. Let Derrick know we leave before dawn. Move that bag you've been filling to the back porch tonight, before you go to bed."

Nam nodded, carrying the chamber pot to the door.

"And Nam?"

They turned.

"Pack your stupid comics. You're coming with us."

This time, there was no argument.

✦✦✦ ✦✦✦ ✦✦✦

Morning dark was full of menace and twitch. There was something both seductive and terrifying about a darkness that insisted on change without reason, turn without halt. It would be day, and it would be soon, and nothing could stop that. The minutes before dawn were headstrong and without doubt.

Rose had stayed up, scared to close her eyes in case she slept too deeply and they ended up missing their opportunity. She had been stretching and keeping limber, flexing her arms or kicking her legs or doing crunches until her stomach screamed. She was ready. The threat of the Chief on top of her, of life as a swollen Wife, round and hollow as a paper lantern, made today the day it had to happen.

Nam tiptoed in. Rose was sure it was them because of the way they moved, like a child with parents who shouldn't be woken under any circumstance. They reached for Rose's feet first, unlatching the repurposed belts and carefully laying down the buckles so they didn't clang against the bed frame. Then they moved to her hands. All four limbs released at once, Rose contracted like a drop of mercury, curling in on herself. Then she pushed back out, carefully rolling off her back and the side of the bed that now held her shape, trying to minimize the squeal of the old springs. She reached for Nam's hand, and together they left the room.

CHAPTER 22:
A CAGE OPENS

Nam

THE STAIRS WERE A PUZZLE OF SOUND AND SPLINTER, one that Nam knew well. They took particular steps, shifting their weight so that the creak would be merely a low lullaby if it was noticed at all. Rose peered around the corner into the living room. Six Wives lay around the room on blankets, in chairs, one on the couch. Each one slept in their white garb, so still they turned to shrouds. They made their way down the hall to Derrick's room. He was awake and waiting for them, held to the bed by chains and padlocks. Nam slipped the key from the front pocket of their blazer.

Nam felt every muscle and joint working in concert. They were hyperaware of the quiet in the house. They were so sure Rose and Derrick would feel it, too, that they were surprised when Rose held a finger to Derrick's lips before helping him lift off the bed without a sound, as if noise would change the stakes.

Back in the living room, the Wives looked peaceful, just another family of cult groupies having a snooze. The truth was, they were so far under right now that it would have taken electricity to rouse them. The Chief was the only one who wouldn't wake up—he was lying behind a closed door, his eyes wide open. Nam was glad he had known at the end, glad that he had come to understand that it was his own relative who had caused that end. There was more than one way to steal dreams, and Nam was done with being robbed.

Rose had made a plan, but it hadn't been a good one. She had wanted to wait until everyone was asleep and then sneak out. Nam knew that would be impossible. There was no way to make sure the Wives would all be sleeping at the same time. And the Chief was a light sleeper, waking to footfalls in the hallway or the sound of someone opening the pantry without his permission. Years ago, at the beginning of all the mayhem, Nam had tried to leave but never made it. Today they would make it, and there was only one way to make sure of that.

The Chief had to die. The rest could just be unconscious, because even if some of the women woke early, they would be harmless as long as the Chief was out of the way. He was the battery in the familial machine. Without him there was no movement, no light, no purpose.

To make sure the plan had the best chance of "taking," Nam had to proceed in stages. The first was morphine in their homemade liquor—already a mixture that made them slow and stupid. After the celebration where Nam played heavy-handed bartender came the ceremony, and then there was more morphine, this time mixed into Rose and Derrick's blood. By then, the Chief and his women were slurring and moving like litter caught in a current. Nam suggested they turn in early, that perhaps the booze had come from an exceptionally strong batch, that the ceremony had probably been doubly effective.

"Get to your beds," they told the group with false excitement. "The dreams are on the way!"

Half the Wives cried, stumbling over chairs and the bubbles in the water-rotted rugs to get to their nests. The Chief gathered Nam in his arms before he retired to his bedroom alone, his skin sweaty and cold at the same time.

"You make everything possible, little bird. You are the original dream catcher. I hope you see prophecy tonight, like I did years ago when I first laid eyes upon you."

Nam kept their eyes wide open and bore the revulsion of his touch by emptying everything of value from their mind, from their skin, leaving nothing for him to reach, not like before. For years, they had called him Uncle Bear, not for his protection or size, but for the shadows he threw on their bedroom wall in the moonlight, creeping softly in at first, then without care later on when there were no adults left to hear or stop him.

"Good night, Uncle." Nam snapped their hand at their side, and the plastic bag unfurled.

There were some signs that all was not well. Some gurgling, a gasp or two, the cacophony of a blind stumble into chamber pots around midnight, but all in all, it was without the pomp of the usual household ceremony. The Wives wouldn't wake up for hours, maybe a whole day. And when they did, they'd be alone and useless. Maybe some would choose to join their leader. Maybe others would wander off into the woods. But no matter what happened now, they were no longer a threat.

Nam read comics by candlelight while listening to the Wives stumbling around, a few retching into bowls, one continually crying until she was breathing deep and heavy, hung over the arm of the couch. Nam took their time turning the pages, seeing more color now than they had ever noticed in the muted drawings. They wondered if Rose and Derrick knew, if they had felt the Chief's struggle through the floorboards, up through the walls, as he tried unsuccessfully to untie the knots that held the plastic bag tight around his neck and over his head.

You're just being paranoid, they told themself. *They don't know. They can't know.* Decent people—the kind of people you wanted to take with you, to make part of a normal family—didn't do these kinds of things. Nam knew that much.

After leaving the Chief for the last time, still and stiffening on his bedroom floor, Nam finished filling an oversize hiking backpack with supplies: antibiotics, vitamins, bandages, a stitch kit, tins of food and bottles of water. They left it outside the back porch door as per the original plan. Rose had instructed them to gather these things slowly over the last few days, but taking precious supplies from a madman was an impossible task. It never would have worked. So they did it now, taking time to read labels and wrap bottles in protective fabric. Then they went up to release Rose.

Outside now, running through the overgrown yard toward the shadows of trees, Nam had a moment of panic for the first time, a sinking kind of fear that threatened to flush them away, out of reach. They turned around to look at the house, the windows dark, the left side sinking into the muddy earth.

"Nam, come on. We gotta go!" Derrick called. In front of him, Rose waved them on, terror and excitement making her dark eyes shiny.

One last look back. The house was just made of wood after all, not metal bars. The windows weren't fortified. The back screen swung wild on its hinges like a mute woman screaming. And this time, they felt nothing. There were no eyes watching, no white ghosts floating, no bears stalking. There was just an old house being swallowed by the forest, one plank and one bone at a time.

"Coming."

Nam jumped through the last knot of anxiety and off into the woods like a bird from an open cage.

CHAPTER 23:

THE LIGHTS COME ON

French

"IT SEEMS THAT ONCE AGAIN, YOU ARE HAVING DIFFI-culty following the rules, Mr. Dusome."

Agent Mellin glared at me over the thin frames of her spectacles. I fought to maintain eye contact even though it was making me nauseated. Because that's what was required: eye contact when requested, complete subservience when demanded. Fear had grown in my body since I'd been here. It reached new places at a higher volume than ever before. It was more intimate, more immediate.

I opened my mouth to speak, but there were no words. What should I say? That the notes had already been in the mattress? That I'd never seen them before? Would she believe me if I told her that I'd written them myself? I couldn't be responsible for the punishment—sorry, correction—of the entire isolation block. Their names bubbled up in my throat, slipped around my fingers.

"You know that having any personal items in your quarters is strictly forbidden, do you not?"

"Yes, ma'am." I wished I had thought to bring something, anything, to stuff in my ears while I was in the Correction Room. Not that you could block out that wail. Its pitch was set to shake your brain on its stem. I lowered my eyes to my lap, watching my fingers hold and release every name. Kirby . . . Marsh . . . Shell . . .

"And so can you explain this?"

I looked up, but the desk was clear. No napkins, no bag of evidence. Nothing. I looked at Mellin, and there in her hand was a pen, the pen Mitch had left behind. The one I had stashed under the toilet tank.

The relief made me blink hard, pushed the air in and out of my body quicker. To an observer, I must have seemed on the verge of tears, and maybe I was. They hadn't found the notes after all!

"Well, what do you have to say for yourself?" She allowed the pen to roll off her palm and hit the desk like a single die.

"I'm so sorry, ma'am. I . . . I found it in the hall. Someone must have dropped it." God, there was so much room in my head right now, so much movement. I wasn't trapped, not as bad as I'd thought I was. I could handle this.

"I didn't know what to do. I wasn't sure anyone would believe me that it was just in the hallway, so I hid it in my room. I didn't use it at all. I just kept it there until I could figure out what to do."

She watched me speak, checking my eyes, which direction I looked, my breathing patterns—anything that would betray a lie.

But I was so relieved that this version of the truth came easily. It was convincing, even to me.

"Mr. Dusome, you know the rules, do you not?"

"Yes, ma'am. I do."

"This is contraband."

"Yes, ma'am. It is. But I promise, I never wrote a single mark with it." That much was the god's honest truth. I softened my gaze, opening my eyes wide in a sign of innocence.

She opened a drawer and swiped the pen into it like it was something rancid she'd rather not touch. "Very well. The next time you come across anything like this, the appropriate response is to leave it where it is and to call one of the Watchmen to come and retrieve it."

"That's a great idea, ma'am. I wish I hadn't panicked. I apologize."

"That's enough out of you." She folded her hands in front of her. "You do realize that I am still going to have to offer corrective measures for this infraction, of course."

I nodded. I didn't have words for that. I was going into the Correction Room after all. At least I was only taking myself there and not any of the others. I could live through the screech, holding on to that to lessen the pain.

She buzzed in the Watchmen who had brought me to her office. They stood in the doorway, arms clasped behind their backs, awaiting instruction. I tried to pull myself together for what was to come.

"Return our student to his abode. He is to remain there under lock and key for exactly forty-eight hours—no food, and no privileged Program duties. He is to do nothing but think about his actions and meditate on the Program. After the room is cleaned, of course."

Holding back my relief that I was only going to my room was the hardest con of the day.

✦✦✦ ✦✦✦ ✦✦✦

Two days alone. Two days without interaction was a lot once you were used to a strict schedule that included visiting almost forty voices a day. The worse part was trying to tamp down the unreasonable gratitude I felt. Maybe Mellin wasn't so bad after all. Maybe she was fair and just.

No, I told myself. No, she is a monster, and this is a monstrous situation. I shouldn't be grateful. Grateful meant I was broken.

At least they left the light on. And it did give me time to think, after I checked the mattress, just in case. The slit in the fabric was small, and inside, the notes remained unmolested. I thought about the risk I was taking for the inmates. Was it worth the possibility of discovery to carry hopeful messages out into a world without hope? And how would I even get them out the door? I was sure that on the day they let me out into the field, everything I wore and carried would be closely scrutinized from my naked ass up.

I decided sometime that first night that I was going to have to get rid of them *and* carry them out of here at the same time. I recalled something Mitch had said back in the infirmary about reading the Bible. About how it was ridiculous to think the book was the important thing and not the words themselves that should live inside of you. So, one by one, I slipped the notes out of the mattress, memorized them, and then flushed them. I dared only flush once an hour in case that was being monitored. It took at least that long to memorize some of them, and I was in no hurry. I had nothing but time in here.

The next morning, I finished the entire set. Some of them seemed like they were just for me, or least that's how I took them, maybe because I needed them.

You're not alone. None of us are.

A new day is coming. I can feel it.

I spent the rest of the day running laps around the room, whisper-singing each note back to myself. I made up a song to help me remember them—I couldn't stand to lose even one word. A few of the napkins I hadn't read before. I tried not to get distracted, but a few of them were vague enough that I played a game of Indian Geography. Could this person be a relative? Might one of them be someone I'd met? One in particular stuck in my brain like it was pinned to the inside of my skull. I had no problem remembering it. The fight was in not getting completely hung up on it to the detriment of the rest of the bundle.

I am still Marguerite Eliot. I will always be Marguerite Eliot. Tell my mother that I am alive. She is an Elder and needs help; she don't remember too well anymore. Tell her baamaapii gigawaabamin.

Someone else was missing their Elder. Someone else was putting down the words that held us together. Baamaapii gigawaabamin. In Anishinaabemowin, there was no word for goodbye, only for "see you later." I hoped that was true. I needed it to be true.

Exactly forty-eight hours later, the door swung open. I was less excited than I should have been, almost indifferent, until I saw Mitch standing there.

"Mitch!"

He cleared his throat, straightening his tie as he did. It always seemed to be choking him. He looked up and down the hallway before stepping inside.

"Hello, Francis. I'm here to notify you that your correction period is up."

"Yeah, thanks, I guess." I sat on the edge of the bed, waiting for him to join me like he always did. Instead, he stood a few feet away, as if I were hostile or infectious. He stayed close to the door. It made me sad—so much time wasted listening to his dumb stories, all the days spent looking for, and sometimes finding, little traces of the boy I used to know in his words and gestures, and now I couldn't even get him to sit down?

"I am, of course, disappointed that you chose to break one of the few simple rules that have been handed down to you." He shuffled his feet. He was speaking loud, as if for an audience, even turning his face toward the open door as he spoke.

"Yeah, well—"

"But," he interrupted, "I am happy that you handled yourself well in here. I know that you have spent your time wisely, thinking about ways to be a better Program student."

Before I could answer, he bent down and leaned in, lowering his voice to a whisper. "I know I was the one who forgot the pen in here. Thanks for not telling."

Then he held a finger up to his lips and cleared his throat again. He went back to the performative voice. "I will work harder to be a better mentor as you progress. Do you have any questions for me?"

"Um, I guess, when can I get back to the kitchen?" I tried to speak as if we were under surveillance as well. "I really want to rejoin the Program."

He smiled. This was genuine. Had he already forgotten we were acting? "Excellent. Your escort will be by in one hour to take you for dinner service. It should be a fairly easy shift. Perfect to get back into the swing of things."

He left without another word. My door stayed open, and an hour later, my silent cohort in the grey scrubs meandered down the hall and motioned for me to fall into step beside him.

◆◆◆　◆◆◆　◆◆◆

Mitch wasn't wrong. There were only half as many trays as usual loaded onto my cart. I checked the clipboard. Twenty. That was all. Dread started to fill my muscles. I knew for sure that the napkins hadn't been found, so no one was in trouble over that, but why was the food being rationed down to half the regular number of servings? Was there some kind of revolt while I was locked up, and people were being denied meals? The other alternative, that there were now only half as many mouths to feed, was something I didn't want to consider. It was never good when someone left isolation. It wasn't like they were released back into the wild or enjoying birthday cake in a break room somewhere. They were just gone. Disappeared.

"Hurry up. Half the recipients means half the time. I'm counting, Hemingway," the Watchman said as he let me into the ward. Obviously they had all been informed of my pen-related infraction.

"Yes, sir." I refused to make eye contact—that was my big-man swipe at his authority. Just another small gesture, and yet it pushed fear into my muscles, and I scurried past him. Like a mouse.

More than half the doors had yellow papers tacked on them, the color of caution. I read the page on door one: RESIDENT HAS BEEN

TEMPORARILY RELOCATED. Door two was the same, as were the rest. Resident temporarily relocated. Temporarily—maybe they were in the Correction Room? No, they wouldn't give us the comfort of being anything but alone in that space, so they couldn't all be there at once. Were they all being force-fed? My stomach turned.

I pushed a tray of powdered eggs through the first door without a yellow sign and was shocked by a bright sliver of light. I put my face to the hole instead of the food and looked in.

This was Missy's room. Her note came to my mind easily: *Junior—Lac des Arbres—don't date my sister while I'm gone!* She must have been beautiful at one time; she was still haunted by it around her big eyes, beauty clinging to her cheekbones. She was lying on her cot, staring up at the ceiling. She didn't blink for so long that I was becoming convinced she was a corpse until I caught her halting breathing under the blue scrubs that pooled around her bones.

I tried to push my lips into the slot, to focus the sound, "Missy!"

I moved my head so I could see her. Nothing. I tried again.

"Missy, are you okay?"

I glanced back at the door to see if the Watchman was on his way down the hall to grab me by the scruff of my neck. No movement.

One last time: "Missy, can you hear me?"

She moved her head slightly to the left without unsticking her eyes from where they were fixed, and then, slowly, as if she were operating in a different physical realm, she rolled them to meet mine. The corners of her lips twitched and then pulled back as if caught by fishhooks. She showed me all her teeth, half of them crooked and brown, in a ghastly smile. Saliva slipped out and down her chin. She was not going to talk to me. I wasn't sure she could if she wanted to. I sat in her stare, spit glistening on her face, for a full minute, waiting.

Maybe, in a way, she had also been relocated. I wasn't sure if it was temporary or not. She rolled her eyes back to the ceiling and then her head, the smile still carved into her thin face.

I fed the tray through, let the hatch drop, and made my way to the next door. Nineteen left. Nineteen zombies, lying on their beds, laughing to themselves while sitting on the steel toilets or rocking back and forth with big, stupid smiles plastered on their mugs. Not one of them had words. Not one of them had sense. All they had was whatever was making them so jovial. One old man was crying from it, laughing as he wiped the tears from his wrinkles, then regarding them on his fingers as if they were the most precious jewels. He was Henry (*Sam, Travis, May—move on without me. I can do this knowing you're moving . . . keep moving. —Dad*) and he was unreachable.

What had happened? What was wrong with these people?

I pushed the empty cart back to the door and knocked.

"Not bad. Did you have fun in the loony bin?" the Watchman asked, laughing. I couldn't take any more laughter today. I walked by him without a word, back to the kitchen to pick at my omelet in the quiet of continuing despair, perched on a stainless steel stool while the kitchen staff cleaned up.

There was a soft clatter behind me. I turned and saw a small paring knife on the floor and one of the dishwashers walking away.

"Hey," I called out. He didn't turn. It wasn't a surprise; they were all still ignoring me. "Hey!" I called louder.

This got both his attention and the attention of the Watchman by the door, who looked up from his never-ending book.

"You dropped this." I got off the stool and picked up the knife.

His face went red, then drained to pale. He looked around wildly. "No, I didn't."

"Yeah, you did," I was getting real sick of this shit. Nothing was easy with these guys. "I saw it fall."

"No." He turned and started walking fast to the door where the rest of the staff was lined up. The Watchman got off his stool and grabbed him by the arm, dragging him back to me.

"What's going on here?" He addressed me.

"This guy dropped a knife. This knife." I held it out. "I'm getting tired of not being listened to." Fuck it. Let him get in trouble for being sloppy, for not obeying the programmers. I was done trying to make friends.

"Well," the Watchman drawled. "Isn't that interesting. Are you sure?"

"Absolutely," I said, handing the knife, handle first, to the guard. "I saw it happen."

"Even more interesting, since all knives were supposed to be returned to the locked cabinet and were counted by this very same worm."

"Wait, what?" Oh no, what had I done?

"Seems like we have a rebel on our hands, and a potentially murderous one, at that."

"Oh, no, wait . . ."

"Good job, Dusome," he said, unhooking a pair of handcuffs from the loop on his belt and slapping them on the dishwasher. "I'll make sure this is noted with your superior."

"Traitor!" the man screamed, twisting in the guard's grip. "You traitorous bastard!"

Every face in the line was glaring at me. One woman spat when I caught her eye. The Watchman got on his walkie-talkie, and soon the room was flooded with his colleagues, who patted down every person and recounted all the implements.

Oh dear god, what did I do now? I sat back down on my stool and held my head in my hands, repeating messages from the napkins to myself as if they were for me while the kitchen filled with scuffles and protests.

You're not alone. None of us are.

A new day is coming. I can feel it.

♦♦♦ ♦♦♦ ♦♦♦

That night, I went through each napkin in my head like a meditation. This time there was no music. They were more eulogy than song. When I fell asleep, my dreams were full of their faces, both the inmates in isolation and the kitchen staff with disgust in their eyes. The inmates looked tight and loose at the same time from darkness and hunger; manic jesters in locked rooms. The staff were just angry. They called for my head with their silence.

At one point, I was in the middle of a ring, taped to a chair, the edges of the space swallowed in dark. One by one, the residents paraded around me, giggling, their fingers bent from the girth of their glee, their steps high and awkward as if they were marionettes.

I was startled awake the next morning by the door. I jumped up, tossing the blanket to my knees. Had I slept in? What would the punishment be for that? My bare feet were on the floor by the time Mitch crouched down at my side, and I was trying to apologize. "I'm so sorry, won't happen again, I must've—"

"French, it's me, it's just me. Great news." He was flushed, and even his tie was askew. "We have a meeting with Mellin in an hour. This is it! She's going to give us her decision on the field test. And thanks to your quick thinking in the kitchen, it's bound to be good!"

I tried to shake the echoes of madness from my head. "Wait, what?"

"Agent Mellin—she's going to make a decision about whether you're ready for the final test." He shook my leg. "So wake up. Get ready. I'll set your shower for eight o'clock and be here at eight thirty to get you. This could be it! If you get in, I'm sure to be promoted!"

He stood up, rubbing his hands together.

"Mitch, can I ask you something?"

"Sure."

"Yesterday, you told me the dinner shift would be easy. And then I got there, and half the residents were gone."

"Yeah?"

"And the ones who were there . . . well, they were . . . different."

"Did you see them?" His voice went down an octave.

"Yeah—well, no. I always check the slot before I slide a tray in, and this time the lights were on, and I saw them. Just for a few seconds. But they were, I don't know . . . off?"

He watched my face for a minute. I could see the workings of his mind as he decided how much to share, whether I could be trusted. I was depending on his excitement to make him slip up and offer some information.

"Let me teach you a quick lesson, French. Back in the days of massive slaughterhouses, they would push the cattle through a narrow chute before they put them down. The chute would contract, and the animals got squeezed. That kind of pressure alleviates stress, releases good chemicals."

"Wait, we heard this from Minnie when she came to stay with us, remember?" It felt somehow intimate that we were holding on to the same memory, that it had impacted each of us in some way, separate but together.

He squinted. "No, no, I have no idea what you're talking about. Minnie?" He tapped his chin, then shook his head.

"Our cousin, Minnie? She's, like, two years older than you?" I tried to remind him.

He shook his head. He couldn't remember. "Anyway, it's all well-known science. The squeeze, the chemicals, that lets them relax before the end. Then the meat tastes better without all the panic and fear in it." He spoke as if hosting a matter-of-fact radio program. "We don't have chutes here, but what we do have is a supply of the good chemicals. Let's just say we're looking for new ways, better ways. So everyone benefits."

And then he was gone. And I was left to try and pull myself together for another day of playing model student.

"Christ, if I don't get out of here soon," I told myself, rubbing at the stubble growing out into a lame brush cut on my head, "I'm going to be laughing at my own jokes in a padded room."

I looked into the hall, noticing the eerie pink outside the window, coloring the sky in shades of thinning blood. I couldn't remember what a pink sky meant, so I just got up and closed the door.

"All right. Game on."

CHAPTER 24:
RULES OF THE GAME

French

"I WAS A BIT WORRIED AFTER THE PEN INCIDENT, BUT you have managed to prove yourself. I believe, based on how you reported the theft in the kitchen and mitigated a potentially disastrous attack, that you were indeed telling the truth. You found the pen and did not use it." Agent Mellin had an odd smile on her face, but any smile would have been odd on her face. "See? I am not without charity or understanding. What do you say?"

"We are so honored that you would meet with us. And both your power and your graciousness are well known, Agent Mellin," Mitch jumped in to answer.

She narrowed her eyes at his ass-kissy response, then turned to me. "And you?"

I opened my eyes wide so I looked sincere. I had been learning in this school after all. "Thank you, ma'am. I am very lucky to have you as a supervisor. You are very kind." I stuttered over the *k* in *kind*. Shit.

She closed her lips over her teeth and pushed her glasses up her nose, looking at her open laptop. "Now, let's discuss next steps, shall we?"

Mitch shimmied to the edge of his seat. He gripped his hands together so tight his knuckles were white. He was more excited than I'd ever seen him. I thought about how when he was a kid, he'd work himself up so much on his birthday that nine times out of ten, he ending up puking chocolate cake before we even got to the presents. I moved my legs away from him, just in case.

"There are two threads to this decision, and so I will explain each one." She pulled off her glasses and placed them on the desk, then leaned back in her chair and let it swivel a bit.

"First, the group that you were previously with is on the move."

My bladder squeezed, and I flexed my thighs tight. They knew where Miig and Rose and the rest of them were? *Please don't let them be coming here. Please don't let them be coming here . . .*

"Oddly enough for you, I would imagine, but typical by my assessments, as I have been watching how you people behave for years now, they are not moving in this direction. They are, in fact, going in the opposite direction." She paused to watch how this registered with me. I kept my body as still as possible. I didn't know how to react. I was relieved that they weren't near this horrible place. But then again, why weren't they trying to get me? Wasn't that what we did—stick together no matter what?

"So that's no big surprise. You come from a cowardly lot." Here, her eyes made a quick shift to Mitch. If he saw it, he didn't let on. He was leaning in as far as he could, his knees jiggling up and down.

"We picked up on their movements through informants last night. But here's where it gets interesting. They seem to be in the company of some nurses." She was angry; I could see it now. As much as she wanted to tease emotion out of me, she was desperately trying to hold hers back. So the Agents hadn't known about the nurses, not until now. I felt the power shift a bit. I knew more than she did.

"We now believe they are part of a network that has been in operation for some time, moving inventory right under our nose, sometimes taking it from our very hands. And I don't like being robbed. We don't look kindly on thieves."

She paused again, getting herself under control, though she had barely shown the faintest of cracks. "So, as you can imagine, time is of the essence. So is stealth. And for this, we need someone on the inside."

"Brilliant," Mitch whispered. He couldn't hold it in but knew better than to really interrupt her.

"You have given us important information that leads us to understand that there are some who return to their packs once they manage to leave the institutes. So it should be no surprise for them to find you out in the woods."

I wanted to jump up, to scream and dance. I could go back to them? Was this really happening? Once I was with them, it would be easy to escape, for real this time. I could shake off a Recruiter tail like nobody's business and be back on the trail with my family.

"What we want now is not just to capture your group, but to bring down the network of nurses. This requires having a man on the inside whom they'll trust and allow to join them while they are moving with the network. All the more important, since you explained your group's past experiences with Agents—I believe you called them traitors?" She looked up at me. I couldn't respond, and she kept going.

"We know we cannot infiltrate the network with just anyone, and we need to jump on this opportunity to track them. So, you are to rejoin the clan, as it were, and convince them you are the same old hobo they lost. Then you are to travel with them and gather information on the network so that we have the intel we need to bust up the larger extraction route for good. We have gotten word that they are taking cargo across the border into the United States." She said this last part with so much distaste her nose wrinkled.

"But we don't know how. So, once you are in position, once you are at the border but before you cross over, you will notify us, and we will come to collect everyone."

"Yes, ma'am, I can do that." I tried to seem anxious—willing, but anxious. Really, I was busting at the seams. I wasn't just getting out into the field. I was being delivered right back to my family!

"It is imperative that they not leave our observation while en route. Under no circumstances are they to be lost before we can complete the mission." She pulled her chair back in and retrieved her glasses. "Now, I am going to explain the Rules of Engagement to you."

"Yes!" Mitch clapped. He couldn't contain himself for one more second. I was sure the vomit was on its way.

"Agent Dusome, please," she scolded.

"Yes, ma'am. Sorry, ma'am."

The rules were simple enough—so simple, in fact, that it was hard to find the cracks. I would go with another Agent, and we would be dumped within six miles of the group's current location. We would walk in and join them. To avoid potential complications, we would not carry anything that might give away the mission: no walkie-talkies, no GPS devices. We would instead find one of the trackers left along the border at potential extraction locations and activate it so that Recruiters could be dispatched once the full network was exposed: nurses, transporters, and the route and methods of travel. This would ensure that the entire operation could be shut down as opposed to just the collection of bodies.

We took in every word for different reasons. I was trying to think of ways to slip away or change the route. Mitch was making sure he heard each letter so he could expand his knowledge of field work in order to be a better snitch.

"Now," Agent Mellin said, "let's move on to the regulations surrounding the final test."

"Final test?"

"Yes, of course," she answered. "We wouldn't include you in this vital mission without making sure you were ready, now would we? Frankly, I'm annoyed that we have no choice but to use you this early on."

I only half paid attention while she explained the test that would be the final step before I was sent back to the group. She rattled off longitude and latitude, the appropriate time frames, when I would be deployed, and whatever. I was stuck on the fact that I was going to be reunited with my family. Soon—maybe within days—I would be back with them. Then I realized I would have to convince them everything was okay while also maintaining my cover with the seasoned agent until I could get rid of the second agent for good. But I'd killed before, and I could do it again, especially now with what was at stake.

It was easier planned than executed. Even if I had to maintain the illusion for only a short time, I'd never lied to Miig before. He would know something was up, but he couldn't know, not until I figured out a way to get us all to freedom, out of the grasp of the Recruiters and the school. Then Mellin said something that snapped my attention back into the room.

"Agent Dusome, for this final test, we are putting you out into the field as the senior Agent to ensure that Francis here follows the script to the letter."

"I'm going out? On an actual test?" He sounded breathless.

"Yes. This is your chance to prove that you are worthy of staying on with us in the Program, that you shouldn't be pushed back down to resident status." She made eye contact with him over the rims of her glasses. "Because given all the irregularities we've experienced with this candidate, we have some questions."

He turned green beside me but never looked away from her.

"Lucky for you, we are willing to try to answer these questions. With the grand opportunity to take down a network of weasels that this student has offered us"—she nodded toward me—"we are willing to extend an opportunity your way as well."

"Once more, I am so honored, truly." Mitch was choked up.

"Make no mistake here, Agent Dusome, this is as much a test for you as it is for your brother. And"—she held up one finger, the nail filed sharp and painted red.

"Yes, ma'am. I won't let you down." He actually saluted her like a goddamn soldier.

We left her office and walked the halls in silence. The common room was empty when we passed through. Thank god—I wasn't sure I could handle the accusing stares or whispered denouncements, not now. There was too much else going on. We parted ways at my door. We stood facing each other for a minute before Mitch broke character and grabbed me up in a hug.

"I'm so happy you're here, French," he whispered in my ear. "You're the best thing that's happened to me since . . . well, ever."

I lifted my arms and put them around him. I didn't correct him. It was an act of hope; I hoped that was who I was again: French. I realized then that I was holding my breath, and when I released it, my hands instinctively gripped him tight, pulling the fabric of his shirt into my fists. Oh god. Oh god. What did I do now? I wanted him back so bad, even still, even now.

When he pulled away, there were tears in his eyes. "So, tomorrow at seven thirty A.M. See you then." He hurried away, straightening his tie as he made his way down the hall. I watched him turn the corner, then retreated into the room, closing the door behind me.

"Okay, first things first, French," I said out loud, pacing beside my bed. "First things first."

I had to get my thoughts organized or my heart would take over and I'd spend precious planning time being giddy over the fact that I was leaving.

The final test was tomorrow. I had no idea what it would entail except that I was being released into the woods. And as an added bonus, I'd have Mitch with me. Before the bigger mission was revealed, I had always thought this would be the moment I ran and that my only concerns would be that I had no good supplies to survive on and no idea how to get to the others. But now I knew that if I just passed this test, I would be brought right to them.

So there was just this one thing between me and my family. I had to pass this test, no matter how hard it was.

Logistically, having Mitch with me could go either way. He could prove himself to be helpful and tough, or he could be a huge hindrance whose weight I'd have to carry. But at least we would have some time alone. Maybe being outside would bring back parts of the old Mitch. Maybe out there, we would actually be reunited.

"Okay, bring it on." I stripped down to my underwear and went through my workout. I had to be in tip-top shape for whatever marathon I was asked to endure tomorrow.

I waited until bedtime before I allowed myself to feel the excitement that was eating its way through my belly. I was going to pass this test, and I was going to get back to my family, back to Rose. I let every scenario play out in my head—their faces, their disbelief, their joy. I imagined running through a field with Rose, running toward the trees that would give us cover so we could kiss and touch and hold each other. I imagined more than holding.

And just before I fell asleep, I wondered if my family would have any doubts about me. Would they think I was a traitor? What about the Agent? Would they believe they were just a fellow runner?

"Don't be stupid, French," I told myself, punching the thin pillow to make it comfortable. "They know you. They would never doubt you."

But the thought remained as I drifted off. What if I had changed? Did I even believe myself? And could I possibly pull this off?

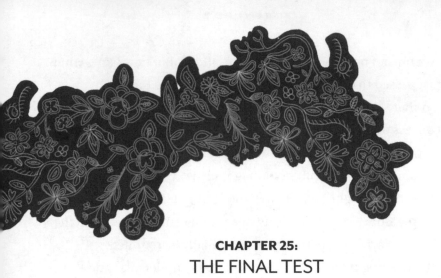

CHAPTER 25:
THE FINAL TEST

French

"I DON'T THINK I'M READY." I FELT SICK.

"You're ready," Mellin answered. There was nothing tender in this reassurance.

I was pacing, patting my pockets as if there were answers in them instead of just an old compass, a worn book of matches, a roll of greying gauze. They'd returned everything I was brought in with. Nothing extra. Why the hell did I have to put these clothes back on?

"Completes the illusion." Agent Mellin answered my unasked question, watching as I took more items out of a plastic evidence bag in the prep room. "And they'll make you feel more in character. These are, after all, authentic items from a runner."

I watched her nose wrinkle in distaste as she said it—*runner*. As if we were cockroaches scavenging in a kitchen instead of people trying to survive state-sponsored genocide. I pocketed a small knife and the worn nub of a pencil.

"Why do I have to be authentic?" My nerves about being released were getting the better of me, and I asked more questions than were good for me. I figured the test would be about how I moved in the woods; maybe it would involve avoiding Recruiters or showing I could survive.

"Because you're going to have to be convincing, now aren't you?" She spoke slow, as if I were stupid instead of just nervous.

"Convincing to who?"

A voice spoke up. "Target is three individuals." The agent in charge of the prep room was reading off a clipboard.

"Wait. Target?" No. This couldn't be happening. "But, this is just a test."

He slow-blinked his irritation at the interruption but continued. "One female in her twenties, one male, approximately midfifties, and a younger female."

"Wait, am I going out to—"

"Yes, Francis, you are going out into the field to extract and return a group of potential residents." She laughed a bit. "What exactly did you think we'd have you do?"

"What else are you people good for outside of a lab?" The prep room agent was annoyed that I was even allowed to talk.

The room was suddenly too bright, my shoes too tight.

"Therefore, for today, you are an Agent," Mellin finished with a small smile, as if she was expecting gratitude. I tried to return it but managed only a grimace.

I reached out and put a hand on a table laid with topographical maps and measuring instruments. I couldn't stand on my own.

Mellin watched me with those calculating eyes, and I fought to stand straight, to be normal and not completely winded by the news.

"Please continue." She motioned to the prep room Agent. He consulted his clipboard.

"Ah, youngest is around eight or nine. Easy cargo," he laughed without looking up. "They're about half a mile from here. Fools don't even seem to know how close they've wandered. You'd be surprised how many idiots are genuinely shocked when they take the short ride in. It's a wonder they're able to survive as long as they do. We're doing them a favor, really. I mean, how long could they get by on their own with those kinds of skills?"

I made both hands into fists before prying them open again through sheer will. I glanced at Agent Mellin, hoping she hadn't noticed my reaction. Thank god, she was busy looking at her own set of paperwork.

"Right, right," I interjected. "But do I need to bring in all three to pass?"

"Excuse me?" She looked up.

"Do I need to make sure all three packages are retrieved in order for this test to be considered a success . . . ma'am? So I can move on to the mission."

"Yes, you do." She was getting suspicious. "And you'll have a partner out there. So you'll have enough manpower to get it done."

Right. I'd almost forgot about Mitch. Or maybe I just wanted to forget. I wanted to forget everything right now. For the first time, I longed for the safety of the narrow bed in my dark room.

"This is such a great opportunity for your brother to prove his mettle. Of course, he's been out in the field before, but only in smaller, lesser roles. But this time, he'll be proving he didn't waste our time and resources when he recommended that we bring you in to the Program."

The door opened behind her, and in stepped Mitch. It was a shock to see him in civilian clothes instead of a suit. For the first time, I could see my twelve-year-old brother in his body. He was wearing brown cargo pants and a muted green hoodie with a black toque. A canvas knapsack slouched over one shoulder, and a torn black bandana was tied around one belt loop. I recognized the bandana and backpack as the ones he'd had when he was first captured all those years ago. They looked small against his new body. Fragile, like playthings. God, did we ever have a chance of making it together back then?

"What do you think?" he asked me, smiling as he turned in a small circle. "Pretty good, right?" He seemed genuinely happy, and his body was relaxed with no tie to fidget with like a slow-working noose.

"Yeah, pretty good." I felt warm toward him, especially in this moment when everything else seemed to be spinning. This is how he would have looked if we'd managed to stay together seven years ago. Oh, why hadn't we been able to stay together? My eyes started to burn. I looked away. I had to get away today. Forget waiting until the mission; there was no way I could pass this test. There was no way I could bring in others.

"Excellent, Agent Dusome," Mellin agreed. "Very convincing. You should both get some filth on your faces and under your nails when you leave, though. You are entirely too clean."

"Right, we'll stop and roll around in the mud like pigs," he laughed. The prep room agent joined in. I managed a small smile to cover the dread in my stomach.

Mitch stood beside me. "Isn't this great, Francis? We were made for this. Even my old limp will be of use. I can make up some story about getting away from Recruiters."

"Please don't offer up too much information. It might be more than you're capable of remembering," Agent Mellin sighed. I was getting real tired of her thinking my brother was an idiot, even though I also thought he was mostly an idiot.

"Right, so we'll go with Agent Dusome and Agent Francis to tell you lot apart. And to be clear, the same rules apply to you both, Agents." She became very serious very fast. "Failure will result in both of you being brought back for radical extraction."

"Yes, ma'am. Understood," Mitch answered, straightening his posture at her harsh tone.

"Yes, ma'am," I parroted back with a little less enthusiasm.

I had no idea what "radical extraction" was, but it did not sound like something I was willing to wager against. All thoughts of a quick dash into the woods were swept away. I was sure I could make it, if it came to that. I could escape, and maybe even get to my family quick enough to warn them. All I had to do was find out their coordinates. But Mitch? Even if he stayed out of my way so I could plan an escape, even if he could hold it together that long, he sure as hell wouldn't make it out of reach of the Recruiters who would be waiting close by. Mostly because he wouldn't want to. He would rather be extracted . . . radically, apparently.

"All right, then." Agent Mellin stood, placing her phone in her blazer pocket. "Let's have the final briefing with the Recruiters you'll be working with and get you out there before noon." She walked out the door, and we followed. Mitch was practically skipping, he was so excited. She kept talking as we walked. "For today's test, you'll have a

GPS tracker. It's installed in the lining of Agent Dusome's bag. You'll need to lure the targets close to the road for vehicular extraction."

Hide, I silently screamed out the hallway windows as we passed. *Hide as well as you can, then go even deeper.* I imagined these three targets we were setting out to capture, like colorful birds in a skeletal tree, without cover, out in the wide open. After these weeks on the inside, it seemed that there was nowhere to hide where the schools couldn't find you. Why did we bother to run? Why not just lie down on the soft ground and take in the stars while you could?

This feeling, this bubbling of despair, was something I wasn't used to. The old French, even at the worst of times, even in the face of death, always had hope. Now there was a heft to life, a weight I wasn't sure anyone could bear. How did people move underneath it? Maybe the Recruiters' steps were so clunky out in the woods because they couldn't bend their knees under the buckle. Maybe the schools' structures were so bland because why bother with design when the people no longer look up?

I watched my feet as they took the steps, and then we were on the loading dock on the first floor and a van was waiting, the back doors open like a mouth.

✦✦✦ ✦✦✦ ✦✦✦

When we reached our drop point, we hopped out and watched the van drive off. It made me nervous how quiet it was, so dark and so silent, like a shadow moving under the trees. I listened close for any tells, anything I could remember for later. I'd have to teach the group about this new threat. There was no chrome, nothing shiny on it. Even the side mirrors and windows had been coated matte so that the sun wouldn't bounce off their surfaces. The only sound it made was the crunch and push of tires over ground, like chewing. There was a new monster in the woods.

"'S go." Mitch tapped my elbow, and we turned into the trees. I eyed the bag on his back as he walked ahead, looking for any sign of the GPS tracker. It felt like he was carrying a bomb. He kind of was.

I wasn't expecting to feel anything to rival the dread marinating my limbs and pooling in my guts. I wasn't expecting to react to the forest. I'd grown numb after so many days on the inside. But as soon as my feet left the asphalt crumble of the road, as soon as my lungs were full of green and my ears full of chirp and trill, I felt it.

This feeling of the familiar and the remarkable cracked the hard crust I'd grown over my senses. It pulled at instincts and habits so that they could no longer lie flat and folded in the drawer where I'd stuffed them since those first sanity-bending days in the school. I was opening up, and all I wanted to do was run.

"You okay?" Mitch was beside me; I didn't realize it until he spoke. "Your face . . ."

I blinked a few times and felt the sting. My eyes were too wet. If I didn't get myself under control, they'd spill over, and I'd have to explain.

"Yeah, yeah." I cleared my throat. "It's just a lot out here. You know?"

"Yeah," he answered, quieter than usual. "It's . . . terrible, right?"

But there was a tone to his voice that sounded like maybe he didn't think it was so terrible. I wondered if he was cracking open, too, even just a little. That was all I needed get through to him, just a little crack, somewhere to dig in. I was determined to use this time to reach him.

"Yup, terrible." I took a deep breath and ducked under a heavy bough bursting with green, sticky with pine gum.

In the institute, I'd heard staff talk about "the wild" like it was empty, like it was an overwhelming amount of nothing, about getting lost in it all. But the truth was, it was easier to get lost in a crowd, to slip into so much that it buried you, slid over your head and made you anonymous. The wild was full—stuffed to bursting.

Out here, I lost my sense of edges, of where I began and ended. Inside the school, I noticed that I smelled; my hair, my skin, my breath—everything carried a scent like meat. It was maddening, inescapable. I could smell my thick sweat on my sheets, tooth decay on my pillow, acidic fear on my clothes. Sometimes I thought I could smell the waste collecting in my bowels.

But now that I was home, my scent was diluted, buried and welcomed. Humanity behind walls is highlighted. Humanity in the woods is insignificant. And because of it, I could take deep breaths and think of things other than myself. It was like the relief you get when you remember your thoughts are not facts, not yet, that they're only just thoughts rolling around in your head. Everything was still possible.

It didn't take long to find the targets' camp. We'd been dropped off close, and sure enough, they were dangerously nearby to both the road and the school. And even worse, they were too close to the danger that was us. I was suddenly angry. Why were they being so careless?

"How do we do this?" Mitch was wringing his hands, nervous now that we were so close to "real Indians" in their "natural habitat."

I fastened the image of my own family behind my eyes and walked into their camp with both hands held up to show they were empty, to indicate that I meant no harm. I was a liar before I even opened my mouth.

The man was about fifty, like we had been told, his face lined from the sun and stress. He was bent over a pile of sticks, stripping the bark off them so they'd burn cleaner. He wore a greasy baseball cap with a blue maple leaf on the front, and there was a cigarette—a real cigarette, like the kind you'd buy at the corner store—sticking out of his mouth. I hadn't seen one in years.

I looked for a gun nearby, and seeing none, I stepped loud on a downed branch. You didn't want to surprise anyone out here more than you had to. But he didn't even look up.

"Excuse me?" I started.

Nothing. He was humming while he worked. Actually humming, like he didn't have a care in the world. "Excuse me," I tried a little louder.

A woman crawled out of a lean-to a few feet behind him. Her eyes got big when she saw me, and she ducked back in.

"I don't mean to alarm you. Me and my brother, we are just passing through this area, and—"

Finally, he noticed me, jumping up and swearing, clutching his chest. "Jesus Henry Christ. Where in the hell did you come from?"

I held up both hands. "We—me and my brother, that is"—I pointed a thumb over my shoulder to where Mitch stood—"we were just passing through and heard you guys, and we thought we'd pop over and say hi."

"Holy mother of god." His small eyes darted between the two of us for a moment. He dropped his hands to his sides. "Whew, thought you were one of those damn school guards for a minute. Scared the gas right outta me." He cackled.

I watched him for a moment. Was the intelligence report wrong? Was he some kind of insane villager who had wandered out into the bush? It would be a relief, in a way. It would mean we could go back without taking anyone in. Then again, who knew what the consequences of that would be, even if it wasn't our fault?

"Ah, sorry about that. Just haven't seen another Native for about a year now."

Okay, so he wasn't insane. A bit stupid, maybe, but not crazy.

Just then, the woman emerged from the lean-to again. This time she had a knife in her hand. She didn't shout a threat or take any steps toward us; she just stood there, making sure we saw that she was armed. I kept my hands up at shoulder height. When I spoke to him again, it was her I kept my eyes on.

"Sorry to surprise you like that. I know there's no good way to come up on someone out here."

"Maybe with a wagon full of deer, that might do it." He was still smiling. He walked toward me with a hand held out. "I'm JP."

I shook his hand. "Fre . . . Francis. And that's my brother, Mitch." We had been instructed to use our real names—one of Agent Mellin's directives in case we were too dumb to remember the con.

Mitch walked over, and they shook hands. He had an odd spring to his step but kept his mouth closed for now, which was probably better. I wasn't sure how I was going to hold myself together, much less police his demeanor.

"Just you and your friend there, JP?" I motioned toward the woman with the knife.

"Oh, Therese?" He looked over to her. "Put that thing down, Therese. These are brothers. Yeah, Therese and me are traveling together for now. And a kid, Sunny. She's around here somewheres. Hard to keep track of a kid. They're so teensy."

I didn't want to know their names. Names meant they were real. Names meant you knew someone, even if just by a phonetic label. I thought of all the names from the napkins—all those real people trapped in a very real prison. A tight slash of lightening illuminated the sky, a kind of warning.

The woman put the knife down, but she stashed it behind her back, hooking it into her belt. She was clearly not as easy as JP. Maybe Therese had a chance out here. That meant she might have a chance once she was taken inside. I pushed that from my mind.

Concentrate, French. Remember the long game.

"No chance she took off on you?" It was more than a question—it was a wish. I mean, what could we do if the target group had split before the mission?

"Nah, she's always around somewhere. She don't talk much, though." JP was grinning ear to ear now, clearly delighted to have company. "Come on in, I was just about to start this fire and cook up some birds Therese grabbed."

"Grabbed?" Mitch was too interested to stay quiet.

"Yessir. She pulls 'em right out of the sky with this slingshot she made out of rope and rocks. Damndest thing."

Just then a massive crack of thunder shook the ground.

"Run!" JP yelled in the pause before the sky was blown wide open by the stuttered cut of lightening. Storms could be deadly, especially when it rained electricity.

Therese put her fingers in her mouth and let loose a high-pitched whistle before the next belch of thunder. Quick as a finch, a little girl ran out of the trees and slid directly into the lean-to, Therese disappearing behind her.

"You can set up real quick or join me in my shelter, but we gotta go now!" JP yelled around the last grumbles before another sheet of lightning settled over the horizon like a piece of tinfoil.

There was no time. At any point, hail the size of your fist could beat your ass from thousands of feet, or the sheets of lightning could tear into bolts, or the rain could come down so hard it would knock your baby teeth out. We ran behind JP as the wind picked up into torrents and ripped the breath from my lungs.

JP's place was impressive for a temporary shelter. It was a lean-to, but he had used pegs to hammer in the pieces. It was tall and narrow, hidden in a half circle of pine that made the enclosure smell like old-timey Christmas and kept the wind from tearing it to rubble. In between the slats, he had shoved moss. Some of that was blowing around the clearing outside, but enough stuck to make it a bit more weatherproof. It even had a door. He opened it just enough to slip inside, and Mitch and I followed him.

"Ahhh." JP settled into a cross-legged sit at the far end of the lean-to and tapped the one slanted side. "Thank god I travel with this old thing."

I looked up. The entire shelter was lined with a crinkly black tarp.

"Waterproof." He laughed.

"Do they have one?" I asked, indicating the second, much smaller structure on the other side of the firepit.

"Them?" He shook his head. "Nah, they didn't pack up as well as me. Gotta think ahead."

"Isn't there enough room in here for all of you?" I couldn't shake the guilt I had, sitting here away from the wind and the rain that was now pelting the wood and plastic around us.

"Maybe, but Therese is not the most friendly, if you know what I mean." He pulled a battered tin from the front pocket of his green flannel shirt, popped the cover, and retrieved a cigarette. "And the little one, well, she follows the big one, I guess."

I wasn't ready for the stench of the cigarette when he lit it. I was expecting wood smoke and maybe herbs, but instead it smelled like chemicals and garbage. I covered my face with my sleeve. Mitch coughed loudly.

"Oh, right, the ol' tobaccy here." He inhaled hard on the tip, and it glowed bright orange in the dark space. "I'll pop a breathing hole for you." He placed the cigarette between his lips and pulled back a corner of the tarp, then dug out some of the moss. A loud whistle filled the shelter—wind furiously trying to push itself inside.

"Better?" he yelled.

We nodded. It wasn't, but god forbid he "pop another breathing hole." We'd be lifted from the ground, walls and all.

"The more reasonable solution would be to just extinguish the cigarette," Mitch said. I wasn't sure if JP had heard him, but I jabbed my elbow back at where he huddled behind me and caught his forearm. That kind of precious talk would get us found out right quick.

"Think the storm'll cover our tracks?"

"What?" I was startled by JP's question. How did he know there were Recruiters lying in wait? Had he lured us here to get rid of us? I checked the door next to me to make sure it wasn't locked.

"If we decided to make a break for it? From the women?" He cackled again.

Relief flooded through me, and I forced a laugh to cover it. I imagined Agent Mellin watching on a monitor somewhere even though I knew that wasn't happening. Part of me was scared to mess up the mission. Another part was scared to succeed. And a smaller piece, one I didn't want to acknowledge, wanted to impress her, to exist in her mind as more than a messy kid. That part was shrouded in shame.

"It's not such a bad idea, really." JP pushed the cigarette butt through the hole and plugged it back up with moss. The room fell quiet, cocooning us from the wild that huffed and blew just outside. "Three men can get much farther without extra baggage. They'd be easy to ditch, what with their little legs and all."

"You would be okay with leaving your partners behind?" Mitch asked. I could almost feel him taking notes. I didn't like how we, the runners, were looking in his potential report. I didn't want him to think this was how we all were. Surely JP was the exception to the rule of community and common decency in an uncommon world?

The older man shrugged. "Why not? It's every man for himself out here."

Suddenly, I didn't feel quite so bad about bringing this moron in to the school. And I agreed with him; it would be easier to do what we had to do without the other two with us. Maybe if they just disappeared with the storm . . .

We waited out the weather this way, crouched, intermittently choking on secondhand smoke, listening to JP, who used to be a long-haul trucker and lived in a place called Timmins. A few times, I jumped when a felled branch crashed onto the roof. Once the ground shook, and I knew that meant the lightening had turned to bolts and one had hit close by. I wondered if Therese and Sunny were okay.

Eventually, the rain put down its dukes, and the wind stopped howling. The silence that followed was haunted by trauma.

"Shall we go see if the world still exists out there?" JP crawled to the door.

I didn't want to go see. I wanted to delay the very movement of time itself. I wanted to stall the inevitable for as long as I could. But then the door was open, and Mitch was pushing me to move from behind.

They would be taken in sooner or later anyway, I told myself. *They're so close to the school. So loud and oblivious. If not you, some other person would've found them.*

The air was wide, blown to expanse by wind and water. But at the edges, you could feel a thick humidity starting to creep in. Weather was impossible to predict, and even harder to survive. I thought about what my family would be doing right now if they were close enough to have been in the storm. Miig would have made sure everyone was safe and together. They had tarps and knowledge. They would be fine. He'd probably used the time they were huddling to tell part of Story, the entire history of us and how we came to be here:

We ran, but not away. We were—we are—running toward. Because running only works when you are running toward something. We are running toward community, toward safety, toward a future centered around what we know and understand to be the good life.

Miig had a gift for making us feel empowered even when we were hiding in the bush and whispering for fear of being heard.

"I think we should pack up and get out of here before nightfall." It was Mitch's voice that brought me back.

"Now? Boy, are you crazy? It's wet out here, and no one wants to be trekking through the mud." JP lit yet another cigarette. I wondered where he was keeping this giant stash that allowed him to be so free with his supply.

"Yeah, but we just passed a road, and this camp is too close to it to be safe."

"A road? Jumping Jesus. Where?"

"Just over that way." Mitch pointed with two fingers in the opposite direction from where we'd come. It was a bold choice, considering we didn't know which route they had taken in.

"Christ, you may be right."

I could see Mitch gain confidence, his shoulders straightening so that his backpack lowered a full inch. It was like watching him get bigger before my eyes.

JP hitched up his jeans, so stiff with dirt they barely moved. "Let me ask you guys something. Do you think we should go get the girls for this move? I mean, we're in the clear to just take off on our own here."

I paused, my anger making my teeth clench. And then I saw this for what it was: an opportunity, a way that Sunny and Therese could be free, free from this man and, most importantly, free from the fate that was about to befall him.

"Of course. You never know when you might need a woman around. Plus, a kid is a good bargaining chip if we need one," Mitch said quickly, the answer already on the tip of his tongue. No hesitation. No ulterior motive. Just the mission.

The man laughed. "True. She might come around to my overpowering masculinity. I could use a wife out here, even if it is in the country way." He ended with a wink, and Mitch winked back, a stunted motion that looked as fraudulent as it was, like a broken eyelid rather than a shared signal.

I lagged behind on the way back to the other lean-to and the firepit, the pile of wood now soaked to useless. Therese was outside, hanging clothing from a low branch—a hoodie, a pair of blue socks, and a tiny pink dress with a duck stitched on the front pocket. That pink reminded me of a pair of boots Riri used to wear before she was killed by a traitor just like Mitch and me.

Long game, French. Family. Rose. Freedom.

Therese watched us with narrowed eyes, like we were the storm returning. She wasn't wrong.

"Hey, now, let's get all this packed up." JP started to kick at the firepit, a half-hearted effort that would have done nothing to disguise human presence from a Recruiter with his eyes closed. "Time to move on outta here."

"Why?" She put a hand on her hip and shifted her weight, one hand still working a T-shirt onto a branch.

"Because I said so," JP answered.

Mitch jumped in. "We're too close to the road. And we heard vehicles before we ducked into the bush. Might be school people trying to take advantage of the bad weather to hunt. People stop moving in bad weather and are easier to find. So we need to move."

The way he called them "school people" instead of Recruiters made her nose wrinkle. None of us called them people. We were more accurate than that. Mitch was going to have to get better at this, and fast.

"Come on, now, rouse the little one and let's get going. Unless you want to stay behind . . ." JP sounded a little hopeful.

Mitch worked hard to keep the prey together and within reach. "No, we all need to leave. If they find one of us, they'll be able to track all of us. Do you need any help?"

She turned and slid back into the lean-to without answering.

"Goddamn women. Must be her time or something," JP sneered, snatching the clothes off the tree and throwing them onto a flat rock before yelling, "You got five minutes."

How had they managed to last this long before we found them? The man was a loose cannon with a loud voice. Chi Boy would have clocked them from miles off. That thought gave me some hope— maybe we were better than the Recruiters out here. Maybe my family hadn't survived on just movement and luck. Maybe we really were going to be okay. Well, *they* would be okay, until *I* showed up.

Therese crawled out of the shelter with the little girl behind her. There was a loud crash and the hollow plunk of branches bouncing off branches. JP kicked at the smaller lean-to again, sending the last bit to the earth. Therese gathered up the wet clothes and tied them to the outside of her duffel bag, an old gym logo on the side faded and cracked. She glared at the man as he scattered the wood, smiling with satisfaction.

"There, all gone. Good as it was before."

Mitch waited by the trees, biting his bottom lip, itching to get going. But suddenly, I realized I wasn't alone. Beside me, down by my waist, stood the little girl, Sunny, staring up at me.

"Oh, hello." I tried a smile. It didn't work. She just stared.

"You, uh, you ready to go?" It was unnerving, having someone so open and direct looking right inside of you.

I opened my mouth to try other words, but something about her face, something about the way her eyes stayed focused—no malice, no suspicion, just openness—reminded me of Riri. Ri was always ready to see, always able to really look. Until someone closed those eyes for good. And then Sunny did something that knocked all the words out of my dumb head. She reached out and put her small hand in mine. No smile, no comment, just a tiny connection, and she was ready to follow me wherever I led her.

"Let's get going, then." JP clapped me on the back as he and Therese passed, the woman giving me another narrowed glance on the way by. It was Sunny who led me out of the clearing and into the bush, following the adults into the dark of the woods.

None of us took any care with our steps. We crunched over old moss and new limbs like peanut shells on a hardwood floor. I bumped shoulders with trees and slapped snagged thorns from my pants, all the while thinking, *What now, French? What do you do now?*

I should have walked slower. I should have asked for a break. I should have broken my own ankle on a braid of tree roots. Because too soon, we were at the road.

"What the hell?" JP looked up and down the crumbling expanse, hands out at his sides. "What the living hell? Did we walk the wrong way?"

Mitch also checked the road, his hands clutching each other with nerves, or maybe it was excitement. "Uhh, maybe? No, let's just, uh, get situated here . . ." He stalled for time. "So, we came from over there . . ." He spun around, pointing at nothing.

"What the fuck is going on?" Finally, Therese used the full expanse of her voice. Just then, two vans came peeling out of a nook in the bush on the other side, headed straight for us. JP dropped his bag and ran, knocking Therese to the ground as he did. She recovered fast and turned to run, making a wild grab for Sunny. I felt the pull of her body from mine and instinctively clutched her hand harder. Why did I hold her so tight? I might as well have been clutching her to me while I dropped off the side of a cliff.

Therese screamed and kept running, her arms empty. The Recruiters were climbing out of the vans, their sunglasses replaced by headlamps with bright lights. Mitch was bent over in the road, his hands on his knees, taking deep breaths. It was over for him. He'd done it. The team would make short work of collecting the runners, and I had secured the smallest target.

I looked down at Sunny, the clomp of approaching footsteps echoing in my head. She was gazing up at me again—no judgment, no fear, just wide-open eyes. We both turned toward the vehicles. The high beams on the vans were too bright. Neither of us raised a hand to shield our eyes. We just squinted in the glare. I squeezed her hand harder; this time it was her who comforted me, because we were there together, and it was too late to run.

Standing by the ditch, I saw a reflective yellow road sign, the faded outline of a deer jumping and the words NIGHT DANGER half covered in dust. I was focused on that deer, jumping into a bright field of caution yellow, when the men reached us, when they pulled her out of my grip, when someone guided me to the vehicles. I reread that word—DANGER—over and over again.

"Great job," someone told me, gesturing for me to climb into the second van.

"Heard we're taking this one right back out tomorrow," said another.

Mitch was in the van already, feet tapping on the floor, hands clasped between his knees to keep them from shaking. He started whispering right away, but I couldn't make out the words.

One step closer to my family, to Rose, I told myself, shuffling into the back seat, backpack still on. But everything was different now. The person I was now after this one single day in the middle of thousands couldn't even see Rose anymore; she was just an idea and not a girl. Because I was a traitor, certified and proven, and not a person.

"Oh, shut up," I said out loud to myself. Mitch stopped talking. My words echoed back to me in the metal hollow as the door slid shut and all the light went away.

CHAPTER 26:
REUNION

French

THE NEXT MORNING, I WAS WOKEN BEFORE SUNUP. OR at least I would have been if I had been capable of sleep. Instead, I had sat in my bed all night and willed my heart to keep working. It felt fragile and frantic, like it was pulled so tight that any palpitation bigger than a blip would tear the tension and it would all come unzipped. I would be left with shreds of muscle, like old wallpaper pulled to the wainscoting. I saw her eyes—Sunny's eyes—in every speck that wandered across my vision, in every corner of the dark room. Worse than being judgmental, they were sweet, steady, familiar. I had already decided that it would never happen again, *could* never happen again. If it came down to hauling someone else in or giving up my life, I would lay mine down. There was no point in surviving if I had to hunt again. There would be nothing of me left to save.

There was only one other time I had felt this rotten—that was really the only word for it. It wasn't just the feeling of loss or frustration or grief. No, those feelings came when you still had a self for them to bounce off. I felt like the part that I knew to be *me* was bruised, caving in, gone rotten. I'd felt this way—the day I'd looked a man in his eye and shot him.

It was months ago now, after the traitors (*like you*, my brain reminded me) had taken Riri and one had ended up falling off a cliff with her still in his arms while trying to escape. When I got there, having caught up to them too late, I ran back to the camp, where the second man was tied up, defenseless, like a dog on a lead. I raised the rifle, hands steadier than ever, and took a full breath before pulling the trigger. In that moment, it felt right—*I* felt right. But later, that breath would haunt me. Something had changed. I had cut off part of myself that would never grow back. That was how I felt now, only this time it was deeper. Once again, I'd had a choice. But this time, I had condemned a kid, one of us, to death just as certain as I'd sent the traitor off with a bullet. And that had been quicker.

There were footsteps in the hall, turning the corner, then in front of my door. Two sharp raps with the knuckles.

"Dusome. Get presentable."

Presentable meant clothed, maybe bathed, and silent. I was still dressed in my grey scrubs, so that was fine. I rinsed my mouth out with water and a squeeze of toothpaste. And I was totally on board with the silent part. I closed the door behind me and followed the

Watchman along the hallways, across the common room (empty, thank god) and up the stairs.

This was it. Today I was being hand delivered back to my family. I put that thought first, ahead of the haunting images from yesterday. And if I was being honest, I was glad I was going to be able to walk away from Mitch, at least for now. After yesterday, I was sure he was lost to me forever. I longed for the chance to grieve him out in the woods.

"Here." The Watchman stood in front of a meeting room. I had been about to turn toward the prep room, but I stopped and walked toward him instead. Through the open door, I was greeted with the unnerving sound of friendly tones coming from evil incarnate.

"Good morning, Agent Francis," Mellin said, and this time she had a genuine smile on her face. "Let me just say, we are all so pleased with the results of your final test."

I couldn't look her in the eye. I burned with shame at the thought of that little girl walking under the shadow of the school's front gate. So I nodded and hung my head, as if with humility.

"Now, let's debrief, shall we?" She spun in her chair after indicating that I should also take a seat at the round table. Pulling back the chair, I checked out the others in the room: Mitch, wearing a suit and a nervous edge to his features, a woman with an open laptop, and an older man, hair still wet from the shower, his face grey and freshly shaved, a pair of round gold-framed glasses magnifying his dark eyes. He seemed familiar, but I couldn't place him. I'd probably passed him in the hallway, or maybe he worked in the kitchen. I sat and folded my hands on the table, trying to be present, trying to breathe and move like a normal person.

"Agent Parisien, if you please?" As Mellin spoke, the woman with the laptop began typing.

"Yes, of course." He referred to the papers in front of him on the wood surface. "The prospects approached the scenario camp at approximately eleven thirty-five A.M., coming from the northwest . . ."

And then I recognized him. Oh my god, I recognized him.

"Both prospects engaged me at the fire. I found their initial contact adequate. Though they may have been exhibiting nerves, it didn't seem suspect, as runners are normally apprehensive when interacting with new individuals."

It was JP—cleaned up and speaking with less color, but it was him. He read out his notes about the storm and the shelter and the return to the clearing, but I couldn't focus on the details; my head was spinning too fast, which is hard to keep off your face. And Mellin was watching both Mitch and me closely as JP spoke. I wasn't sure what the play was—what anyone's play was—so I stayed still.

But I could breathe better. I felt my vision clear up and my heartbeat steady. It was all a fake; the test was one big fake, and the runners were plants. This meant I hadn't become a traitor, not really. I hadn't brought anyone in. Remembering Sunny, I did smile, quick and full. I didn't care that she was a plant, that she was with the school, not right now, not as long as I wasn't the cause of her being there.

"Agent Dusome, do you have any notes for us?" Mellin's voice cut into my reverie.

"No, ma'am. Other than that, the team was impeccable, and I was proud to work with them. Agent Parisien's acting was superb. We had no idea."

Kiss-ass, I thought. Mellin swiveled to me. "Francis? Any notes?"

"In the bush, no one has real cigarettes anymore."

"Pardon?" She looked confused.

"JP . . . Agent Parisien smoked store-bought cigarettes. In the bush, people only smoke roll-your-owns, if anything."

The clicking of keys from the note-taker's laptop reminded me that my suggestions would only help the Recruiters in their work and make their decoys more convincing.

"Anything else?" Mellin asked. I shook my head no, not telling them that the shelter was too perfect, their carelessness almost unbelievable. She wrote a few words in her notebook before continuing. "Good note. We will adjust. Agent Parisien, any closing remarks before we adjourn?"

"Two things of note that I specifically want to commend: Agent Dusome worked hard to maintain the unity of the group and move us to the retrieval site almost completely on his own, even after I gave them an out to divide the group." He looked up at Mitch and gave him a slight nod. Mitch blushed.

"Agent Francis, on the other hand . . ." He shifted his gaze to me. "While he remained quiet for this part of the test, he did in fact secure target two by physically holding her so that the retrieval team had no issues with loading her into the vehicle."

Wait, what? Why were they calling Sunny target two? Why target and not Agent?

"Yes," Mellin remarked. "We were very pleased that both targets were apprehended. Excellent work to all."

Her words echoed in my head. *Targets. Apprehended.* She closed her notebook. The tiny sound was enormous, like a gunshot in the room. Only JP was a plant. The others—Therese and Sunny—were the real targets all along. My vision got narrow again, my heart shrink-ing back under my ribs.

"All right, then. Everyone go grab some breakfast before we recon-vene in the prep room for the mission at . . . let's say eleven A.M." She swooped her notebook under her arm like a purse and left before we could stand. I couldn't have gotten to my feet just then even if I'd had to. Mitch was already busy chatting Agent Parisien's ear off. "Do you think a more forceful approach right off the bat would've worked better? What's it like living with them out there?" They walked out together, leaving me alone at the table.

I was a traitor. For a brief moment, I'd just been a guy who'd passed a setup: no harm, no foul. And now I was a traitor again. Only this time, I was being praised for holding a kid still so the Recruiters could grab her up, nice and easy.

I thought about those moments in the bush, heading to the road. I had held her hand. If I hadn't been holding her hand, would she have run? Would she have been able to duck and cover and get away? She was hidden when we'd gotten to the site; maybe she could have done it again.

I remembered the feeling of her slipping away—no, being yanked away. And I remembered the way I had tightened my grip before we got to the road. And now that moment of shared uncertainty, of kindness on her part—how had she known I needed her hand just then?—had been turned inside out. I put my forehead on the cool surface of the table and stayed there until the motion sensor lights clicked off. Eventually, I got up. But I couldn't go eat. I went back to my room until it was time to meet in the prep room. I sat there on the edge of my bed, reciting messages to keep the other thoughts from my head.

I am still Marguerite Eliot. I will always be Marguerite Eliot . . .
DON'T COME FOR ME. Stay safe . . .

✦✦✦   ✦✦✦   ✦✦✦

"As a reward for such a successful test run, we've decided to keep the team together." Mellin placed her notebook down on the table next to her and crossed her arms, still smiling.

"Wait, what?" I startled to attention. The team?

"Great news, right?" Mitch called from the other side of the prep room. I spun toward him. Sure enough, he was back in his civilian clothes from yesterday, now genuinely dirty, his pack full and already on his back.

I felt dread and panic skip into my gut. I had to hold it together. *Goddammit.* If I were really who they thought I was, I would think this was good news, right? "Yes, great news."

"You did so spectacularly together, we figured we'd give you another chance to excel." Agent Mellin opened a drawer in the desk and pulled out a piece of paper. "This is a signed order that lays out repercussions and corrective measures should these instructions not be followed. It has already been approved and will be executed at the first sign of trouble."

She placed it on the desk, turned it around, and slid it across to me. With Mitch leaning over my shoulder, I read it out loud.

"One. If the field officers do not join the target group or should they make any attempts to go AWOL, the target group shall be terminated immediately.

"Two. The field officers will be monitored by aerial and remote surveillance. Should it appear that the field officers have notified the targets in any way and made them aware of the plan, the entire group shall be terminated immediately.

"Three. If one field officer recognizes that the other field officer is not following instructions, they are required to break from the group and notify local Recruiters (location to be within ten kilometers of target). In that case, the entire group shall be terminated immediately.

"Four. Should this mission be carried out successfully in its entirety, the field officers shall be returned to the school and promoted to Agent and Supervising Agent status. However, should the mission fail, the entire group, including said field officers, shall be terminated immediately."

"Are we clear on what 'terminated' means?" Her voice was an echo from far away. "Not captured, not brought back to the Program or even the ward. Terminated, in the field and without hesitation."

"Promoted to Supervising Agent? Oh man, this is going to be epic!" Mitch was spastic with excitement.

I had planned on just taking down whoever came with me, and Mellin's rules meant anything I did that left Mitch tied up or on his own would get him killed him anyway. So I had only one real option: I had to reprogram him, get him to spit out all the brainwashing so we could run together. It was be the biggest reconnaissance mission I could have been handed, especially now, at the very last minute with no time to plan for it. And maybe Agent Mellin knew the impossibility of the situation I was in now, the one she had put me in.

Of course, the real problems would begin after we'd gotten away, when I'd have to convince Rose not to slit Mitch's throat for being a traitor in the first place, if we ever got to her. And to make sure the others trusted him enough to allow him to travel with us. I wasn't so sure I could convince them to trust me to begin with. Not after yesterday.

No one has to know, French. No one ever has to know.

But I would know. I wondered if I looked different. I ran a fingertip down the small fold in my cheek from the laceration I'd gotten trying to find my mother.

Mitch pulled off his bag to pack some water, and I remembered something. "You still have the GPS tracker?" I asked, trying to sound nonchalant. "Because you know they'll find it. This is a longer mission, and they're no fools." If I could make sure we weren't tracked, it would buy me more time and space to figure things out.

"The device from yesterday has been removed from the bag," Mellin answered quickly, letting me know my questions were not welcome. "Enough. Time to go."

Soon we were loaded back into a van, going over our story to make sure it fit together seamlessly. Seams could be ripped.

"What will you say about the institute?"

"Only that I was held without speaking to anyone the entire time. But I was fed and had access to water."

"And did you see any others inside?"

"No one. I heard voices, but that's about it."

"And what did they say?"

"Not much, but they sounded content."

"Excellent."

After hours of driving, with one break to empty our bladders on the side of the road, the vehicle stopped, and we jumped out the back and into the day I had been dreaming of for weeks. We checked the map for final directions, making sure we were pointed the right way, that we understood where the targets had last been sighted, then burned the paper and buried the ashes under a silver birch who watched with knotted eyes. The rest of the day was walking, nothing but movement and the soft torture of knowing I was getting closer with every step. Every muscle in my body wanted to shape the movements of 'RUN.' I just wasn't sure in which direction.

"I'm hungry," Mitch said. I had heard this four times in the last hour alone. "And tired."

Finally, I stopped. "Okay, this is as good a place as any." I dropped my pack and stretched my arms over my head. "We have enough time to make a small fire and maybe even a lean-to."

"Here?" He looked around at the endless trees, fallen and standing. "There's nothing here."

"There's everything we need here." I pointed around my feet. "Dry wood, level ground, heavy ferns for concealment . . . everything."

"What are we going to eat?" Okay, now he was starting to piss me off. I tried to remember that he hadn't even made it out of the suburbs when we first ran. This was all very new for him.

"All right, listen. You know as well as I do that we have to do this right. And showing up with full bellies after running away from the school is not exactly realistic."

"How would they even know?" He kicked at his bag like a kid.

"Trust me, we . . . they notice things like that. Just . . ." I sighed. "I'll make you some cedar tea. It'll fill you up a bit. 'S got lots of vitamins, too."

"Whatever." He folded his arms across his chest.

I walked the perimeter, wishing we had some bells to hang so we weren't so vulnerable. It hadn't registered yet that we were the ones people should be setting alarms for. I avoided Mitch with work. I found a balsam poplar with not too much debris underneath and a lower branch study enough to hold the crossbeam I'd foraged from the wreck of a jack pine lying nearby. Then I collected enough branches to latch together and crisscrossed them on either side. Mitch sat nearby while I worked. I was frustrated, but then I saw him making the small motions one does when they feel overwhelmed in the bush, the ways you start to orient. He picked up a snail and let it crawl over his finger; he peeled a patch of moss off a tree and sniffed it; he took a deep breath and held it for ten counts. I left him alone to this important work. By the time I set out to collect the ferns that would finish the walls and provide cover, he was back at my side.

"I don't mean to be this way, you know."

"And how's that?" I kept working

"Useless." He plucked a small plant and held it up. "Is this right?"

I looked up from my stoop. "Sure." His face was painful with the need for approval and laid bare with embarrassment at the same time. I stood up.

"You'll want to gather fuller ferns, like these." I pointed my lips to the pile at my feet. "And avoid the ones with red leaves at all cost."

"Poison ivy, right?"

"Right. You don't want to be grabbing those with your hands. And we sure as hell don't need to be sleeping under a roof of them, either."

He started laughing, an odd bubble of sound he wasn't used to producing. "Hey, remember when Uncle Ford passed out in a full patch of poison ivy?"

I paused. "Holy shit, yeah. He rolled around in there, too."

"It was in his mouth, for god's sake. Probably dreaming about his neighbor again and started making sweet love to the bush." He closed his eyes and moved his head side to side, mouth open, tongue sticking out.

I laughed hard. "Yeah, yeah! His whole head swelled up. He looked like a frickin' monster for days."

"And then Mom, she got calamine lotion in his eyes when she was trying to help." He was having trouble getting the words out. "She was laughing so hard she couldn't keep a steady hand."

I remembered it clear as day. Us rolling around on the floor in our matching pajamas in fits while Mom cackled over her brother, who was slumped, red and blubbering, at the kitchen table.

I wiped water from my eyes. "I learned my best swear words from him that day."

"She . . . she damn near pissed her pants." Mitch was laughing so hard he started tearing up, too. It was contagious. Soon we were bent over, wheezing. Oh my god, it felt so good. Like the weather had suddenly warmed up and there was more than enough food waiting and there was nothing to fear. For just a minute, I was with my big brother and we were happy and free. For just a minute, everything was open and possible.

I watched him try to compose himself and break out in another a fit of giggles. If only I could make things stay like this. But before I could will it away, I saw him leading the way to the road, Therese and JP on his heels, and then me walking hand in hand with Sunny. He didn't hesitate then, did he? No, he took charge and finished the mission: three for three, every Indian accounted for. All the laughter was knocked out of my body.

"Grab any dry branches you come across. For the fire."

"Ah, ha, sure thing, boss." He saluted me, dropping a few fronds as he did.

Eventually, the shelter was done. It was a little pathetic-looking, but it would do. We rolled out a tarp on the ground inside and pinned another over the top in case of rain. Or worse, hail. Hail these days was bone shattering, like even the sky was digging for marrow.

"All right, let's get some water boiling." I made the fire and picked the cedar and filled the small cast iron pot, just big enough to hold a cup and a half. Mitch watched everything I did, so I did it all a little slower than usual. Neither of us talked, and it was a comfortable silence, the kind that lets you learn, lets you teach.

"Hey, French?"

"Yeah?"

"Did you ever see Mom again? Is that why you were looking for her before, when you were hurt?" He spoke low, as if hiding the question from his own ears.

"Nah, never." I stirred the pot. "But I never stopped looking for any of you. And I found Dad." I turned a bit to see how this landed on his face. I'd been saving that information for when I needed it, for when I thought it could do the most work of tearing him down. He pulled back a bit when others would have leaned in. He leaned so far back he had to put an arm behind him to hold him up.

"Oh. He's . . . out here?"

I was cautious. How much of Mitch was in this question, and how much was Agent Dusome? No way to tell.

"Yup. Lost a leg, but he's okay otherwise."

"His leg? Seriously?" His eyes jumped around the clearing, landing everywhere but on me. His lip twitched. He put a hand over his mouth to cover the small movement.

"Yeah. It's not like we're out here playing tag or some shit. This is life and death. Things get messy. Things go missing." I tried to stay calm, like I didn't have any skin in the game anymore.

"Well, he's lucky it was just a leg," Mitch responded. "You have two of those suckers. Not like losing a heart or something."

"Yeah, well, he had two sons, too, and look how that turned out."

Mitch gathered his words carefully. His voice was shaky, and he paused in weird places. "Are we going to . . . I mean, is he . . . with the . . . target group?"

"No idea."

We sat in silence for a few minutes. I waited for him to offer a rebuke or question my newfound loyalty. When he didn't, I decided to push it a bit. I handed him his tea and grabbed my backpack. I rummaged around in the front pocket, threw it on the ground, and sat on it.

"Mitch, do you remember the tree house?"

It took him a few seconds to answer. "What tree house? Like, the one we're about the sleep in?"

I didn't believe him. He knew. How could he forget the last time we were together? When we were both running in the same direction? When he'd been taken in and changed?

I balanced my elbow on my knee, straightened out my arm in his direction, and slowly opened my fist. Balanced on my palm was a small green army man, the kind that used to come in bags of a hundred, the kind that stood on small, usually uneven, plastic platforms. Mitch looked up from blowing on his tea to cool it down.

"W-what's that?"

I didn't answer right away, watching his face. But he had put space between us, more miles than this forest had. I took a deep breath and told him what was really our coming-to story: how we'd gotten here, how we'd become who we were.

"We had lost Mom, in the city and we kept walking, together. We ended up in someone's backyard out in the suburbs. The houses were all empty then. The people had moved on or were made to move on. We looked through some of the places for food and supplies, and then we found a tree house. Remember that? I know you remember, because that's where you broke your leg and got brought in."

He sipped his tea, eyes downcast.

"And we fought. I'll never forget it—yelling and carrying on like we were regular brothers in a regular world. But we weren't. We were too loud. And then you pulled out this bag of chips. I was an idiot kid, so that's all it took to make me feel better. Imagine, an orphan already so used to messed-up shit that chips made me smile? And then they came."

I stopped, remembering the Recruiters' whistles filling all the space in the yard and every cell in my head. I remembered the way Mitch had reeled in his fear so he could do what he did next.

"You told me to escape. You told me, 'They know someone's up here, just not how many someones,' and then you made me jump into the trees. I stayed there for a long time with my eyes closed. But I could still hear everything. Yelling, whistles, banging, your leg breaking . . . And then, after a while, there was no more noise. And I came down. Before I left, I found this, this army man lying in the grass."

He kept his eyes down, but his shoulders shrugged slowly. I couldn't tell if he was being dismissive or reverting back to that kid who'd been taken away.

"I knew it was yours. You'd snagged it from a ransacked store, kept it in your pocket. So I picked it up and put it in my pocket, and I've had it ever since."

"Why are you telling me this?" He sat still, but the muscle in his jaw flickered.

"No reason." I tipped forward and placed the little man by his foot. "Just talking."

I got up and carried my bag to the lean-to. I wasn't tired. There were too many thoughts in my head, too many possibilities. But I wanted to give him some time on his own to think, to really, truly be in those memories. Who knew how often he got to do that at the school?

♦♦♦ ♦♦♦ ♦♦♦

My body must have relaxed into the familiar smells and chill of the woods, because I was asleep before he made it inside. In the morning, there was a moment of peace, lying there with the world waking up around me, when I forgot why I was there. I was just plain old French, out on the run but still inside. . . . And then reality poured into my consciousness, and I felt my bladder pinch. I rolled over. Mitch was beside me, his face more familiar to me now in sleep. I wondered what he was dreaming about. Then I wondered if he could dream at all anymore.

I carefully slid out of the shelter and into the day. It was still so early an owl hooted indignantly from a nearby tree. The morning birds hadn't yet started their daily ablutions.

I relieved myself beside a blueberry bush grown vascular with strangler vines and clapped my hands to warm them up. Since we weren't in any real danger and we were still far enough away from the group, I decided on a small morning fire. The pit was cold. Mitch must have put out the fire before he came to bed. I worked until there was a small bundle of flame in the center of the ashes, just enough to heat up some water. I didn't have anything to add to it, but it would feel good to drink in warmth. I'd get some boiling and then wake Mitch so we could pack up and get going.

As I positioned the small vessel in the center of the flames, something caught my eye. I grabbed a stick and moved the ashes around. There, melted to a nub, the platform warped enough to curl, was the plastic army man I'd left with Mitch.

"Fuuuck," I sighed. Well, so much for that. I picked it up and slipped it into my pocket anyway. Now it was a reminder of the second time I saw my brother for the last time.

When the water was bubbling, I went to the shelter to wake Agent Dusome.

CHAPTER 27:
REUNION, PART TWO

French

THEY WERE JUST UP AHEAD. THERE WAS NO COLOR, NO movement, no sound to betray them. Only the intelligence we'd been given by the school and the feeling in my gut, the incredible pull, the urge to rush ahead. This was exactly what they'd been talking about—the danger of having people, how connections could be ruinous in these times. They made you want to do stupid things like run through the bush, throw away a month of preparation, face deadly consequences because of nothing more than a feeling.

We'd walked all morning in silence. I didn't mention the army man in the fire, and neither did Mitch. The silver lining of his quiet was that I didn't have to hear about how he was hungry or tired. I also didn't have to hear any more plans for his first day as Supervising Agent. But even in that silence, I knew something had changed. I couldn't put my finger on what, exactly, and I hoped beyond reason that the pendulum in Mitch's brain was swinging-back in my direction.

I stepped over a small hill roiling with ants—they seemed to form alliances in these times—and paused. There were no more birds, just the soft thrum and scuttle of insects burrowing and alighting on dense moss and curated sand. It was like the sound of velvet being folded.

"They're here."

I knew it as fact. They were close. They were watching. I had never felt more like a prisoner than I did at that moment, knowing that I was here under false pretenses, that I had few to no choices, that I was going to have to make one soon, and that either way, someone was going to pay a huge price.

Reel it back. Reel it in, I told myself, literally imagining my heart at the end of a fishing line I was gathering up.

"Okay." Mitch did some jumping jacks like he was getting ready for a race, and maybe he was; it was just that we had different ideas about what was at the finish line. "You ready?"

"Yup." I couldn't say more. Opening my mouth to let out more words meant running the risk of revealing that we weren't on the same page right now, never had been.

We walked on, slowly now. I knew we had to be a bit louder than usual to be certain they would "find us." I didn't want to surprise anyone and end up with one of Wab's arrows in my neck. It wasn't hard; Mitch was snapping branches and sliding around in the mud-soaked peat like a real amateur.

I knew they were on the way before I saw them. Something under my skin burned bright, like a beacon of blood and bone. Then there was a soft *thunk*, and something large and dark ran full tilt at us. I braced myself. I barely had time to put out a hand to motion Mitch to stop when Tree jumped the last foot between us and threw himself into my arms.

"French!"

I gasped from the weight, but more than that, from the feeling of all his familiar limbs tangled up in mine. I took the deepest breath I had taken in more than a month. I felt lightheaded from it. Then there was more jostling as Zheegwon joined in, running his long fingers over my short hair.

"Shit, I'd know that noggin anywhere, even without the luscious locks."

I was crying, but I stifled the sobs in Tree's shoulder, gripping both twins with everything I had. There are no words to explain the feeling of clicking into the exact spot you belong. Your muscles move differently. Your blood has weight all the sudden.

"We heard you were dead! But we knew you weren't dead. Legends don't just die." Zheegwon stepped back with a clap on my shoulder and sized up Mitch.

I pulled away from Tree, wiping my eyes with the back of my hand. "This is my brother, Mitch. Mitch, this is Tree and Zheegwon."

Tree put out a hand. "We're his other brothers. Good to meet you. Damn, French, you're really rallying up the half-breeds out here."

"Nice to meet you both," Mitch said, a little too stiff. "Where is everyone else?" He was already looking past them to the green expanse beyond. It made me angry. I wanted to shake him, to slap his face. He was in such a hurry to collect that he was missing the beauty of these identical boys and the warmth they offered.

"Waiting to see who we bring in," Zheegwon answered, oblivious to the intent of the question. "And wait till they get a load of this guy!" He put his arm around me.

They peppered me with questions, the ones I knew would come: where I had been, how did I get away, how long was I in the woods before they found me? These were the questions we had rehearsed on the drive to the drop-off. What I couldn't have anticipated was the way giving each simple, practiced answer felt like dropping pieces of myself on the path, parts I was sure I would never get back. With every word, I pushed them closer to danger. And I couldn't get Sunny out of my head, the way her hand had gone limp in mine before it was yanked free with the quick violence only a badge could bring, knowing there were no arguments to be had unless you wanted things to get even worse.

I wasn't sure my feet were touching the ground anymore. Every part of my awareness was caught up in the forward momentum, in the curve of Tree's shoulder up ahead, in the loud pounding of my heart pushing blood. And then, just like that, I was home.

Everything happened in slow motion. Slopper let go of a pot of beans, and they spilled into the mud like lava dipped in pork fat.

"Holy hell," he exclaimed, but stayed where he was, brown sauce splattered across his shins.

Wab—who was huge now!—and Chi Boy looked at each other as if registering the truth before breaking into huge smiles. I thought there may have even been tears in her eyes, but it was hard to say. Could have just been a flash of anger; that was more likely from her.

A short woman with the longest, blackest eyelashes I'd ever seen crossed her arms and observed how the camp reacted to our appearance, how everyone seemed to be coming undone. Later, I'd learn this was Rania, the nurse who was going to lead us across the border. At dinner, I would meet the other nurse, Theo. But right then, I didn't care about a new face, not when I was searching for the old ones.

"Look who we found." Zheegwon clapped me on the back, squeezing at the tension buried in my neck. He walked ahead, tucking his baseball cap into his back pocket. He stopped by Slopper, still standing with the upended pot in one hand, beans pooling around his taped-up sneakers, and pointed at the mess, "Apparently, lunch is ready, if you guys are hungry." Then he laughed, jogging over to the thick brush where tents were hidden from aerial view.

"Where the hell have you been?" Wab reached up and touched my cheek with a delicacy I didn't know she could hold in her body, finding the scar newly etched there. "We heard you were dead!"

"Dead? Nah, I'm good."

"Obviously." She punched me in the arm. There, that was more like it.

Chi Boy grabbed me in a one-armed hug, pushing me back while he rubbed my hair. "Nice cut."

I ran my palm across the top of my head. "Yeah, I know. The barber wasn't taking any new clients." It was hard to be casual. I searched the area for her; I had been searching since the twins had found us. Where was Rose?

"FRENCH!" Miigwans yelled from the edge of the clearing. At the sound of his voice, my breath caught. This was what it felt like to come home—relief and joy and new pain for the time away and the unshakable need to be held, all at once.

He pushed past Slopper, his pace all off—fast, then slow—his head held at different angles as if trying to see from them all at once.

Then he rushed toward me, stopping just a few steps away. "But . . . but you were dead. You . . . you died."

"I didn't. I got out."

"But then . . ." He leaned in, looking clear into my eyes, tilting his head one way and then the other, looking, searching for something—the truth of me, of who I was then.

I closed the gap between us in two strides and clasped him in a hug, burying my face in the front of his shirt. He smelled of smoke and fire and sunlight and hide, and I had never smelled anything more beautiful in my life. I'd never thought I would be here again; I'd never thought I would know what it was to have him this close. I took him in and tried to remember each nuance of his smell, his skin, the way his hair felt when the breeze blew it suddenly over the back of my neck. The next time I was in a dark room, I would need it. Or I would die. I knew that now. This was oxygen. This was why I breathed.

After a few seconds, he gripped me back, taking handfuls of my clothes in his fists and holding tight. He leaned down and kissed the top of my head, speaking to me in Anishinaabemowin. I felt those words under my ribs. In that moment, everything snapped into clarity. I knew for certain, regardless of the odds or risks, that I would do whatever it took to keep them safe, all of them. Even my asshole brother, who had big dreams of being a Supervising Asshole. I would do whatever it took.

The twins had taken Mitch to start setting up our temporary camp and show him where to pitch the tent, a place to dry wet boots. Wab and Chi Boy were getting some plates ready, and Slopper was still trying to pull himself together.

"Where's Rose?" I couldn't wait another minute.

Miig sighed a bit and held me at arm's length. "Before you go worrying, she is fine—she's always fine, that one. But still, you'd better come sit. Slopper, is there tea left?"

Come sit? Tea? Oh boy, this couldn't be good . . .

◆◆◆ ◆◆◆ ◆◆◆

"Derrick! She left with Derrick?"

I was on my feet and couldn't sit back down. Rose was somewhere, headed toward a school, and she was with that insufferable show-off who was so obviously trying to get in her pants. "When did she leave?"

"Right away—we couldn't keep her back. Almost six weeks ago now. Made a decision and then left the before the sun." Miig folded and refolded his hands, not making eye contact.

I was being irrational, and I knew it. Why did it matter who she was with when she was in danger? I should have been happy she wasn't alone. But still . . . *Derrick*?

Then another thought occurred to me. "That's too long to be gone. What if she got taken?" Then I sat because all feeling left my legs. Rose could be in a dark room. Rose could be huddled in the middle of a siren screech. Rose could be in an isolation cell, scribbling words on a napkin with spaghetti sauce.

She wouldn't survive. I knew it. Rose would never break, never falter. They'd weed her out and lock her up first chance they got—her passion was contagious, and that was the last thing they allowed in the schools.

"Why did you leave without her? Oh god, she's dead, isn't she?"

"We don't know anything yet. You can't think the worst," Miig responded. "We left because we received some news that forced our hand—there was no way we could safely stay. There's a train that'll take us across the border, out of the schools' reach. And the schools, they're changing. We had to get Wab—"

"I know the worst, and that's all I can think of," I interrupted. "She's dead. What else could it be?" The end of the sentence was pinched. I ran out of breath and forgot how to put more into my lungs.

"Okay, easy, there." He rubbed my back. "Slow down, in and out. You're here with us now. In and out. We got you." I matched my breathing to the pattern he massaged into my skin.

No, I wanted to tell him, *I got you. I am here to get you.*

"I have to go." The more I thought about it, the more resolved I became. "Now. I have to go get her before it's too late. If it's not already too late . . ."

I tried to stand, but the hand on my back held me firm. "My boy, it's too late for you to set out from here. Where would you even go?"

I started to protest, but the truth was that I had no idea where she was or if she was even anywhere anymore. "I can't just do nothing," I finally said.

"French, trust that she knows what she's doing. This is Rose we're talking about. The girl who survived for years without us. The girl who fought alongside us. The girl who puts us to shame with her resourcefulness, her outsize bravery. Just have faith."

He wasn't wrong. Rose was the best of us. If anyone had a shot at surviving, it was her. In and out. My breath came back. I saw her in my mind now, hiding in a tree, blended in perfect.

"And besides, Derrick took a gun with them, so they'll be eating good," Miig continued.

Derrick. That was it. I on my feet, running.

Miig shouted, but I didn't turn back to answer. "French! Wait! We need to talk. I need to know—"

I found Mitch setting up a borrowed tent by a small circle of rocks set for an evening fire.

"We did it!" he loud-whispered. "We actually did it! And did you see that woman? She's a nurse. We're gonna bring down this whole friggin' network!"

"I'm leaving." I shouldered my pack and pulled my hood over my head.

"What? Wait, what do you mean, you're leaving? You can't leave!"

"I can. I am. Right now." I retied my laces with double knots and started folding up the tarp to slide under the flap of my bag.

"No, French. You can't." Something in his tone made me pause. He stood very still, all the anxiety and excitement gone from his face. He looked like a stranger. "If you leave, the mission will be called in. It'll mean we've failed. It'll mean I've failed, and I cannot fail, not when I'm so close to getting exactly what I deserve. I won't let you slow me down, not again."

That hurt like a punch to the gut. I was the reason he'd gotten caught in the first place, me and my little legs, me and my young hysteria. I had made running hard when we were kids, and he'd paid the price for it. But now I knew that he knew it, that he blamed me after all.

"Mitch . . ."

"No, French. There's nothing to say. If you leave, I will call in the recruitment team right now. At least that way, they'll know I wasn't in on this." He pulled a small device from the inside of his waist-band. So Mellin didn't trust me after all. She had made sure Mitch could get in touch.

I sighed. Suddenly, my bag was too heavy. Eyes still on me, Mitch opened the device and hovered his finger over a button. "I swear to god, Francis. Don't make me turn the tracker on. Because it's not going to come out in your favor."

Frustration was the worst emotion to cry over. But the tears still threatened. "You don't understand, Mitch. I have to go get her. Rose left, she went after me, and now she's in danger."

"So she's going to the school. Isn't that just perfect?"

"I have to find her. Please."

Once more, I sounded young and hysterical, slowing down his pace. I was helpless, waiting for him to make all the decisions, hoping that this time, the loss wouldn't be so big, so complete.

CHAPTER 28:
A ROAD, A SCHOOL, AND AN AMBUSH

Rose

BECAUSE OF DERRICK'S STILL-HEALING INJURY, THEY had to take it slow, slower than Rose could handle, but she did it anyway. She focused all her nervous energy into taking care of Derrick. At first, he was resentful—he didn't like being babied and sure as hell didn't like being one-upped in the providing role. But after the first night, when Rose slept up against him, not bothering to ram blankets in between them for extra space, he seemed to come around. Rose knew his mood had a lot to do with the fact that they were still going after Frenchie even after the house of horrors, even after the bear trap. But this was the mission, and she was still on it.

Rose could tell Nam loved the woods as much as you could love something so vast and terrifying. But as much as they loved the spongey ground, the smell of air without mold, the freedom of being an individual, they obviously had trouble falling asleep without walls.

"I'm going to keep an eye out for a bit," they said, watching the other two settle into the tent. "I'll be in later."

"Thanks for taking first watch," Derrick answered. He really was grateful. He needed to rest, as much as he didn't want to admit it.

There were a few moments when it seemed like Nam had something to tell but didn't, like when Rose stopped to set a foot trap on their path in case anyone was pursuing them, or when she resisted lighting a fire to cook dinner in case it was seen by the Chief. Surely he was close behind them?

The next morning, they all heard it—the sound of rubber on cement and the low squeal of mechanics.

"The road."

Rose fought every instinct in her not to run full tilt and burst out of the bush into the road. Instead, she paused.

"We need a tree."

"Plenty of them out here," Nam responded.

"One big enough to see what's near," she continued, "but not sparse enough that we'll be seen."

They circled until they found one. Rose dropped her bag and stretched.

"You're going up there?" Nam's head tilted all the way back. "It's so high."

"Yup. It's how we scout. You'll learn." Rose didn't hesitate any longer. She launched herself up the trunk like French had taught her, hand over foot like a monkey. When she reached the first thick branches, she climbed them, swinging from one to the other, using momentum and that first push to keep up her speed. Nearing the top, the footholds got thinner and the trunk began to sway, so she matched her movements to the tree's and found a spot to perch.

There it was, like a black creek with a cracked bottom: the road, stretching out through the sticky pines and birches. Rose felt excitement pouring out into her chest. Even better, about a mile up as the crow flies was a squat brown building. The school. She took a minute before she climbed down to do something she hadn't done since Minerva died—purposely head to the road to attempt a rescue. The wind and height making her feel huge, the anticipation and fear making her feel small, she closed her eyes and prayed.

Her feet hit the ground, and she immediately shouldered her pack. "School's a mile north. Let's go."

Nam and Derrick exchanged worried glances, then followed her determined steps, each one bringing them closer to what they knew was certain death. They made good time now that there was wind in their sails and a destination in sight. They stopped once for half an hour to drink some water, share a couple of cans of tuna, and rest. Rose wouldn't sit down, not even while she ate, using two fingers to spoon the fish into her mouth.

"What's the plan, exactly?" Nam was nervous, both about getting to the school and about pissing off Rose.

"We get there. And we look for any entrances, any weak points, any ways in." Rose spoke around the food in her mouth.

"And then what, Morriseau? We friggin' storm in with one hunting rifle and a sharp stick?" Derrick was less worried about Rose's reactions at this point. He was either an hour away from dying or an hour away from losing Rose. He was in no rush to get to either.

"No, smart-ass. We see where we can get in and out, and then we . . ." She waved her dirty fingers in the air. "We just figure it out."

"Figure it out? We just *figure it out*?" He raised his voice. "Oh, that's rich."

"And what's your plan, then?" she spat back.

"My plan is to go back to the camp. This is a suicide mission, and I didn't just survive a horde of bloodthirsty—literally bloodthirsty—maniacs to die at a school!" He was on his feet.

"You survived the maniacs because of us!" She pointed to Nam and herself. "You need us, not the other way around! So maybe sit the hell down and let the grown-ups talk!"

"Uh, guys . . ."

"Shut it, Nam!" Derrick turned on them.

"Don't you yell at them. They didn't do anything wrong."

"Guys . . ."

"What?!" they both screamed at Nam.

"There's someone coming . . ." They pointed behind Derrick, into the thick green between them and the road.

It was too late to reach the gun. There were two bodies dressed head to toe in black running through the trees and headed directly for them.

The first one crashed into the clearing and grabbed the gun where it lay against a rock. The second jumped over a log and landed beside Nam, grabbing them around the shoulders and holding a hunting knife to their neck.

"Everybody calm down." It was a woman's voice. "Just calm down. No sudden moves."

The person with the gun kept it down, pointed toward the ground. Derrick thought about making a grab for it, but they sensed it and lifted the rifle in his direction. "Easy now, big guy. Easy." Another female.

"Who are you?" the first one asked, knife still millimeters from Nam's skin.

"No one. We're no one," Rose answered.

"If you're no one, what are you doing this close to the institute?" She didn't sound angry. Stressed, out of breath, maybe, but there was no anger in her voice.

Rose looked from one to the other, trying to find the words to stay safe, trying to find a way to keep the mission alive. She couldn't find an angle. She was tired and hungry and out of ideas. "We've come for someone."

Derrick's eyes got big. "Rose, what the—"

"Real stupid," the shorter one said, still pointing the gun at Derrick.

"I know," he answered. "Real stupid."

"You need to get out of here now."

Rose was confused. "What?"

"Go on, get out of here. Walk back the way you came. There's no way you're getting in, never mind getting back out." She relaxed her grip on Nam and pushed them away. "Now."

The knife wielder pulled off her balaclava, revealing a pleasant face and close rows of box braids. Her eyes were friendly, but she still held the knife out at chest level. "Listen, you gotta go. It's not a good plan. You'll just get taken in, and not in any way you want."

Rose had never seen a Black Recruiter before. Even now, with weapons drawn and a standoff underway, the medicine of seeing someone who resembled her was fortifying. "Who exactly are you?"

"Nurses. Allies," the one with the gun said, pulling down her bandana. "And we're telling you to get lost before the Recruiters head this way. It's hard to know when a new patrol's being sent out. They keep it random."

"Don't have to tell me twice," Derrick said, reaching for the gun. After a nod between the women, she handed it over. "Let's go."

Nam picked up their bag and slung it over a shoulder.

"I'm not leaving." Rose stiffened her legs as if she were planting herself in the earth.

"Jesus, Rose." Derrick was exasperated now. "Come on. You heard them. It's impossible. Let's just head back to camp."

"We came all this way, dealt with bear traps and a goddamn vampire cult, and you just want to walk away without really trying?" She was resolved.

The women exchanged a look. "Vampire cult?"

"It's a long story," she sighed. "But we're here, and we're not leaving without him."

"Who?" one asked. "Who did you come for?"

"Frenchie." Saying his name out loud made breathing difficult. "Francis Dusome."

Again, the nurses exchanged a look, this one holding more than confusion. Rose picked up on it.

"What? What is it?" A dozen different answers ran through her mind.

"First of all, I'm Alice, and this is May," the woman answered, putting her knife back in her belt. "And you'd better have a seat here for a minute."

But Rose had taken her stance, and now, with news on the horizon, news that she was pretty sure was going to be bad, she couldn't move. "I'll stand."

Alice sighed. "Okay. I'm not sure if you guys know about the Program?"

They all shook their heads.

Alice went on to explain how some of the residents of the school were taken in to be reprogrammed. "Sending out decoys has been pretty successful over the years."

"We ran into a few," Rose remarked. "They grabbed one of our family, a little girl. We made sure neither of them made it back to do any more harm."

May lowered her head and kicked at the rocks by her feet. "I am truly sorry for your loss."

"It takes months to go through the Program. Used to take years, but they've introduced new methods. Your friend, Francis, he was here."

"Was?" It was the word that stopped all her relief from bubbling up.

"I'm sorry to tell you that Francis was fast-tracked through the Program. By all accounts, he was successfully integrated and is now working for the Department of Oneirology." Alice paused to let it sink in. "He's out in the field now."

Rose narrowed her eyes, repeating this over and over in her mind. Then she started to make noises, small pushes of air and voice like at the beginning of a wail. Her knees bent, and she hunched over on the ground.

"I'm sorry to have to be the one . . ."

Alice stopped. Rose lifted her head, and she was laughing. She laughed so hard tears filled her eyes. Laughed so hard she fell all the way onto her bum and then laughed some more.

"Rose?" Nam took a tentative step toward her.

When she calmed down enough, she said, "Oh, that's brilliant. Brilliant!" She was back on her feet, looking at her friends with a crazy intensity. "Don't you see? He escaped! He totally duped them all and escaped!"

She spun around to face Alice again. "When did he leave? We've got to catch up to him!"

The woman looked to Derrick and Nam for help, then back at May, who remained silent.

Why wasn't anyone answering her? Did no one see that this was the best possible news? Now they didn't have to try to get into the school. He was out here, in the open. He'd done it! She should have known he'd find a way.

"Listen, he's not faking. He really did go through the Program, and he really is working for them now." Alice talked a little slower, trying to calm the girl down.

"Lady, there's no way—no possible way—French is a traitor. He's as solid as they come. If you knew him, you'd never say otherwise." Rose was still full of mirth. "Where's my bag? We gotta get going."

"He brought in a family." May said it low. She didn't want to say it, but she had to. There was no way she could let this girl walk into a trap, not without knowing the truth.

"What?" Rose stopped halfway to her pack. "What do you mean?"

"He brought in a family. The day before yesterday. Two people. A woman and a little girl."

"No. No!" Rose was shouting. "He wouldn't. He couldn't!"

Derrick ran to grab her, squeezing her tight, trying to get her to shut up. "Come on, Rose, be quiet. You're going to get us all taken in."

"I'm sorry, but it's true. Seven years old. They're going through processing now," Alice finished.

Now Rose was crying for real. She thrashed in Derrick's grip and broke free.

"He would not, he just—"

"Rose." Derrick was as gentle as he could be while trying to shush her. "What would you do? What would any of us do, really?"

"Not that!" she screamed. The sound of her own voice echoing in the shadows shocked her to quiet and then to action. She gathered herself and took off into the trees before another word could be spoken.

Derrick sighed, watching her back get smaller. He turned to the nurses, who were both scouring the space around them in case they'd been heard, then he pointed his lips at Nam.

"Grab what you can," he instructed, hoisting his bag and the satchel of food and gripping the gun. He dared not put it away, not with all the ruckus they'd just kicked up.

"I'm sorry, but you had to know." Alice was pulling her hood back over her head. May had already repositioned her bandana and started back into the bush.

"No, thank you. We appreciate it. Take care." Derrick waved, and then they were off, the allies back to the road and the runners into the trees after their hysterical friend.

◆◆◆ ◆◆◆ ◆◆◆

They found her pretty quick. She wasn't thinking, wasn't even seeing clearly, and so she wasn't too fast for them to catch. They walked behind her without saying anything, and after a while, she turned back and grabbed her pack to carry herself. That night, they camped without tents or a fire—they were too close to the school. And early the next morning, they started back toward the resistance camp. Without hope, the journey seemed twice as long.

It was days before they saw the first syllabics telling them the camp was nearby. Nam was getting nervous. What if they weren't welcomed once they got there? Derrick assured them as best he could that there was a place for them. But between being the sole navigator and making sure Rose didn't hang herself from a low branch because of French, he didn't have time for niceties.

"Just trust me, it'll be great." That was the most he could offer them right now.

The trio hadn't eaten much, and their pace was a little off. It took forever to make their way in. So when he finally saw the first scout high up in the split elm, Derrick was so relieved he cried out.

He broke into a jog, whistling and waving up to Manny, who gave the all clear signal from the branches.

"We're here," he called back. "We're home!"

CHAPTER 29:
IN THE PINES

French

I STAYED. WHICH MEANT THE MISSION WAS FULL steam ahead. Only now, I had a harder time imagining that there was a way out. I never should have come here, never should have put them at risk. Stupid. So stupid. Now that I knew Mitch had a tracker, one he was guarding with his life, I knew the bush would be lousy with Recruiters the moment he had an inkling I had told the group about our true identity. So I kept my mouth shut until I could figure out a way to get the tracker and slip away, leaving Mitch to the mercy of the forest and the wrath of Mellin.

There had always been a part of me that held out hope, ever since I could remember. Hope was a gift my mother had given me when I was little. It was a small gift at first, the way she always trailed off at the end of a sentence, like "Oh, you never know . . ." or "One day . . ."

From there, it built itself up like a sandcastle until I could live inside of it, even if the walls were a bit shifty. She let us dream without holding back. She refused to put boundaries on our plans. For a long time, I thought I would go to a real school one day . . . and I guess that one came true, in a way. But in my head, it was a good school for children, with colorful classrooms and nice teachers and long recesses. She would ask me to be more specific about my daydreams: "What's your teacher's name? How many swings are there on the playground? How high can you swing? Do your feet touch the tops of the trees?"

Hope is a wonderful thing until it becomes your downfall. And I was edging closer and closer to the fall with each and every step we took toward the train station where we would be whisked across the border to safety.

Mitch was in great spirits. Not only would he be bringing in the rogue Indians who had been causing so much chaos, but he would also almost-single-handedly uncover and tear down an entire refugee network. You couldn't get bigger than that. He was moving fast through the bush; it was hard to even make out his limp at this pace. And he had questions.

"So, tell me about this girl."

"Nothing to tell." I refused to even think of Rose right now. I couldn't.

"There must be something," he teased. "I mean, you were about to blow our whole mission for her."

"Was not." I thought of the device nestled against his lower belly and chose my words carefully. "I was just going to bring her back."

Mitch laughed. "Yeah, sure."

"How would you know what I'm thinking, anyway?" I was getting angry. Pretty soon it would be obvious, because I would have my hands around his throat.

"Well, because if you really were worried about her getting away and not about her staying out in the wilderness, you would be happy that she was headed to the school. It means less work for us; she's hand delivering herself. Imagine her face when you walk in with the rest of them."

And then I did imagine it, her face. I imagined walking in with Miig and Slopper, Chi Boy and Wab and the twins, and seeing her there. And her seeing me, the traitor. Maybe I could convince her to play along, to join the Program so we could escape. It was a risk, and it would cost me exactly six tickets to ride that ride, each one of them a member of my family. How could she ever forgive me for that? For trading six lives for her own? I knew the answer. She couldn't. She wouldn't.

"It might work out, French. I mean, it will. She'll understand. Maybe she can join the Program with us." In a weird way that was about as off as you could get, Mitch was trying to make me feel better.

"Sure."

✦✦✦ ✦✦✦ ✦✦✦

"So, what's the difference between owl eye and angle vision?" Mitch interrupted my thoughts, huffing at my side as we climbed a rocky incline. We were ahead of the main group, scouting the trail. Not too far ahead, since we weren't sure of the path, but not too close so that they could still get away if we stumbled into danger. They had no idea that the very danger they were trying to avoid was playing fifty questions beside me.

I sighed. "Why do you need to know now?"

"Why not?" he countered. "I've been out of the bush since forever. Gotta keep sharp."

"You planning on staying out in the bush?" There was that hope again, busy building new rooms.

He laughed, "No. I couldn't. But once this is over, I'll be a legend—*we'll* be legends—and there'll be lots more missions."

A wall toppled over, halfway built.

"Owl eye is when you cup your hands around your eyes to concentrate the light in the darkness so you can make out objects better. Angle vision is when you move your whole head side to side so you can gauge distance and depth." I spoke in monotone. I had to get better at hiding my anxiety and disappointment or he'd catch on. I didn't need him blowing the whistle yet, not before I had a chance to figure out a new plan.

"You're like a whole Indian now." He cuffed me on the shoulder. I tried to grin. It was more of a grimace. I didn't like him saying *Indian*. It didn't feel the same way it felt when one of us said it—casual, reclaiming. It felt mocking coming out of his mouth. He hadn't earned it. You need to love something before you can tease about it.

"You could be, too. You're maybe just half at this point." It came out sharper than it should have been.

He stopped. "What's with you, man? You're really grumpy."

"I'm tired." I slowed down but kept walking. "That's all. This is tiring, all this damn walking and climbing trees and bush work."

He jogged back to my side. "At the institute, we won't have to do any physical activity unless it's PE time, and even that's inside.

When we get back, your privileges will be extended so you can do it, too. Just keep the goal in mind, and it'll be easier to make it through this."

I couldn't believe he actually thought being in a school was better than this—being able to pick your own direction, carry your own weight, and be your own person.

"Isn't it weird, though?" I tried. "Following all those rules and knowing that it's not real?"

"What do you mean, not real?"

"It's just, out here, you make decisions based on your gut and your head, not because you're following a schedule. And when you do something or don't do something, it's because it has a real impact on your life."

"So it's better to be almost dead or close to dying every day than to be safe and fed?" He laughed like I'd told an awesome joke. Maybe I had. "No thanks, man. I'll take the institute any day."

I had to shift gears. I was wasting precious alone time.

"It's gotta feel strange, even for you, even after all this time, being at a place that's a prison for us." I had to tread lightly but still make sure my point was getting across. "I just feel like, I don't know, like a second-class citizen there."

"Ummm, I mean, sometimes it's weird. But they really take you on your own merit, you know? Like, you can work your way up from the bottom. It's all about pulling yourself up." He was practically skipping along. "I appreciate that. It means I can get to where I want to be for no other reason than that I earned it."

"Okay, but aren't you beginning a hundred yards back from the starting line while everyone else is already at the gate, just because of what they are and what you aren't?"

He didn't answer right away. A good sign. I kept going.

"Out here is where you can really prove yourself every day. And nature doesn't judge anyone before they are called to task—it can't."

"You seem awfully skeptical, Francis." His voice had gotten low.

I pushed him a bit, smiling. "Nah, just saying, is all. I don't want to be a part of something where people think I'm a moron before I even have a chance."

"Yeah." He pushed me back. "Better they give you the opportunity to prove you're a moron." Then he took off running. I had no choice but to chase after him, like I hadn't a care in the world and nothing better to do than goof around with my brother. Like I wasn't trying desperately to amalgamate my two families before I had to choose one over the other.

"How far you figure it is until we get there?" he shouted back over his shoulder. He still hadn't gotten the hang of being quiet out here. I guess it was all playacting, anyway. Was he really in any danger? Certainly not from the enemies the rest of us were avoiding.

"No idea."

He stopped at the top of the hill and put his hands on his hips, catching his breath. "So, is Rose your girlfriend or something?"

I winced at her name. "No." I still wouldn't offer up any details about Rose, not to Mitch.

"You sure? 'Cause that could be a problem." He was skeptical.

"How so?" I was standing beside him now, taking in the thick trees and uneven ground all around us. Looking back, I could make out branches moving in a pattern not explained by the wind—the rest of the group on our trail.

"Well, I don't want you going all soft on the mission because of some girl."

"She's not 'some girl.'" I paused, remembering to add, "And she doesn't make me soft."

"Oh, so she makes you hard, then?" He busted out laughing. I wanted to punch him in the lip. I was jealous that anyone could make those noises, could feel that mirth. I thought about Riri at the bottom of the rocks, one pink boot still on, her head a mass of dark hair and crusty blood. I thought about Sunny holding my hand while I delivered her into darkness.

"Why do you keep bringing her up, anyway? Enough."

"Okay, okay, easy." He held his hands out in front of him. "Just making conversation, is all. Anything to break up the monotony of this damn walk."

"Well, just shut up, and let's go." I waved him on. "We gotta find a good camping spot for the group for tonight."

I started down the hill, kicking my heels back into the soil as I stepped to avoid spilling out. I didn't bother to explain the technique to Mitch, who skidded and overstepped and fell on his ass. That was the first time I smiled for real all day.

◆◆◆ ◆◆◆ ◆◆◆

Miig was acting strange. He didn't tell Story that night. In fact, he wouldn't even sit with us. He kept to the perimeter of the camp, even when Isaac sat with us to eat. Mitch horsed down his food, and I was embarrassed. It was ironic behavior from someone who thought we were the primitive ones.

"Come sit, my love." Isaac patted the tarp beside him.

"Not hungry," Miig responded, arms folded over his chest.

"Okay then, more for us." Isaac gave him a coaxing smile.

I hadn't gotten a chance to see them together before I was taken. Back when Isaac only existed in Miig's stories, they were the best couple I could imagine. Now, in person, they were everything I had imagined them being—loving, respectful complete; a goal I wanted to reach in my own life.

I felt Miig's eyes on me as I spooned watery rice into my mouth, not tasting it. I refused to make eye contact.

"So, Wab, when's the baby coming?" I tried to make conversation, to seem too busy to seek out my Elder.

"Whenever they damn well feel like it," she sighed. "I'm ready now."

"Not *right* now, though." Chi Boy put a hand on her distended stomach as if offering instructions to the ears inside. "We need to get outta here first."

"We had no idea that people were still able to procreate without help," Mitch said, careless with his guard down.

"Who's we?" Isaac asked.

Mitch lowered the spoon before he could shove the contents into his face. His eyes got wide. I put my bowl down. The clatter of the spoon against the rim was like a warning bell in the silence. All eyes on Mitch.

"Uh, just me and the guy I was traveling with . . . before. He was a doctor. So we talked a lot about medical stuff."

"What happened to him?" Slopper asked, oblivious to the new tension.

"He died. An infection. Got hurt and it got dirty, and that was that." Mitch was pulling the story together as he spoke. I wondered if anyone else noticed the odd pace of his words.

"Hmm. You'd think a doctor would have some supplies with

him," Isaac continued. "Or at least know how to avoid a simple infection."

"Yeah, well, I never said he was a good one." Mitch offered an awkward laugh.

Just then, Zheegwon slipped in from lookout, pulling the bow and quiver off his back. "Save some for me?"

"I'm going next." I jumped up and grabbed the weapon from his hand. I had to leave now. I couldn't lie, not one more untruthful word, and I still didn't know how to solve this problem that affected all of us, so I fled.

"Wait, French." Miig stepped toward me. "We need to talk."

"Not now." I kept walking. "I'm done eating, and I haven't taken a turn yet."

"French . . ."

"Later, Miigwans." I took off at a jog, leaving Mitch to his story and the others to their skepticism and rice.

In a circle of pines, I found a tall maple covered in new vines, neon and muscular in their infancy. It took me longer than usual to scale the trunk. I was out of practice. But tearing at the green climbers and grunting through the flex, I made it to a branch high enough and strong enough to offer a good view while holding me up. The trees always held me up. I was better out here. I took a moment to feel the space I filled.

People used to seek out the abandoned. My father had told us about that. "They'd take road trips and pay money to go on tours. Shut-down parks, old mansions, falling-down buildings, and a whole Russian city ruined by a nuclear accident. They wanted so bad to be in that intimate space, close to nothing."

I think now that they just wanted to be in a place that looked like how the world really was. They wanted proof that we were alone in a crowd. That the world had quickly pushed us into little cubicles so we could cause minimal damage and then gave us stupid shit to amuse ourselves with: games, toys, politics.

I wondered if those tourists saw the truth of an abandoned place. That it was fuller than a mall, more bustling than an old freeway. Because the Earth didn't stutter. It moved ahead, smooth and elegant, and uncoiled its fingers into every last place, hooking nails under crook and groove. Now so much of the country was abandoned, and we had never lived in a more crowded space.

Clouds nuzzled at the bottom of the sky where the teeth of the tree line poked it, and it slowly bled to dark. Different birds tagged in and took over the symphony. I stretched out my legs, relaxing into the bones of the tree like a parent's lap. And then I heard rustle below.

"Pssst. Francis?"

Mitch.

"Francis, you up there?"

He was calling into the pines. Of course he couldn't find me, even though I'd left my mark all over this trunk, vines torn and ground stomped.

I sighed, pulled the bow over my head, readjusted the quiver, and started down. There was no way he could get up to me. Not with those noodle arms and school smarts.

I jumped from the last branch and landed a foot in front of him.

"Ahh!" he screamed, clutching at his collarbone.

"Shut up, Mitch. You can't be so damn loud out here."

"Holy Jesus Lord, you scared me." His breath was coming in pants.

"No need to pray about it. What's up?"

He composed himself just long enough to switch gears into a different kind of tremor. "We're almost there!"

"Where?"

"At the rendezvous point!" He clapped his hands together, grinning ear to ear. I saw rot in his back teeth.

"How do you know?" My stomach felt funny, like the bottom had dropped out. There was new weight in my muscles. All the lightness and peace of the tree was gone.

"I heard the nurse talking to the old guy," he said.

"Miigwans," I corrected. Not even a perceived slight was too small to bother me. Not from his mouth. Not about Miigwans.

"Right. That guy. And she said we should be there by noon tomorrow!" He clapped again to punctuate his glee.

"Oh." Here it was—the last possible minute.

"*Oh*? That's all you can say?" He took a step toward me and leaned in. "Francis, this is it. We're almost there, and then we will be heroes!"

"Great." My head was spinning. I examined my boots, the ground, anything to avoid looking at his face, shining with excitement, glowing with accomplishment.

"I know, right? And we'll be back in time for the transition to start, and we can help. Be actual architects of the new stage! And, oh God, I cannot believe this, we will be bringing in one of the first mothers!"

He lifted his feet, one and then the other, almost to knee height, a movement that reminded me of the jigs our uncle used to dance when he was real happy or, as my father used to say, "feeling his oats."

"Wait." I looked up. "What do you mean? First mothers?"

"Oh." He grabbed my arms and squeezed. "I guess I can tell you now. I mean, why not, now that we're helping to herald it in? Oh God, this is so exciting!" He paused to throw his head back and giggle. It was an odd combination—such a dramatic motion for such a small sound. It seemed all wrong. "The schools are transitioning to a more proactive model."

"What the hell does that mean?"

"It means, dear brother, that they've been researching and studying the whole time. The best marrow comes from young donors, the newest carriers." He started walking in circles, talking with his hands, trying to remember all the words to this particular tune. It drifted into the branches like a funeral song.

"See, young people, babies, they have immature cells—stem cells—and their tissue is weaker, easier to break down, like Jell-O. So they carry the cells that can become anything to anyone, and they're easier to extract." He shrugged, exaggerated, like he was explaining simple facts to a child.

It was getting cold. It had to be, because my hands were getting numb. I balled them into fists, then the fists unclenched, then they were running up and down the strap holding the bow and quiver.

When I didn't answer, he continued. "Soooo, I mean, why waste precious resources and time on older donors? Especially when dreamers are still so fertile, even now?"

The blood returned to my extremities in a torrent. Suddenly, I could feel everything, see everything.

"If we change the institutes to focus on farming newborns, we can cut out all the messy in-between bits. And it means there will be a chance for more of us to integrate. To live like normal people." Mitch flapped his arms now, spine straight, head back. "We, brother, can make it so that more Native people have a chance to truly live. As productive members of a reborn society."

The bow was in my hands. I saw Rose at the school, defiant and stubborn as ever, even under those circumstances. She wouldn't have to get ready. She stayed ready. I saw her in the common room with a fist held high. I saw her in the Correction Room, singing louder than the siren. I saw her fading away from me, because I would never get to see her again, not after this.

"See, there will be the herd, and then there will be everyone else. Not divided by race, exactly. Just divided by purpose. And the purpose of Indigenous people will be to give birth to the answer. What more noble purpose could you ever ask for?" He paused, reaching into his waistband and pulling out the tracker.

"Now we'll send a signal so the team knows to get ready. That way they can start heading in this direction. And then tomorrow, our futures are secure!" He looked up, waiting for me to join in the celebration, the absolute joy of this new world where we were, if not architects, at least laborers. And then his face fell.

I stood in front of him, arrow nocked, bowstring drawn. Rose was gone. Mitch had taken away any outcome where she existed, where I could hold her and breathe in the smell of her hair, the salt of her neck. And now he was coming for Wab and her baby.

"What are you doing?" He spun around, checking the woods behind him, looking for a target other than the obvious.

He took a half step back, hand out. "Seriously, cut it out, French."

"Francis," I reminded him. "You're not family. I'm Francis."

"French—Francis—listen to me. Don't you see? We can save so many of our people this way, for just a small sacrifice."

I closed one eye and moved the aim to his heart. "My people. Not yours. Mine. Yours are back at the school."

He froze, one hand still up, the other by his side, holding the tracker. "Let's just stop and think for a minute, here. You don't want to do this."

That's when I looked at the device. It was blinking green, the small thrum of light bouncing against his leg.

"You're right, I don't." I took a full breath. Then I released my fingers from the string.

The thing about arrows is that they are quiet. So if your prey doesn't know you're there, you have a better chance of it staying still, of being hit exactly where you aimed. But an arrow is not a bullet. It's slower, less exact. Things like wind and muscle tension and shadows can impact the blow.

But this time, everything that could have made the arrow arc or question its intent held its breath. And the tip entered just to the right of his sternum, burying itself in the striated muscle of his conflicted heart. And unlike legs, you only have one of those.

Mitch staggered, placed a hand on the shaft protruding from his chest, and looked up at me, incredulous. "French?"

His voice bent one way, then the other, wavering as if the breath that pushed it was too much, too fast, too temporary and rushed.

A thin line of blood slipped out of the corner of his mouth, and his features began to change, animated by confusion, fear calling across the distance. He blinked, long and stilted, one eye opening after the other, focusing on my face. "We need to run." He staggered instead.

Now I recognized him again—the scared boy running through the streets of a hostile city, dragging his little charge behind him. The confused boy trying to find shelter and food for two mouths in the absence of a caretaker. The brother looking for a way to survive without knowing what survival looked like anymore.

He lifted a hand toward me. "Come on, French. We gotta get out of here. Just us. Please . . ."

Oh god, he was crying. He rolled his eyes to the treetops, to the sky, and turned, one foot forward, then thrown back to try to keep him upright. My breath was quick, too quick; I was panting. I wanted to grab him, to hold him, to run with him, anywhere, anywhere but here. Anywhere but now.

The tracker dropped as he walked, uneven and halting and in no particular direction. He was pushing his breath out now, wheezing it back in, a forced series of mechanics that showed the absurdity in the work of living. In and out, again and again.

He reached the base of a large pine and put a hand on the bark to hold him up. Once more, he turned back to me. His breathing was slow, and slower, and gone. Blood covered his chin so that his face looked like a skull with no jaw. Dead already. Dead long enough for there to be nothing left to see but his bones and the dreams they could hold, the dreams he dreamed while lying next to me. The dreams he hid, maybe even now, waiting for the night when he'd be free to let them spill. I hoped they were there now. I hoped he was dreaming already.

"We ran, Mitch." My voice cracked. "We ran all the way home."

A small twitch, something close to a smile, and then he fell into the dark bush, one shoe left empty beside the tree, his body curling fetal like a plastic figurine in a fire.

I didn't know how long I stood there, bow still raised, chest heaving, but it was the blinking tracker that called me back, sure and exact as an alarm clock. Time was ticking by, one blip to the next.

I dropped the bow and ran over and stomped on it, smashing the plastic to bits, pulling out its wiry guts and tearing at the connections until there was no more light, until I was sure it was not broadcasting. Even then, I tossed pieces in different directions. Then I gathered up the bow and quiver and ran as fast as I could. I was already out of the pines when the crows started cawing.

I burst into the clearing. Miig sat by the fire, probably waiting for me to return so we could talk. He shot to his feet. "What is it? What did you do?"

I gasped for air, looking at him, and I knew. I knew that he knew. He knew exactly who I was, exactly who Mitch was. He knew, but I had to convince him to follow me anyway. "They're on the way."

He paused for only a second before turning and sprinting toward the tents. "Let's go, everyone! Pack up, now! No time to hide our tracks, just grab your gear and run!"

I hunched over, hands on my knees, catching my breath, while the others flew around, tearing down tents and folding up tarps. In the corner of my eye, where the dust and floaters swam, all I could see was Mitch, his shoe, the crows I knew had arrived at the scene, and I couldn't move.

I remembered when the Recruiters took Minerva from the old barn where we were hiding. She had insisted on staying on the ground while the rest of us nestled high in a hay-strewn loft, safely out of sight. I remember us finding old tin can lids she had kept and rolled into cones for a jingle dress that one day some girl would wear, when we were allowed to make noise again, when we were allowed to heal and dance and live. And the words Chi Boy had spoken came back to me right then.

Sometimes you risk everything for a life worth living, even if you're not the one who'll be alive to live it.

I stood up and started packing so we could run. This time, together.

CHAPTER 30:
THE WAY HOME

Rose

ROSE REMEMBERED HER GRANDMA'S HOUSE ON THE rez. It was small, just a kitchen that opened onto a small living room, a bedroom with a twin bed and a dresser with broken drawers, and a tiny bathroom that consistently smelled like a bleached outhouse. The front mudroom was always crammed with boots, snowsuits, toboggans, and hunting gear. On the back porch was a stack of plastic chairs that sat under snow for months at a time and a round table rusted to leaning. There was a huge backyard her grandma refused to mow until one cousin or another dragged a mower up the dirt road and did it for her while she glared at them from the sliding doors. "All those flowers chopped up so I can have a golf course," she'd mutter. "And I don't golf, me."

But Rose loved that backyard. She even built a small fort back there out of old wood pallets steadied against the gnarled trunk of an apple tree. Out there, she could be alone. No smaller cousins popping at her knees like corn, no rez dogs snouting her hands for scraps, no grown-ups pestering her to get something or do something or say something. But to reach it, first she had to get down the steps from the deck. They were rickety and wide, and the railing had long since rotted off. So she'd position her bum at the top and slowly descend, stretching each little leg out to touch the next step before carefully lowering herself onto it. This approach was a double-edged sword, since underneath the deck was the most terrifying place on earth. Damp and cold even in August, it housed sharp hedge trimmers long abandoned, antlers and skulls her great-uncles never got around to mounting, the skeleton of a snowmobile from the seventies, and boxes that had melted into a kind of tan flesh sculpture near the back.

One summer, her mother surprised her with a satellite dish, and Rose stayed inside for two whole months. During this time of discovering real horrors on late-night movies and, from reality TV, just how big and stupid the world actually was, she grew four whole inches. So by the time she was dragged to her grandmother's house for a dinner to celebrate the new school year, everything looked different. She kissed her granny hello, now having to stoop to reach her head, and slipped out onto the back deck before she could be put to work. Suddenly, the stairs looked just like stairs—surmountable, unremarkable. And no one had managed to cut the grass in a while, so it was up and out in all its wild glory.

The stairs were not to be feared. They weren't actually scary, like the zombies she'd watched ripping into scalps or the crooked cops she'd seen chasing the good guys into old factories. So she positioned her newly elongated feet at the top and stepped like a normal person. No more climbing on her hands and butt. She was past all that.

But the first step never rose to meet her feet. She underestimated the distance and faltered before she could find purchase, pitching her upper body off balance. And then she was in the air.

Every place her bones could connect with the splintered wood, they did. She smashed her cheek, her shoulder, her ribs, her tailbone. It was like a slow-motion blast from a shotgun, each pellet finding its mark with heat and sting. After what seemed like an excruciating amount of time, she lay at the bottom, gasping through bruised ribs for air, trying to keep the tears from coming before her breath did. No one had seen her fall, so no one came, and maybe that was better, because the thing that hurt the most was the humiliation, the shock of it all. She wasn't past a slow climb after all. Thinking she was safe when it was clear she was still vulnerable broke her to pieces. She was breathless.

That's what it felt like in the days after they ran into the nurses, walking back into the camp without French, knowing that she would never be with him again. Even now, Derrick was filling the Council in on the truth of it, that the French they'd lost was dead and that a new kind of predator was out in the woods wearing his skin. She hadn't considered that they wouldn't get him back, not for one moment—not when he'd been taken, not even when she'd been strapped to a cot, being drained of blood. There wasn't one moment she hadn't thought about finding him, holding him, surrendering to the truth of how she felt about him. And now? Now she was breathless.

There was only one place she could imagine being, only one place left in the world that could hold her together.

"Where's my family?"

Clarence glanced at Bullet and stepped toward her. "Listen, my girl. Things have changed since you were gone."

"Where are they?" She couldn't listen anymore. She needed them—Miig and the twins and even Wab. They would know how to put her back together.

"Rose, they had to leave. We got word that Wab was in imminent danger, so they—"

No. Not this. Not now. She dropped her bag by the cave and took off running to their campground.

"Rose!" Derrick shouted after her. She didn't falter for a second, running as hard as she could, pushing past startled kids and quiet couples, not even noticing the empty circles on the ground and bundled belongings where people had started packing up.

She heard footfalls behind her and was determined to outrun them. She had to get there. She couldn't be alone for one more second. She wouldn't make it without Miig telling her she'd be okay. That was the only thing she needed to hear.

She burst into the clearing, her chest lifting and falling with the demand for air. She put her hands on her knees and swallowed hard, finally taking in her surroundings.

Nothing. Not one tent. Firepit buried, branches moved back to cover any signs of occupation. She spun. Had she gone the wrong way?

Then Derrick was behind her. "Rose, they left. They had to leave," he pushed out between heavy breaths. "Had to get Wab across the border."

"What are you saying?" She got in his face. "What the hell are you saying? Where is my goddamn family?"

He looked away, then back into her face. He wouldn't let her down, not now. He'd tell her the truth, no matter how much it hurt her. He would always tell her the truth.

"They're gone. It's just us now."

Watching her unravel was harder than he had ever imagined it could be, because there was nothing he could do to make it stop. She just lay there at the bottom of someplace dark, feeling every sore spot on her body all at once.

✦✦✦ ✦✦✦ ✦✦✦

"They had to go," Clarence explained. "The nurses were here, and the time was right. But they didn't leave you. The rest of us waited for you to come back. That's the only reason they agreed to leave so they could make the arranged pickup."

Rose didn't answer him. She just stared straight ahead, somewhere over the low fire, a blanket wrapped up over her shoulders. Nam sat quietly on her other side, holding a mug of tea in case she needed a sip. Derrick had brought her to the Council meeting area. He thought she'd feel better being by the lodge, huddled in the corner of the space like a sleeping child under layers of blankets. And she did. But not all the way through; there were parts of her that remained untouched, unreachable. She wasn't sure they would ever open up again.

"They know about French?" Her voice was monotone.

"They think he's dead. We all did until Derrick told us about the nurses at the school. Our informant told us his name was off the register, and we assumed the worst."

"Being dead is not the worst. Being a traitor is."

"Rose, they didn't want to go without you," Bullet interjected. "It killed them not to be able to wait. They almost didn't go, but they had to, for the sake of the baby. They made the nurses leave instructions, directions. Even though it's against network rules."

"Instructions." She sneered. "So I can try to find them again on my own?"

"Miig said if anyone could do it, it would be you," Bullet offered. She looked to Nam, beseeching, as if Nam could help here. They just looked at their feet, still unsure of their place.

"Ha! They didn't think I'd make it back."

"That's not true." Jean limped into the light. "Not at all. They knew if anyone could get my boy back, it would be you. And they always knew you'd return."

Everyone at the fire jumped. They hadn't heard him approach. They'd already decided not to share the news of Frenchie's resurrection and defection to the school army with him. If his son's death hadn't killed him, then this surely would. Bullet paid attention to the way he moved to see if he'd overheard.

"I knew it, too. Knew you were a fighter the second you showed up." He smiled at her. His demeanor was calm, focused on making the girl feel better. There was no way he'd overheard the traitor part.

"And you know, my girl, you don't have to go. You can stay here with us. I always wanted a daughter."

This touched Rose. She hadn't been anyone's daughter for so long, hadn't worn that title since she was a little girl, before her parents were hauled away and she was left hiding from Recruiters in her grandmother's backyard. She'd hidden so well that it wasn't until early the next morning that her great-uncle Jake found her while sneaking to his sister's house through the back.

"Holy hell," he'd yelled, hand over his heart, when her face appeared from between the pallets. "You scared the piss right outta me. What are you doing?"

She could do nothing but cry. It was the last time she'd shed tears until the day Minerva had died. Now it seemed like she couldn't stop crying. When would things just stop so she could go back to the luxury of not crying? The truth was, she was the only one who could make it stop. She had to find a way to be at least okay, if not happy, or she would never stop. She would die, a dehydrated girl floating in a pool of her own tears.

Nam moved closer so that Rose felt their leg against her own. "This community is big, bigger than any I can remember seeing."

Rose nodded, sniffling. "Mm-hmm."

"If . . . if we stay, I think . . . I think it could work." They watched as Rose wiped tears from her cheeks.

"Oh yeah?" She cleared her throat.

"I mean, no one even questioned me," Nam continued. "They just shook my hand."

"Well, why would they say anything? Anyone would be glad to have you in their family." Rose looked at Nam for the first time since they'd sat down.

"You're my family, Rose. You." They put their hand over Rose's, and she grasped it. They sat in silence.

Time did what it did best—slipped by regardless. One by one, people went to bed. Eventually, even Nam left to pass out in the cave on a small pile of blankets one of the women had prepared for them. And then it was just Rose and Derrick, sitting side by side under a sky exploding with stars so that all the ancestors sat waiting for what would come next.

"Rose, we need to talk." Derrick's voice was low but a bit shaky. "I don't want to upset you. You have to promise not to get upset."

"Derrick, I don't think I have any energy left to be upset." She was solemn, kept her head down and didn't even raise a hand to bat away the loose hair by her face.

"I want you to think seriously about what Jean said." He paused, choosing his words carefully so as not to spook her into flight. "About staying with us."

"I don't belong here."

"You do!" This brought him to his feet. How could she even think that? "Of course you do. You did from the moment you showed up."

"I showed up with my family." She stood now as well, slower than him but steadier, too. "I belong with them."

"Do you? Because they left without you." It was too far. He flinched from his own words as soon as they left his mouth. "I'm sorry . . . but it's true. I would never leave you." The last part was quiet, bashful.

"I know."

"You do?"

She nodded, and he caught his breath.

"I would literally do anything for you, Rose. Hell, I would follow you through the woods with a bear trap stuck to my leg if that's what you wanted." He laughed, and she smiled. And for a moment, she even looked up, watching his mouth while the laughter fell out.

She could almost see it, like thin smoke lifting toward the canopy of stars, an offering to those who watched over them. It made her feel lighter. Like maybe she could lift, too.

He got softer now that he'd broken through. "Do you want to keep chasing ghosts, or do you want to fight these bastards from the safety of a good home, your own home? We're going to leave here and find a new spot, and you can help build it from the beginning so it can be exactly what you want." Derrick felt like a salesman trying to pitch this idea.

She didn't answer, so he kept going. Silence was too heavy. Silence was too close to a no.

"Aren't you tired of running?" He was getting panicked. He could hear it in his voice. So he took a breath to slow down.

"I know you carried a torch for French, but he's gone now. For good. There's no rescue mission that's gonna bring him back from where he's at. I don't mean to be an ass, but that's the truth. We tried, we really did. But he didn't try back. Not hard enough, anyway."

Her shoulders curled in a bit under the weight of those words. He leaned toward her, close enough that he could hear the air that slouch pushed out. "Rose, it's okay. Maybe not now, but it will be. And I'm willing to wait until you truly understand that. I will wait for as long as it takes. I'm in, totally in. For every minute you are sad, or so angry you want to claw the bark off a tree, and maybe even the times you're happy enough to smile. I'm in. And better yet, I'm the one who's already here."

He reached a shaking hand across the new distance between them. "I can wait, I promise. You're worth every minute, however long it takes."

"Derrick . . ."

He cut her off. "You know how I feel about you. Christ, every-one knows how I feel about you. I'm not exactly subtle, you know?" He dropped his hand against his thigh. "And I know I can be . . . a lot, but you and I, we're a good team. We were amazing out there, weren't we?"

She nodded, slow, to make the time to think.

"And we can keep being a good team. But for that to happen, you gotta stay with me. Please stay with me." He tried to exhale, but the air hitched up in his throat.

That was it. He was done asking. Now it was her turn to give an answer. And she wasn't sure she had one, not one that she could bear to hear herself say out loud. She remembered him in the bush, how he took care of her when she couldn't take care of her-self. She remembered lying beside him in the tent, pretending to still be asleep so she could enjoy the weight of his arm over her. She remembered the dream she'd had where they were strung together like Christmas lights. She knew how she felt when he was around: like everything might just work out. Like she was safe.

She just wasn't ready to say the words. She took a breath and, for the first time in weeks, looked him directly in the eye. She had an answer.

CHAPTER 31:
TRAVELING SONG

French

FOR A WHILE, I THOUGHT MAYBE I COULD JUST LEAVE, go running after Rose, now that Mitch was gone. But the tracker flashing in the bush before I could smash it meant the Recruiters were on their way, might even be in the area now. The only good chance I had—that *we* had—was to stick together and run forward, and fast.

"What happened out there, anyway?" Tree asked once we slowed our run to a fast walk.

"Recruiters." I couldn't give details. Not now. I wasn't ready.

"But where's Mitch?"

"That's for later, Tree," Miig jumped in. "Let's give French some time now."

I nodded my thanks to Miig, who nodded back. I had to deal with both the loss of my brother and the potential loss of the rest of them once the truth got out. That would take time. He offered that to me.

✦✦✦ ✦✦✦ ✦✦✦

I hoped the tracker had been destroyed before it could transmit a readable signal to Mellin's minions, but I had no way to know for sure. We kept up a fast pace because it was possible we really were being hunted. We made it to the rendezvous point about an hour after dawn and stayed vigilant. We couldn't afford real rest, not now. Not when we were so close. Everyone took turns scouting and sleeping while we waited. I stayed in a tree, refusing relief.

"I'm fine," I shouted down whenever someone offered. "Not tired. You go grab some shut-eye. I got this."

✦✦✦ ✦✦✦ ✦✦✦

At the appointed time, the train slid over the land like a smooth snake and paused without shutting off the engines.

We boarded one by one, helping Wab up first, though she complained about it. "I can do it myself, Jesus. I'm not an invalid. Watch your hands!" She slapped us away as best she could, but her roundness made her aim less accurate.

"You'd better get your beating arm back in shape before this kid starts walking. You're gonna need to land a swat or two," Isaac joked.

"That's old-school parenting," Slopper interjected, bent with hands on knees so Wab could use his back to steady herself as she climbed into the car. "Besides, this is Wab we're talking about. She'll just have to raise an eyebrow, and they'll duck and cover. I do."

Even Chi Boy laughed. They were all a little giddy now that the train was here and we were actually getting onboard. We didn't have a plan beyond getting to the States and staying in a safe house for a few days, but that was enough right now. Everyone was buoyant—everyone except Miig and me. We watched the trees for movement and bodies. Even now, the rest of them didn't know how close we had come to capture. The Recruiters were probably waiting by the closest road. I watched the sky for unknown lights, listened hard for the roll of tires or the crunch of feet past the dark edge of trees beyond the tracks. I wouldn't relax until we were over the border and under new jurisdiction.

"We'll be up front. We have papers that say we've been given permission to visit New York State hospitals to see where they're at with a cure," Rania explained as she moved boxes and packed our bags into one wooden container. "The U.S. likes to think that we're moving toward their way of thinking."

I was the last to board the train. I thought about what Mitch had told me. Farms. They weren't ditching the schools; they were repurposing them. How could dreams be transferred in to such poisoned heads? I couldn't imagine minds capable of making schemes like that also being able to create nighttime cinema of swimming through the stars or losing teeth by the handful. But it didn't take depth to build cruelty, only a profound lack of hope.

Theo and the conductor placed each of us in our own wooden box, long and narrow with small breathing holes drilled in them, stamped with labels like MARITIME BLUEBERRIES and 100% PURE MAPLE SYRUP that weren't so obvious at first glance. Then they screwed the tops down tight. Lying still, I listened to the grind and squeal of the metal against wood with an intoxicating mix of fear and relief. We were trapped, but at least we were away. On the move to somewhere else, somewhere far away from schools and the dead boy in the woods. Away from the truth that had put him there.

The box was hard; it was not forgiving, but I didn't deserve forgiveness. I wasn't sure what I deserved. Maybe exactly this—to be trapped in a coffin-shaped pine box with just enough space to scratch an itch as long as I didn't have to bend a knee or turn on my side. Or maybe this box was what Mitch deserved. When I closed my eyes, all I could see was his feet sticking out of the underbrush—one shoe, one sock. I could spot his ruse clear as day—the sock was clean, no holes. The school officials really should've take those details into consideration. A traveler with clean socks was unheard of. I made a mental note before realizing what I was doing—gathering intel like a good little agent.

I shook my head. What the hell was the matter with me? No, the information wasn't for them. It was for us. Keep the note, but use it for the group; check the socks of any future strangers we might come across. As if I'd let anyone get that close to us ever again.

On this journey, I had nothing but time. I wasn't used to being so passive, to letting the miles slip by without the effort of physically gaining them. I used all these minutes to imagine what Rose was doing right now as we trundled over the land along unending tracks in boxes stacked under more boxes. Correction: what Rose and Derrick were doing. On the one hand, I was glad she wasn't alone. On the other, why did it have to be Derrick, of all people? And why just the two of them? I didn't trust that guy farther than I could throw him, and right now I couldn't even flex to reach my own neck, let alone anyone else's.

The journey wasn't the smoothest. The rails were knitted by overgrowth in some places. Everywhere it could, the Earth was taking back space, one brick and one track at a time. The movements of our car were louder than they were jostling. I settled into the small rocking motion, back and forth, back and forth, trying to move with the sway instead of fighting it with tightened muscles. I wondered if this was how Wab's baby felt when she walked around. At least she wasn't running now. And if this worked out for us, she wouldn't ever have to anymore.

After years of sickness and mismanagement, the U.S. had finally elected a decent president. She was the one who called for the no harvesting law. Down there, it was illegal to scoop dreamers up. Not that that stopped people from doing what they thought was best for themselves, which was why it was still dangerous for us there. They had gotten used to brown lives being disposable, used to it being okay to throw us into cages because of something as shallow as politics, being okay to kneel on our necks until breathing was impossible. It was easy to imagine what they would do if they thought their lives were in danger and that we, the disposable, could bring that danger to an end. But at least there, we'd have the law on our side, for once. I stopped my brain from reminding me of all the times we'd been the exception to the rules—the forced relocation that history forgot to account for, the missing women no one looked for, the crimes against us that had gone unpunished . . .

That was enough. I needed to sleep. Nothing to do but rest before the next leg of the journey, and who knew what waited for us on the other side. We never knew. We just knew we had to stay ready for anything.

I closed my eyes. But the nagging feelings of both having forgotten something and having committed an unforgivable act weighed heavy on me. So heavy I started to feel claustrophobic. My breathing got sharp and shallow. I whimpered a bit, and that sound amplified the panic. I had to calm down. We had been told this journey would last hours, and now was not the time to freak out. Instead, I focused on the tracks clacking below us. If I paid enough attention, the sound turned into music, a muffled shuffling and gentle clicking. I tried to find the rhythm and match my heart to it.

Words came to mind now instead of horrible images, words I had memorized to keep them safe. They became my traveling song, and I offered them up into the confines of this box and my broken heart.

I have to get out. Help me. I am forgetting the words. I forget my children's faces.

They're changing the game. Tell the leaders to burrow. Tell them to take up arms. It's the only way.

One thought kept breaking through—Rose. Where was she? I couldn't do any of this without her. I thought about the way she laughed with all her teeth showing. How she kept her eyes clear of anger even when she was shouting at me so that I knew it was temporary and that if I said the right words or did the right thing, her anger would melt away like summer snow.

"Oh, Rose," I whispered into the anxious corner of my moving tomb. "I don't think I'll find you. I can't hold on without you."

✦✦✦　✦✦✦　✦✦✦

I must have successfully matched my heartbeat to the rhythm of travel, because it was the train slowing down that pushed me awake—gasping, slamming my forehead when I tried to sit up to catch my breath.

THUNK.

"Ow, Christ." It took me a few seconds to remember where I was: in a box on a train speeding toward the United States of Freedom and not strapped to a wheelchair or hooked up to machines in a bed in some residential school, waiting to be drained. But then, why was I still so scared? My armpits stung with nerves and new sweat. Something was wrong. Something was very wrong. I knew it before I heard the first yell.

"Get out! Nice and slow, that's right. You too, missy. Hands up where we can see them."

I lifted my palms and pushed against the lid of my box. Still screwed into place.

"Shit."

Nothing to do but lie here and wait and try to be as small and quiet as possible. Luckily, I had learned that lesson well at the school. So instead of panicking, I listened, trapped inside what might turn out to be my coffin after all.

"What do we do with the driver and this one up here?" one called.

"Neither is the brand we're looking for. Tie them up and leave them. They don't deserve any better than that," came the answer.

"There's a woman here!"

"Indigenous?"

"Can't tell."

"Pack her up and bring her. Waste not, want not."

"Search the cars!"

"You search the cars, they're dirty."

"Well, who told you to wear white on a mission?"

"Excuse me? How are you any kind of expert? I mean, how many cat sweaters does one person have to own before they are officially considered insane?"

"Ladies, ladies. You can both search the cars. Look for the signs: smells, sounds, dark corners, piles of material, and containers with breathing holes. And do not think for one minute that the cargo is tame. Remember the drill. We must remember that the hostile will act . . ."

"Hostile," a chorus answered.

And then the doors starting sliding open, banging back against the walls so hard the insides of the train shook—*my* insides shook.

And then a whisper in the dark of the car:

"Here, piggy, piggy, piggy . . ."

I held my breath. And waited.

CHAPTER 32:
MOTHERS, DEAREST

Three Days Before

MOMS DO WHAT IS BEST FOR THE CHILDREN. ALWAYS. It was rule number one in the handbook. There were twenty rules in total, each with bulleted points, but this one? This one was number one.

Adelaide McKenna had argued that it should be the organization's motto instead of being grouped in with "Cleanliness is next to godliness," with its twelve sub-points.

"It's the central principle of MOMS. It should at least be in a bigger font." Adelaide had issues with the formatting of the handbook in general. She'd brought it up every meeting since they'd been distributed. It started with the fact that the manual consisted of typed pages in an inch-and-a-half-thick binder labeled with hand-lettered stickers. "These holes aren't even reinforced," she'd remarked the first time she'd seen it, tearing out the first page to demonstrate.

"Highlight it, then, if you feel so strongly," Shirley-Rachel Mitchell responded. She had typed up each page herself and wasn't budging. "Besides, we already have a motto."

And they did, drafted by all twelve of them, including Adelaide McKenna, and approved by Elizabeth Purdue, the Founding Mother herself.

"Securing Our Future By Any Means Necessary"

—The Mothers of Meaningful Slumber (MOMS), Inc. 2041, Albany, NY

It was on page one of the handbook in bold eighteen-point Times New Roman. Underlined, even. And centered. That was as extravagant as President Purdue would go. Someone had once suggested changing it to Helvetica, and she had retired to her upstairs bedroom to lie down.

Ten years of hardship had beaten them all down, Adelaide included. "My Jimmy has been put into an induced coma. The meds came too late for him. And now I am back to changing diapers and singing lullabies. And he was on track to be the next governor of New York State."

Everyone knew Adelaide's son had been a stoner with bangs that covered his forever-red eyes and a penchant for sending unwanted pictures of his privates to random classmates even before he got the Plague. But the MOMS sat quietly while she spoke, as was their way.

Not one of them breaking the code, not one of them pointing out that before the coma, Adelaide had been in the middle of signing little Jimmy up for military school down in Georgia. She had cut his bangs the first day he was put under, not that he needed to see better. His eyes remained closed day in and day out. But at least now she recognized her boy as the boy he was in her heart, the boy he was meant to be all along.

"Damn meds are doing nothing but making us into zombies," said Shirley-Rachel. She was respected in the group—she was a great secretary and always brought the snacks—but there was the matter of her smoking. Not that she did it indoors, but she went outside so many times for quick breaks that her clothes and skin reeked. And because she was the secretary, they had to wait idly each time or fill her in on everything she'd missed so it could be entered into the official minutes.

"Honestly, the same damn four dreams every time. Every damn time. You'd think they'd get HBO involved in the lab so we could at least have some variety. I'm about to jump off a damn bridge. And I would, except jumping off a bridge is already one of the four dreams, so why bother?"

Veronica Smythe was the newest member, and Adelaide was still suspicious of her. She wasn't alone in the feeling, but she was the only one who spoke her distain out loud, even if it was mostly after the meetings, when a few of them would meet for coffee or quilting. "What's with the name? Veronica seems a little fussy, doesn't it? And Smythe with a *y*? Well, that's just putting on false airs."

Veronica had gone from a shamed teenage mother to a local celebrity when it became clear that her unexpected pregnancy nine years ago was one of the last few in the state. She was even in the paper, in between stories about the goings-on in Canada and the updates on dream enhancers that were announced monthly by the president and her chief medical officer from the White House lawn.

The MOMS had good reason to be suspicious. Veronica had only joined at the insistence of her friend Maggie McConnell, and she had yet to join in on any of their darker deeds. Like their latest plan to secure their future by any means necessary.

"Do we really think we can do this?" She was holding her coffee mug with both hands like a small child. "I mean, I'm just not sure I could."

"We are all going to do this. Not one of us is hanging back," Adelaide began with a sigh. "That's why we gather in the first place: to take action where our woman president will not. I mean, come on. There's a viable cure right there in our faces, and we're just going to ignore it and keep lining up at the dispensary for her ridiculous potions?" She threw her hands up. "Jimmy doesn't have time to wait around for her to grow a pair."

"It's just . . ." Veronica's voice was as small as her grip.

Adelaide had had enough. "It's just what, Veronica? Do you really want your child growing up in a world without art? Without literature? Without innovation? Because that's where we're headed. People can't dream anything but these manufactured dreams, and the whole progress bus takes a detour to Broken Town. Maybe not as fast as people without the meds, but we'll get there, sure enough."

Veronica bowed her blond head and sniffed.

"Right?" Adelaide was leaning forward so far on the edge of her folding chair that the back legs lifted. She waited for an answer. She got one in the form of a reluctant nod.

"Good." Adelaide continued, now that she held the floor. "Now, I think we need to talk about our home base again. I still maintain that the best possible location is my house. It's detached, so there's no worry about close neighbors. And it's a quick drive to Walmart for supplies and the Super 8 for those who choose to stay close."

Elizabeth Purdue cleared her throat. She had been sitting on the settee by the window, where the best light poured in this time of day. Her lavender pleated skirt fell gracefully to her calves. Her waist was cinched with a simple white belt, showing off an admirable figure for a woman nearing eighty. She still had her hair set once a week and wore lipstick to match her outfit. She was an Easter parade in the living room.

"Adelaide, dear, we've already settled this. We are making Shirley-Rachel's home our headquarters. It's located outside city limits. She has a pool house with cement walls and enough room in the main house for some of us to stay overnight." She turned to Shirley-Rachel to make sure she took the note. "We'll figure out a way to determine the order; those who stay there will not get priority over those who don't. We'll always wait until we gather. And of course, I will be staying at my own home. There's just simply no way I could sleep out."

"Of course." Shirley-Rachel made the note.

Adelaide tipped her chair back to the ground and folded her arms over her chest. None of these bitches knew how to be a vigilante. In fact, they refused even the word *vigilante*. But that's what they were, striking out on their own to provide what the government could not, would not. She was starting to think maybe she should strike out on *her* own, especially since she knew something the others did not . . . not yet, anyway.

"I would like to just say," Kelsey Jones interjected, lifting a well-manicured finger, "that I offer up my house as an alternate. Seeing as my sweet mother-in-law is in critical condition, it might be easier for me to be close to home, just in case."

"In case you get a chance to slip her some of the goods before the rest of us get it?" Adelaide hadn't meant to say it out loud, but there it was, hanging in the room, floating above their heads inside the embossed wallpapered walls. For a few seconds, there was nothing but the loud ticking of Elizabeth's grandfather clock.

"Adelaide McKenna, you take that back. I would never—"

"Ladies, please." Elizabeth cut Kelsey off before it could get heated. After all, she was still the undisputed queen of this small kingdom, even if her fiefdom ended at her gated driveway. "The decisions have been made, and everyone knows the rules. We have worked too hard to get someone on the inside, and this opportunity is too perfect to tear down with selfish squabbling. And let's not forget, it's not just the government we need to worry about. It's all the groups sprouting up, running around like wild men, snatching anyone with a suntan. We don't need to lose our prize to a bunch of backwoods drunken hunters, not when we've come this far."

Kelsey's face was vivid red under her powder, mostly because she *had* been planning on skipping the line. "Yes, Mother."

Elizabeth turned to Adelaide, locking eyes with her until the younger woman bowed her head like Veronica Smythe and nodded just as timidly.

"Good. Now." She clapped her hands to indicate the matter was settled. "There is cargo retrieval left to suss out. Shirley-Rachel? You have the map?"

"Sure do." She put her notebook on the coffee table and reached for her spring jacket. "Let me just take a quick break, and we'll get right to it."

Every woman in the room exhaled at the same time. Another break.

"Shirl, why don't you just leave the map while you go out for fresh air so we can start studying it?" Veronica said kindly.

Kiss-ass, Adelaide thought.

"Suit yourself. Map's in my tote bag." She flapped her hand toward a canvas bag with a picture of two cats on the front. "And the train schedule. In the green folder." Then she let herself out onto the back deck, flicking her lighter even before the door had slid back into place.

Veronica got the papers and spread them out on the coffee table. The women pulled their chairs in closer. Those farther back in the room, the half dozen lesser members, stood in the spaces in between.

Miranda had done good. She was their mole in the nurses' smuggling network. She also happened to be Adelaide's first cousin. It was through her that Adelaide had the inside scoop on the Canadian schools and what they were offering. And it was a good offer. One that, depending on how this went, she might take them up on.

"Okay, so we have enough vehicles lined up to take the whole group?" Elizabeth asked.

"Three minivans, a pickup, and my Fiat," Veronica answered.

"Excellent."

"That car is ridiculous. Looks like a regular-size car took a dump." Adelaide had had quite enough of Little Miss Uterus today.

She couldn't wait until things got back to normal and they could go back to shunning her for getting knocked up before she had her braces off.

Elizabeth chose to ignore the comment. They had work to do if they were going to pull this off. "Miranda went to great lengths to infiltrate the network," she said. "She has assured us that the next delivery to Albany Station will be Wednesday at precisely noon. Of course, we will be there well before then. The route is not often used, and I had Frank take care of the stationmaster already. Turned out he hadn't been paid in over a month so it didn't take too much cajoling."

Frank was Elizabeth's husband. He could cook a decent croque monsieur and was quick with his checkbook, so they'd enjoyed a lovely fifty-year union. Now they had four children and six grand-children. Elizabeth's life was full. Starting MOMS meant keeping that fullness healthy. Frank was getting odd lately, and she was worried about the possible side effects of the dream meds. It was either that or senility.

"Do we know how many we're getting?" one of the lesser MOMS inquired.

"It is unclear at this point, but we do know it's going to be more than one individual, so we don't have to worry about being too . . . fragile." Elizabeth thought that was a lovely way to put it.

"And the nurses they're traveling with? What do we do with them?"

Elizabeth settled against the cushions and adjusted the gold rings on her fingers. "Well, dear, I suppose we let them go, and the conductor as well. No use in harming them. What they're doing is illegal, so there's no need to worry about any of them going to the authorities. And it would be just dandy if they kept right on doing their jobs so we had more deliveries to look forward to."

Veronica sighed, pulling back from the group huddling around the map and the handwritten schedule.

"What is it, dear?" Elizabeth asked her quietly while the conversation continued about who was bringing guns and who would be riding with whom.

"It's just . . ." She winced. It was hard to even imagine participating in violence. And what if there were children? "It's just, if we do this, aren't we no better than the rest?"

"What rest?"

"The domestic terrorists. The backwoods drunks running around grabbing the Natives. Aren't we doing the same thing? Aren't we exactly the same?"

Elizabeth laughed. It was a rare sound that shocked the room into silence. "Oh, my dear, no. No, no, no." She patted her lacquered chignon. "We are doing this for the children, because, as dictated by rule number one . . . ladies?" She raised her hands like a conductor in front of an orchestra, and the group responded like a well-timed overture.

"Moms do what is best for the children. Always."

"Exactly." She approached Veronica and put a soft hand on each shoulder, her Cheshire Cat grin matte lavender. "And my dear, we follow the rules. After all, *we* are civilized ladies. Not some gang of wild savages stowing away on a train."

"And when they get here?" This was what Adelaide really wanted to know—the action part. Just how action-y would it be?

"Well, we'll secure them, we'll conduct some research and test- ing, and we'll carefully measure out the cure." Elizabeth was already tired, and annoyance was slipping into her tone.

"Research? Measure out? What about those of us who need a solution, like, yesterday?" Jimmy needed Adelaide to stay angry if he was going to get better.

"Meeting adjourned." Elizabeth clapped. She was done.

So was Adelaide.

On the drive home, Adelaide used voice messaging to text Miranda, their woman on the inside, the one who'd spent months getting into the inner circle. Also the person she'd first gotten drunk with at thirteen and whom she'd stayed close to when the shit started to hit the fan.

"We need to talk."

She didn't mince words. She never did. Mincing was for Presi- dent Purdue and that wimp Veronica. They could mince all they wanted. Adelaide was ready to take what was hers. The Canadian schools were offering a reward for the return of "lost assets," and not something stupid like a bag of cash or the key to some Podunk Canadian city. No, they were offering special dispensation for an informant to relocate to Canada with their immediate family. Can- ada, where you could have all the straight-from-the-source dream serum you needed. Forget the MOMS and their hesitant and mea- sured pace. Adelaide could make sure Jimmy got more than enough to come back to her and then some.

"I think it's time to reach out to the school people. I'm tired of this shit." Her phone beeped to confirm the message was sent.

If there was one thing Adelaide knew, it was that being tired didn't mean you would be able to sleep. She was lying in bed, wide awake and reading a romance novel, when Miranda texted back:

"Roger that. I'll make a call."

Her phone screen was still glowing when she put a receipt between the pages to mark her place and set the book down on the nightstand. Then she settled into her pillows in a bed made too wide by her husband's recent absence and fell asleep. If she could have dreamed, it would have been a good one.

CHAPTER 33:
WELCOME TO THE LEISURE DOME

French

"TAKE THEM 'ROUND BACK."

The voices were muffled, but I could still make out the words. The box tipped and swayed dangerously. I banged my head twice before the motion stopped, and I was dropped so abruptly the wind was knocked out of my body. The women were conversing as they worked.

"Jesus! Be careful. Don't be bruising them up."

"They're not fruit. And, I mean, does it even matter at this point?"

"Yes, it does, Kelsey. We're not sadists, for Christ's sake."

"We should have asked the men to help."

"Adelaide, you know we can't. No one is to know what we're up to until we can make sure it works. Remember, we don't need to be building anyone up for yet another letdown."

"It better work. This morning I found my curling iron in the freezer. So either I'm losing it, or Larry is."

"Larry didn't have it to begin with."

"I heard that, Shirley-Rachel. And you are being very unkind."

"Well, to be fair, it coulda just as easily have been you. I'd say you and Larry are a matched set."

"Thank you . . . wait a minute . . ."

In between their bits of conversation, I could hear my family. Slopper kept asking "What's going on?", Wab swore a blue streak, and the twins called for each other while Miig tried his best to reason with our captors from inside a coffin.

"Hello? I think we can talk this out. There are children here, and we need to consider what this means for all of us, especially them. You don't seem like the kind of people who would want to harm children."

"We don't harm children; we happen to be in the business of saving them. And you? You're hoarders, keeping all the dreams for yourself. Why even bring up our children?" one woman answered.

Miig was quiet after that, maybe scared for the first time since we'd been hijacked off the train. Once you realized the shapes under the bed were actually monsters and they didn't speak your language so you couldn't even reason with them, it was time to panic. We had obviously been grabbed by monsters, even if they did smell like floral perfume and strong soap.

The loud screech of metal and wood. I took a few deep breaths, preparing to spring out, wondering what the others were planning. I was greeted by strong beams of light from flashlights, then arms reaching.

"Let go!' I squirmed away from one hand, only to be grabbed by another.

"Adelaide, get the needle," someone shouted. There were more hands, shadows of faces behind the flashlights, then a sharp pinch in my thigh. Then the edges of my vision started to shrink in. There was only one light, and then a face leaning in, all teeth, no smile, a halo of blond curls and the flash of gold earrings.

"Nighty-night."

✦✦✦ ✦✦✦ ✦✦✦

At first I thought I was back at the school, in my room, waiting for a grey-scrubbed man to swing by and get me for morning kitchen duties. It wasn't a bad feeling, just one without any lightness, any curiosity or hope. But at least I was alive. I tried to wipe my eyes, they were so heavy, but I couldn't get my hand to my face. I pulled and got it to my chin, but that was all. Then I heard the others.

"Can you push the side? Lean back and put your feet up on the opposite side. Now push!"

"It's not budging. Dammit."

"Okay, okay. Rania, can you reach the cage?"

"The chains are too short."

Cage? Chains? I opened my eyes and looked around.

The room was small and beige. A single bare bulb hung in the center of the ceiling. Around the perimeter sat every member of our group: Rania the nurse, Miigwans, Isaac, Slopper, and Chi boy, and on the other side of a doorway, Tree, Zheegwon, and me. And between the nurse and me was Wab, locked in a cage not much bigger than a kennel. In fact, that's exactly what it was: a modified dog crate. And every one of us was restrained—tied, locked, or chained to metal loops embedded in the cement walls. Above the door was a long, narrow wooden sign painted a cheerful ocean blue; written in cursive letters was WELCOME TO THE LEISURE DOME. To the left of the door was a stack of faded life preservers. The air smelled of chlorine and sweat. There was one small window high up in the wall above me, but it was closed and covered with short curtains on a wire rod.

"Where are we?"

"A shed or something. In a backyard." Slopper sounded tired, but his eyes were wide. "There's a big pool outside. With water in it. Never seen one with water before."

"A pool?" I couldn't put the pieces together. We had been on the train on the way to America. Then there were voices—women, maybe a dozen of them—and then a car ride, and then the struggle. I remembered the hands and the light and then the jab. I had been sedated.

"Were you all drugged?"

There were nods.

"Not me," Slopper spoke up. "I pretended to be all calm. So I could watch."

"Nice one, Slop," Tree said. "How many . . ."

"Wait . . . where is Theo? And the driver?" Rania sat up all the sudden, fear overcoming lethargy.

"I heard them. They left them at the station, tied up." Isaac tried to make eye contact with her while she shuffled around, pulling her body one way then the other with little give.

"So we made it? We're . . ."—I looked around, pulling at my restraints to test them—"safe?"

"Apparently." Wab's arms were folded across her chest, resting on the top of her belly. She snorted. "Welcome to the land of the free."

"Jesus." Rania managed to get on her knees, straining to see how much movement her ties would allow. "Vigilantes."

"Vigilantes?" Slopper screwed up his face. "Who is that?"

Miig sighed, pushing his back against the wall. "There's always vigilantes. They're groups of citizens who decide to take matters into their own hands."

"They're bad down here." Rania rubbed her forehead against her shoulder. "People aren't happy the government doesn't support mass experimentation or the collecting of Indigenous donors for the dream deficient. So they do it on their own. But how the hell did they know we were coming?"

"Never mind that now. How the hell do we get out of here?" Zheegwon bent his head to examine Tree's restraints. "Yours are rope, the nylon kind. Better get to work . . ."

"We have to mind it now!" Rania was growing frantic. "Do you know how many shipments the network makes every week? We're talking about hundreds of people. We need to plug the leak now. I need to get word back." She looked around the space. There was nothing visible that could possibly help, not unless she planned on swimming back and needed a life jacket.

"We can only do that if we get out." Zheegwon was steady, especially for a guy who had already suffered at hands of "regular citizens" along with his brother before Miig found them hanging in a barn with pieces cut out of them. He tried to reach Tree's restraints with his teeth. Tree took over speaking without pause. "So, you think someone talked?"

"Someone had to have talked." Rania shrugged, "But who would do that? I can't think of anyone in the network . . ."

Wab, who was not tied up inside the cage, turned to lie on her side and cleared her throat. "French, what happened to your brother, though, for real? Could he have, I don't know, been captured and interrogated?"

"No." My voice was low, but everyone leaned in to listen. Obviously, they'd had their own conversation about this already. A missing kid doesn't exactly go unnoticed. "Not a chance."

"I'm not saying he's a rat, I'm just thinking maybe they, like, forced it out of him," she continued. "Maybe—"

"He's dead." I spat it out. "He died before anyone could get to us. Like I said, not a chance."

Chi Boy made eye contact with her, and the twins stopped fidgeting.

"What happened?" Slopper's mouth was agape.

"This is a good time to remember that we tell our own stories when we are ready," Miig interjected. "This is part of Frenchie's coming back story, a part that is painful and wholly his. All *we* need to know is that French knew Recruiters were on the way, and that he got us to safety, and that Mitch was not capable of sending word to any group that might have been down here, not while French was with him."

I had to come clean. This was my family, and who knew if we'd even get out of here. I owed them the truth. At least Rose wasn't here to hear it. I exhaled slow and loud. Here we go.

"Things were crazy inside. People, they have to do things—"

"The important thing right now," Miig interrupted, staring straight at me, not even blinking, "is that we need to stay together, undivided, and get out of here. Any distraction, any rupture, could put all our lives at risk."

The room fell silent for a minute. He was right. Now was not the time. I swallowed hard, pushing the bundle of grief and guilt and torment back inside. It was a painful relief. In the pause, we heard voices outside.

"I think we should start right away. Why sit around waiting?"

"Because we have to do this right. And we've already gotten into the celebratory chardonnay."

"Damn right, we did." There was the crash and tinkle of glass exploding on concrete. "Woo-hoo! That's what happens when you leave us alone to stand guard all night with a cabinet full of good white wine. Ha!"

"Jesus, Kelsey. Elizabeth is gonna be pissed if she hears about this."

"Ooooo, what's Elizabeth going to do? Banish me? Strangle me with her mummified hands?" She groaned like a movie monster, then laughed. "Just because she's old doesn't make her god."

"This is a bad idea . . ."

"Just shut up, Shirley-Rachel. And help me get the door."

There was rustling just outside: grunting and the sounds of chains dropping and locks popping. Zheegwon sat up, and Tree shuffled back against the wall. Wab sat in the far corner of the cage. Everyone tensed. We waited.

The door creaked open, and flashlights shone in. One beam hit Chi Boy in the face, and he squinted hard but refused to look away, his mouth set in a hard line.

"Shit, the overhead light is still on."

"So? What do they care about a light when they're tied up in a damn pool shed?"

The flashlights went off, and two women entered. The first one in was dressed in a beige tracksuit and running shoes, her red hair in need of some new dye. She stumbled over the stack of life jackets not two steps in.

"Oh, shit." The flashlight went rolling across the floor and stopped in front of Miig. No one had free hands to grab it. She recovered quickly and scooped up the light, glaring at Miig as if he had tried to take it, burying any embarrassment in anger. "That's mine."

The second woman stepped carefully over the pile of life jackets and kept her back to the door. She held her light tucked under an arm so both hands could hold a small .22. "No one get any ideas. This isn't just purse candy," she remarked, eyes moving around the space nervously. She wore pajamas in a soft mint color and flip-flops on her feet, each nail on her fingers and toes painted bright pink.

"Wow," the first woman said. "Look at all this!" She held her hand out and looked back at the gunslinger. "So much meat!"

"Shirley-Rachel, don't be crass," the woman replied, her shiny bob (no grey here) bouncing at her shoulders. "You know what, let's just get out of here before someone comes to check on us."

"Jesus, Kelsey, relax. You want to help your family or not?" She was obviously drunk, swaying on her feet, talking too loud.

The brunette hesitated, then tilted her chin up and adjusted her grip on the gun. "Hurry up, then."

The redhead walked the small circle of the room, looking each of us over, pointing as she passed. "Eenie, meenie, miney, mo . . ."

"Just get on with it!"

Shirley-Rachel spun to face Kelsey. "Calm down. What do you feel like? I think we should go with something young." She spun to face Slopper, who recoiled into Isaac's shadow. Then she grimaced. "But nothing too fatty. I'm on a diet." This made her laugh, and she snorted.

"Shirl . . ."

"Okay, okay, back to shopping." She turned back to where she had left off. "Well, nothing fatty leaves you out of the equation," she said to Wab.

The look on Wab's face? Holy hell, if there hadn't been bars between them, Wab wouldn't have been the only person missing an eye tonight.

The woman in the beige tracksuit approached, head held at an odd angle, her face twitching. She took small steps on white sneakers until I could feel her breath on my cheek. I closed my eyes. I could hear her teeth snapping open and shut and then the low rumble of a growl, like a spool of ribbon uncoiling up her throat.

At the last minute, she turned and zeroed in on Zheegwon. "This one." She pointed a thick finger at him, and Kelsey swung the gun in that direction.

"No!" Tree struggled to reach his brother. Zheegwon had gone pale and silent, not even breathing. There was a new look in his eyes, as if he had left his body. His lip quivered. He had been through this before, years ago. His eyes said he wouldn't make it through a second time.

"Leave him alone!" Tree was frantic. Shirley-Rachel pushed the screaming boy, and he fell onto his side, arms twisted painfully behind his back. She started fiddling with the bike chain that held Zheegwon.

"Dammit, why'd we have to use this thing?" she snarled, kicking at Tree as she spun the numbers on the inset lock.

"Ran out of cuffs and rope. So much for being prepared," Kelsey answered before yelling at Tree, "Calm down before you get shot!"

"Okay, okay, got the first three numbers. Do you remember the last two?"

Wab kicked at her cage. Slopper was wailing now, and Rania was trying to reason with them. "This is ludicrous. You can't just take their dreams like this. I'm telling you, you're making a mistake . . ."

"If you want the best dreams, you take the best dreamer." Miig's voice cut through the panic.

"What's that, old man?" Shirley-Rachel answered without looking up.

"I'm just saying, if you have one shot at this and you want the most potent magic, you'll take my marrow. I am the Elder of this group. Therefore, I have the best dreams." He sounded calm and spoke evenly.

She stopped spinning the dials and looked over at him. "Is that so? And just why would you volunteer?"

"Because that's the thing about being the leader. You have to make sacrifices. You know what I mean. You're out here doing this because you are making sacrifices for your children, right?" Miig was playing a dangerous game. I watched and listened with nothing to offer. Should I stop him? But then what—let Zheegwon be taken?

"How do we know your bones aren't all dried up?"

"Well, you'll just have to take my word for it. But you know old Indians can't lie," Miig replied, clearly betting on the fact that mainstreamers were vastly undereducated about Native people, that they relied on hokey stereotypes and romantic tropes. "Might as well unlock my cuffs—no combination to remember. I won't fight. Just take me instead."

Isaac leaned toward him. "Miig . . ."

"I gladly offer up my dreams in place of the boy's. It would be a noble sacrifice. Who do you think has more to give, anyway? A young boy who's only ever known struggle? Or a man with a life-time's worth of experience and joy?"

She dropped and chain and nodded to Kelsey, who nodded back, then swung the gun in Miig's direction. "No funny business, now, old-timer."

She retrieved a ring of keys from the front pocket of her hoodie and made her way to Miig. I tried to yell, to tell them to stop, to tell them to take me instead. But all that made it out was a long, low groan. What now?

✦✦✦ ✦✦✦ ✦✦✦

Once he was led out, the rest of us sat in a haze of thick fear. It hurt to breathe in that space without Miig. Surely they would kill him. How could they not? They had barely led him out of the room without bumbling around, and he was cooperating.

"I'm sure he has a plan. He'll escape and come back for us," I tried. But no one answered.

We listened for sounds of escape or pain or the report of a gun ending our hope. There was nothing. Nothing but crickets in the weeds and Slopper whimpering in the corner. We'd fallen asleep from exhaustion and the remnants of the sedatives we'd been given when the door finally opened again. I slid back up the wall, sitting as high and alert as I could. I knew from the shuffling around me that everyone else was awake now.

"*Shit, shit, shit . . .*"

"Shut up, Kelsey, just get him back in his spot. Lock him back up. Hurry!"

"What's wrong?" Isaac was zero-to-a-hundred frantic.

Miig groaned as they dragged him across the floor, the side of his shirt rust-colored and wet. One of the women hit her head on the hanging bulb, and it swung wildly, making the room an abstract rendition of itself, illuminating one face, one scene at a time—Wab's fingers clenching the bars, Isaac's wide eyes, Miig's head hanging between his shoulders as they laid him down in his original spot.

"We are in so much trouble." Kelsey's voice was high-pitched. She put a hand over her mouth to stop it.

"He'll be fine. He'll be fine," Shirley-Rachel repeated.

"But I've never seen so much blood."

"Kelsey, stop it! Knock it off. Jesus, why did you let me do this?"

Kelsey stepped backward, trampling one of the life jackets. "Me? This was your idea!"

Shirley-Rachel finished securing Miig. Isaac strained, trying to reach him. "Yeah, well, you're the one who went all Annie Oakley in here with your damn teensy gun."

"Ladies, ladies." Rania raised her voice, and surprisingly, they stopped. "I'm a nurse. I can help him."

"How? We're not untying you." Even now, Shirley-Rachel was hard and calculating. "It was just a cut. Well, a few . . . the first one wasn't big enough, so we had to kind of go sideways . . ."

"All you need to do is tie my hands in front instead of behind my back. Leave them a little looser so I can reach him, and I can stop the bleeding."

The women looked at each other, thinking. "Maybe they won't be so mad if he can still be harvested, right?"

"For god's sake, do something! He's still bleeding!" Isaac screamed.

That snapped Kelsey into action. She pulled out her gun again and pushed it into Shirley-Rachel's hands before retying Rania's rope so that her hands were in front with a few more inches of give.

"Good, now run inside and get me some supplies. I need a sewing kit and clean towels. And antibacterial cleanser, if you have it."

"Why the hell would we have that?" Shirley-Rachel was getting calm again. She was also getting sober.

"Saline solution. Like for contact lenses. Hand sanitizer. Or bring me hot water and salt." Rania was already pulling Miig into a better position. Now I saw where the bleeding was coming from. The whole front of his shirt was soaked through.

"I'll go. I don't want to lose a whole unit. We'll get kicked out for sure," Shirley-Rachel huffed.

"*We'll* get kicked out? I didn't plan this," Kelsey squealed.

"Yes, you idiot. This happened on both our watch." Shirley-Rachel was angry now.

She turned and ran. We waited for long minutes while Rania bit the edge of Miig's shirt until there was a small tear and then ripped it straight up the middle. The gash was on his right side, just above his stomach, and it was wide and oozing. Thankfully, he had passed out.

"What the hell did you take?" Rania asked, pushing gently around the edges of the wound.

"A rib. Well, a piece of one, really," Kelsey answered.

"Monsters," Isaac hissed, tears on his cheeks.

The older woman came back with a round cookie tin, a stack of dishcloths, a personal-size hand sanitizer, almost empty, and a cooking pot filled with steaming water. She carried a glass saltshaker in her mouth. She put everything down beside Rania and spat on the concrete floor. "Yuck. Salt."

"We'll need drinking water as soon as possible, too," Rania said, already opening the tin and assessing the contents—needles and thread and an assortment of useless buttons and thimbles. "And pain relievers—aspirin, ibuprofen, whatever you have."

"Look, lady, this isn't the Hilton. You get what you get." Shirley-Rachel scratched her forehead with the barrel of the gun and turned to her friend. "We need to get back up there and clean up before the next shift arrives. We can hide this for a while. Maybe come up with a story. Maybe he tried to escape?"

Kelsey nodded enthusiastically, better now that she had a task and maybe a way out of this. They left without another word or a glance back. They locked the door securely, and I heard them run around the pool and up to the house.

"How bad is it?" Wab called from the corner.

Rania didn't answer right away. She threaded a needle and mixed salt into the water before speaking. "Let's just hope he stays unconscious for a bit." Then she cleaned her hands with the sanitizer and got to work.

✦✦✦ ✦✦✦ ✦✦✦

It was hours before we heard anything else from outside. Rania kept us updated on Miig.

"He's running hot. When the water's cooled off, I'll try to keep his temperature down by wetting his forehead."

"Wound is closed, and the blood is clotting now."

"Swelling is a bit much, but cold water will help. It'll be ready to use soon."

"He's a champ. Already looks a little less pale."

The sound of cars coming up the drive made me hopeful for minute before I realized new people could mean a repeat of last night's attempt at extraction. I caught Chi Boy's eye. "You hear that?"

He nodded.

A few minutes later, there were voices just outside, and the door opened. In the sudden burst of full sun, I saw four figures. They stepped inside, including an older woman in a floral print dress. "Ladies and gentleman, my name is President Purdue, and I am . . ." She stopped talking and her small smile disappeared when she saw the streaks of blood on the floor and Miig with his shirt off and his middle bandaged with dish towels and Isaac's sweater.

"What in Jesus's name happened here?"

Three other women stepped forward to look, each one carrying a wicker basket. They gasped and muttered amongst themselves behind the older woman, never raising their voices. Clearly, she was the one in charge.

"The idiots you left us with last night cut open my husband." Isaac was all fire and wrath. "Took his rib like animals and brought him back here to die."

"Is he dead?" she asked, leaning in but not coming any closer.

"Not yet."

Rania jumped in. "But if you want him to be okay, and you do, we need ibuprofen and ice and some drinking water, to start."

The woman turned back and nodded to a blond in a white sweater set, who handed her basket off to another before heading back to the house.

"Anything else?"

"Freedom would be nice," Wab remarked from her cage. "Or a gun, so at least it's a fair fight. Hell, I'd take a pointy stick right about now."

The old woman smiled again. She waved the women forward, and they placed the baskets on the floor in front of the nurse. "You'll find food and water in there. Some empty jugs so you can relieve yourselves, and a few moist towelettes to clean up." She turned to Wab. "But no weapons, I'm afraid."

Wab gave her a fake smile in return.

The woman turned and spoke only to Rania. "Veronica will bring what you've requested. It would be a shame to lose one, but we have so many, so . . ." She shrugged, and Isaac threw all his weight in her direction.

"We'll be back later to check in and begin. Right now we have an important meeting, with one of your own, actually—a nurse on the inside, as you would say." She savored the look on Rania's face. "Yes, that's right, we aren't some hillbilly crew of hooligans. We have a mole, and she has been quite useful, as you can tell from your current predicament."

"Who is it?" Rania fought to keep her voice even.

"Oh, don't you worry about that, dear. You just tend to the herd as best you can and keep them fresh for us." The blond came back in with a canvas tote bag and placed it beside the baskets. "There, now you have everything you need. Behave while we are gone, and maybe I'll give you another hint. For now, be a dear and take care of these." She waved a hand around the room.

She clapped, and the women all stopped whispering. "Okay, ladies, let's see what the big update is, shall we?" She paused. "Oh, I am putting an armed guard outside for all of our sakes. And Veronica?" The blond woman snapped her attention back from Wab. She'd been having a hard time looking away since she'd gotten back with the medicine and water. "You're to remain here at the house in case someone is needed."

The woman lowered her gaze in deference, taking one last peek at the caged mother-to-be.

"There will be no more unplanned procedures. From now on, everything will be followed to the letter like it's supposed to be. And I will personally deal with Kelsey and Shirley-Rachel. The fools."

She turned on a low heel and walked out, her flock falling in behind her. The door slammed shut, and the sound of chains and locks echoed inside.

"Stay here," the old woman barked to the sentry outside. "And for god's sake, don't move for anyone. We could be a while. After the mole, I have another appointment. Recruiters are crossing the border now and are requesting a meeting as soon as possible. Someone from within the organization saw fit to inform our Canadian friends about our guests, and now I have to deal with them. Do let me know if you hear who might have broken confidence, will you?"

"Yes, ma'am," the sentry replied.

Footsteps retreated up the path to the house, and then the small pop of a sliding door pulled closed.

Slopper's eyes were big. "Did she say Recruiters?"

And that was the exact moment Wab's water broke.

CHAPTER 34

SOMETHING WICKED THIS WAY COMES

Agent Mellin

AGENT MELLIN INSISTED ON COMING SOUTH. IT TOOK some cajoling to make it happen—after all, she had made the decision that had allowed the escape to happen in the first place. Why the hell had she believed those idiots? How could two half-blooded rejects have pulled this off? Well, almost pulled it off. They'd found Agent Dusome's body that morning, his eyes pecked out of his skull. What had he expected, throwing his lot in with forest hobos? He'd gotten what he deserved.

Sitting in the back of a black government-issue car, Mellin traced the shape of the arrow on her thigh with her finger. "Idiot," she said under her breath, and leaned forward to look through the front window.

They were stopped at the border: two cars with diplomatic license plates and a paddy wagon behind them. An immigration officer with a semiautomatic was looking over papers handed through the open tinted window of the first car.

"What's taking so long?" She threw herself back against her leather seat.

The driver regarded her in the rearview mirror but said nothing.

They were on a schedule. The group had been detained by some gang of roving women, one without the wherewithal to know what the hell they were dealing with. Mellin had taken the call herself.

"I know where your Indians are," the voice had told her.

"How do I know you're telling the truth?" She'd been skeptical but still excited, snapping her fingers for a Watchman to start a trace in case she didn't get a location.

"There's an old man, and a pair of twins, and one with a shaved head . . ."

"Shaved head? A male? About seventeen?"

"Yup, that sounds about right. Anyway, I want assurances—"

"What kind of assurances?" Mellin had written ASSEMBLE TEAM NOW! on a small pad of paper as she spoke and tossed it at the Watchman, who took off at a run.

"Me and my boy, we want to get to Canada. He needs the serum."

"Of course." Mellin was oil slick. "We can do that for you. Where exactly did you say this group is?"

"Oh, they're in our custody. I can give you an exact address."

By the end of the call, Mellin had the name of the informant, Adelaide something or other, the location, and the men ready to bring back their stolen goods.

It was nearing nine o'clock and dark as only the country could be when their engines purred across the border. She had reached out to the people holding her property—better to negotiate a peaceful return herself than risk any involvement with the U.S. government. They were apt to offer the runaways political asylum, and then none of them would end up getting what they wanted. A meeting had been set. After that, if things were still uncertain . . . well, Mellin had a backup plan. No matter what, she would return with her cargo. Her job depended on it.

Sliding along the road under a fingernail moon, the Recruiters synchronized their watches and loaded their weapons. Soon, things would be back the way they should be, with every Indian accounted for.

CHAPTER 35:
BLOOM

French

THE MOON NEVER LOOKED LIKE ANYTHING OTHER than itself, even when it changed, chasing itself from sliver to full to sliver. But it had this ability to remind you of exactly the thing that haunted you.

It was night. I knew that because the curtain on our one window was open about three inches. The sky was navy, but in layers, and the moon was low and slight. Tonight, that moon was a gentle curve of creamy white. Tonight, the moon was the rib sawed from the scaffold of Miig's chest and ripped out. Tonight, it wasn't something in the sky; it was a spot taken out of it. It was a hole. It was loss, a rib-shaped absence.

The room was full of the smell of pennies and salt. The concrete walls and floor and that one high, locked window had kept the space cool. But now a new, dark humidity muddied the air. It was easy to be quiet in this new atmosphere. It was like a church after the incense has been swung down the aisle.

Wab held the thin cage bars with both hands, each finger red at the tip and pale white at the bend. She strained and shimmied in the cramped rectangle. I couldn't watch. I couldn't look away.

"Breathe. Don't forget to breathe." Rania kept her voice even, calling over her shoulder while she tried to clean Miig's stitches with the small bottle of hand sanitizer and the hem of her T-shirt. She'd done the best she could with what she'd been given, but the stitches were starting to look puffy. I could see the worry in the way she scrunched up her eyebrows, like they were acting out while she herself tried to remain calm.

The real electricity in the room came from Chi Boy, who strained against his cuffs, every muscle in his chest flexed, his neck a terrain of cords and pulse. He'd been like that for six hours, since Wab's water had left her and started trickling down the drain in the center of the room. A slow drip of blood beaded off each thumb from the metal slicing its way through his skin and into the meat of his hands. He hadn't even noticed. I wasn't sure he was even breathing regularly.

Wab was on her back, her head tipped back against the cage, her hair tangled with sweat.

"It doesn't even make sense. It's unfair." Her words came out with pauses, like exhales.

"What is, Wab?" I leaned as close as the rope would allow so she could hear me.

"Pain. It's like being pushed under a freezing wave before you can cough out the last one and take a full breath." Her head lolled to the side and rested on her shoulder. "There's no way to say what it is, you know?"

I didn't know, so I stayed quiet.

"It's like, you could scream the edges, yell the borders, clench at the height and width, but there is no way inside the thing with words." The last part of her sentence was hissed, and she pushed her legs straight until her feet were flat on the opposite wire wall. The cage rattled as she pushed at the top with her palms.

"Easy, Wab, easy. Try to breathe through it." Rania's eyebrows were arched now.

After a full minute of very deliberate breaths, she bent her knees and rested her hands on her hard belly.

"You okay?" What a stupid question, but it was all I had at the moment. All I could think about in the moments between her screams was the potential of Recruiters. Would they take us back to the school? Truthfully, I wasn't sure it even mattered. Either way, we were as good as dead. Maybe it just came down to who would do it quicker.

"I can tell you one thing for sure, French," she said through closed teeth. "It hurts less to lose a fucking eye."

I felt like I had to pee, I was so stressed, and I was just a witness, a useless, inexperienced witness. God, I wished I could have traded spots with Rania. She could at least say the right things in that soothing nurse voice while keeping a close eye on what was going on instead of trying to twist around and only getting half the picture. And here I was, just trying not to piss myself.

It was terrifying, but there was also something darkly sacred about this work, about the excruciating turn and pull that threatened to knock Wab unconscious. I watched her fight against blacking out, wanting in spite of it all to truly live in each minute, to be present for the ordeal. She was having a hard time getting her muscles to relax, which Rania kept reminding her to do; it looked like she would sever her own fingers with the grip she had on the little bars. But she tried, flexing each one then letting it go, pushing her breath out as evenly as the spasms would allow. And when she could, she locked eyes with Chi Boy, who had barely blinked since labor began. Silent and out of reach, he told her everything she needed to hear. I avoided looking his way, it was so intimate.

On the other side of me, Tree was holding his bound hands out behind his back, twisting them in opposite directions at the wrist, back and forth, back and forth.

"What are you doing?"

"Creating slack," He answered.

"Why?"

"If I can get the rope looser, someone can use their teeth to start pulling on the strands."

"That works?"

He glanced at Zheegwon, and they both nodded. I thought about them before they'd come to us, captured and held in a barn. If anyone knew how to get out of a rope, it was them.

I tried to mimic their movements.

"Won't work," Zheegwon said.

"Why not?"

"You have to keep your wrists a bit open when they first start tying you," Tree responded.

"Damn," I hung my head. "You should've told us before."

"When? When you were passed out cold?" Tree sneered.

"Maybe we should have asked them to wait. We could have been like, 'Excuse me, ma'am, I just need to do a bit of an escape tutorial here, could you come back in twenty minutes when my friend comes to?'" Zheegwon was the more sarcastic of the two, though neither was chatty enough to really be hurtful.

"Fair point," I agreed. "At least now one of you will get out. Then you can help the rest of us."

"Maybe," Tree said.

"Not any time soon," Zheegwon assessed.

I looked back at Wab, who let out a long, anguished groan before hooking her feet on opposite walls and grabbing her own thighs. "Hopefully soon enough."

✦✦✦ ✦✦✦ ✦✦✦

Things only intensified and then stayed that way for hours on end. None of us could bring ourselves to talk about the threat of Recruiters, not now. Now we needed to hold space for Wab. Miig had roused an hour into her labor and was starting to feel a bit better. He and Isaac sang old songs for her. Tree keep trying to get free, twisting the skin straight off his wrists, though that didn't stop him, and I whispered whatever sounded encouraging to the back of Wab's head. Slopper slept on and off. That was his go-to in times of high stress: sleep. I envied him. But Chi Boy, he never stopped his vigil, not for one second. Both his hands were covered in thick red blood, his eyes rimmed pink and bruised blue underneath.

The key was to help Wab stay calm. Once or twice, she flipped right out, kicking the cage until the metal screeched against the concrete floor. Rania gave her instructions. Wab had to be her own midwife, checking progression, moving into position. Sometimes Rania had to yell, and sometimes she was able to whisper. All we could do was wait. No one came to check on us. But then again, why would they? As long as we were making noise, it meant their marrow supply was alive.

When the baby started to come, oh man, those were the longest minutes in history. I'd always known Wab was strong, but I had no idea what that even meant until I watched her deliver her own baby. She was on her hands and knees, rocking back and forth. We all rocked with her, counting, yelling out encouragement, breathing with her. The head appeared, and she turned onto her side, holding it. She had to scoop out the mouth and clear the nose. The baby was all grey and quiet as she guided the shoulders free. The rest came quick, and she rubbed at the little body with her sweater, getting the blood flowing and the warmth back. Right away, it turned from grey to brown and sneezed. Wab laughed. After all that, she actually laughed, and the baby started crying.

We cheered. It had really happened. It had seemed impossible, but Wab and Chi Boy had a child. We had a child. Even now, our family was growing.

"Hi, Daddy." Wab held the tiny baby, downy skin and curled fists, up to the side of their cage. The steel grid couldn't hide the shock of dark hair, starting to lift as it dried. Couldn't mask the quiver of her bottom lip. Couldn't hide her father's eyes, looking steady across the dim room at the man she'd inherited them from.

Chi Boy opened his eyes and blinked, the first tear escaping. He cried out like a bird, like an animal, like nothing I'd ever heard before, and then he wept, the tears streaking clean marks down his face.

"Ishkode," he said, his tears striping down his chin like paint.

"Mmmm, a good name for one who's going to bring change." Miigwans grinned and spoke a little louder. "I can't wait until you can tell us who you are, little one, until you can share your coming-to story. Until then, we'll do our best."

Wab tried to hold back her own tears, but they came anyway, covering the baby in her water again. "Ishkode," she repeated, whispering it into her hair. "Ishkode. Like your daddy. Like your family." Wab placed her on her lap and set about delivering the placenta and severing the cord with her teeth.

"It's beautiful," Rania said. "What does it mean?"

Slopper had been studying Anishinaabemowin since Minerva was killed, working to keep us all alive with the words she'd left us, the ones she'd carried forward against all odds, so we could make sure the new kids coming could curve their tongues around those sounds, could rattle the consonants against their baby teeth. He was the one who answered. "Fire. It means fire."

Miigwans was tired again, his face covered with sweat. "Things are different now." He closed his eyes, sighing as he lay back. "Sometimes you need fire to clear the path forward."

"Guys?" It was Zheegwon. "I think I found a way out."

CHAPTER 36:
WHAT'S YOURS

Adelaide

JIMMY WAS ALL PACKED AND PROPPED UP IN HIS wheelchair. Adelaide wheeled him to the front door before she did her final walk-through of their bungalow.

The family portraits were still on the wall. She didn't need those. They all included Harold, and since he had left them for a woman in Duluth, they would leave him here to fade in the wooden frames. She hadn't bothered giving their food and linens away. That might draw attention to their departure, and she didn't need anything coming between her and the north. North was where she was going to find a new home. North was where Jimmy would come back to her. Plus, fuck her neighbors. What had they ever done for her?

She packed their toiletries and a couple changes of clothes and the medicine they soon wouldn't need. The school lady had told her to bring no more than a duffel bag each and maybe a back-pack. There wouldn't be room for more. She'd been far more help-ful than Adelaide had assumed she would be, walking her through the next steps: meeting with the MOMS, loading the cargo, swinging by to pick her and Jimmy up . . . and she'd assured her that no one would know the identify of the squealer. They'd figure it out when she didn't show up for the next meeting, but by then, what would it matter?

"As soon as we take possession of the runaways, your agreement will be formally set, and we will come by and pick up you and your dependent," she'd said.

"And you're going to get them for sure, right?" Adelaide was nervous about this part. What if Purdue was uncooperative? What if they refused to make a deal?

There was a short laugh on the other end of the phone. "Oh, we will get them. For sure."

Adelaide had laughed, too, not sure if it was just nerves. She wasn't used to being nervous. She was used to taking charge and moving forward with her back straight. And that was just what she did now, closing the bedroom doors, throwing a few granola bars into her purse, and returning to the front door.

"Any time now, Jimmy. Any time. And we'll be on our way to the promised land."

After an hour, she went outside and sat on the front stoop. The wind had picked up, and she crisscrossed the sides of her sweater over her chest, glancing at her watch.

"Any moment now . . ." she whispered to herself. Behind the screen door, Jimmy slept through it all, his blank dreamscape as empty as their driveway.

CHAPTER 37:
HERD

French

ZHEEGWON HAD REMEMBERED THAT HIS BIKE LOCK had almost been opened when they'd come for Miig. In the turmoil that had followed, none of us had given it a second thought. "She got the first three numbers, right?"

I nodded. "I watched. There's two left."

"So, I mean, eventually we'll get the right ones, right? It's only two, and there are only ten possibilities each."

"Ten for the first number—you knock one possibility off the second digit from the first combo on digit one if you're looking for a specific order. That means there's a hundred possibilities," Slopper answered. We all turned to look at him.

"What? I'm little, not stupid," he answered.

"Good boy, Slop." Chi Boy beamed at him.

"I mean, that's assuming she got the first three numbers right. She was pretty wasted."

"Well, it's worth a shot." I shuffled as far to my right as I could get. "Let's give'r."

Taking turns, Tree and I reached and flicked the two remaining knobs one at a time, panting from the stretch as much as the moments when we held our breath, waiting for Zheegwon to try to pull his hands apart.

"Nope."

Another try.

"Nope."

And another.

Miig had gotten new dressings and taken a bunch of pills, some of them vitamins that had been helpfully slipped into the tote bag. Whether or not one-a-day vitamins were really going to help a man who had been deboned like a smallmouth bass was questionable, but Rania added them to the aspirin and ibuprofen anyway. "Couldn't hurt," she'd said, shrugging.

Now he was able to talk a bit and drink some water. The rest of us ate slices of buttered bread off our knees and drank Gatorade out of squeeze bottles held by the person beside us behind their back. Wab was the only one who could eat normal because her hands were free, but her bread had to be folded up to fit into the cage.

"Great, an origami lunch," she joked, but she ate it as fast as she could, dropping crumbs on Ishkode's fuzzy head as she nursed. Chi Boy refused his share and gave it to her. Wab paused to smile at him before downing that slice, too. She was softer and also somehow more cutting than ever. There was a new desperation in her features now that there was more than her, more than us, to worry about.

The baby was mostly quiet, sleeping hard and working to get milk from her mother.

The day had changed from a soft haze outside the window to a howling rage of rain by the time the blond returned. We had time to sit back and pretend at lethargy before she got in, since the door was firmly chained. We'd been through sixty-two permutations of the combo by then.

"Hey, y'all," she stepped timidly into the shed.

We didn't answer.

"I brought you some more food." She shook a Tupperware container stacked to the lid with cookies.

She held out the container, then awkwardly pulled it back. "Oh, I guess you can't really get to them." She pried the lid off and tucked it under her arm. "I baked them just now, so they're still warm."

The room was flooded with a smell I'd never smelled before, and my whole head filled up with saliva.

"Chocolate chip," she giggled nervously. Here we were, tied up, cuffed and caged, about to get ripped inside out, and she was the one who was nervous. "My daughter's favorite."

She shuffled her feet in her cheap sandals and tried not to make eye contact. "I'll just, uh, I'll just do this." She walked around and placed two cookies in front of each person, close enough so we could bend over and pick them up off the ground with our mouths. She hurried past Miig with a hand held just below her nose.

"Yeah, blood isn't the best smell, is it?" Rania scoffed. "Better skedaddle before the harvesting really begins, then."

"I'm so sorry," the woman whispered.

"Veronica, is it?" Miig asked in a small voice.

"Yes, sir."

"Thank you, Veronica. We appreciate the food." He didn't reach for his share. She placed a third cookie on top of his pile nonetheless.

Sometimes Miig and his damn manners really pissed me off, like now. Why should we be thankful for scraps of food when we could be out in the world getting our own without having to worry about getting slit open and pulled apart?

Veronica paused at the cage and crouched down. She picked out half a dozen cookies and broke each of them in half. "Oh my lord, the baby!" She grabbed the bars, dropping crumbs everywhere. She craned her head this way and that. Wab stayed very still, following her movements with her eyes only.

"Oh my gosh. Oh, that baby is sweet! I have a daughter myself. Angel. She's nine now."

"How nice for you," Wab answered sarcastically, arms crossed over her swollen chest at the back of the cage. "Maybe one day, our kids can play together. Oh, wait . . ."

"I'll just give you a few extra." She fumbled with the container. "I know how much fuel you need to feed a new baby." She tried to smile, but there were tears in her blue eyes. She could not look directly at the baby anymore.

"Oh, and did you also give birth in a dog cage?" Wab refused to reach for the treats as they were pushed through the bars, so Veronica placed them inside on the floor.

"I'm really sorry," she sniffed. "I had no idea they would really go through with it. I mean, I have to think about Angel. And I certainly had no idea one of you would be carrying." A single fat tear plopped onto the front of her sweater.

"Then do something about it," Wab challenged. "Open the cage."

"I cannot. I just can't. Never mind what they would do to me—what might they do to my sweet Angel? Well, I just couldn't live with that."

"And you can live with keeping a newborn in an animal cage? I can't even stretch out. It's all blood and water in here. I'm in pain." Wab was bordering on pleading but wouldn't go that far.

"It won't be much longer. Mrs. Purdue called. Recruiters want you back, but they don't know about this one, the baby, so we get to—" She stopped herself. "Anyway, at least she won't ever know those schools." Veronica tried to sell this news as mercy.

"No! You can't have her!" Chi Boy was as loud and abrupt as I'd ever heard him. The baby startled and began to whimper.

"When are the Recruiters coming? How many!" I was frantic, panic climbing up my guts. All I could see was Mellin. All I could hear was the loud pitch of the Correction Room siren. And then I remembered there would be no Correction Room for me, for any of us. It would all just be . . . over.

Veronica spun around, like she had forgotten the rest of us were even there. "I mean, don't you want the baby to stay out of those terrible places?" She looked around and stood up when she saw us all staring.

"So if she stays here, you'll let her live? What, give her a nice nursery and get on a wait list for a good daycare?" Isaac sneered.

"I . . . I really shouldn't be telling you this." She picked up the container and placed the lid on, rushing back to the door. "I shouldn't be telling you any of this."

"Veronica," Wab called, sharp and loud, before the woman got to the door. She refused to turn around but paused, hand on the knob.

"Are they going to eat my baby? Are *you* going to eat my baby?"

The container slipped out of her grip and crashed to the ground, cookies pinwheeling over the cement. She didn't answer, not directly. She just whispered, "I'm so sorry," and left in a rush so that the guard, a short woman with a shorter hair, had to close the door behind her.

Immediately, Chi Boy began pulling against his cuffs, straining so hard his neck was a bundle of cord and blood. He grunted with the effort.

"Chi Boy, stop, you'll pop your arms right out of the sockets!" Rania warned. Miig struggled to sit up, but she pushed him back down. "And you, you stop that now."

"We'll get it, the lock," I yelled. "We have to be close!"

"Hurry, French." Wab was pleading now, and the panic in her voice shot adrenaline into my limbs. "Before they come back and take Ishkode. Oh my god, please hurry! I can't believe they know now."

"Wait." I was confused. "You knew about the baby farms?"

"Rania told us. That's why we left in such a hurry," Miig answered. "We wouldn't have left Rose and your dad unless it was urgent. You have to know that."

"Dammit, Miig, you popped a stitch," Rania chastised him, opening the cookie tin sewing kit to repair her work. "Just lie still for a minute."

She rummaged around in the tin and then pulled her fingers back. "Oh my . . ."

"What? What is it now?" Miig tried to twist his head to see what was wrong.

The nurse lifted her hand to eye level as if to confirm it was real. A pair of shiny silver sewing scissors. They had been right at the bottom, under the packets of needles. Kelsey and Shirley-Rachel had been too drunk or too scared to check the tin, and now Rania was holding sharp, narrow sewing scissors.

Isaac exclaimed in Cree and laughed. "Wab, you see that? You see what we have? Scissors!"

Wab, who was cooing to the baby, rocking back and forth, looked up for a second. "Do something with them, and now. My baby will not die that way, not by their hand."

"Just hold on," Chi Boy called across the room, still trying to pull his blood- and sweat-slick hands through the metal cuffs.

"Leave the stitch for now and try to get free, hurry!" Miig hissed.

Rania opened the blades and used them like a saw, furiously running them up and down her ropes. After a minute, the rope began to fray. "It's working!"

"Okay." I pulled to the end of my reach. "Tree, I can get to the lock easier. You take the scissors after she's done. We're the only three with rope ties. Cut yourself free while I do this." He nodded, eyes glued on the nurse and her thinning bonds.

"Wab, we got this, you hear me?" I shouted over the din of everyone talking and shouting encouragement at once. She didn't answer me. Her face was smashed up against the sleeping baby's, rocking back and forth, eyes closed.

I pushed the combo dial one notch.

"Go!"

Zheegwon pulled his elbows wide. "Nope."

Another notch. "Go!"

"Nope."

"I got it! I got it!" Rania scrambled to her feet, the coils of rope dropping to the cement. She hobbled on stiff limbs to Tree and started sawing.

"Leave me, I'll do it," he said. "Go fix up Miig so we can get out of here the second we're all free."

"You sure?" She waited. He nodded, and she opened the blades and tucked the metal between his palms so he could get a good rhythm going. Then she ran back over to Miig and threaded a new needle.

"What about us?" Slopper called out. "We're in shackles!" He rattled the chains for emphasis, and my heart sank, even as I kept running through combinations.

I looked over at Wab, who had her eyes closed, and yelled, "Don't worry, Slop. Once we're out, we'll get you. We're not going anywhere unless it's together. All of us. We'll figure it out."

I clicked another notch on the dial and yelled, "Go!" I rolled my aching shoulders, ready to try again, but this time, there was a small click and the clatter of the lock hitting the floor.

"That's it!" Zheegwon tried to spring to his feet but had to sit back down when he almost fainted.

"Easy, now, we don't need any more injuries in here. Take your time." Rania tied off the new stitch and started pulling out new cloth to dress it.

After a few seconds, Zheegwon slowly stood. He pulled the baseball cap out of his back pocket and put it on, then leaned over and helped Tree with the last of his ropes. When it fell loose and his brother was free, they embraced, tight and short, and then Tree took the hat and put it on his own head.

"You're next, French."

"I can't get out of these cuffs." Slopper was getting flustered. "How am I going to get out?"

"Don't, little man, just hold on, we got you." Tree made short work of my ropes, and then I was free, and the twins crossed the room to get to Slopper. "Let's see. Maybe we can pick this thing."

I had just gotten to my feet and was reaching for the cage when we heard a car pulling into the driveway.

"It's too late, they're here!" Slopper's face crumpled. Isaac, who had been bouncing his upper body in excitement, slumped back against the wall and hung his head. Rania yelled for us to hide the scissors, so I kicked them over to her. She slid them under her thigh.

Footsteps approaching from outside. Three, now four voices.

"Everyone get back in your spots! Hide the cut ropes!" I knew we didn't have time to plan, but we could at least keep the element of surprise on our side. "Everyone ready?"

The door chains were being unlocked. I looked around. The twins had their backs to the wall with their hands behind then. My own ropes were under my butt. Miig was groaning but conscious, and Slopper had clean marks down his face from tears. Then I looked into the cage.

Wab was still rocking, but she was different, mechanical, not there. One hand held the baby, supporting her head, and the other hand was placed securely over the baby's mouth and nose. She was singing a traveling song slow and soft under her breath. Someone was leaving. Who was she singing for? Then I realized her hand was making a tight seal over the baby's face so no breath could get in or out.

"No! Wab, no!" I screamed, and the door opened.

"What's all this yelling in here?" Elizabeth Purdue stalked in, hands going to her hips.

"Now, Zhee, now!" There was no more time to wait. Not another second, not with the baby turning blue. Zheegwon sprang from where he sat directly in front of the old woman and tackled her to the ground. Her head hit the cement, and there was a loud crack. She never moved again. Then a gunshot rang out, and Zheegwon slumped against her.

Tree jumped up and over the fallen bodies and grabbed the guard who had shuffled in, rifle still hot in her hands. He struggled to take it, and they fell out the open door.

Another gunshot and another, so loud my ears rang and my vision tunneled. I couldn't make out particulars at first. I was focused only on the things I had to do right away—those came in clearly, a specific list to get through. I slid across the floor, banging up against the still-warm body of old Purdue oozing blood from her broken head, and pried the keys out of her hand. I tried key after key in the lock, swearing and shaking, until one fit and Wab's cage popped open. I yanked the door wide and grabbed the baby, blue around the mouth like she'd been eating Popsicles. Wab was shaking, eyes vacant, her body rebelling against the movements of her hands just a moment ago.

"C'mon, come on," I whispered to the baby, careful to cradle her dark head even as it lolled against me. I got to Isaac and laid the baby by his legs while undid his shackles. He grabbed up the baby so I could free Miig and the others. I unlocked Miig first, and he moved like a man without a wound, tackling an older woman in an oversize cat sweater who was brandishing a knife. At the same time, Isaac crawled along the wall toward Chi Boy. He placed the still baby down in front of her father and started the mechanics of getting life back into all the tiny places it should fit, tilting her head back and pushing with delicate fingers. Rania was staring up at the ceiling, our struggle reflected in her unseeing eyes. I hadn't even seen the bullet enter the shed from outside, but she was gone. I felt under her thigh for the scissors and closed them in a fist. The light bulb was broken, and the shed was darker than before. I turned on my knees toward the turmoil and came face-to-face with the open end of a gun barrel.

Veronica was holding the gun with shaking hands. Gone were the tears and cookies. When it came down to it, there was nothing left in her body but anger. Anger that we felt we deserved to fight for our lives. Anger that we would take something from her, from her own precious child. "You asshole!" She was screeching, wasn't giving directions, wasn't even trying to get me back into captivity. She was bent on killing, on nothing more than the math of bullet plus flesh equals removal.

"Drop it," she instructed, and the scissors clattered to the cement. Out of the corner of my eye, I could see Isaac still working on the baby, Wab still rocking in the cage, Slopper and Chi Boy being unlocked, and a flurry of movement in every corner. No one noticed this small standoff. Everyone was busy. And now I was going to die.

I closed my eyes and waited for the heat and tear, and then came the shot, loud and sudden and more like a scream than a bang.

And then, nothing. Just . . . nothing.

I opened my yes. Veronica was on her knees now, too, so that we were the same height, finally seeing eye to eye. The anger was gone; now there was only shock. Suddenly, with the anger ripped off like a wrapper, there was so much to be read in her face, and most of it was childlike confusion.

I could practically see her thinking, *This is not how it was supposed to end.* Where were her loved ones? Where were the lilies and platitudes? Where were the silk sheets and foreign doctors? She was dying in a dirty garden shed surrounded by strangers, barely even real people—a herd of animals.

Behind her stood a figure lowering their rifle—the shooter. Their face was covered in shadows, and their clothes were dark with dirt. Was this another vigilante, one who had gone rogue? Another nurse from the network who had been alerted to our predicament, maybe? I looked at Rania, dead in the corner because she believed in something beyond herself. Who else had we lost? I scanned the room, but it was impossible to guess. Bodies lay everywhere, so much carnage in this small space. Then the shooter reached up and pulled back their hood.

I didn't trust my eyes at first, with only the moon and the weak blue light wavering from the pool outside. Then she smiled, and I would have recognized that face anywhere, under any light, even if it was just the stars, so far away they were beads in a velvet sky.

"Rose?"

CHAPTER 38:
HOW ROSE ARRIVED—
A DIFFERENT COMING-TO STORY

Rose

SHE HAD LEFT DERRICK IN TEARS IN THE WOODS. SHE had grabbed up her supplies, "borrowed" Derrick's bundled tent and a flask of water from beside the firepit, and slunk back into the trees. She was half a mile away before she heard footsteps behind her.

"Derrick." She spun around. "I told you I have to go!"

Only it wasn't Derrick. It was Nam.

"Nam, what are you doing? Go back." Rose turned and kept walking, a little slower now. But they didn't turn back. They kept following until they were walking one step behind.

"I'm serious. You should go back. You're safe with that group. I have to find my old group."

"I'll stay with you." Nam's voice was soft.

"Why?" Rose threw up her hands. "I don't even know where the hell I'm going." She laughed a bit. This was the truth. She had Miig's directions and a good sense of where south was but had no idea beyond that. She had almost nothing.

"Just want to," Nam answered.

"I don't know what to tell you, kid. That's a bad decision."

"It's fine."

They trod on together in silence until Rose was sure they were far enough away that they wouldn't be found. There wasn't enough light left to walk safely. They set up the stolen tent and fell asleep almost right away, then started out the next day before the light even had a chance to fully return.

It went on like this for two days: walking to exhaustion, eating random greens, conserving water with sips, sleeping like the dead. And then they came across a small group—just a man and a small child—living in the middle of a circle of spruce. Like she had done years before when she'd first been on her own and found Miig's group, Rose watched from the periphery. When she'd clocked that their only weapons seemed to be a couple of steak knives and that the man was old and slow, they approached.

They didn't stay for a meal or accept his invitation to set up their tent for the night. What they did do was get as much information as they could. Word was that the network of nurses had been uncovered. There was chaos and death in the forest. The man said things were heating up at the border. People were starting to head south. If you could get through the flatlands—and that was a big if—the Appalachians and the swamps below them were supposed to be safe.

Without wavering, Rose thanked him for his information and wished them well and, with Nam beside her, pushed through the spruce.

"Wait," he called out to her. His voice cracked like the skin on his hands. The breath whistling through his loose teeth smelled of sickness, something deep and solid. "You have to take the boy."

He pointed to the five-year-old sitting quiet by their lean-to. If the boy heard, he didn't let on.

"He's real silent. Raised him without words, mostly." The old man approached them, walking like one does near animals—slow and even, no sudden movements. "He can't stay with me. I'm . . . I'm dying."

Rose looked him in the eye. "I know."

"So, so then, please . . . *please*. You have to take him with you. I can't imagine him all alone out here. He can't hunt yet." He tried to smile, putting his fingers together in the universal symbol of prayer.

Nam took a step toward the boy, and Rose grabbed them by the arm. "We can't."

"You can. You have to." The man was getting desperate. Nam swiped their eyes, wiggling the slightest bit to release their arm from Rose's grip.

"We aren't headed anywhere good. He's better off here, with or without you." Rose turned quick and slipped through the hard needles on the branches, pulling Nam behind her. Walking away, they heard the old man wail. They kept walking, didn't stop for the night until even the moon turned away from them and into the clouds.

Huddled under a tree that night, Nam refused Rose's body warmth and turned away instead.

"Nam, are you mad at me?"

"No, just sad," they answered, their voice small in the curve of a bent elbow. Crickets chirped in the grass around them. "Why couldn't we take him, the kid from back there? Why'd we just leave him?"

"We have to move fast, quiet. And we're not headed anywhere safe. It wouldn't be right to put him in more danger." Rose was tired, her muscles ticking into exhaustion, but she knew they had to talk this out. There was no room for space between them.

"We're taking risks for your family. How do we decide who's worth that risk? Maybe that kid was."

This made Rose stop. "I guess we decide. We have to. Look," she sighed, "you haven't spent a lot of time out here. You were probably barely walking when you left the rez. Shit's bad. You can't imagine."

Nam turned suddenly. "Oh, I can't imagine? What do you think would happen to me at the schools, Rose? Huh? I have more to lose than just dreams."

"Yeah, we can cease to exist," Rose shot back.

"I'd cease to exist before they ever cut into me." Nam was getting loud. Rose put a hand on their forearm, and they took a breath before continuing, low and urgent. "How do they keep us, do you think?"

"What do you mean?"

"Do they organize us based on size? How about age? Or more likely by gender—boy, girl, boy, girl. And what about those who don't fall into those categories, all neat and tidy?" They paused. "I would have so much taken from me—my name, my identity, my autonomy—before they even exposed the first bone."

Rose counted three crickets calling as she took all this in. Holy shit, how could she have dragged them out here, taken them on this crazy journey without giving a second thought to what they were truly putting on the line?

"Nam, I'm sorry. I didn't think. You should have stayed with Derrick—"

"Again, *you* are deciding who is worth the risk. No, I decided. I decided that getting to your family is worth it. I decided that I am the kind of person who acts, who goes out into the dark, who goes all out when they're needed. I decided I'm a community member the day you showed me community." They rubbed their face with a sleeve, their breath hitching.

Rose collected them in her arms, with the crickets singing and the stars starting to pop through the clouds above them. "You're my community, Nam. We got this. Whatever this is, whatever happens, we got this."

The next afternoon, they came across a rebel nurse. She was a little worse for wear but still eating. Her name was Simone, and she had chosen to stay out while others fled, in case travelers needed her. Turned out she was needed. She led Nam and Rose to a farmer who let them sleep in his barn overnight, even bringing out a big plastic bowl of instant chicken noodle soup for them to share.

"Donovan is headed across the border tomorrow. Delivery. He brings crops across once a week. A lot of farms on the other side were abandoned during the Plague, so the state is short on supply," Simone told them as they ate. "You can go across with him, but it's not gonna be easy."

"What is these days?" Rose replied between mouthfuls. The soup was still hot, but she couldn't wait for it to cool to eat.

"Especially now." Simone sighed. "One of our trains got stopped. Word is the driver didn't make it out alive and a nurse was brought back for questioning."

"Who stopped the train?" Rose asked. Nam was quiet, eating and listening.

"Not sure, vigilantes? Or maybe Recruiters?"

"Recruiters?" Rose dropped her spoon. It disappeared into the broth. "What the hell are Recruiters doing south of the border?"

Simone shrugged. "Someone must have tipped them off. They don't usually cross into the States. Too busy working towns and fields for the schools. Plus, it gets messy down there with jurisdiction and all."

"Wait." Rose felt panic rising in her throat. She tried to breathe through it. Throwing up her only real meal in a week wouldn't do them any good. "Was anyone on the train? Any . . . of us?"

"We're not sure. Probably." She saw the look on Rose's face and added, "But there's no report of anyone else getting caught. They must have made a run for it."

Rose stood. She was done eating. "What time do we leave?"

In the morning, they said goodbye to Simone, who was staying for others who might need her. They left their tent and some supplies with her, all but the refilled flask of water, a single backpack between them, some jerky and nuts crammed into their pockets, and Rose's knife. There was no room for anything else.

"I'll pass these along to other runners who need them," Simone assured them. "There's more than one way to save a life."

Donovan helped them into the false bottom of his truck, a claustrophobic space that really only had enough room for one, then piled crates of greens and bales of hay on top. Each new weight above them caused the wood to creak and bend. Nam was breathing quick and shallow.

"Stop that—you'll hyperventilate, and you can't exactly get some air now." Rose breathed deep and loud so Nam could mimic her. Then the engine chugged to life, and they began to move.

It was hours before they came to a stop. There were voices, muffled and quick, and then the truck bed was pulled down. The whole truck shook.

"Oh god, oh god," Nam whispered.

"Shut it!" Rose hissed.

Crate by crate, Donovan's load was pulled down and searched. Rose was sure this was it. Any moment, there would be the squeal of wood and metal, and then sudden light, and then . . . well, she wasn't sure. Death or capture, and she wasn't sure which one she hoped would come.

It took a minute to realize that the next sounds were the crates and barrels being slid back over them, then the thuds of bales being tossed into place. Then the engine chugged on again, and they were on the move. Rose cried without sound. It wasn't until Nam squeezed her fingers that she realized they'd been holding hands.

It was well into the afternoon when the floor hatch opened and Donovan helped them out. They were inside some kind of warehouse space, and they weren't alone.

"Welcome to the United States," a woman yelled. She had a machine gun slung over her shoulder. Two younger men stood beside her, each with an automatic rifle.

Rose shook her legs awake and jumped down from the bed. "Nice guns, jeez."

"We're gonna take you to a safe house. You can stay there for a few days, then we'll get you farther in, into a neutral zone," the woman continued, reaching to give Nam a hand down.

"Neutral zone?" Nam repeated.

"Well, that name's a little deceiving. No place is really neutral right now, but they're parts of the country that are not seeing much violence. We should give them a better name, but 'a slim shot in hell' is a little too long." She smiled. Her front tooth was gold.

They all sat down for sandwiches and coffee before Donovan left again, tipping his greasy baseball hat at his travelers. "Good luck."

"Thank you," Rose called after him as he climbed back into the driver's seat and the gates were opened so he could leave, off to deliver non-Native goods for non-Native people now that the Natives were handed over.

"Come, sit, finish." The woman with the gold tooth waved them back to the picnic table. "We should talk about where it is exactly that you'd prefer to go, which zone, if you end up having a choice."

She refilled their cups with strong coffee and was opening a tin of cookies when a new man, this one older and dressed in all black like the rest of them, burst in a back door.

"Fi, we got a report in!" He waved a piece of paper and jogged over.

"From the border incident?"

"Yup." He handed her the page and bent over with his hands on his knees to catch his breath.

"What's it say?" Rose was on her feet.

The woman read in silence.

"What the hell does it say?!" Rose felt that same panic from the barn.

The woman, Fi, looked up at her, took in her anxiety, weighed her options, and told her the truth. "A group of travelers, including a pregnant woman, were taken by one of the vigilante groups around here."

"Oh my god," Rose gasped. "That's Wab. It's them. Where are they? Where did they take them?"

"Relax, Rambo," Fi said, reading the rest of the page. "Ah, shit."

"What?"

"Says here the Canadian government has sent officials over to repatriate them."

"Repatriate them?" Nam asked, confused.

"They're coming to take them back," Rose answered, plopping back down on the wooden seat. "To take them to the schools." It took her a minute to regroup. "Are the Recruiters here yet?"

"Uh . . . they are expected to cross over tonight, a few hours from now," Fi said.

"You asked where we want to go, right?" Rose leaned across the tabletop.

"Yeah."

"There."

It was Fi's turn to be confused. "What?"

"I want to go there. You know the vigilantes, know where they are?"

"Yeah, but—"

Rose cut her off. "I want to go there."

There was a few seconds of quiet while everyone took this in.

"We can't engage. That would put the network in jeopardy, make it impossible to get other refugees across," Fi said.

"I didn't ask you to engage. Just take me there, as close as you can, and then leave." Rose didn't even blink.

"Us," Nam piped up. "Take *us* there . . . please."

Fi looked at the man in black, who raised his eyebrows. She pushed a hand through her short, dark hair. "Listen, you know that this is not exactly a neutral zone. In fact, it's kind of the opposite," Fi answered.

"Yeah." Rose was already on her feet. "But it is a slim shot in hell."

CHAPTER 39:
SUBTRACT AND ADD

French

WHEN THE BODIES OF THE WOMEN WERE ACCOUNTED for, we knew that we had lost three: Rania, Tree, and Zheegwon. But the baby had recovered, breathing on her own and back in her mother's arms with Chi Boy's wrapped around them both. Before grief could push us to our knees and make us frantic and useless, Miig started giving orders.

"Pick up our family—they come with us. No time to grab anything else but the weapons and water. We cannot go into the house. There'll be others arriving soon. We need to put some distance between us."

"But carrying them will slow us down. We have—" Isaac started.

"They come with us." Miig shut his lips tight.

Chi Boy stepped forward. "Miig, Uncle, we can't bring them, not now. Besides, this isn't them anymore."

Emotions played over Miig's features: anger, frustration, resolution, grief. Finally, he agreed to bring them into the trees behind the pool house—carefully manicured and trimmed, but still wild in a small way—and lay them on the earth.

Chi Boy pulled Tree over his shoulders, carrying him like a sandbag. Slopper and I shared the weight of Zheegwon, a weight heavier than I could have ever imagined. When their shared baseball cap fell off his head, we stopped to retrieve it. With both hands under his arms, I carried the hat in my teeth. It smelled like sweat and wood and home.

Isaac picked up Rania, her head lolling back on the stem of her neck, eyes watching the stars that witnessed our struggle. Rose gathered the guns and water, and then she and Miig closed up the shed, putting the locks and chains back in place to buy us time before our absence was noted.

We laid our dead under the low branches and stood quiet until we knew we risked adding more bodies to the pile, and then we walked away. Miig and Chi Boy took the twins' hat and a silver medal from the chain around Rania's neck and trailed behind us.

Wab had popped Ishkode inside her shirt and held her there with both hands, reminding the tiny girl's heart how to beat with the rhythm of her own. Her eye patch had been knocked loose in the fray and hung around her neck. Her ruined eye was a pucker and a slash, and for the first time, she didn't try to cover it, both hands tending to the baby, rubbing her back, smoothing the thin fabric over her bottom. She was in her own world, a world where she had to reckon with the fact that she had almost ended her baby's life before someone else could end it more brutally. She was different, quieter, pulling inside herself to somewhere we couldn't follow.

Headlights cut across the lawn.

"Shit." Chi Boy tensed, moving in front of his partner and child.

A truck headed straight for us, cutting up the sod and knocking over a low fence around color-coordinated flowers.

"Scatter!" Miig yelled.

"Just wait." Rose held out a hand to stop him. "Just wait a minute."

The truck screeched to a stop, turning at the last minute so the lights illuminated the side of the house, its neat trim and clean windows with jaunty drapes way creepier than any abandoned building I'd seen.

The driver's side window rolled down, the engine revving. A small face appeared.

"Get in," the driver said.

Rose's shoulders dropped in relief. "Oh, thank god it's you. Where the hell did you find this?" She turned to us. "Guys, this is Nam. They're with us."

Nam gave a short wave and answered, "It was parked out front, keys in it and everything."

We piled into the truck, Wab and the baby in front with Nam and Rose, the rest of us in the back bed. Slopper leaned over the side and yelled in the window, "You sure you know how to drive? You look pretty young."

"Bitch, I'm from the rez," Nam called back. "I've been driving since I got out of diapers." Then they pulled the truck around and lumbered back over the grass and onto the road.

I watched the house get smaller, the wind screeching between us and the property as if measuring distance in sound. The blue light from the pool marked the grave site we'd left; the tires crunched over the packed gravel.

"Where are we going now?" Slopper yelled over the wind.

I turned to look in the small window in the cab and saw the back of a head, curls escaping wild from a loose braid. And I couldn't look away. It was her. It was really Rose. She was back.

"Home," I answered. "I think this time, we might be headed home."

CHAPTER 40:
BEGIN AGAIN

French and His Family

MIIG, ISAAC, AND NAM TOOK TURNS AT THE WHEEL. We drove south until the needle was below empty. Then we refilled the tank from a canister stashed in the toolbox in back, which we smashed open with a rock. We kept going, driving until the truck sputtered and slid to a stop at the side of a back road surrounded by fields gone wild, sunflowers and vines between jagged rows of dusty cornstalks. It was a different landscape than we were used to, more flat and open, more terrifying than the darkest woods.

"Rania said the south is better—fewer people."

"Fewer vigilantes, too?" Slopper was obsessed with the idea of roving groups of dreamless militants. I supposed it was a break from the monotony of the one enemy we had grown accustomed to all these years.

"I don't know." Nam kicked a rock into the ditch, and the high-pitched screams of bugs paused. "Doesn't it kind of feel like they won? They chased us out of the country, for god's sake. And now we're down here."

"That isn't our border." Miig gestured north. "That's an imaginary line drawn by politicians and land prospectors. The only thing we have to worry about is who the original people are so we can honor the lands we are on. And if we do that, remember to keep doing that, they don't win. They never win when we remember."

We emptied the truck of supplies, then pushed it into a ditch and covered any parts that showed with handfuls of grass and overgrown crops. Eventually they'd blow off, and if anyone cared, they'd find the vehicle. But by then we'd be gone.

We crossed the first field and found a small thatch of trees.

"Here." Miig indicated a shallow curve in the ground under the boughs where a small pond had once been. Then he pulled out his bundle so we could make offerings and sing our lost ones on their way. We dug as best we could with no tools, enough to bury the hat and the medal. Miig ran his finger over the indentations on the front of the round charm before covering it.

"St. Roch's medal—patron saint of healing." He smiled, touching his fingers lightly to the wound on his side. "We are here because of this woman, because of what she did for us. I am alive because she raised her voice for me, even in the worst of times. That's what matters most. How you use your voice, and sometimes even your whole body, when things are at their worst."

The hat—the twins—that was done without words. Because there were no words elegant enough, no statements solid enough, to hold the weight of their loss. We concentrated on just breathing, on just standing. We were loud with breath and quiet.

When we were done and we'd watered the holy ground with our small grief—we still had to keep it small—we walked on. Later, we would cry, we would scream, we would laugh and tell stories of the beautiful boys who had been with us for so long, but not nearly long enough. But for now, we walked.

I wanted to talk to Rose, to hold her, to tell her exactly what she meant to me, but I had to talk to Miig first. I couldn't find words to begin to be with her again until I'd dealt with the burden I was carrying.

"Miig, you know, don't you? About how I got out of the school?" It was a question even though the answer was obvious.

He paused for a moment. "I do."

And even though I knew he knew, hearing him say it hit me like a rock to the face.

"I also know you only did what you had to do to get to us, to keep us safe." His eyes hadn't moved from the path ahead, the rest of the smaller family walking in front of us. We were at a loss, always at a loss.

"But what if I could have done more? Or less, I suppose?" I was edging on panic again. It was always so close by. "What if I'd just stayed and found another way, or even if I hadn't? What if I'd just refused? How can I live with this, with what I did? It's too heavy."

He slowed down to match my gait. All I could feel was Sunny's small hand in mine. All I could see was Sunny's eyes on me.

"Frenchie, weight is what holds you to the ground, to this ground. Otherwise, you might just blow away. And it can be unbearable unless you remember that our ancestors are there not just to pile onto the load you carry, but also to shoulder some of the weight."

I concentrated on my breath. In and out. In and out.

"When should I tell the others the truth?" It was barely a whisper, but he heard me.

"That's not for now. For now, we have to move. For now, you'll carry this alone. No one else can take that on right now. We've lost too much, and now we have a new life that needs all of our attention." He motioned with his lips to Wab and the baby. "So for now, it's only yours. Maybe you need that weight right now. So you don't blow away."

The sun was getting low in the expansive sky. Soon we'd have to stop, and we barely had enough supplies for another day. I heard what he was saying, that there were more pressing matters to worry about. Then I remembered something else.

"Miig, what was Minerva's last name?"

"Why?"

"Just thinking. Do you know it?"

"Yes, she was an Eliot."

I felt that knowledge in my spine, the understanding of it mapping out the contours of the very lattice that let me walk straight. I spoke the words on the napkin out loud.

"I am still Marguerite Eliot. I will always be Marguerite Eliot. Tell my mother that I am alive. She is an Elder and needs help . . ."

"What?"

"Her daughter, has to be. It's a message from Minerva's daughter. She's being held at the school." Once I said it out loud, I knew it as fact. "It has to be her."

Miig was quiet for a moment. He rubbed his chin, his eyes getting bright. Then he reached out and put a hand on my shoulder. "Then we have one more reason to survive. One more responsibility to take care of."

"We need to get through this so we can help the others, too," I said out loud. "The ones I had to . . . the ones I brought in."

Miig said nothing, but he kept his hand on me, so I knew it was still there. Even now, now that he knew everything, all of it, he was still there.

✦✦✦ ✦✦✦ ✦✦✦

I jogged ahead and caught up to Rose, who was walking with Nam. I wasn't sure if I could keep a secret from her, but I knew I couldn't stay away, not for another minute. Nam smiled and then split as soon as I fell in beside Rose, catching up to Slopper, who lit up a bit when they fell in step with him. Being so close to Rose was maddening, and we had to stop walking. She grabbed my hand and pulled me from the group, running just far enough away that we felt privacy.

"Rose, oh my god, Rose." It came out as movement pushing me into her. She touched my hair, the line of my cheek, my lips, and then met me halfway. And oh, it was everything.

"I knew it." She pulled away and spoke into my neck, arms wrapped all the way around me. "I friggin' knew there was no way you'd join them. Not you. Not after Riri. Not ever!" She squeezed me tight, and I couldn't breathe. I could barely stand.

She took my face in her hands. They were shaking. "French, I never gave up. They told me some bullshit story about you bringing in some people, but I knew it wasn't true. I knew they were wrong!"

I tried to respond. I tried to tell her that I knew she would never give up, that she was the very best of us, but there was too much in between the thought and the words. If I opened my mouth, I would scream.

"I almost stayed at the camp," she said, pulling her shoulders down and then back. I wondered if by "camp" she meant "with Derrick."

"But it just wasn't home. And Nam"—she turned a bit to indicate the slim figure walking with Slopper—"they came with me. We followed the map Miig left and ran into an old guy who told us—"

"You can't just talk to anyone out there! You never know who's real and who's . . . not." I grabbed her arms as I spoke. The thought of her stumbling into JP or someone like him made me panic, even now with her safe in front of me.

"Jeez, I know." She shrugged me off. "God, like I'm new to this?"

"How did you get across the border?" Fear had given me use of my voice again, and I needed to know everything that had happened every moment that we were apart, no matter how horrible or heartbreaking. "Did you . . . did you come with Derrick?"

"Derrick is not with me." She took a moment to make sure I was really seeing her. "Derrick was never really with me, French."

"But how'd you find us here, at that place?"

"Found the network, and they had information about a captured group. I knew it was you. I just . . . knew. So we made our way in. Then we had an opening, and we took it. And you, French? How did you get out of the school?"

So here we were, finally, and I held my truth: the truth of how much the Program had gotten to me; the truth of sacrificing two people so I could make it home without stopping to save even the youngest of them; the truth of all the moments I had hesitated, waiting on Mitch, hoping he would come with me, even when it put my family at risk. I held it all in one long, shameful scroll, and then I started folding, right there with Rose's hands on my cheeks, her smile exposing every tooth and crinkling up her dark eyes. I folded it over and over until it was tiny, until I could roll it down the insides of my ribs like a papier-mâché ball—one at a time, a bony staircase—and into the pocket below my heart, black and wet and empty till now. I had a secret. One day maybe I'd write it on a napkin, or I'd tell it at the fire, or maybe I'd expire with it there, soaking up my blood, swimming in my dreams, expanding until it made breathing impossible and I died in the pines like my brother, one shoe off, curled up like a fiddlehead. But I wouldn't speak it, not today.

"We had an opening, and we took it."

"We?"

"My brother, Mitch. He was with me. He . . . isn't anymore."

She squeezed both my hands, and we stayed there a moment, just that small connection, and it was enough for now.

✦✦✦ ✦✦✦ ✦✦✦

We rejoined the group and walked on until we came to a grove of dead trees, all of them tumbled to the ground and in different stages of decay. It was at the top of a gradual hill, so we could see the messy patchwork of fields all around us.

"Farmland. And I can smell salt in the air. Must be getting close to the ocean," Chi Boy said, softly bouncing the baby on his shoulder.

Miig shook his head. "I think that's just wishful thinking."

"Not too much, you'll make her spit up," Wab called. Rose was helping her get cleaned up with the supplies she had in her over-stuffed backpack. She was speaking again, which was a good sign, though she couldn't take her eyes off the baby, not for a second.

"I got her, don't worry." Chi Boy could barely stop smiling, even now. He couldn't stop marveling at the perfect beauty of his baby's face.

"I'll take first watch," I told him. "You have your hands full." I touched the back of my hand to the sleeping baby's side. She was warm and she was breathing, and that was enough for now.

I walked the perimeter of the hill while the others tried their best to set up a camp for the night. Some of the wood was dry enough for a small fire. We didn't have much hope of a hunt, so when Nam pulled a packet of dry noodles and a full bottle of water from their bag, everyone cheered. I watched Rose as I walked, too far away to hear her, memorizing every move she made as she spoke. She talked with her hands a lot. I'd never noticed before now.

In the distance, I could see roads still smooth enough for vehicles to take, the moving lines of herd animals traveling, the furry dots of tree clusters and a real forest or two, and a curious collection of decayed construction lifting above them. It took me a minute, but then I remembered why it looked familiar. It was an amusement park—there used to be places where people paid and lined up for the chance to be scared by dangerous rides and make themselves nauseated by spinning mechanics. I laughed. Oh man, what a weird place this used to be.

Eventually, the sky started to fill up with stars, so many at once it was like the Earth had moved closer to them, as if we had walked into the sky. I sat on the side of the hill and tried to count them. The distraction didn't last. I started worrying about our food supply. About the bullets we may or may not have left. About the direction we were headed and what would be waiting there for us.

The wind kicked up, and I wrapped my arms around myself, holding everything in, keeping everything out. A star pulled itself from the others and arced across the sky like a gesture of direction. And I was brought back here, to the place where this is what mattered: the people up the hill, the truth locked under my ribs, the very stars shifting and holding still at the same time.

I was warm and I was breathing, and that was enough for now.

Rose

NIGHT WAS PEELING BACK FROM SKY, REVEALING thinner layers and gauzy light as it went. Rose couldn't sleep. Out here, the grass swam with whistling insects, was pushed down by quiet paws. The sky was too big, too vast, too much space to get lost in. Nothing was holding her down except the weight of a boy's arm, the warmth of a boy's love, and those, too, could be too much. She slid out of French's sleeping embrace and crawled outside the circle. She stood and walked into the thick of the field, so riotous she could hear it working pulpy braids into the abandoned agriculture.

In the distance, the bones of an old amusement park scratched the horizon with splintered loops and creaking chairs held together with climbing vines where the rust had broken them free. If she closed her eyes, she could hear the echoes of excited screams and old laughter caught up in the wind. There were no remnants of greasy popcorn, no cotton candy, no animal shit or off-brand cigarette smoke. The smells were gone. The people were gone. But the sounds, those lingered somewhere in between the open sky and the snaking grass.

Sound has a way of living on and being noticed. When you are drawn forward, you say something is calling you. When you have a passion, you say it's a calling. Something was calling to Rose now. Something under the grass, beaten into the ground loosened by so many new roots. Or maybe something up in the stars, hanging like the ancestral portraits in the night gallery just above her head.

When Rose was a girl, she wanted to dance, but her feet wouldn't cooperate, and her pride made her stand still. She'd wrap her mother's old Fancy Dance shawl around her shoulders in the comfort of her bedroom and pull the yoke on top, some strings loose so that when she moved, beads fell to the floor. She didn't watch herself in the mirror, because then she would remember she couldn't do this. She couldn't dance. What she could do was fight, so she did that instead. Punching second cousins when they teased her for her curly hair. Putting townies in headlocks when they called her names she didn't understand but knew were poison by the way they festered under her dark skin. They couldn't decide if they hated her more for being from the rez or being Black, so they made weapons out of words, all the words they could find, and threw them at her. And now, even now, even after all that, she still couldn't dance. So she kept fighting.

Rose was a fighter, and sometimes that's nothing more than the choreography of survival.

Rose wanted to be a Jingle Dress dancer, but she never asked for regalia. By the time she was five, those dresses existed only in stories. Making noise drew attention, and attention brought in outsiders. So to be safe—to stay alive—the people had gone quiet. Except for the stories.

Eagle plumes fastened to the backs of their heads, small purses with tobacco offered in return for prayers, hundreds of silver cones hanging from bias tape tabs around bright material, Jingle Dress dancers were the healers. They made the noise that brought the healing; the first one came from a dream and allowed the girl who wore it to overcome her own sickness with a sound like nothing else in the whole world. Rose wanted to make that noise, but instead she made the sound of a knuckle against a tooth, a fist connecting with a kidney, the suck of breath being knocked out of a chest.

Rose was a fighter, and sometimes that's nothing more than the choreography of want.

She had never been to a powwow, had never seen a real Jingle Dress, but she knew the pattern by heart. Her grandmother had taught it to her, sitting at the kitchen table, drawing out the lines with a finger through spilled sugar. People had different versions of where the dress first came from, but her grandma asserted it was from Treaty 3, her own territory.

"The skirt goes below the knees, and it's heavy 'cause of all the jingles. Most people do three hundred and sixty five, one for each day in a year. Hang 'em close together so they hit each other when you move. Boy, you could hear some of those dancers walking into the field from the fry truck. Like shattered glass being put back together."

Now the loudest sound was the Earth uncurling and flexing into every space. Tree bark popped its seams from the sudden changes in weather. Weeds strangled the geometry of cultivated spaces over-night. Bees swarmed broken streets, made hives out of green-clotted houses, the wallpaper shot through with moss. Foxes traveled in covens, noses to the ground, throats safe from the wolves that slunk across barricaded highways like silent motorcycles. The moon was blocked by the flight of dark birds moving into new territory. Not every fight was violence. Some fights were resistance.

The Earth was a fighter, and sometimes that's nothing more than the choreography of reclamation.

Rose turned back to the camp and went to her backpack, full of medical supplies and tinned food, a knife, and a small tarp to collect water. She was more grateful than ever that Nam had scavenged the pantry before they'd escaped the house in the woods. She reached into the front pocket and pulled out a small bundle. Then she made her way around the perimeter of sleeping bodies to the place where Wab and Ishkode shared the only remaining blanket. The baby was sighing in her sleep. She didn't cry much, already attuned to the danger of that pitch. This soft exhalation fringed in voice was more useful, letting her mother rest swaddled in the certainty of her baby's steady breathing.

Rose slunk forward, pulled the bundle from her pocket, and unwrapped the cloth. Minerva's jingles, the ones she'd carefully crafted from tin cans and discarded lids. Minerva, who hung in the night gallery beside all the other Grandmothers now. Minerva, who had known that one day there would be someone in a dress that made a sound like nothing else in the world. Minerva, who had known that one day, the people would be loud again.

Rose rewrapped the handful of jingles, already dangerous with potential, and tucked them in beside Ishkode. They were hers now, and one day, Rose would help her make the dress that would hold them. This child would make noise, like shattered glass being put back together. And they needed it, because a new cacophony was breaking in. It was just up ahead. Rose could feel it, cresting the audible edge of tomorrow. It was coming on dark wings, making short work of time and distance. And this would be the way they resisted. This would be the reclamation. This was the girl who would be loud.

Ishkode was a fighter, and sometimes that's nothing more than the choreography of being born everything the ancestors ever dreamed of. And those ancestors,

they

never

stopped

dreaming.

Author's Note

There was not going to be a sequel to *The Marrow Thieves*. And then the very people I wrote the book for asked for more. So this book is dedicated to the kids who wrote me letters, the Reserves and communities who invited me to speak, the students who asked big questions, and every person who identified with these characters and demanded that their story continue.

I am from a specific community with a specific history and an ongoing culture. I cannot and do not speak for all of us—no one can. The fictional characters in these books come from a diversity of land, families, backgrounds, languages, teachings, and identities. I wrote it this way to include as many of us as I could, to show us together resisting and holding one another close through a dark time, to reflect the readers who deserve to see themselves in print. If I got something wrong, I am truly sorry and will try to do better. If I got something right, please accept it as both a gift and a responsibility to honor our ongoing cultures.

For all readers, both *The Marrow Thieves* and *Hunting by Stars* are works of fiction. They reflect people and places I know, love, and respect, and echo a very real and very dark time in our collective history. But they are still fiction from one imagination rooted in the specific community I am from and fostered by the many teachers and mentors I've had along the way. Please reach out to teachers, read other books, and find resources to learn more about individual nations and histories, including the residential school system and Indian boarding school era in both Canada and the United States.

Shortly after *The Marrow Thieves* was published in 2017, it became clear that this story had found a home with readers. And I am so grateful to be allowed to tell this story. I've spent the last years since the first publication visiting, listening, and learning. I hope you see yourself—both your difficult anxieties and your remarkable dreams—in these pages.

Acknowledgments

I am so grateful for the careful eyes and open hearts of Melody McKiver (Anishinaabe, Lac Seul First Nation, Frenchman's Head, Treaty #3), Erin Konsmo (Michif, Métis Nation of Alberta), and Waubgeshig Rice (Anishinaabe, Wasauksing First Nation) who read drafts of the manuscript, taking on the huge task of guiding my steps when the story asked that I veer from my own community and identity. I respect and value their opinions and views as friends, family, and brilliant minds. Author and advocate Wab Kinew (Anishinaabe, Onigaming First Nation) worked on the Anishinaabemowin in the text with great care and specificity, ensuring speakers and community members would see themselves reflected in those passages. The talented and inspirational Stephen Gladue (Métis, Cree) took on the delicate and work-intensive job of creating art for the book, inside and out, and I am honored to have his gorgeous imagery alongside my words. I am so privileged to have such incredible people in my life on a daily basis, and especially when I need someone to throw me a lifeline when I'm writing! We cannot do any work that is for community without community, and I am so lucky to call this small group of geniuses my community for this book.

There are so many writers and artists whose work inspires me; here are a few: Eden Robinson, Janet Rogers, Smokii Sumac, Lee Maracle, Maria Campbell, Christi Belcourt, Ryan McMahon, Gregory Scofield, David A. Robertson, Marilyn Dumont, Terese Mailhot, Alicia Elliot (and Miles!), and Devery Jacobs. Thank you for continuing to share community with me and for reminding me I was not alone even when it really felt like it. (This section can also serve as a "Who to read/watch/experience" for those interested in the very best in Indigenous arts.)

To the Penetanguishene Halfbreed Community, now called the Historic Georgian Bay Métis Nation—especially my family: the Dusomes, Greniers, Trudeaus, Beausoleils, Secords, and so many others (it's a huge family), my undying gratitude and love. Let's have a kitchen party soon.

To my brilliant editors, Lynne Missen and Maggie Lehrman, thanks for always listening and for the countless hours you invested in this story and these characters. I appreciate all the effort and belief you placed in this project, and for not letting me slack off, especially during a pandemic.

Huge thanks to Jennica Harper and Alexandra Raffe, who worked with me on adapting *The Marrow Thieves* for the screen and who taught me how to better serve my own stories in this new-to-me medium. Your mentorship and patience is so appreciated, and even more so, your true friendship.

I would not have a house to write from or a contract to fulfill without my amazing agents Dean Cooke and Rachel Letofsky. I also wouldn't have anyone to give unasked-for Ted Talks to on conference calls, or to take me out for martinis as a distraction while you set my life in order.

For my kids, Jaycob, Wenzdae, and Lydea, and my husband, Shaun, thank you for following me around the world and through every risky venture. You guys are the best Apocalypse Survival Team a person could ask for. To my parents Hugh and Joanie, and my brother Jason, thanks for always having my back and loving me through everything.

All my stories are dedicated to my mere, my grandmother Edna Dusome, who gave me stories and love. This time, I'd like to also include my grandfather, Fred Dusome, a fisherman and guide on the Georgian Bay who made bad decisions and lived a life far from the stories and love of my grandmother. Because there is room for all of us —the beautiful and the broken. When you have a place that includes room for all of us, that's when you know you are finally home. I welcome your bones home, Grandpa, and know that somewhere in them, there are dreams that no one could take.